By Freda Lightfoot

House of Angels
Angels at War
The Promise

a&b

House of Angels

FREDA LIGHTFOOT

Allison & Busby Limited
13 Charlotte Mews
London W1T 4EJ
www.allisonandbusby.com

A CIP catalogue record for this book is available from
the British Library.

Hardcover published in Great Britain in 2009.
Paperback first published in 2010 (978-0-7490-0724-9).
Reissued in 2011.

10 9 8 7 6 5 4 3 2 1

ISBN 978-0-7490-1019-5

Typeset in Adobe Garamond Pro by
Allison & Busby Ltd.

The paper used for this Allison & Busby publication
has been produced from trees that have been legally sourced
from well-managed and credibly certified forests.

Printed and bound in the UK by
CPI Bookmarque, Croydon, CR0 4TD

House of Angels

Chapter One

1908

There was barely sufficient light in the musty loft to judge the pallor of the woman lying on the filthy sheet, rank with blood and urine, but the young girl tending her could tell by the way her mother's eyes had sunk deeper into their sockets that the end was not far off. Even so, she put the cup to her lips, urging her to drink.

'Try a sip, Ma. It's good beef tea and you need to keep up your strength.'

The woman attempted to obey but a fit of coughing took hold and she turned her dry mouth away from the succour offered to deposit yet more mucus and blood in the filthy rag she pressed to her lips.

When the spasm passed, she managed a smile and squeezed her daughter's hand by way of thanks for her efforts. Despite the gloom in the airless loft, lit only by one tallow candle, she could see tears glimmering in the girl's eyes, and the mother's heart swelled with fear for this child she was about to leave alone and unprotected, in Fellside of all places.

This whole district of Kendal comprised a chaotic assortment of dingy cottages clinging drunkenly together on the western slopes of the town, their walls blackened by soot and peat smoke; a veritable warren of dwellings linked by a labyrinth of dark alleys, cobbled passages, and seemingly endless flights of stone steps that climbed the hillside in a haphazard fashion. An entire family with five or six children could occupy one room, and think themselves fortunate. Those streets worthy of the honour bore such names as Sebastopol, Sepulchre Lane, Hyena Row, or The Syke, and tucked behind many a hovel could be found the family pig sty or cess pit. The area was peppered with unsavoury taverns, dark corners for striking deals outside of the law, and foul workshops where shoes were cobbled, watches, chairs or saddles mended. And in many a grimy loft, woollen cloth was woven by weary men and women old before their time.

'Listen to me, Mercy. There's summat you needs to know, summat you must do.'

Again the woman was taken by a coughing fit and her daughter held the frail, bony shoulders until it eased. The girl herself was barely more robust, being small and skinny, her features sharp with hunger, the colour of her lank hair indeterminate beneath the grease and filth, scabs and sores marring young flesh that rarely saw the sun. In the gloom she appeared a pale, almost elf-like creature, with a face that rarely smiled, having seen far too much sadness in her short life of just sixteen years. Only the eyes hinted at the beauty that might have been present had poverty not done its utmost to destroy it before ever it bloomed. At certain times, such as in the rare brilliance of a summer's day, they would be a bright translucent blue, at others the light in them would transfuse almost to aquamarine. Now they were dark with desperation and dread.

'Hush, Ma, hush. Don't try to talk. It's rest you need, not chatter.'

Fear lay in the pit of the girl's stomach like undigested cold porridge. She had no interest in anything her mother had to say at this juncture. She wanted only for her to sleep and wake refreshed and reborn, to see again her bonny smile, her cheeks flushed with sunshine and happiness rather than fever.

From somewhere behind the wainscot came the scuttle and scratch of a rat, but Mercy didn't even turn her head, too used to such an occurrence to let it trouble her. They paid sixpence a week for the privilege of not sharing this verminous room with any other family, and the rats and cockroaches came free.

It hardly seemed possible that this ravaged skeleton was her own mother: Florrie Simpson, a hand-loom weaver who'd lived her entire life on Fellside, where she'd birthed four children with only herself, the youngest, having survived infancy. Since Mercy's father had disappeared before ever she clapped eyes on him, her mother had devoted almost every waking hour to weaving the linsey cloth in the famous checks or stripes for gentlemen's trousers in order to feed and clothe herself and her only child in little more than rags. Six days a week she'd worked her two-treadle loom, carried her bundles of cloth to the foreman to collect a pittance in payment, then made her weary way home again, weighed down by bundles of yarn for the next batch.

On Sundays, Ma always insisted that, humble though it might be, the room should be made spic and span for this special day. But by six o'clock on Monday morning she would be off weaving again and within hours the loft was once more filled with the pernicious, lung-choking dust from the weft.

Now Florrie lay in the last throes of consumption.

Where was the point of it all? Resentment burnt like bitter gall in the girl's breast. Ma had never seemed to stop working, slaving from dawn to dusk for starvation wages with never a minute to rest or snatch a breath of fresh air. Weaving was notoriously badly paid in an industry that had been dying ever since the huge factories sprang up to produce cheap cotton. No one wanted soft linsey petticoats these days.

When weaving was hard to come by, like the other women of Fellside she would knit stockings, for which Kendal was famous, using her crooked pins or sticks, and a carved wooden knitting sheaf tucked into the belt around her waist to hold it.

Now Florrie's work was done and this once pretty young woman would soon be dead and buried, though never forgotten, not if Mercy – the daughter who loved her, heart and soul – had any say.

It would be her responsibility now to mind the loom and go on without her, to carry on living in this rat-infested hell-hole, this hand-to-mouth existence, with barely a penny left over after rent and food had been paid for, and the woollen masters had taken their cut. There'd been much fearful talk lately among the tenants that the landlord, Josiah Angel, who owned these buildings, intended putting up the rents, though he did nothing to improve the condition of the place and justify that rise.

Not that her mother ever complained. What can't be cured must be endured, was Florrie's motto. Mercy was only too aware of the few options open to her, if she was to survive. She could either work herself to death in the unhealthy miasma of Fellside, as her mother had done, or earn a better living on her back. And even at sixteen she understood precisely what such a job entailed, and nearly vomited at the thought.

Florrie slept for a while, which was a relief. But much as Mercy longed for sleep herself, having not closed her eyes for a day and a night, not since Mrs Flint, her neighbour, had brought the beef tea, she remained alert, fearful her ma might slip away when she wasn't looking.

It was late evening now, and she became aware that her mother was awake and speaking, in weak but insistent tones. Something of great importance, or so she claimed. Mercy leant close to listen, her eyes stretching wide as Florrie whispered the secret she'd carried in her heart for sixteen long years, choosing at last to speak because of fears for her beloved daughter's future.

'Your da didn't run off to be a sailor like I told ya. Truth is, I were never married, never had any other bairn but thee.'

The exertion of this confession brought the expected penance of another coughing fit, and in something of a state of shock Mercy persuaded her mother to take a sip or two of the tincture she'd bought from the herbalist with their last few coppers. It seemed to quieten Florrie, calmed her sufficiently for her to continue in soft, rasping tones.

'No miscarriages. No still-born bairns afore you. No husband. It were all a lie. You were my one and only precious girl. I might never have had you 'ceptin I grew careless. Not that I regret having you, child, not for a moment.'

The warmth and love in her eyes as she looked at her daughter was unmistakable and Mercy's own eyes filled with ready tears.

'Don't fret yourself, Ma. I don't care if you weren't never married. You don't have to try to be respectable for me. Don't I love the bones of you?'

Florrie smiled sadly and squeezed her daughter's hand. 'There's little more than bones left of me now, so I'm glad you do. And I love you too, my lovely girl.'

After a moment's rest to gather her strength, she continued, 'Your father were Mr Angel, the gent what owns the big department store in town.'

Mercy gasped. 'What – the bleeding landlord? Him what owns these buildings?'

'The very same. Him and me…we had a bit of a thing going once. Lasted for a year or two, s'matter of fact. He were right good to me, was Josiah.'

Little by little, and pausing between sentences to allow

14

for coughing spasms, the story slowly emerged. Florrie Simpson had worked in the town's department store, known as Angel's, in the household linens department where she'd caught the eye of the owner, Josiah Angel. Against all odds the pair had fallen in love. Not that young Florrie had expected this great man of wealth and prestige in the town to abandon his wife and children for a mere slip of a girl such as herself.

'Oh, but he made it very plain that he loved me,' she whispered, her face going all soft, and her blue eyes glowing at the memory.

So why did he leave us to live in near starvation in this hell-hole all these years? Mercy longed to ask, but buttoned her lip as she'd no wish to distress her mother in her last hours. Seeming to guess her daughter's troubled thoughts, Florrie strove to explain.

'I was obliged to leave the store when I fell pregnant with you. Wouldn't have been right for me to stay on, even had that been possible. None of the other girls would've been allowed, so it'd look odd if he made an exception in my case. But, like I say, he did what he could for a long while. Set me up nice and comfy in a lovely little cottage in the Shambles. Proper pretty it were, and handy for Josiah to pop in on his way to and from the store.'

A look of blissful contentment crept over her face and Florrie fell silent, reliving those sweet, precious encounters in her head; the loving hours they had spent together while the child quickened within her. It was as if she were losing her grasp on the present and slipping back into the past, where she much preferred to be. Mercy gently brought her back. 'Why did he stop coming?'

Florrie shook her head. 'I don't know. He just did. One day I was expecting him to call on his way home, as he always did, but for some reason he never arrived.' A tear slid down the hollow cheek, and Florrie wiped it away. 'I'm sure it weren't his fault. He had his family to think of.'

'Did he know about me?'

'Oh, aye. Took quite a shine to you, he did, when you were a bairn.'

'But then he just stopped coming, without any explanation?'

'Aye, when you were about twelve months old.'

'And sent no more money?'

Florrie sighed. 'Not a penny. I thought at first it were because you'd been teething and making a row, as bairns do. But then I hadn't been too good meself, suffering some sort of infection in me tubes. He saw to it that I had a proper doctor, fetched me a few tasty bits to eat and suchlike. He could be a kind man when it suited him, though I'll admit he hasn't a reputation as such. Eeh, but we had some good times together for a while…then he just stopped coming.' Sadness cloaked her ravished face. 'I never blamed him. I reckon it all came to be a bit too much for him, what with his other responsibilities. Or happen his wife found out. I don't know.'

'And you've not seen or heard from him since?'

'Never.'

Anger, hot and raw, was building inside Mercy at the treatment her mother had suffered at this man's hands.

16

'Then he wasn't the gent you thought he was.'

'Nay, don't say that!'

'Didn't you ever go and ask, at the store I mean?'

Florrie looked shocked. 'I could never do that. Wouldn't have been right. He were the boss, the owner. I were... I were nowt.' The conversation had exhausted her and she closed her eyes, her breathing growing ever more laboured, her face crumpled with pain.

Mercy said, 'Don't ever say such a thing. You're not nowt to me, you're my ma, and I love you.'

'I know, lass. I know.'

As Florrie stroked her daughter's cheek, Mercy held on tight to her other hand, willing her mother to keep on fighting, not to give in to the exhaustion that was claiming her. She urged her to rest, not to talk any more, but Florrie was determined to somehow find the strength to finish what she had started.

When she spoke again, she spaced out her words, struggling to catch a painful breath between each. 'I – want – you – to – ask – him – for – a – job. A future. He owes me that, and he could do so much for you, lass.' She turned her head slightly to indicate the box they kept under the bed, the one in which they stored their few precious belongings. 'Letter – give it to him. Tell Josiah I allus loved him – selfish old goat.' A smile lit up Florrie's face as she fought to breathe, her eyes locked with love on her daughter.

It was all over. Just as Mercy had glimpsed a lightening of the sky through the narrow loft window cut high in the sloping roof, her mother had breathed her last. Mercy

17

thought she would remember that last rasping, rattling breath for as long as she lived. For some hours afterwards, the girl had lain unmoving, holding her mother close, intent on trying to warm the rapidly cooling body, praying she was mistaken and that the loving arms would come round her as they always did when she needed comfort. But it was Jessie Flint from the room below who did that, prising free Mercy's tight grip.

'She's gone, lass. Her soul has already flown. Let her be,' the old lady gently urged. Then she'd gathered the child close to her soft bosom, letting her sob while she murmured a few inadequate words of comfort and condolence before briskly fetching wash cloth and water to do what had to be done.

Now Florrie lay stiff and cold, as neat and clean and tidy as she'd liked to be in life. Mercy sat dry-eyed beside the bed, still waiting for her mother's head to turn and her lovely face to break into a smile as it would do every morning when she woke.

'We can make the sun shine in our hearts, even if it's wet and cold outside,' she would say.

But this morning there was no response from the shrunken, withered figure that lay unmoving on the ramshackle bed, a mere shadow of the lovely young woman she'd once been. Even now, in the hour of her death, she was but thirty-six. Far too young to be meeting her Maker.

Heavy footsteps sounded on the narrow stairs. Men coming to carry her precious mother away. With no money for a funeral, Florrie would be put in a pauper's grave and Mercy felt her own small body begin to shake at the dreaded prospect.

'Na then, don't tek on, lass. Bear up, as yer ma would wish,' old Jessie soothed.

But Mercy shook not with grief, of which she'd barely begun to comprehend, being still in shock, but with the degradation and humiliation of it all. She was outraged that her lovely, young, caring mother could be bundled up in a sheet and carried away like a roll of bad cloth to be dumped in some dark, musty hole in the ground; that her last resting place would be unmarked and uncared for. As if reading these thoughts, old Jessie clucked softly, patting and stroking the young girl, offering what comfort she could where none was available.

The men had no difficulty in lifting the woman, light as a child. They carried out the task with sombre respect, but it was all too much for Mercy. She could barely take in what was happening; unable to comprehend how it was that her quiet, orderly, albeit simple life could suddenly be turned upside down. How one day her mother had been happy and laughing and filled with her characteristic energy to work hard in order to get her daughter out of this place, and then within a few short months, be dead and buried.

All that stuff she'd told her at the end about who Mercy's real father was. Not some common sailor after all, but a man of consequence, a man of class and position. And this gentleman, so-called, had cruelly deserted Florrie and her child. Having set her up in some pretty little cottage in town, no doubt only to assuage his guilt, he'd soon grown bored and abandoned her to cope alone as best she might. Probably found himself some other pretty maid who'd caught his eye, and forgot all about poor Florrie. A sad but familiar tale which made Mercy burn with shame and embarrassment on her mother's behalf. Within months, Josiah Angel had forgotten his lover sufficiently to stop sending her money, or even paying the rent on their one-time love nest. Was it any wonder her mother had ended up living a life of penury, hard graft and near starvation?

Even then she couldn't escape him entirely, but was compelled to pay the man an inflated rent for the privilege of living in this rat-ridden hole.

Now her poor mother was dead, and her daughter left to fend for herself.

Mercy was filled with a bitter resentment. Not for one moment did she imagine Josiah Angel treating his own precious family with such callous disregard. No doubt his three daughters were coddled, spoilt young misses possessing all they could ever desire. Mercy hated each and every one of them with a venom that burnt to her very soul.

Chapter Two

The sound of the strap singing through the air was the last thing she remembered, that and the hot searing pain before darkness enfolded her. How long she lay unconscious Livia had no way of knowing, but it couldn't have been more than a second or two as she became aware of her father's craggy face leering over her, the rancid smell of his cigar-tainted breath suffocating her, and his icy fingers pinching the soft flesh of her cheeks. He hated it when his victims were not sufficiently alert to savour his torture.

'I'll teach you who is master here if it's the last thing I do.'

Josiah Angel grabbed his eldest daughter by the wrists and began to drag her across the floor. Livia let out a scream, knowing what awaited her, but even as the sound echoed around the dusty emptiness of this claustrophobic little room, she knew no one would come to her aid. Certainly not her mother, who had taken to her bed more than ten years ago as the only means available to evade a brutal husband, and quietly gone into a terminal decline, making as little fuss by her departure in death as she had done in life. The servants knew better than to interfere in family business, as well as which parts of the house were barred to them. This tower room, or torture chamber, as Livia and her sisters caustically referred to it, was the place they feared the most.

The House of Angels was what the locals called this fine Victorian mansion situated on Brigsteer Road, high above Kendal. With its crenulated towers, gothic arches and tall slender windows beneath frowning eaves it resembled a fortress more than a home.

But only the Angel sisters who lived within its dark walls knew that it was ruled by a devil.

Josiah Angel was a great bull of a man, his face as hard and unforgiving as the crags that formed the landscape of his birth, high cheekbones protruding sharply beneath folds of skin grown slack with age. His temper was as dark and brooding as the thick cloud that blanketed the tops of the distant mountains that dominated the skyline in this part of Westmorland. But then he was a man who demanded attention as did Great Gable or Scafell. He might attempt to soften his appearance with the silk cravats and silver cufflinks of the country gent going about his business, but beneath the fine worsted cloth of his expensively tailored suit lurked a heart as cold and rancid as the bogs beneath the lush green grass of the lower fells.

His three daughters had long since learnt to listen for the heavy tread of his highly polished boots so they could better judge his mood. The louder the creak on each stair, the more vile his temper. The sound of his menacing approach would allow them a few precious moments to take evasive action: to slip quickly down the servants' stair and run helter-skelter to hide among the exotic leafy plants in the conservatory, or climb the hill to Serpentine Woods above the house, their hearts racing with giddy excitement at their daring escape.

He had never been the kind of father any daughter would run to for a hug and a kiss, but rather one to be avoided. A man without pity; a tyrant and a bully who would have his way at any cost simply to prove that he possessed the power to do so.

A stray shaft of spring sunshine from the long window that reached almost from floor to ceiling cast its dusty rays into the furthest corner of the room, where Livia's two sisters huddled together, powerless to help her. Alike they may be in many ways, certainly with regard to their angelic fair hair and soft grey eyes, yet they were so very different in temperament. Romantic, spoilt Ella, so self-absorbed, so sure of her pale elegant beauty that she'd steadfastly believed herself to be immune to their father's torment. Now her childlike grey-green eyes were rounded in disbelief beneath fine winged brows, revealing shocked outrage at finding herself in this predicament.

Practical, uncomplaining Maggie, the youngest of the three, was begging their father to desist his torment; her sweet, heart-shaped face turned pleadingly up to his, soft grey eyes pooled with tears. Not that he would pay heed to either of their pleas. Witnesses to his cleverly devised punishment were an essential feature of their father's reign of terror, all part of his evil plan.

Josiah Angel maintained control over his three daughters by the cleverest, vilest form of cruelty. Too often he'd experienced their stubbornness over the years and had come to see that to bring one to heel, he must hurt one of the others. The trick never failed. On this occasion it was Livia who was being made to suffer for Ella's obduracy. And, since the strap had failed to bring about the desired surrender, his second choice of punishment was the iron cage, small enough to accommodate one person and of sufficient height to keep his eldest daughter's long legs from touching the floor.

But Livia had no intention of making it easy for him. She drummed her heels on the unyielding floorboards, wriggled and fought in a futile effort to free herself. Sadly, her strength was puny against her father's iron grip. He held her by her long golden tresses, which she took such care to brush one hundred times every night, wrapping them tightly around his great fist. She could feel clumps of hair tearing from her scalp, splinters from the rough boards digging into her bare feet as she attempted to hinder his progress in any way available to her. In spite of her pain, Livia managed to raise her head sufficiently to look up, and wished at once that she hadn't.

It was Ella who let out a half-strangled gasp, and Maggie who found the courage to defy him. 'Not the cage! Please, Father, not the cage. Have pity.'

Ella began to weep and Maggie's pleading went unacknowledged as Josiah tied Livia's thin white wrists

24

to the leather strap that hung from the central hook. He half smiled, revealing the handsome good looks he'd once enjoyed before ill temper, age, and overindulgence had taken their toll. '*Only a bird in a gilded cage*,' he disdainfully trilled in his hoarse, grating voice as he closed the door of the cage and turned the great key in the lock, leaving his daughter hanging an inch from the floor.

Livia's blue eyes welled up with tears as she courageously kept her gaze fixed on Ella, teeth gritted against the pain, arms stretched to breaking point as she gasped out her plea. 'I'm all right, Ella. *Please* don't give in. You…really…*mustn't*!' She saw how Maggie drew her sister close, which caused Livia to strive all the harder to hold on to her own courage. 'Don't let her, Maggie. Don't let her agree!'

Livia could say no more, needing the last of her strength to deal with the agony.

Ella was watching her sister's torment with growing despair, desperately striving to still her own trembling, knowing it would serve only to anger her father further. There seemed to be no escape for her now, let alone for poor Livia. No more secret meetings with Danny Gilpin in the shadow of the castle ruins, no more lovers' trysts, heartfelt promises or sweet, stolen kisses. She was to be sold to the highest bidder, auctioned off like a heifer at Kendal Auction Mart to a cold-hearted farmer in need of a wife.

Pretty, scatter-brained Ella, at just turned twenty, had endured her own beating with remarkable fortitude, but quailed at witnessing the more brutal torture inflicted upon her beloved and brave sister. And she knew that if Livia, with her fierce rebellious nature, refused to concede defeat to their father's tyranny, he would turn next on the softer Maggie, whose weak chest and nervous manner made her an easy victim.

She could not let this go on. She had to say something, anything. She had to save Livia, as well as herself.

Brushing aside Maggie's restraining hands, Ella took a tentative step forward and faced her father with reckless defiance. 'I would marry this man, this Amos Todd, but I doubt he would have me since I'm carrying Danny Gilpin's child.'

Maggie pressed her hand to her mouth, stifling a cry of dismay, while Livia groaned, knowing all was lost. But Ella stood resolute, her chin held obstinately high even as her eyes brimmed with tears, her beauty and distress surely sufficient to melt even the coldest heart. Unfortunately, not Josiah's.

Josiah drew a walnut from his pocket and cracked it in his palm while he considered his daughter in all seriousness. 'Don't lie to me, Eleanor. I've always been able to tell when you were lying. But just in case it's true, we'd best look sharp, hadn't we? If we marry you off quick, Amos will never know. At least, not till it's too late.' Tossing aside the shells, he turned on his heel and strode from the room, taking the key to Livia's prison with him.

Josiah did not trouble to lock the door of the attic, knowing Maggie and Ella would not stir from their sister's side while she hung like a joint of meat from a butcher's hook. As ever, they would cling together, stubbornly united against him. Until he finally broke them, that is. Which he fully intended to do.

They accused him of being harsh but in Josiah's eyes he'd been far too indulgent. It was long past time all three of his daughters were wed. Most women of twenty-two, as Lavinia now was, were married, yet she'd refused every suitor he'd found for her, resisted every attempt to do her duty. Now he'd turned to the next in line, deciding to deal with Ella first, and come to Livia next. Maggie, he would keep at home a while longer. He had other uses for his youngest daughter, and was in less of a hurry to dispose of her services.

Josiah proceeded at a leisurely pace to his study, showing no sign of haste as he dealt with several pressing matters of business, determined to allow his rebellious daughters ample time to fully appreciate Livia's distress. He wanted them to share her agony and reflect upon the consequences of their disobedience.

He certainly had no intention of being sidetracked by Ella's hysterical nonsense. A barefaced lie if ever he heard one. But just in case the tale was true, he'd make sure the nuptials took place promptly, before Amos Todd could get wind of it.

As ever, there was a great deal of business in need of his attention. In addition to the family department store, Josiah owned property around the town and was involved in a number of lucrative deals and land speculation. Kendal was expanding rapidly and he intended to share in

27

its success. Then there was the town council, of which he was a member, with every hope of being elected as mayor in the next year or two. Later he might consider applying to become a Member of Parliament. And why not? In fact, he had his fingers in several interesting pies that would increase his wealth and standing in the community, so his patience with foolish, recalcitrant daughters was thin. Why did they persist in their obstinacy? Why were they not obedient and biddable, as girls were meant to be?

He'd been deeply displeased and disappointed when Roberta had failed to give him sons as a wife's duty demanded, but where was the use in even having daughters if they couldn't be married off to good purpose?

Josiah Angel was a self-made man who'd begun his working life apprenticed to a draper. It had soon become apparent to the young Josiah that other men did not appreciate the fact that although his employer's daughter might be plain, her father was a man of means in poor health, clearly not long for this world. Josiah had made it his business to court and win the girl. In a very short space of time he'd married her and inherited the family's draper's shop, which he then set about successfully developing into a fine department store, using his father-in-law's substantial savings, plus a few judicious loans over the years. But then Josiah was never afraid to take a gamble when there was a possible profit in sight.

Admittedly his fortune had suffered something of a beating in recent months, due to one or two ill-advised property speculations, and other, possibly unwise, commitments. But that would all be put right soon, if he had any say in the matter. His latest project was the acquisition of a plot of land along Sedbergh Road. He intended to make a tidy sum by building several fine villas for the aspiring middle classes: the merchants and thrusting young managers of the district, assuming he could lay his hands on the necessary funds.

All it would cost him was his daughter's hand in marriage. A small price to pay.

The project, once completed, promised to make good his losses with a sizeable profit on top, thus ensuring a substantial increase in his fortune. He could see no reason for the plan to fail, so long as he could bring Ella to heel. Which he fully intended to do. But then Josiah generally found a way to curb the excesses of female histrionics and stubbornness which seemed perpetually to blight his life.

On his return to the attic, he took with him a towel, tightly knotted and wringing wet with ice cold water.

As he entered, Ella was on her feet in an instant. '*No!*' she screamed. 'Don't hurt her any more. It's not true. *I lied!* I *lied*! Dadda! I'll do it! I will, I will. It was all lies about me being with child. Let Livia go and I'll marry this farmer, I *swear*!'

Maggie sobbed while Livia cried out in dismayed protest. Josiah offered what might pass for a smile, twisting his mouth into a grimace. Nothing about his face was symmetrical, neither side quite matching the other. Even his nose was slightly crooked and off-centre. The eyes were a dark, chilling charcoal, hooded beneath heavy lids, one tilted slightly upwards while the other dragged down at one corner. His mouth, more often than not, was clenched in a firm tight line, the chin jutting strong and square, evidence of Josiah Angel's iron resolve to bend the world to his will.

'I am mightily relieved to hear it, and thankful you've come to your senses at last, Ella. You could have saved your dear sister a great deal of suffering if you hadn't proved so stubborn. Clearly you are in dire need of a husband to control this wilfulness you've displayed of late, this emotional instability. A man of maturity and sobriety will steady you. Amos Todd, I believe, is perfectly suited to the task.'

Ella stared at her father, mute, drained of any further protest.

Had she possessed one jot of Livia's courage, she might still have fiercely repudiated his argument. She longed to maintain her obdurate stand, to scream at her father that he'd only agreed to this match because it suited him financially to do so, all too bitterly aware that the marriage was nothing more than a business transaction. Yet she could not find the strength to resist.

Ella had once been considered her father's favourite, the only one who called him by the pet name 'Dadda', and the one least likely to suffer from his unpredictable temper. Yet she knew that even she could not win this time. Her cause was lost. Everything had changed the day he'd discovered her in the conservatory with Danny Gilpin. Her young lover had been dismissed without a reference from his job as groom to the family, and arrangements were at once put in place for Ella's hasty marriage.

She shuddered at the prospect of marrying a man she barely knew: apparently a religious fanatic with three young children already from a previous marriage. It was like something out of a cheap Victorian melodrama. They'd entered a new century, and already the emancipation of women was reaching new heights, with some daring ladies embarking upon golf and cycling, tennis and even wearing bloomers. Yet she was to be allowed no say even in a choice of husband.

Josiah strolled over to his two trembling daughters, and as Maggie instinctively shrank from his touch, he dropped the key in her lap.

'When you've let your sister out of the cage, see that the key is put back on its hook in my study without delay, then return to your duties. I want no more histrionics. I trust this episode will serve to reinforce the importance of obedience, something you all seem to have forgotten. Ella, you come with me. We have arrangements to make.'

Ella cast her sisters one last anguished glance before trailing from the room in her father's wake, shocked into silence as she contemplated her fate.

The moment the door closed, Maggie rushed to release Livia, tears rolling down her cheeks as she rubbed and massaged her sister's numbed wrists and hands, fetched warm water to bathe the fresh wounds on her back made by the shining leather strap.

They did not engage in any discussion over what had just taken place. Nor did they allow themselves the luxury of bewailing their lot. Much as both girls loved their sister, they were only too bleakly aware that further resistance was fruitless. Their tyrant father had won, getting the better of them all as he had done so many times in the past. Livia might now be allowed out of the cage but there seemed to be no escape from the prison he'd erected around all three of his daughters.

Chapter Three

Nothing changed in Fellside in the weeks following her mother's death, save for Mercy being faced with the day-to-day reality of living without her. She still rose every morning at five to riddle the clinker left in the stove and make herself a brew from the leftover tea leaves in the pot. She would empty the slop bucket down the privy out in the alley, then wash her hands and face using the bit of hot water left in the kettle, mixing it with a splash of cold from the pail she kept in the corner. There was no running water up here in the loft, a tap being a luxury enjoyed only by those who lived on the lower floors. If she was lucky, she'd nibble on a heel of bread, or Jessie might bring her up a bowl of porridge left over from her own family's breakfast. She was generous that way.

Once she was dressed, Mercy made her bed every morning exactly as her mother had taught her, emptied the night soil bucket out in the yard, then got on with the weaving. The clack of the loom at least filled the deafening silence. How she missed her mother's lively chatter, her laughter, and Florrie's cheery certainty that tomorrow, or the day after that, things would get better.

But Mercy knew things could only get worse now that she was alone. And how she would find the rent each week, let alone food to fill her young belly, was still a mystery to her. She'd have starved already if it hadn't been for Jessie and her family.

There was talk of change in the neighbourhood, of buildings being threatened with demolition. 'Slum clearance', they called it. A proud town like Kendal didn't much care to have any part of it described in such a way, although finding the money to make the necessary improvements always took second place to the needs of the wealthy, to men like Josiah Angel, who ran this town. It could be years before they ever got round to the task.

Little, in fact, had altered in the district over the last two centuries beyond some necessary attention given to the sewers and water supply, which had originally come from the Tea Well at the top of Fountain Brow, and had been closed almost half a century ago because of the risk of typhoid. Overall there still hung the sweet-sour stink of mouldy decay, shared privies, household refuse, and the waste and sweat of too many bodies crowded into too few dwellings.

Old women still sat on stools at their doors while bare-footed children played hoop-la or marbles in the filth of the gutters, if they were fortunate enough to own such treasures and not otherwise employed helping to work the hand-loom, or run errands for their mothers. Yet despite this evidence of a close-knit community where loyalties were strong and everyone knew the business of their neighbours, it was not a place to linger, nor one in which to risk taking short cuts unless you were sure of your bearings.

Mercy ventured out only to buy a few essentials. She kept herself very much to herself, wrapped in a private world of grief. She missed her mother desperately, and, despite her good intentions, would often waste hours each day just lying on her bed weeping. She might never have found the courage to carry on at all had it not been for Jessie. It was the older woman who had gently bullied her into working again by fetching her the yarn. She'd remind her to eat, insist she wash her face, even comb her tangled curls. And when the day's shift was done, she'd fetch her up a bit of warm dinner on a plate.

Jessie Flint was a large woman with breasts like cushions that shook when she laughed, which she did surprisingly often. She had smooth white hair fastened in a knot at her nape, and dark watchful eyes, few teeth, but plenty of grit in her soul. She was the mother of nine children, all of whom seemed to have miraculously survived, no doubt due to the canny ingenuity their mother instilled in each and every one of them. They were all of them streetwise, never missing a chance to earn an easy penny, whether by holding a gentleman's horse or sneaking off with his purse. Jessie's view of right and wrong was tempered by the necessity to earn a crust, if not always an honest one – the needs of her precious brood coming well above any fancy law devised by the rich and the blessed.

The Flint family made their living out of weaving, and

from knitting stockings, the younger ones knitting in the thumbs. Jessie had readily passed on all she knew to Florrie when she'd first come to Fellside. Like her mother before her, from whom Jessie had learnt these skills, she would stand at her door in her old coal-scuttle bonnet, swaying or 'swaving' as the knitters called it, moving gently with the rhythm of her knitting sticks. There were few knitters left in Kendal now, the trade almost gone, but Jessie clung on to the old ways because she loved the work, and needed every penny she could earn.

Mercy didn't know how she would have coped without her friend, or Jessie's eldest son, Jack, who was yet again urging her to carry out her mother's last wishes.

'Damn it, Mercy, just swallow your pride, go to the store and ask for work. It's what your ma wanted for you. That bastard Josiah Angel owes you that much at least.'

'I want nowt from him,' Mercy said, her small voice tight with pain. 'The man has ignored my existence for sixteen years, why should I go to him now with me begging bowl?'

'Because he's your da, and as much responsible for your well-being as your ma was.'

'No he ain't. I loved me ma, but I hate him.'

''Course you do, but who else do you have now that she's gone?'

'I have you and Jessie. Leastways, I thought I did.'

Jack patted her head in a rare show of affection. ''Course you do, lass. Always, you know that. But we're stretched as it is, and this man could give you so much more. You deserve better than this.'

Mercy was accustomed to listening to her old friend, whom she admired and revered, turning to him whenever she was in trouble. Jack was older and wiser than herself, a man now at twenty-three, and with a growing reputation for toughness. He led a band of followers who lapped up his every word, ready to do his bidding with no questions asked. But Jack was no one's fool, and not a man to cross. If power helped you to survive on Fellside, then Jack Flint ranked high in the pecking order; top of the tree in these buildings, although there were rival gangs down other yards and entries.

He could be as boisterous and rowdy as the rest; drink most of them under the table when he had coins in his pocket, but was also pig-headed, stiff-necked, and naturally perverse and argumentative. He was perhaps a mite too impulsive, and certainly never slow to take on a fight if challenged. But he was also a man of strong opinions with a mind of his own, the sort of person you could turn to when in trouble, always ready to take on the world if he sensed an injustice, albeit judged by a set of principles forged by the tough life he'd led. Jack Flint was impervious to danger and readily flouting all normal rules and conventions.

In Mercy's eyes he could do no wrong. He was deeply caring, supportive and protective; not only her best friend but her hero, and she had adored him for as long as she could remember. Even the look of him delighted her. His hair, the colour of burnished mahogany, sprang back from a wide brow, reaching almost to his shoulders, as wild and untamed as Jack himself. His velvet brown eyes were dark and brooding beneath winged brows, the chin strong and square, the lower lip full and sensual beneath a straight, almost aquiline nose. A face that might have marked him out as an eighteenth-century gentleman, had not the set of those broad shoulders proved he was very much able to take care of himself in the tough world of Fellside.

Of late, Mercy had begun to see him in a rather different light from that of big brother, a role he'd readily adopted on her behalf, although not through any encouragement on his part. Much to her disappointment, Jack still saw her as a scrawny child in need of care and protection. But it had long been Mercy's secret desire to alter this view he held of her, given time and opportunity. She dreamt he might one day see her as a young attractive woman. For this reason alone, if for no other, she paid heed to what he had to say.

'You don't have to give a toss about the greedy bastard. I'm not asking you to turn into Josiah Angel's devoted daughter, or to love and respect him. Why should you, for pity's sake? But you could use him, as he used your ma. Play him for all you're worth and relieve him of some of his ill-gotten brass.'

Mercy gave a vigorous shake to the head. 'Oh, I could never do that. I couldn't just walk in and ask for money any more than I could ask him for a job. I just couldn't.'

Jack let out a heavy sigh, and looking into the young girl's pale face with bruises like thumb prints beneath those big turquoise-blue eyes, judged that she might be right. Mercy Simpson was not nearly as tough as she might pretend, which was something she'd need to change in the months ahead.

'How about if I make the appeal on your behalf?'

'Oh, I couldn't ask you to do that for me, Jack. It wouldn't be right.'

'Why wouldn't it? It's no skin off my nose. He can only say no, can't he? Though he'd have to give me a damn good reason why, if he refused to do owt for you. Here, give me that letter, and I'll see what I can do, eh?'

'I'm not sure.' Mercy glanced at the letter, which lay between them as they sat cross-legged on the dusty wooden floor. She stared at the familiar handwriting penned in her mother's carefully rounded script, and thought of walking into Josiah Angel's fancy store, looking like the scarecrow she was. Mercy quailed at the thought. She'd be tongue-tied. Even if his minions allowed her in to see him, she very much doubted he'd listen to a word she said, let alone read any letter she held in her filthy paws. And yet...

'No, Jack, it's my responsibility. I'll do it. I'll make an extra effort and clean mesel up a bit. Happen ask your mam if she can find me summat decent to wear. Then I'll go and see him. Beard the lion in his den, as it were. Anyroad, I'm curious to know what he looks like. He's me da, after all.'

Jack felt a nudge of pride for her spirit, but he also felt very slightly cheated. There was nothing he'd have liked more than to find some excuse for challenging that man, anything to use against the bully who so pitilessly exploited folk in order to satisfy his own greed.

The cottages and lofts that Josiah Angel owned and which Jack's entire family inhabited, along with several others, were naught but damp, rat-infested fleapits, with insufficient privies to serve all the poor souls who occupied them. People had taken to using the streets rather than face the stink of lavatories that often overflowed. Yet rents were going up time and again despite the fact that the amount of weaving work available, much of it provided by his friend and colleague Henry Hodson, was rapidly decreasing. The weaving trade was dying before their eyes, nothing was being done to save it, and yet the workers were still being screwed for every last penny.

Oh, aye, Jack had his own reasons for doing battle with the man, besides supporting Mercy.

He'd privately relished the prospect of giving him a punch on the nose for what he'd done to poor Florrie, and by default little Mercy here. Course, he could always make a few enquiries on his own account; sniff out the opposition, like, test the waters, check out the lie of the land. Jack trotted out all his favourite catch-phrases in his head, savouring the thought of these investigations.

He resolved to keep a close eye on what went on, and if the man didn't treat her right, he'd soon find that Mercy was not alone in her current difficulties. Josiah Angel might be able to fob off Florrie and her child, but the fellow would find that he, Jack Flint, was a very different kettle of fish. He'd soon discover that the lass now had friends capable of protecting her, ready to stand up to bullies like him. And by challenging the evil bastard, Jack would be doing all the occupants of these buildings a favour.

Chapter Four

Mercy hesitated as she reached Angel's Department Store, desperately trying to summon up the courage to enter. She'd done the best she could with her appearance, scrubbing her face with Pear's soap and water till it shone, and Jessie had washed her hair with lye soap, and combed the tangles out of it. Mercy had rarely done such a thing more than once a month in her life, and since Mam had been ill, hadn't bothered at all, soap being something of a luxury. She'd been astonished to rediscover her own fairness, and how soft and slippy and clean her hair felt. Really quite wonderful. It had grown so long, Jessie had pinned it up for her into a sensible chignon at the back of her head. The new style made Mercy feel very grown-up.

Jessie had also insisted upon laundering her only blouse and good skirt, although it meant Mercy going about clad in nothing but her shawl until they were dry and ironed. Then her flannel petticoat and vest, worn next to her skin, which to her certain knowledge had never been washed, were dunked in the wash tub too. Mam had always considered it highly dangerous to remove underthings, particularly at night. Now the clean flannel felt all scratchy and stiff, and full of shaming holes as the shock of the hot water seemed to have made the fabric fall apart. Fortunately no one but herself would ever see these, and Jessie had assured her the flannel would go soft again, with wear.

Jack had managed to find some boot polish from somewhere, which he'd used to good effect on her one decent pair of boots. They pinched her toes a bit but Jessie said that were she to secure a job as a shop assistant, a uniform would be provided. Perhaps accommodation too, as many of the young women employed by Angel's were housed either in large dormitories above the store or in various quarters around the town.

Standing before her friends Mercy had felt unexpectedly optimistic and excited, but now she was sick with anxiety. She felt insignificant and out of place, the stuffed mannequins with their knobs for heads in the shop windows looking far better dressed than she was. But then Mercy couldn't recall the last time she'd worn anything new, if ever.

Giving a little gulp in a futile attempt to moisten her dry mouth, Mercy pushed open the shop door and walked in. She was as quickly marched out again with a stern reprimand from a man in a smart morning suit. Spruced up and clean she may be by Fellside standards, but not respectable enough to be seen shopping in Angel's emporium.

Back out on the pavement, Mercy chewed on her lip, wondering what to do next. How was she ever to get a job if she wasn't allowed to set foot in the store? It suddenly occurred to her that, like any grand house with a servant's entrance, the store itself would no doubt have a back door for employees, who likewise mustn't be seen cheek-by-jowl with the esteemed customers. She set off down a side alley in search of one and soon found what she was looking for. No one answered her timid knock so she turned the handle and crept inside.

The door Mercy had found opened onto a long corridor which, in turn, led to a labyrinth of similar passages. Mercy tiptoed along them, feeling very much like a mouse who might be pounced upon at any moment by the resident cat.

Finally, and to her great relief, she opened another door and found herself in a large room. Her first impression was that it was filled with boxes, stacked high on the floor, on tables, on every possible surface, but then she saw that people were engaged in unpacking them: young boys, and girls in black dresses with their sleeves rolled up.

There were shelves all around the perimeter of the room filled with bolts of fabric, lace curtains, blankets, mantles, shawls and even furs; a strange looking collection of brass stands that held an assortment of hats, muffs and umbrellas. One was completely decked out in feather boas. A group of the same mannequins she'd seen in the shop window leant drunkenly together in one corner, their knobbed heads close together as if gossiping over some naughty secret. And through a half-open door Mercy glimpsed a second room, which appeared to be filled with girls operating machines of some sort, perhaps sewing the fine garments that she'd seen on display.

Mercy was so overawed by the scene that she might have been content to stand transfixed for hours, drinking it all in, had she not been approached by a tall woman with a stern face and a spine that looked as if a steel rod had been inserted into it.

'And what might you be doing in our stock room, young miss? If you're seeking employment you should have rung the bell and waited.' She cast a jaundiced eye over her shabby blouse and skirt, and the too-large coat she'd borrowed from Jessie.

'I never saw no bell,' Mercy murmured.

'And I presume you have no experience either? Where was your last employment? Do you have any references? Can you even read? Standards are high for Angel assistants, and we don't make a habit of taking in wastrels who drop in uninvited off the street.' She folded her arms across her bony chest. 'Well... I'm waiting.'

Mercy struggled to recall all the questions, and to remember the little speech she'd practised with Jessie and Jack before setting out. Sadly, her mind had gone completely blank and all she could do was to stare at the woman with her jaw hanging open.

'Speak up, girl,' the woman chided her. 'I suppose you do have a tongue in your head? Come along, I don't have all day.'

Only when she felt her collar being grasped in an iron-grip, which surely meant she was to be evicted yet again, did she spring to life and speak. 'I want to speak to Mr Angel... If you please, ma'am' she added, remembering her manners.

'What did you say?' The woman sucked in her thin mouth, looking very much as if Mercy had asked to be admitted to an audience with the King himself. 'I – beg – your – pardon!' punctuating her words loud and long, so that heads turned and noses twitched, sniffing trouble brewing.

But having got this far, Mercy wasn't going to be easily put off. She shook herself free, smoothed down her skirt and said rather primly. 'Please tell Mr Angel that his daughter is without, and would like a word if he could spare five minutes of his time.' This little practised speech, finally remembered, was triumphantly offered and it gave Mercy great satisfaction to see how the shock of her words sent a dozen expressions flitting across the woman's ashen face in quick succession, from disbelief, through outrage, to nervous uncertainty.

In the end discretion won and Mercy was indeed shown into the inner sanctum of Josiah Angel's office. At last, she thought, excitement and trepidation warring within, I shall meet my father face to face.

Not for a moment had Mercy expected Josiah Angel to gather her to his bosom or weep with joy over being reunited with his long-lost daughter, but neither was she prepared for what did happen.

46

He was standing behind his desk when she entered the office, a large man dressed in a frock coat and trousers of unredeemed black, seeming to fill the small room by his dominating presence. He rocked back and forth on his polished heels as he studied her for a long moment, his silence making Mercy feel all hot and bothered about the collar. And she could see by the cold fury of his gaze and the tight curl of his upper lip, that he was not impressed by her ploy to gain entry. His opening salvo confirmed her worst suspicions.

'It's not often that I get to meet such a consummate liar. I've seen some nifty tricks played in my time in the fond hope of gaining employment, but this takes the biscuit. I assume it is work you're after?' He didn't wait for Mercy to answer but hooked his thumbs into his waistcoat pockets and began to pace about the room, his gaze raking over her with critical disapproval as he calmly continued with his lecture.

'Unfortunately for you, you've mistaken your target. I do not normally conduct interviews myself. Miss Caraway, whom you met just now, is the person responsible for hiring and firing shop staff.' He made an impatient clicking sound at the back of his throat. 'And you've most certainly cooked your goose so far as she is concerned. Whatever possessed you, girl, to issue such a barefaced lie? What possible advantage did you imagine it would give you to pretend to be one of my daughters? Do you not realise that it is an offence against the law to attempt to pass yourself off as someone else?'

At this stage, having at last come face to face with

her father, Mercy experienced a sudden urge to speak her mind. She longed to tell this man how her mother had suffered after he'd so callously abandoned her; how Florrie had been forced to live in the meanest of slums and work all the hours God sent to earn an honest crust. How she'd developed consumption and passed away a sad and broken woman believing the man she still adored no longer loved or cared about her.

But all she could do was to gaze, mesmerised, at this man who had the reputation of being a tyrant, and was in fact her living, breathing father. Her tongue was cleaved to the roof of her mouth. She felt overcome by nerves, and some strange emotion she couldn't begin to analyse, perhaps the knowledge that the man she'd longed to know for all her childhood years was now standing before her, that he did in fact exist. She'd believed, wrongly as it turned out, that her father was a sailor on the ocean blue. Yet here he was, in the flesh, and not at all as she'd imagined. The thought that this bull of a man might have bounced her on his knee when she was a small child seemed incredible. Impossible! Had he really teased and tickled and kissed her, as Florrie had claimed? Had he been in the least bit fond of her, or loved her just a little? If so, how could he then have gone off and left them both to starve?

Mercy was mindful that she'd promised her mother she would be tactful and polite when she reminded him of his duty towards herself. This man was powerful, after all, and in a position to help her earn a living. And, illegitimate though she might be, he was still her father.

Her fingers closed over the folded sheet of paper in the pocket of her skirt, and, gathering all her courage, Mercy handed him her mother's letter. He read it in silence, glared at her for a long, heart-stopping moment, then read it again.

'Your mother – Florrie – she's dead, I take it?'

'She is, sir, yes. Died a few weeks back, if'n you please, sir.' What a silly remark to make. Why should it please him that her mother was dead?

'How old are you, girl?'

'Sixteen.' She told him her birthday and he nodded, the lines of his craggy face tightening a little, almost as if he had no wish to be reminded of her birth.

'And you now have no means of subsistence?'

Mercy shook her head. There was the bit of weaving and knitting she did, but neither amounted to much with the prices currently being paid, and taking into account the poor state of her own skills. Jessie might be able to knit a jersey in a day, but Mercy could never match her speed, not in a million years, and even her friend struggled to cope with all them mouths she had to feed. She certainly couldn't afford to take on one more.

He was still glowering at her, then he instructed Mercy to wait and strode from the room. The click of the door as he softly closed it behind him seemed to echo chillingly in her head.

Mercy stood on the fancy Persian rug and waited. For how long, she couldn't afterwards recollect. It felt like hours. Long enough for her fast-beating heart to slow and her shredded nerves to calm down, and begin to gather her scattered wits. Sufficient time for Mercy to think of all she *might* have said: how she should have spoken with calmness and some show of intelligence. Instead, she'd just stood there like a gormless idiot while he'd read that letter, as if she didn't even have a tongue in her head let alone a brain.

She suddenly noticed that the letter her mother had written with such painstaking care as she clung on to the last threads of life had been blown from the desk in the draught from the door when it closed behind him. Or he had tossed it there. Whatever the reason, it now lay crumpled and rejected on the floor. For some reason this annoyed her and, picking it up, Mercy smoothed out the creases, reading the words again as she did so:

I know you will do this small thing for me, Josiah dear, because of what we once meant to each other.

The mere sight of her mother's handwriting brought a lump to Mercy's throat and tears momentarily blinded her. She gulped, rubbed away the tears, which would do her no good at all.

'I'm here, Mam. I'm doing just what you told me. I've come to ask me pa for help.' But would he give it? That was the question.

Hearing a sound at the door, and still with the note in her hand, Mercy panicked, then quickly slid it into the letter rack that stood on Josiah Angel's desk. At least there it wouldn't get lost or crumpled. By the time the door opened, she was once more standing smart and straight on the Persian rug, chin high, heart pounding. She was disappointed to see it was the woman, Miss Caraway, and not her father, who entered. She remained framed in the doorway, arms folded. 'This way, girl.'

Mercy registered this as an order, not an invitation, and did as she was bid without question, obediently following the woman back along the labyrinth of corridors until they were once more out on the backstreet that ran behind the store. Her heart sank like a stone as disappointment hit home. Oh, no, she was being thrown out, yet again.

'Where you taking me? Don't I get no job then?'

'Since you appear to be destitute, accommodation has been found for you,' Miss Caraway informed her, rather tartly. 'Get in.'

Mercy blinked, and noticed for the first time that a carriage, or hansom cab as she believed it was more rightly called, pulled by a black horse, stood patiently waiting at the kerb. Hope soared within her. My word, this was something. They were offering her accommodation, no doubt to allow her time to settle in and get her uniform fitted before starting work at the store. *And* she was being taken there by cab. By heck, this was a turn-up for the books. 'I've not brought me things,' Mercy told the woman, in a sudden panic as she thought of her few bits and bobs at home.

'Don't worry about that, girl. All you require will be provided. Come along now, get on board. We don't have all day.'

Mercy settled herself with some importance upon the leather seat while Miss Caraway firmly closed the door. She'd never travelled in so much as a wagon before, let

51

alone a fine carriage like this one with windows, and a proper roof to keep out the rain. Moments later the driver, who was standing behind the cab on some sort of ledge, flicked his whip and they were off, the horse clip-clopping along at a fine gait.

Mercy settled back in her seat unable to believe her good fortune as the cab drove through the crowded streets of Kendal town, forcing people to step out of the way and allow it to pass.

She couldn't believe it. The interview had gone ten times better than she'd expected. A thousand times better. By heck, what would Jessie have to say when she heard about her being taken to her lodgings in a cab? If this was the sort of transport they used for staff, Mercy couldn't wait to see where she'd be living, somewhere a lot better than Fellside, that's for sure. And there were still the delights of the uniform to come. She must also remember to ask what her pay would be. Eeh, God bless Mam for revealing this long-held secret and making sure her future would be safe and secure. She'd fallen on her feet good and proper. It was all too exciting for words.

It was only when she reached her destination that Mercy realised quite how ruthless Josiah Angel really was.

Chapter Five

Ella's wedding followed a few weeks later at the unfashionable hour of twelve noon on a Friday in early May, and with very little jollity about it. No rose petals strewed her path to the church, no carriage with high-stepping horses, not even any pennies thrown to the town's children from the church gate. But then Josiah Angel didn't believe in wasting his hard-earned brass, particularly not to the scavenging poor. All of the local gentry were present, since Josiah was a man of stature in Kendal. The repast he provided: a selection of cold meats, bread, cheese and the smallest of wedding cakes, all laid out on trestle tables on the lawns at Angel House, was considered somewhat penny-pinching by many, although none would ever risk saying as much to his face.

The bride looked somewhat pale rather than blushing and blooming as brides were supposed to look on their wedding day, and wan in an outmoded wedding gown, its lace yellowed with age, probably having originally been worn by her mother.

The only person who seemed entirely happy with the proceedings was Josiah himself, who beamed triumphantly upon all and sundry.

'It may well be the happiest day of Father's life, but not dear Ella's,' Livia muttered behind her hand to Maggie. 'Did you see the anguished glance she cast her new husband? How will she endure it?'

'I shudder to think.'

Livia and Maggie watched with unashamed curiosity as Amos Todd moved among the guests, one hand clasped firmly to Ella's elbow, as if to make sure he didn't lose her at the eleventh hour. They noticed how his pale, some might say washed-out brown eyes carried no spark of interest, rarely showed expression of any kind, but maintained a polite disinterest throughout. It was almost as if he were nervous of meeting anyone's gaze direct, save for when he spoke of his passion for his land and his animals.

'Poor Ella,' Livia whispered. 'He looks terribly serious. I've never seen him smile yet. Imagine kissing that sour mouth, those dry, thin lips. Oh, Maggie, I've let her down. I promised Mamma that I'd take care of you both, and I've failed Ella completely.'

'No, you haven't. It's not your fault, Livvy. There was nothing more you could do.'

'But he's so *old*! I believe he's thirty-two, *twelve years* older than our Ella. And he's so short and skinny!'

Amos Todd was barely two inches taller than his bride. A wiry man with large hands and feet, the kind of physique considered ideal for a hill farmer. He wasn't, Livia admitted, ugly as such, but nor could he be termed handsome. His face was plain and rather long, with ears that lay neat and flat to the side of his head, wearing an expression more sombre than joyful. Weather-beaten it may be, the cheeks bearing the ruddy hue typical of a man who spent his days out on the fells. Yet there was a blandness to it, a kind of serene calm, as if he'd resolved to remain untouched by the ills of life. By contrast, his hair, an indeterminate brown, was cut brutishly short, and Livia had an image of him sticking his head under a cold-water pump to wash it, something she could never imagine her demure sister ever doing.

He took out a handkerchief to mop his brow, revealing some of the strain he must be under. At least the handkerchief is clean, Livia thought, which brought a new concern into her head.

'Is there a housekeeper or washerwoman at Todd Farm, or must Ella do all of the chores herself?'

Maggie frowned. 'It's quite large, hundreds of years old I believe, but Father insists she will have help. I'm not sure though that we can entirely trust him. I do worry that may not be the case. Amos is every bit as mean as Father, being a strict Methodist. How Ella will cope with a harsh, lonely life out on those fells at Kentmere, I dread to think. You know how lazy and spoilt she is, never doing a stroke unless forced to it.'

Livia tried to smile. 'I dare say she'll learn, if she must, as we all will. What is to be *our* fate, Maggie? Have you considered that? Father can beat me till I expire, but I'll not marry Henry Hodson. Never!'

Maggie sighed. 'Oh, Livvy, don't sound so fierce. You frighten me.'

Following the service and simple repast, a country dance started up in response to a neighbour tuning up an old fiddle. The assembled guests seemed determined to salvage something out of the day, even if the bride and groom themselves seemed not in the mood for celebrating.

The sun was beginning to drop in a hazy blue sky by the time Maggie and Livia hustled Ella upstairs to help her change for the journey. Not that the newly-weds were having anything so frivolous as a honeymoon. Livia asked why this was, as she unbuttoned the row of tiny pearl buttons down her sister's back to allow Ella to carefully step out of the gown.

She explained that Amos could not leave his livestock, even for a day. 'Cows still need milking and sheep tending, wedding or no.'

'How very sad.' Livia knew all too well that romantic Ella had once dreamt of a continental tour to Italy for her wedding journey.

'I don't care in the least,' Ella said, her face pinched with despair. 'The last thing I want is to be alone with that man.' There was an edge to her voice as if she were on the verge of tears, and her two sisters quickly wrapped their arms about her to hold her close.

The night before as they'd sipped hot milk together for the very last time, outspoken Livia had bluntly asked her sister if she were a virgin still. 'Even if it was a lie about the pregnancy, did you and Danny ever…you know?'

Tears had formed on Ella's lower lids, causing the grey-green eyes to shimmer and seem as fathomless as the sea. She had loved Danny Gilpin for two long years, ever since she was eighteen. But because he was only a humble groom they'd both known that Father would never allow them to marry. It had meant that their love must be kept hidden and their meetings take place in secret. The result had been that Ella had drawn a little away from her two sisters, occupying a world of romance and dreams. Now she was facing stark reality, and felt crushed by it.

She gave the smallest shake of her head. 'I never dared. Oh, but I wish we had. I do so wish Danny had been the first. We were too afraid, too nervous of…of getting caught.' A sob caught at her throat. 'And now it's too late.'

Maggie quietly asked, 'You do know what will be expected of you, Ella? What will happen?'

A small nod, the lovely eyes wide with fear. 'I do. Mama told me once, years ago.'

'Don't resist,' Maggie warned. 'It will only make it worse. It can be quite painful…or so I believe…the first time. After that, well, you get used to it. Close your eyes and think of—'

'Of my darling Danny? No, I could never do that,' Ella cut in. 'It would be a sacrilege.'

Her father's voice boomed up the stairs. 'It's gone four o'clock and you'd best be making a move if you're to be home before dark.'

Ella felt panic rise in her breast. '*This* is my home. I

don't want a new one. Oh, and I shall miss you both so much.' She was trying hard not to cry, to hold fast to her failing courage, but Ella felt as if her heart were breaking in two. How would she survive without them, without Livia's energy or Maggie's sweet gentle comfort, both of them fussing over her like mother hens? Since the death of their beloved mother the three girls had formed a special bond, supporting each other through good times and bad.

'Be strong,' Maggie said. 'Be brave. Don't forget you'll have his children for company. I'm quite sure they will love you, and you'll come to love them as your own.'

Ella was silenced by this thought. She'd forgotten all about the children. How might they react to a new stepmother? She shuddered to think.

Maggie and Livia both put their arms around her, holding their sister close in a tight, we'll-keep-the-world-at-bay sort of hug while Ella clung to them as if her life depended upon it.

Then she stepped bravely away, dried her eyes, striving to be as sensible as her newly acquired and very serviceable navy blue serge coat. She'd chosen it from a selection at the store for that very reason, as it would do well for chapel. Even so, Ella hadn't been able to resist trimming the collar with a small pelt of grey fur, even if it was coney. Her matching navy hat bore a dashing flower with petals made from the same fur. Livia assured her that she looked as beautiful as ever, even if the coat wasn't quite so stylish as the kind of outfits she usually wore.

'Oh, my gloves. I've lost one of my new kid gloves. I was showing my going-away outfit to Mrs Crabtree in the parlour earlier. I must have dropped one.'

'Don't worry,' Livia said. 'I'll run and find it for you. Wait here, and don't you dare leave without saying goodbye.'

'I won't, I won't, I swear!'

As expected, Livia found the kid glove behind the sofa in the small parlour, but as she turned to hurry upstairs to her sisters she saw a man's face peering in at the back window, clearly not one of their guests. Incensed by this apparent invasion of their privacy on this special day, Livia marched outside to remonstrate with the intruder.

'Miss Angel, would it be?' the stranger bluntly enquired, with not a scrap of courtesy or good manners, and before she even had time to ask what he was doing in their back garden.

'Indeed, and who might you be?'

The man dipped his head in a mocking bow. 'Jack Flint, if you please. I dare say you'll have heard of me.'

Livia's mind ranged swiftly over various possibilities where she might have met him, all of which seemed highly unlikely. Yet as she studied him more closely, she found herself thinking that surely she would have remembered if she had. He was not a man one would easily forget, being disturbingly good-looking in a rough and ready sort of way. Judging by the wildness of his dark hair and the stubble on his jutting jaw, Livia supposed it must be some considerable time since he'd last visited a barber. He wore dark fustian trousers, a crumpled tweed jacket that had seen better days, its collar turned up against a white silk scarf knotted loosely about his neck. The kind of clothing that very much set him apart from the rest of the wedding guests. Yet there was something about his stance, the proud tilt of his head, and the way he lounged before her with his hands in his pockets, that told her such sartorial matters were of little concern to him.

Seeing how she observed him, his dark eyes glimmered with amusement, showing he was all too arrogantly aware of his own masculine charm; the long aquiline nose, straight and true, giving him almost a condescending air.

Livia watched as the wide mouth with its full lower lip curled at one corner into a wry parody of a slow smile as each measured the other with studied carelessness.

In his turn he saw a woman who was tall and slender, shapely rather than the waif-like fragile females common among her class. No milksop beauty this, but strong and spirited, matching the fire that undoubtedly burnt within and revealed itself in the glossy glory of her titian hair. She possessed the most beautiful gentian eyes he'd ever seen, deeply fringed by dark lashes fanned out in star-like wonder as if she could see into a future she clearly intended to plan for herself. Her mouth was wide and softly curved as if smiling at some secret she held close to her heart. A woman you might like to dominate but could never own. And one who would most certainly never be dull.

'I'm afraid I have no recollection of our ever having been introduced,' Livia tartly informed him. To her shame she realised that her response was really quite rude, sounding more like Ella in one of her pets than the supposedly more mature, sensible Angel sister. But the man's attitude had, for some reason, rubbed her up the wrong way. His entire demeanour loudly proclaimed that he had no time to waste on niceties, and he clearly didn't believe in showing respect for his betters.

The stranger stifled a snort. 'Your father knows me well enough, since I'm a tenant of his. So if you wouldn't mind telling him I'd like a quick word.'

It came to her then in a flash of inspiration who the man was, the facts rushing with clarity into her mind. Jack Flint had led those very same tenants of Fellside into a riot only last year – had, in fact, threatened to burn the place to the ground unless her father saw fit to reduce their rents. The riot had quickly petered out when Josiah had called the police, whereupon the rebels had scurried like rats back into their holes.

Livia was only too aware that her father was not a good landlord. No doubt his poor tenants had a just cause in that he was again threatening to raise their rents to unprecedented levels, but she could not approve of riot and arson. Such criminal acts achieved nothing.

She lifted her chin, stiffened her spine and looked the man straight in the eye; a gesture that took some effort on her part since he was considerably taller than herself. 'You may not be aware, *Mr* Flint, but this is a private celebration. I don't believe you were invited.'

He gave a low chuckle that sounded very like a

growl deep in his throat, and Livia realised that he was dangerously close to laughing at her.

'I reckon you're right there, but I'm sure you can forgive the inconvenience, since this could be termed a matter of some urgency. So go and tell him I'm waiting, love. My time is limited.'

Livia blinked. How dare this man, this rapscallion with bad manners and dubious origins *dare* to issue orders to *her*, never mind address her in such a familiar manner? Oh, dear, now she really was turning into snobby Ella. But if Father ever got his hands on this villain, he'd have the interloper thrown in jail.

'I would not advise disturbing my father at this precise moment,' she announced, cool but studiously polite. 'You may be surprised to learn that he has far more important matters to attend to on this, his daughter's wedding day, than to speak to the likes of you. And I am not *your love*.' She couldn't resist adding this last, although instantly wished she hadn't when she saw how the remark made him smile.

'So it's not *your* wedding then, even though you are the eldest?'

Livia found herself flushing. 'It's my sister Ella who is getting married today, *if* that is any of your business.'

'My congratulations. I'm sure you're delighted for her. Never mind, your turn next, eh?'

'I have no plans for matrimony,' Livia snapped, before she could quite stop herself, which again caused him to snort with suppressed laughter.

'Is that because you haven't yet found anyone who

quite suits? Or because you haven't received any offers?' he teased, that wide mouth lifting at one corner into a smile of pure amusement.

Livia was appalled to find that the heat in her cheeks had actually increased, and came swiftly to the decision that she must put an end to this embarrassing conversation forthwith. 'To answer your enquiry, I can only repeat that my father is unavailable. Whatever cause you are fighting will have to wait for a more suitable occasion. Were one ever to arise,' she finished, somewhat caustically.

'I cannot argue with your sound common sense,' Jack Flint blithely agreed, with a sad shake of his handsome head. 'Perhaps I should beg your pardon for intruding?' The words hinted at an apology, yet he posed them in the form of a question, and his tone bore not the smallest degree of remorse, which stoked Livia's ire all the more.

'Unless you take your leave now, Flint, I shall be obliged to call for assistance.'

'*Flint* now, is it? Oh, dear,' he tutted softly. 'I rather liked the way you called me *Mr* Flint. Yet it seems all civilities are now gone, eh? Kid gloves off,' glancing at the one she held in her hand. Then he slid his own hands, the skin rough with calluses although surprisingly clean and scrubbed, from his pockets, and moved closer. He was near enough for her to feel the heat of him, to note the perfect conformity of his handsome face, and for that non-quantifiable element that marked his masculinity to assail her nostrils. She'd rather expected him to smell of – well, something unclean – instead there was the unmistakable tang of soap mixed with the scent of peat smoke from the old musty jacket, as if he'd taken some trouble before coming out.

'I would recommend, Miss Angel, that for his own good, you should warn your father that Jack Flint intends to pay him a call, at *my* convenience, not his. I wish to speak to him on a most delicate and important matter, and it would not be wise for him to refuse.'

Touching his forelock in a mocking salute, he turned and strolled leisurely away. Rooted to the spot, Livia watched him go, the sound of his low chuckle sending a thrill of emotion rippling through her in a most unexpected and startling manner. Goodness, was she turning into a romantic now as well as a snobby harridan? She, who had turned her face against matrimony and eschewed men completely? But then, she'd never met a man like this before, had she?

'Who was that you were talking to?' Maggie wanted to know when Livia returned to her sisters, slightly out of breath. She looked out across the gardens at the rear of the house but saw no sign of him, and shook her head.

'No one. No one at all.'

'It's all coming to an end, isn't it?' Ella said, clutching tightly to their hands.

'Never!' Livia protested, as fiercely protective as ever. 'We're still the Angel sisters, and always will be. Nothing and no one can ever change that. I promised Mama I'd look after you, Ella, and I will, even if you do now have a husband to do the job. Just remember that you can still turn to me, if needed, and you'll surely visit Kendal every market day with...with Amos. We'll have such a lovely gossip.'

'And at least you get to be free of Father,' Maggie added, with a hint of envy in her tone.

Out on the lawns they kissed and hugged one last time, and helped Ella to climb up onto the farm cart while Father stowed her box behind. Then, as Amos clicked the reins and told the horse to walk on, Livia stood at the gate with family and friends to wave the pair off on their new life together. The last view they had of their dear sister was when Ella turned to look back, one hand clutching her hat with its frivolous fur flower, the other holding tightly to the edge of the cart as it bumped down the rough drive towards the road and the open fells. Never had she looked more vulnerable and alone.

Chapter Six

It was a long, uncomfortable journey, the cart bumping and bouncing over stony tracks that seemed to lead forever upwards into an empty wilderness.

Kendal, and Ella's childhood home, slipped further and further behind, becoming ever more distant until the town was nothing more than a huddle of grey houses in the valley. And with each extra mile Ella's heart sank further.

Amos drove the cart onward through the village of Staveley, where he stopped at a shop, Threlfall's Grocers, to buy provisions and animal feed. There were other items in the cart too, as if the trip to Kendal for his wedding needed to be made more worthwhile. Ella would have liked to get down from the cart and visit one or two of the other shops, perhaps take some refreshment at the Fat Lamb Inn. But when she asked about this, you'd have thought she'd suggested stepping into the jaws of Hell by her husband's icy response.

'I never set foot in a public house,' he coldly informed

her. 'I'm a member of the Staveley Abstinence Society. We meet at the Temperance Hall on Station Road, and campaign tirelessly against strong drink. We don't stand for any rowdiness or drunken behaviour.'

Having been put firmly in her place, Ella waited patiently in the cart while her husband loaded it with sacks and boxes. My goodness, was he always so righteous?

Leaving the village behind them they continued alongside the fast-flowing River Kent, which drove the machinery of the bobbin mills in the district. Ella spotted a heron standing on the weir, keeping an eye out for an easy supper. Her own hunger had completely gone now as her nervousness increased with each mile. The road into the dale beyond became little more than a track, rough and stony as it progressed along the narrow valley of Kentmere.

'St Cuthbert's Church,' Amos suddenly announced with pride in his voice. 'It's thought it was built here to commemorate the place where the monks of Lindisfarne rested on their escape from the Viking oppressors.'

'Oh!' Ella wasn't much interested in churches, or their history, but she gazed politely upon the small cobblestone building set on a hummock from which protruded a scattering of gravestones surrounded by a dry stone wall.

'I'm a local preacher and attend both the Primitive Methodist in Staveley and St Cuthbert's, which is more convenient. It's a close community, and you will of course be expected to join. You'll meet everyone, come Sunday.' He clicked the rein to urge the tired horse to walk on, following the curve of the track.

Ella cringed at the thought, wondering what was involved in being the wife of a lay preacher, who these people might be, and whether any of them would become her friends. It puzzled her where they could all live in this empty landscape, as there were precious few farmhouses visible in the scattered hamlet. It seemed desolate, for all it was the most spectacular setting.

Ella found the silence oppressive, broken only by the sound of gushing water from the many rivulets that came down from the mountains, spilling into the Kent and the Gowan. How much longer would this journey take?

She hadn't slept well the night before and she felt tired and bruised from bumping up and down on the hard wooden seat, her bladder near to bursting. Deep inside she nursed an increasing sense of outrage that this should be happening to her. What right had her father to bully her into marriage with a man she neither knew nor liked? Hadn't he always dubbed her his favourite, the one daughter who was spared the worst of his punishments? Until now.

In these last three weeks, caught up with the sewing of her dress and trousseau, she'd tried not to think about the future. The arrangements for the wedding had been made with shameful haste, and throughout all the preparations Ella had felt as though she were standing outside herself, watching events from afar.

Reckless to the last, she'd gone on seeing Danny. How could she resist when she loved him so? Their opportunities to meet had been necessarily scarce since he was no longer employed by the family, but she'd told not a soul about their trysts, not even her beloved sisters. Ella would slip out at night while everyone was asleep, and creep up to the woods behind the house where they'd kiss and weep and swear undying love for each other.

On the night before her wedding Ella had forsaken her pride sufficiently to beg him to take her and make her his. Panicked by her desperation, Danny had refused, claiming he respected her too much. They both knew, of course, that his reluctance was really because he was too afraid of her father.

But he promised to keep a look out for her on market days, when Ella hoped to come into Kendal town with her husband and visit her sisters. They would most definitely see each other from time to time, he assured her, even if they could never again meet like this. Which only made her cry all the more. Where was the point in Danny continuing to love her, if she was married to another man?

A thin cold rain began to fall as the cart bumped along through marshy ground following the river, Amos naming the mountains as they passed: Rainborrow Crag, Ill Bell and Froswick ahead, and on the opposite side, Kentmere Pike and Harter Fell. The sombre line of hills seemed the physical embodiment of all her childish nightmares. The light was fading and the long narrow valley felt claustrophobic, hemmed in by its ridge of hills on all sides, and the huge slabs of rocks and boulders jutting out of the boggy earth.

They drove on past an area where local slate and stone

were quarried. Amos pointing out the barracks where the men were lodged. He followed this with a stern warning about the dangers of the quarry workings, ordering her to keep well clear.

'They are the sort of men who visit the Fat Lamb the minute their wages are paid at the end of the month.'

Ella smiled to herself, not certain whether her new husband was more concerned that she might get caught up in the explosions or run off with one of the lively young men seeking solace after a hard month's labour.

Her feet itched to jump down from this hateful cart and run home. She wanted to keep on running, back to Kendal, or over the mountains to Windermere, and never look back. Even as the thought sprang into her head it died at birth, knowing she was trapped, with no hope of escape. It was too far, and it would be quite impossible for her to find her way over these lofty mountains alone and on foot. She had no choice but to face whatever fate had in store for her.

Nevertheless, as they approached the reservoir at the head of the dale, its surface as black as her father's heart, Ella made a private vow. If she did not care for her new home, did not grow to like her new husband, then she would refuse to remain in this dreadful place. She would demand to be released from this marriage and insist he take her home, no matter what scandal might ensue. Livia would protect her.

Before her stood a long, low farmhouse, its thick, whitewashed stone walls built to withstand the harsh

Lakeland weather. A storm porch enclosed the front entrance with one shuttered window on each side of it and three above, signifying, she assumed, the same number of bedrooms. Attached to its west wall stood a ramshackle pele tower, two stories high and in a more ruinous state even than the one at Kentmere Hall. These were said once to be used as a fortification against the marauding Scots. Ella was to learn later that it housed the dairy, where she would spend many long freezing hours in the coming months.

Without doubt the old house had seen better days, was smaller than she'd imagined, and for all the magnificent grandeur of its setting, her heart quailed at the prospect of living here alone with a man who was little more than a stranger.

No one came to the front door to welcome them as Amos jumped down from the cart. Neither did he make any attempt to assist Ella from her seat. He swung her box on to his shoulder and, with a jerk of his head, indicated that she should follow him as he set off round to the back of the house.

Ella was outraged. She was wet, cold and tired, and never in her entire life had she entered a house by the servants' entrance. She certainly had no intention of starting now. Stubborn and cross over this rude reception, she flounced down from the cart and stood by the front porch, clutching her umbrella and tapping one small foot in annoyance. The rest of her belongings were scattered about her.

When no one came running to her assistance, and the

thin drizzle turned into a downpour, she finally admitted defeat. Ella snapped shut the umbrella, gathered up her bags as best she could, and followed the path in the direction Amos had taken. It was difficult carrying all her baggage when she was obliged to also lift her ankle-length skirts, and tiptoe carefully to avoid getting mud on her new shoes.

As Ella finally entered the kitchen her heart quailed with foreboding. She was instantly appalled by the overpowering smell of livestock, and the stink of peat smoke from an open grate where a kettle hung from an iron crane. Cold struck through her thin shoes from the slate flagged floors, and the thick stone walls seemed to press in upon her as she regarded her new home with something like dread.

Her gaze took in the paucity of her surroundings at a glance, the cavernous fireplace that took up one entire wall and from which hung a great pan suspended by a hook like some sort of witch's cauldron. Blackened oak beams seemed to press down upon her from above, and the panelled walls might be elaborately carved, with a wooden settle either side of the fire, but they were black with smoke and pitted with age. Two grubby children with snot running from their noses sat on a pegged rug playing with a mangy kitten. A young girl of eleven or twelve stood washing dishes at a stone sink, and an old crone with a wizened face and no teeth was muttering something to Amos about a ewe having been cast during the day, whatever that might mean.

None of them paid her the slightest attention, save for

an old dog, which raised its head for a moment before sinking back to sleep again on a sigh.

Ella dropped her bags and umbrella, folded her arms across her chest and waited with undisguised impatience. It was growing quite dark outside and she could hear the wind whistling through the cracks around the door and windows, despite them all now being closed. And having eaten barely a crumb at the wedding breakfast, she was cold, hungry, and tired beyond endurance, as well as bursting to relieve herself. What kind of welcome was this to give to a new bride?

Her eyes came to rest upon a plate of oat cakes and clap bread, a chipped blue milk jug and a wedge of yellow cheese on the none-too-clean wooden table which stood in the centre of the bare, comfortless kitchen. Not much hope there then.

Without a glance in her direction, the old woman shuffled over to the fire where she began to stir what smelt like mutton broth. Ella's stomach rumbled, even as she perversely resolved not to eat a scrap.

'*I'm not staying here,*' she cried into the silence, stamping her foot and startling both husband and housekeeper, if that's what she was. Even the children looked up from their game with the kitten, and the thin silent girl stopped washing dishes as they all turned to look at her for the first time.

Ella put her face in her hands and began to weep.

'Put supper on t' table, then take her things upstairs,' Amos instructed the old woman, ignoring his young bride's outburst. 'We'll all be wanting an early night tonight.'

Ella's tears dried upon the instant. It was in this moment that she longed most for her sisters and the sanctity of her own bed. For if this day had been bad, worse was surely to come when night fell.

Livia tossed and turned, quite unable to sleep, haunted as she was by images of a dark-haired young man with a mocking, arrogant smile.

After Jack Flint had gone, almost against her better judgement Livia had found herself filled with admiration and respect for the courage it must have taken for him to approach her as he did. What could possibly be so important that he would risk coming within a hair's breadth of Josiah Angel, the man who itched to fling him into jail for inciting a riot, and throw away the key?

He might be rough and blunt of manner; Livia might not approve of the way he'd fought his corner with regards to that rent revolt last year, but there was no doubting his sincerity. He did at least possess a set of morals, however flawed. She very much doubted Hodson knew the meaning of the word. Entirely self-serving, the wealthy businessman seemed to spend much of his leisure time at the card tables frittering away the profits he made at the expense of others, as did her father.

When she'd returned to the guests at the wedding breakfast, Henry had clung to her side like a fat limpet, all unctuous affability and sycophantic insincerity. Livia couldn't help but compare her would-be suitor with Jack Flint. She sensed that at least you'd know where you were with a man like that. With Hodson, on the other hand, you never quite knew what he was thinking. There was a slyness to him, to his secret thoughts and studied diplomacy. He'd say whatever seemed appropriate to get what he wanted, and he very much wanted her.

Fortunately, Livia had managed to put him off thus far, and would continue to do so if she had any say in the matter. She had no intention of allowing her father to force her into the match. If she had her way, she wouldn't marry at all. She'd never met any man worth giving up her independence for, what little independence she had, that is. Being controlled by her father was bad enough, willingly putting herself under the thumb of a husband as well would be folly in the extreme.

Livia longed to be a modern woman. She wanted to join the family firm and learn the business of managing a department store from the floor up. All her life she'd yearned for her father's approval and to make him proud of her, but had never yet succeeded. Surely working alongside, rather than against him, would be a start? Apparently, he didn't agree. He point-blank refused to allow her to do any such thing.

Livia sighed as she pounded her pillow and tried yet again to settle to sleep, knowing her dreams would never come to fruition, that no matter how hard she fought him, Josiah would get his way in the end. Didn't he always?

A shudder rippled through her, as, tucking her nightie round her toes against the cold, Livia turned her mind to what it would mean to be married to Henry Hodson. To be kissed by that wet, slobbering mouth, fondled by those sausage-like fingers; to be taken to bed as his wife, rather as her poor sister was no doubt enduring right at this moment. Livia felt sickened by the thought this might indeed be her fate, as it was Ella's.

Why did life have to be this way? Why did she never meet decent men, real men like... She stopped, shocked by where her thoughts were leading her.

Yet she'd felt almost flattered by the way Jack Flint's eyes had appraised her, as if in admiration. He'd made it clear that he did not dislike what he saw. And there'd been an athletic grace to his strong muscled body as he'd strode away across the garden. As exhaustion finally claimed her, it was not Hodson's face she saw but quite another altogether, and another mouth she tasted. If she shuddered then, it was surely with pleasure.

Maggie was also far from sleep. But unlike her sisters, she had never viewed her own bed as any sort of sanctuary or safe haven. She'd tucked her diary away in its secret hiding place beneath a cracked floorboard, and now lay listening with dread to the familiar heavy step upon the stair. The sound, when it came minutes later, seemed to reverberate in her head. Maggie held her breath, waiting for her bedroom door to open.

Even as she shrank, mouse-like, into a tight little ball, she knew there was no escape, no place for her to hide. Hadn't she discovered that fact years ago? The door creaked open, the heavy tread drew nearer, accompanied by the grunt and rasp of whisky-tainted breath. The next instant the covers were being pulled back and the bed sagged with the weight of him as he sank beside her.

Maggie's every instinct was to turn away, to cling to the far side of the bed and press her knees tightly together, but she stayed where she was, flat on her back, knowing resistance was fruitless. She'd tried many times in the past to escape, even to run, but had learnt to her cost that it was safer to close her eyes and endure. That way it was over and done with all the sooner, and with less pain and fewer repercussions.

He'd first come to her bed when she was just eight years old. Maggie hadn't understood back then what he was doing. She'd thought that his kisses and cuddles were meant to prove that she was special in some way, perhaps because she was the youngest; and that she was his favourite. She'd revelled in the attention, at least for a while. And then everything had changed. His attentions had grown more demanding, far too intrusive for a shy young girl, and instinct had told her that this was wrong. Trying to tell her father so, to resist these demonstrations of affection, was another matter altogether. Josiah wasn't a man to take no for an answer.

She used to hide in the cupboard, holding her breath and covering her eyes with her hands, hoping and praying that if she couldn't see him, then he couldn't find her. But he always did. He'd make a game of it, a sick sort of hide and seek, where he would call her name softly as he opened drawers and doors, the lid of her toy box, and even look under the rug, saying 'Now where can my special girl be? I know she's here somewhere.'

When he found her, which he always did, he'd carry her back to bed and climb into it with her, start to kiss her and stroke that secret private place, as if this were all a part of the game to prove how very much he loved her. He described it as their little secret, something special which must be kept only between the two of them. He couldn't seem to understand that she really didn't like what he did to her, and was far too ashamed and embarrassed to tell anyone.

There had been a time, when she was approaching womanhood and he began to demand more than simply touching and stroking, that Maggie had tried to actually fight him. She'd smack his laughing face, punch his solid shoulders with small fierce fists. At first he found her resistance amusing, then he'd smack and punch her right back, and his 'attentions' following such demonstrations of rebellion had been far more brutal. Thus Maggie had learnt the wisdom of obedience.

'Shove up, my pretty,' he said to her now. 'Be a good girl and be nice to your dadda, eh? Let's enjoy our little secret business.'

Within seconds he was on top of her, pushing her legs apart, his sharp nails digging into the soft flesh of her inner thighs. Maggie kept her head turned away in a vain attempt to disassociate herself from what was going on below as he fiddled and poked, stroked and licked her tender parts, grunting and panting all the while. Tears rolled silently down her cheeks, but she made not a sound, long since schooled to endure in silence.

Next came the part she hated most, when he pushed her head down under the covers till she was in close proximity to his own private parts, and it was her turn to pleasure him. His choice of word, not hers. The sweaty stench of his hairy loins alone made her gag, let alone the thrust of his loathsome member being rammed into her mouth. Maggie did what was required of her until she could bear no more and did indeed almost vomit.

By the time he entered her, pinning her down on the bed with his strong hands and his cumbersome, ageing body, coming to a violent and brutal climax, Maggie was beyond caring, beyond thought or emotion of any kind, save to wish that the sheer weight of him might crush her into nothingness. Maggie loathed her father for what he did to her, and loathed herself even more for allowing him to do it. She ached to disappear completely, to sink into some hole in the ground and vanish for ever; longed for it with all her heart. Maybe one day she would succeed and find some way to escape and make herself disappear altogether.

Chapter Seven

The sun was high in the sky by the time Ella woke that first morning, indicating that it must be quite late. She stretched and stirred, savouring that warm half-doze for another few moments, that half awareness which made her imagine she might be in her own bed. And then she remembered. The bed, the place, her situation, was entirely new and strange. She was married. She was a wife, in name if not in truth.

Last night Ella had lain shivering in the marital bed, although whether with cold or fear was hard to define. It felt like a combination of both. She certainly didn't experience the sense of excitement and joy a bride was supposed to feel on her wedding night, and she'd dared not even allow herself to think of Danny.

She'd left the mutton stew largely untouched, its greasiness making her come over all nauseous so that she'd had to run outside and vomit into the bushes, much to her shame. The housekeeper, a Mrs Rackett (strange name for such a silent old crone) had been most disapproving.

'Waste of good food to chuck it up minutes after you've eaten it,' she'd complained. Ella couldn't argue with the logic of that. But the woman had put the rest of the untouched stew from Ella's plate back into the pot, which had made her retch all the more.

Ella hadn't troubled to unpack but collapsed into bed, dreading the moment when she heard her husband's tread upon the stair. She'd waited with her heart in her mouth, very much as she would listen to the approach of her father to the tower room when he intended to use the strap on one or other of her sisters. She hadn't suffered this fate half as often as Livia, but the memory was sharp all the same.

Would this man, her new husband, be another such? Would he use her kindly or take what he wanted without a care for her own feelings? Ella curled herself into a tight little ball and waited.

But he had not come. Sleep had claimed her instead. Now it was morning and she stumbled out of bed, splashed her face with cold water from the jug and pulled on one of her prettiest gowns. It was a pretty print sarsenet with a pin-tucked bodice. But Ella had trouble with the long line of buttons at the back so was obliged to take it off again and find something simpler and more sensible. A skirt and blouse came to hand and she dragged those on with a sigh of irritation. She did so like to look pretty.

Pinning up her hair took another age without a maid to assist and Ella grew flustered and frustrated, cursing her father for not having spared her Kitty. He could easily have got himself another parlour maid. But he'd insisted that a farmer of modest means could not afford the luxury of a ladies' maid for his bride.

'But *you* could easily afford to pay her for me,' she'd stubbornly pointed out. Very reasonably, so far as Ella could see. To which plea her father had snorted his contempt, informing his daughter that it was no longer his responsibility to spoil her any more than he had already, and that she must speak to her husband on the matter.

Now, dropping hair pins all over the floor and being decidedly dissatisfied with the result when she'd finally tucked every lock of shining, silver fair hair into some sort of order, Ella made a vow to do exactly that at the very first opportunity. Really, it was quite unreasonable to expect her to manage without the assistance of a maid.

The kitchen was empty, the great table scrubbed bare by the time Ella emerged some time later, still rubbing sleep from her eyes. There was no one in sight, not even the sour-faced old crone. She found a heel of bread languishing in the bread bin and poured herself a mug of fresh milk from the jug in the larder. Then she began to ransack the shelves in search of some other delicacy: peaches perhaps, or cold sausage, youthful hunger suddenly returning with renewed vigour after her prolonged fast.

'Breakfast was over and done with hours ago.'

The voice made her nearly jump out of her skin, Ella having thought herself quite alone. She swung around, the two eggs she'd been considering putting in a pan to boil flying from her fingers and smashing to the slate floor. Amos frowned at the resulting mess, and silently handed his young wife a cloth. Ella dropped quickly to her knees and began to wipe up the pool of sticky yolk and albumen.

'We allus has us breakfast reet after milking. Six sharp. I didn't wake thee since it were your first morning, so I'll let thee off this time. But see thou isn't late again.'

She didn't quite understand what he meant by 'let thee off'. After all, at Angel House she could rise when she pleased, take breakfast or not according to her mood and appetite. No one would ever presume to wake her. And did he always talk in thee's and thou's? Ella had never noticed that in him before, but then she'd hardly exchanged half a dozen words with her husband, save for the few words he'd spoken on their journey here, and hearing him read his Bible at the kitchen table last night.

He was still speaking, issuing further instructions, or so it seemed. 'Now tha'd best get theesen over to the dairy.'

She looked at him askance. 'The dairy? But it's Saturday.'

'There's still work to be done. It's not Mrs Rackett's job to do it, not now we've got thee.' He glowered down at Ella's ineffectual efforts with the broken eggs. 'Nor is it her job to clean up after thee. You might find a drop of water would help.'

Ella considered this, wondering where she might find such a thing as a tap.

'The pump is outside,' Amos informed her, reading her mind.

She looked at him blankly. 'Pump? Outside?' As if she couldn't quite work out where that might be, or what, exactly, a pump was. Angel House was equipped with the very latest in bathrooms and plumbing, even in the kitchen. Ella suddenly recalled that the privy, once she'd finally been allowed to relieve herself the night before, was tucked behind the house amongst a patch of nettles. She shuddered at the recollection. What sort of a place had she come to?

'Aye, where else would it be?' Amos was saying. 'And look sharp about it,' he grumbled, turning to walk away. Ella remained on her knees for a full heart beat, then jumped up to hurry after him. 'But, Amos, what is it, exactly, I'm supposed to do in the dairy?'

He blinked at her as if she were suddenly speaking an unknown language. 'Churn butter, mek cheese, do whatever needs doing a' course.'

'B-b-but...' She was stammering now, uncertain, fearful, as she had used to do when she was a child and her father had been cross with her over some supposed misdemeanour. 'I've no idea how to do those things, how to make b-butter or cheese.'

'Then tha'd best look sharp and learn,' he calmly informed her. 'This isn't Angel House, and we don't have no servants here. As well as the dairy, there's the calves to feed, and the hens to see to. Mrs Rackett will show you what's what, so look sharp.'

Looking sharp, by which he seemed to mean the necessity for both speed and the facility of learning, appeared to be his byword, although what all the rush was for, Ella really couldn't imagine. Even had she the first idea how to set about making butter, didn't she have all day in which to manage it? What else was there to do in this godforsaken place? She could quite see herself being bored out of her mind by nightfall.

Watching her husband stride away in his lolloping gait, Ella thought that perhaps this might not be the moment to mention the problems she'd encountered dressing and attending to her hair by herself, or to ask for a personal maid.

Instead, she toasted two slices of bread at the kitchen fire for her breakfast, spread them lavishly with fresh butter and honey, and began making plans for a visit to town. She certainly had no intention of languishing here for very long, nor of spending her days churning butter. Nor did she have any intention of becoming involved with whatever it was you were supposed to do with calves or hens. The very idea made her shudder.

Ella chose to ignore his instructions to find either Mrs Rackett or the dairy, and went back to her room where she set about unpacking her few belongings. She shook out her dresses, left in a crumpled heap after her indecision over what to wear, and hung them in the cavernous wardrobe beside Amos's best Sunday suit and an old tweed jacket. She put the few books she'd brought with her on the table by the bed, and her shoes and other possessions, such as her writing case and sewing box, in an empty chest which stood at the foot of the bed.

If she'd known how stark her surroundings were going to be, she'd have brought much more. She started writing a list of what she would bring the very first time she visited Kendal.

The room itself afforded little in the way of home comforts, with its uncarpeted bare boards that were rough to the feet, the shuttered windows with no sign of curtains, and basic, rustic furniture. Ella supposed a bedroom was not a place a farmer would have much time to linger, since the nature of his work demanded he rise early. She nursed a wild hope that perhaps she could make the room into her very own little hideaway, somewhere she might escape to, to read her romances or write letters home to her sisters.

She groaned as a wave of homesickness struck her. It already felt like days rather than hours since she'd last seen them, her wedding day having gone by in a blur.

Why had she ever allowed herself to be bullied into this match? Why had her father turned on her, the one daughter who had always been his favourite, or so she'd believed? And all because she'd fallen in love with a groom, a working man instead of a man of property. Why was it that he valued land, money, his business, everything in fact, above his three daughters' happiness? It was so unfair.

Amos made no comment on her defection from her duties, perhaps because it was a Saturday, and her first day at the farm. Ella read for a while and worked on her list; she ate bread and cheese with Mrs Rackett and three silent children at lunchtime, then took a walk as far as the clapper bridge in the afternoon, desperate for a breath of fresh air.

A flock of pink-tinged grey clouds chased each other across the blue sky, as if lining up to take turns crossing Lingmell Fell. Perhaps they were heading for Scotland via High Street, the old Roman track that traversed the tops of the fells. Ella longed to go with them. Better still, she wanted to go home, to Livia and Maggie. She so longed to keep walking, on down the valley through the village of Staveley and beyond to Kendal, that it took every ounce of effort to turn around and walk back to Todd Farm.

Her courage was further tested that night as yet again she lay in the cold marital bed, waiting for her husband to come to her. The click of the latch was like a gunshot in the quiet of the night.

Dear God, what had she done?

He looked smaller and thinner by the light of the candle he carried, like a cadaver rather than a living, breathing man. Setting the candlestick down on a washstand he poured water from the jug into the basin and began to wash his hands. Ella was surprised by this, knowing Amos had already washed and shaved in the outhouse before supper, using the cut-throat razor and strop that hung behind the scullery door. Whatever he had found to do since then, which would necessitate this further thorough scrubbing and washing, Ella really couldn't imagine.

When he was finally done and towelled dry, he sat on a bentwood chair to remove his boots and socks. Shadows loomed as he moved about, but she was grateful for the semi-darkness as he began to peel off his clothing. Seconds later she saw a white nightshirt billow over his head, and fear clutched at her stomach.

Ella's heart beat slow and hard in her breast. What would he do to her? Would he be gentle and patient? Or had Father given the impression that she was no virgin, that she was very much a woman of experience, which was not at all the case. Should she remind Amos of that fact now? Ella opened her mouth to explain but as quickly closed it again. How could she possibly discuss anything so intimate with this man, this stranger?

Once ready for bed, she expected him to extinguish the candle and climb in beside her. Instead, he took his time smoothing out the towel, hanging it to dry on a wooden rack that stood close by. Next, he knelt beside the bed and began to pray. His prayer was largely silent, little more than a mumble with few words distinguishable beyond the obvious, such as 'Father in Heaven' and 'cast your eyes upon a poor sinner'.

There must have been several prayers for he took an interminably long time over the task before finally he blew out the candle and climbed into bed beside her. The flock mattress sagged beneath his weight but he brought no warmth with him, and precious little comfort. Still without uttering a single word, he turned towards her, tugged up her nightdress, and lay on top of her.

Ella stopped breathing. Was this how he intended to go about it? Were there to be no preliminaries, no soft kisses such as the kind Danny would shower over every glimmer of silky bare flesh he could find: her mouth, her eyelids, behind her ears, even the inside of her wrist, oh so deliciously sensitive.

She really mustn't think of Danny, not right at this moment.

Ella could feel something soft and warm against her thigh, which surprised her. She might lack experience with regards to the actual act itself, but she was by no means totally ignorant, and well accustomed to the hardness of Danny's manhood, as well as the way he struggled to control his need after all those sweet kisses. Amos seemed to have an altogether different problem.

There was much grunting and gasping, pushing and shoving. He indicated that she should part her legs for him, and obediently she complied, although still he didn't speak. Ella could feel the heat of him through the thick stuff of his nightshirt, and prepared for the worst as her husband began to sweat.

Would it hurt? she worried. Would there be blood on the sheets to prove her virginity? She rather hoped there might be, if only to prove her innocence. Amos pawed at her breast, squeezing one as if testing a fruit for ripeness. He sucked at her nipple, which startled her but did nothing to light any burning desire within her belly, or bring that familiar pulsating glow between her legs. And his penis, flopped against her thigh, remained stubbornly inactive.

This agony seemed to go on for hours, yet was probably a matter of moments only. She could almost smell his anxiety, along with his sweat, which had a strong odour of farmyard about it.

Ella could feel the anguish growing in him, a fretting frustration.

Desperate to help him she put up a hand and stroked his hair, which felt surprisingly soft and clean. She tried to kiss his cheek but it landed clumsily on his ear instead. He made no reciprocal move to kiss her.

Wanting this whole thing to be over and done with, she suddenly said, 'I don't know what Father told you about Danny Gilpin, but I swear it's not true. We did nothing we shouldn't, not much anyway. So if he said anything different, he's lying.' Rather tentatively she added, 'Would you like me to...' and sliding her hand down between their two bodies attempted to drag away the thick fabric of his nightshirt, searching for bare flesh.

On a cry of horrified disgust he flung himself off her, almost leaping from the bed as if he'd been stung. 'You've been with another man? You Jezebel! No wonder I can't do my duty by you. I should have realised there would be problems marrying a pretty girl like you. Women are all the same.'

Instinct drove her to defend herself. 'You're not listening to me. I've done nothing wrong.'

Amos snorted his disbelief. 'You lie! A virgin is without fault before the throne of God – "but thou didst trust in thine own beauty and played the harlot because of thy renown, and poured out thy fornications."'

'What?'

'I will not have you play the whore with me, woman!'

Ella was struck dumb, not having the first idea how to respond.

To her horror he proceeded to again wash his hands, as if merely by touching her he had defiled himself in some way. Then he got back into bed, turned his back upon her and amazingly, seconds later, was snoring.

Ella lay unmoving, quite unable to sleep, staring into the darkness in a state of total shock and misery. Her husband couldn't even bring himself to make love to her, or show her the least tenderness. And when she'd tried to help, to explain, he'd called her by that foul name. Oh, how different this night would have been had Father allowed her to marry Danny. Fat tears rolled down her face, soaking into her pillow.

How would she endure?

At some point in the early hours, when there was still no crack of light for her to see properly, Ella was woken by a strange sound. She became aware of a shadowed figure huddled in a corner of the room, presumably that of her husband. His shoulders were shaking, which quite mystified her. What he was doing she had no idea, but he was giving odd little gasps and sobs and whimpering sounds.

It came to her then with a new wave of shock that he was crying. She hadn't realised that grown men could cry. But why would he? What could possibly have upset him? What had she done, and why wouldn't he believe in her innocence? Had her own father blighted all hope of that?

Or could he perhaps still be grieving for his first wife? Ella's heart filled with sympathy, for him, and for herself, trapped in this loveless marriage.

The noise went on for some long moments and when finally it stopped, she again heard the sound of water being poured, and the washing ritual begin all over again. After that, he climbed back into bed on a trembling sigh. Ella turned her face to the wall, as far from him as she could get in the big double bed, and wept her own silent tears of anguish.

Chapter Eight

If Fellside had seemed like a hell-hole, then Mercy thought she must surely have arrived in Hell itself.

She'd walked from the hansom cab in all innocence, not appreciating exactly what this great mausoleum of a building really was. She'd thought it was the lodging house where some of the girls who worked at the store must live, having assumed she was to be given employment.

Now she understood how cruelly she'd been tricked. Mercy saw to her horror that she was in a worse situation than before she'd asked Josiah Angel for help, or shown him her mother's letter. He hadn't given her a new future at all. He'd sent her to the workhouse.

What kind of father was he? What sort of man would condemn his own daughter, albeit one from the wrong side of the blanket, to incarceration? A devil, no less.

What had gone wrong? How had this all come about? More importantly, how could she let Jessie and Jack know where she was and what had happened to her? They'd be so worried, although what they could do to save her was beyond Mercy's imagining.

The woman now searching her and stripping her of her clothes, her very identity, paid no attention to her claim there'd been some mistake and that she shouldn't even be here. Nor did she listen to Mercy's plea that her friends be informed of her whereabouts. Her protests fell upon deaf ears.

'You've no right to keep me here,' Mercy cried. 'Josiah Angel has no right to send me here without my agreement, not even a by-your-leave. Surely I should have a say in the matter?'

'He's *Mr* Angel to you. Mind your manners, girl. And you're destitute, so where else would you go?' Her voice was weary and disinterested, making it clear she'd heard it all before. The very fact Mercy's pockets were empty with not a penny to her name proved her parlous state.

The woman, or Matron, as she instructed Mercy to call her, was tall and thin, her face composed of a number of planes and sharp angles that tapered to a long sharp nose. Dressed in a striped blue dress covered with a white bib apron, her tightly scraped-back hair was topped off with a fancy white cap, firmly tied under a narrow pointed chin.

Mercy was duly stripped of the clothes Jessie had so carefully washed and pressed for her, and put through the indignities of being bathed and deloused, her hair cut to no more than half an inch all over her head before being dressed in a scratchy cotton nightgown several sizes too big for her. When she protested about this too, she was smartly informed that head lice were not welcome here, and didn't she know that prayer, self-sacrifice and cleanliness was the way to reach the Kingdom of God?

'You should be grateful Mr Angel took the trouble to find you proper care and accommodation.' As if to emphasise her point, on the way back from the bathrooms Matron permitted Mercy to look through a window to see the long line of tramps, known as casuals, who were already queuing up for a night's board and lodging.

Mercy was appalled at the thought that anyone would actually volunteer to get in here. 'Why does the man in charge send some of them away?' she asked, curious over the way the line was being managed.

The woman sighed heavily. 'Because they've come begging a bed once too often lately. Those who are allowed in will be given the order of the bath too, just as you have, missy, but tomorrow they'll be out on the streets again. So thank your lucky stars you're at least sure of a bed every night. You're a very lucky girl.'

Mercy didn't feel in the least bit lucky. She felt as if she'd been abducted, kidnapped and locked up, and someone had thrown away the key.

A fracas broke out and seconds later the tramp appeared on the stone-flagged corridor ahead of them, frogmarched along by two officers and thrown into a cell. Mercy was allowed to peep through a slit in the door as they passed by, her insides turning to water at the sight that met her eyes.

The poor man was bent double, a huge hammer in his hand, which he swung time and again to break a pile of huge stones. He was already shaking with the effort, near to collapse, probably from lack of food as much as anything.

'He'll have to break them small enough to push through that grid set in the far wall,' Matron told her. 'When he's finished all the stones in the cell, he'll be let out. Shouldn't take him more than twelve hours or so, then he'll be given breakfast and sent on his way. Serve him right for being feckless and quarrelsome. Not a bad bargain for a night's accommodation, eh?'

It didn't seem much of a bargain to Mercy. But the point hadn't escaped her that clean and neat though the place might appear at first glance, there were rules to be kept, and darker issues at work beneath the surface.

With shock still blurring her mind so that she found it hard to think straight, Mercy followed the woman along endless dark corridors, and was finally allotted a bed in a large dormitory.

The room seemed huge, the ranks of beds numbered fifty or more. Nobody spoke to her and the place stank of stale sweat, urine and vomit. Mercy curled up on the straw-filled pallet, pulled the single red wool blanket over her head and wept silently for her dead mother, overwhelmed by despair.

How she wished, in that moment, that she'd never gone near Josiah Angel.

Mercy endured her first night with fortitude and no small degree of bitterness. She barely slept a wink for all the snorting and coughing and weeping she could hear going on in the other beds. It was the longest, coldest, most miserable night she could ever remember, far worse even than the Angel buildings at Fellside. How she longed for her mother, or for Jessie to come bounding in bringing her a warm barm cake and a morning kiss.

Instead, she lined up with the other women for the lavatory and to wash her face in cold water. After that, dressed in a blue cotton dress and a pinafore that might once have been white she followed them to the dining hall, where she ate a silent breakfast of salted porridge and a mug of weak tea. She saw that the staff sat at a separate table on a platform at one end of the hall, Matron in the centre, clearly in charge. And although Mercy was aware of many sidelong glances and curious stares in her direction from the other girls, no one said a word to her.

Since she was too old now for school, Mercy had rather assumed that she'd be put to weaving, knitting or carding, since she had skills in these tasks. But she soon learnt different.

A large girl a few years older than Mercy, a Nurse Jenkyns with a round face, red hair and a cheerful smile, was delegated to take her on to the wards. Mercy's task, she explained, as they set off at a cracking pace down a long corridor, would be to scrub floors, make beds, empty chamber pots, turn mattresses and other menial tasks.

'We calls 'em scrubbers, since that's what they do.

Matron is very particular that everything be kept spanking clean, which includes patients' bottoms.' She laughed at the look of shocked distaste on Mercy's face. 'You won't find it as bad as it first appears, once you get used to it,' she told her kindly.

Mercy was not reassured.

'It's a bit of a facer at first, I will admit. We get some odd sorts in here, and quite a few nutters. Still, the food isn't bad and nobody knocks you around, eh? Leastways, not if you mind your Ps and Qs. Anyway, if you've any problems, come to me. I'll put you right.'

'Thank you, Nurse Jenkyns, I'll remember that.'

The other girl grinned, revealing two missing front teeth. 'Call me Prue, and sorry about the missing gnashers; me pa knocked them out for me, which is why I come here. No place else to go.'

'*I* shouldn't be here at all,' Mercy burst out. 'It's all a big mistake.'

''Course it is. No doubt you've got a bleeding palace somewhere. Right, we go through here. Don't panic, it'll look a bit like bedlam but that's upstairs actually.'

Mercy looked at the other girl in horror. Where had she come to? What sort of place was this?

The ward did indeed seem to be packed with people, many wandering about aimlessly, singing or shouting and making a lot of noise. Others were lying comatose in their beds. Prue explained that they were mostly old, or abandoned by their families in this the final refuge for the unemployed. It seemed to Mercy a cruel fate.

A group of patients were huddled together round a mean little fire shielded by a large fireguard at the far end of the ward as the two girls passed through. They didn't seem to have any sort of occupation, or conversation, which seemed sad, used as Mercy was to the women of Fellside who were always gossiping or busy with their knitting sticks. These people sat unmoving, their eyes dead, their gaze unfocused, as if they'd given up the struggle and were simply waiting to die.

There were no pictures on the wall, save for one of Christ on the cross. Even the walls themselves weren't plastered, the open brickwork painted a bluish white, and over all hung the sweet-sour stench of cloying sickness and decay.

The next ward was the children's, which was even more distressing. One giant cradle, filled with half a dozen babies, was being rocked by a young girl who smiled at Mercy as she passed by. Infants stood holding on to their cot rails, many of them too frail to even cry, let alone smile or laugh as children should. Prue explained that deformities were common, the result of rickets, infections, or injury.

'Some have had all the sense shaken out of 'em, quite literally,' which made Mercy shudder at the thought that anyone could hurt such small children.

Prue picked up one baby and gave her a hug and a kiss before handing her over to a young attendant. 'That sheet is wet, Nurse. Best change it before Sister sees it.'

None of the babies had napkins on them, Mercy noticed, but they did at least look pink cheeked and well fed. She said as much to her new friend, who clearly held some status over the other attendants.

'Oh, aye, they get well fed here; plain fare but substantial. All food and schooling provided by the local council. Just as well since most are orphans, or illegitimate, with no loved ones of their own to provide for them.'

That word – illegitimate – made Mercy shiver. This could so easily have been her own fate. At least she'd been more fortunate than these poor mites, having been brought up on Fellside with her mam.

One girl was rocking herself back and forth, banging her head in a tragic rhythm against the end of her cot. She must have been doing this for some time as there were large blue and yellow bruises on her forehead. The young nurse in charge put the child in a strait-jacket.

Mercy could hardly bear to watch as the child stiffened and became rigid, screaming her protest at being so confined.

'Is this where I'll be working?' she asked, a thread of hope in her voice. Surely she could try to make the babies lives more cheerful, perhaps by telling them stories or finding something to occupy them. She knew any number of games she used to play with her mam. All she needed was paper and pencil, or a bit of a string for cat's cradle. Prue shook her head and hurried Mercy out through the big swing doors.

Crossing an open courtyard they came to a large door, which her companion proceeded to unlock with a key hanging from her wide belt. A small knot of unease lodged itself in Mercy's chest, some instinct warning her this wasn't quite right. She wanted to ask why the door needed to be locked, but her tongue had somehow cleaved to the roof of her mouth, and her heart started to pound against her rib cage. All she wanted to do was turn on her heels and run. The trouble was, there was nowhere to run to.

'This is where you'll be working, for now at least.'

Mercy could barely believe the sight that met her eyes. She stared in horror at the inmates, all male with hair cropped as close to their heads as her own now was, dressed in unbleached calico suits, complete with waistcoats, although they wore no necktie at the collarless shirt. As she hesitated, Prue bustled her inside, locking the door carefully behind them.

'Don't panic, love. I'll have you moved soon as I can, but all new girls start here. They might look odd but they're harmless enough.'

Clearly curious about the newcomers who'd suddenly appeared in their ward, the men came shambling over, looking very much like a herd of cows examining a stray dog who'd wandered into their field.

Mercy took a step back. 'What's wrong with them?' At least she'd found her voice, weak and trembling though it might be.

'Nowt, so far as I know, 'cept they're imbeciles, or so they call them. Real sad cases. Your job is to keep them – and the ward – nice and tidy and clean, which I'm sure a fine strong girl such as yourself can do quite easily. You won't get much help from them, mind. These poor souls barely have the sense to wipe their own bums.'

Mercy looked at her aghast, but Prue gave her a nudge. 'Go on, get along with you then. Go and report to Nurse Bathurst. You'll find her in her office. Keep your head down and do exactly what she tells you to, that's my advice to you, love. Batty Brenda, as we calls her, isn't exactly the patient type, and doesn't much care for shirkers. Just keep your head down and get on with the job. That way you might survive.' And having issued this bleak warning, her new friend turned on her heel and left Mercy alone in the ward.

Mercy had barely taken two paces when she found herself surrounded by men. They stroked her hair, pinched her cheek, fingered the buttons down the front of her dress as if trying to count them, or perhaps undo them. She was too terrified to decide which. One untied her apron strings and Mercy hastily retied it, in a double bow this time. Another patient, clearly male with stubble on his unshaven chin, was dressed like a woman in a stuff gown. He even wore a bonnet.

'I like your dress,' he said. 'Have you got drawers on?' And he lifted up the hem of her dress to see for himself, making his comrades giggle and grin like naughty schoolboys.

Mercy tried to tug her dress free. 'Please don't do that,' she begged. Close to panic, she longed to slap him, to push them away, but was doing her utmost to remain calm, remembering how Prue had told her that these patients might be simple-minded but were largely harmless. It was hard to believe this as one reached out and squeezed her breast, chuckling with delight when she squealed.

'Stop it,' she cried, trying to sound like a disapproving schoolmarm. 'Stop this at once.' But they weren't even listening to her. They had her apron entirely off now, followed by her cap. The men were crowding her, pushing and shoving, stroking her breasts and hips, and Mercy found herself helplessly cornered, unable to escape.

Quite how it came about she could never afterwards explain. Maybe she slipped, or one of the men pushed her, but suddenly she was on the ground and they were all over her like a troop of inquisitive monkeys. She could smell their tainted breath, feel the roughness of their hands as they poked and probed at her.

She let out a stifled scream, unable to help herself, recognising something like joyous madness in their eyes, and knew they could easily turn into a rabble out of control.

Fear cascaded through her. What did they intend to do to her? She was quite incapable of fighting them all off. As she pushed one away another quickly took his place. Mercy felt trapped. One lifted her skirts, exposing her legs and she cried out in terror. Where was this nurse Prue had mentioned? Why didn't the woman come and help her?

And then she saw her, standing by what must be her

office door. She seemed perfectly aware of what was going on as she stood watching, arms folded across her flat chest, saying nothing, and making not the slightest effort to step in and help her new assistant.

'Help! Get them off me,' Mercy cried.

The man who had pulled up her skirts was now on top of her, grunting like a rutting animal and his mates were cheering and egging him on.

'Go on, go on.'

'She *is* wearing drawers,' he cried in delight, hooting with laughter, as if he'd made a great discovery. 'See, she is, she is.'

'Let me see,' cried another, pushing the first one away.

Hands reached for her, and for one terrible moment Mercy was quite certain they meant to strip her entirely, but then a voice rang out. Not that of the nurse but a high-pitched falsetto.

'That's enough, boys. We've had our bit of fun, now no more rough games. Let her go.' It was the man in the dress, and, by a miracle, the rabble obeyed. One moment they were like rampaging lunatics, the next they melted away, chuckling and giggling together, quite happy with their little joke. Some even redid the buttons of her frock, tied on her apron and tried to put her cap back on.

'I like you,' said one young man, giving her a kiss.

Mercy was shaking, quite beside herself with terror, but somehow managed to thank him.

The man, or woman, whatever he was, helped Mercy

to her feet, brushed down her skirts and found her shoe, which seemed to have come off in the scuffle. 'They can get a bit enthusiastic at times, bless them. Are you all right, love?' His voice this time was deep and throaty, a man's voice, and he held out a large calloused hand. 'The name's George, by the way, but everyone here calls me Georgina.'

He shook her hand, grinning all the while. Then, leaning closer, he – or she – whispered softly in her ear. 'You won't tell on them, will you? It was only high spirits. They meant no harm, and they don't get much chance of a laugh in this place. Only, if they get punished, it could all turn very nasty.'

Mercy thought of the tramp in the cell breaking stones, and again glanced over to the office door. The nurse in charge of the ward was nowhere to be seen. Shocked as Mercy had been by the assault, she realised it would do her no good at all to make a complaint. Perhaps they were simply testing her, and she really didn't seem to have any choice over which ward she was assigned to.

She managed a tight little smile. 'No, of course I won't tell,' and then, adopting a slightly scolding tone, added, 'But can we make sure it doesn't happen again?'

Georgina giggled behind her hand. 'We'll try to behave better, but you're so pretty. And I do like your drawers. We couldn't resist finding out if you had any on. Will you show me how to make a pair just like them, with the frill round the legs and everything?'

And suddenly Mercy found herself laughing too. 'Can

you sew?' she asked. 'Any of you?' And as heads were shaken and frowns gathered, she laughed again. 'Then I'll have to teach you. But the other men won't want a pair of drawers. What can we teach them?'

'Dignity,' said a stern voice from behind her. 'Something in which you seem to be sadly lacking, girl.'

Chapter Nine

It was Saturday afternoon, Maggie was taking a rest and catching up on her diary, and Livia decided on a short walk. She was already missing Ella, even if her sister had only been gone a few days, and had some serious thinking to do, for which she needed a clear head.

She opted to walk right up to the castle ruins, quiet at this time of day, and settled herself on a grassy mound. A cow lifted its head to stare at her, its jaws working, before ambling away. Livia loved the peaceful solitude of this place. The castle was built back in the twelfth or thirteenth century by one of King John's powerful barons, so far as she could recall from school History lessons. By the fourteenth century it was in the hands of the Parr family, and some said Catherine Parr herself was born there, and had spent much of her childhood in Kendal. She too had been married off against her will to two geriatric husbands before accepting the dubious honour of becoming the sixth wife of Henry VIII.

What was it about men? Why was their father so

hard on them? Livia knew that her father worshipped power. Craved it as others might crave whisky. She heard occasional talk in the town that Councillor Josiah Angel took bribes. That a suitably substantial sum slipped quietly into his bank account would earn you the right to build where you wished, expand your factory, or treat your employees in whatever manner suited you. Such gossip distressed her greatly as Livia felt a natural pride in her father's achievements as a self-made businessman.

It also upset her that he made little more than a perfunctory show of caring about the welfare of the poor, being of the view that their penurious state was due to their own fecklessness, and in no way connected to the high rents he charged them to live in the property he owned.

Kendal was a prosperous town and Livia was aware that she lived in one of its better class districts, with everything she could wish for by way of material comforts. She couldn't imagine what it must feel like to share a room with ten others and be uncertain where your next meal was coming from. But the old saying that money didn't necessarily bring happiness was certainly true in her eyes. There were other ways of bringing misery into a person's life beside poverty, and surely the lack of love was the worst cross to bear.

Her father had made her mother's life a misery, constantly criticising her and finding fault as if to prove that he was better than her, no longer the young man who had joined her father's business as a mere apprentice. He seemed to carry a chip on his shoulder because they came from different ends of the social spectrum, and Josiah never missed an opportunity to put her down.

In the end the poor woman had taken refuge in ill health, thankful to be out of the firing line of his caustic remarks and cruel tricks. Livia felt her loss keenly, but the responsibility of caring for her two younger sisters, as she'd promised their dying mother she would do, harder to bear than she'd ever imagined.

Things had got steadily worse once his three daughters were his only target. Whatever dissatisfaction or disappointment he felt in life, he took out on them, viewing them as mere pawns to use in his empire-building. Ella had been married off to a man she barely knew, and poor Maggie was so fragile and vulnerable Livia feared for her health. She felt quite anxious about her, but then she'd always been a sickly child who needed care and rest. Yet Father made no allowances for that fact.

He seemed to expect to control every part of their lives and Livia was fully aware that if he had his way, he would marry her off to Henry. Livia had no intention of marrying anyone.

She stared out over the view of the town she so dearly loved, the huddle of grey stone houses, Victoria Bridge that straddled the river, and the Helvellyn range visible on the distant horizon. Despite her strong loyalty and love for the town of her birth, Livia longed to pack her bags and walk away and be free. But that was impossible. Where could she go? Besides, nothing would induce her to leave Maggie.

Yet the fact that she stayed didn't mean she had any intention of being bullied as her poor sisters were. She meant to resist him to her last breath.

Dinner that evening was reasonably civilised, if rather quiet. Maggie was troubled by an irritating cough, as was so often the case, and picked at her roast lamb before taking herself off to bed early. Livia issued a whispered reminder for her to take a sip of her cough mixture before retiring, and worried in case her departure might create a fuss. Their father seemed to revel in punishing his younger daughter for her apparent intransigence over the poor state of her health. Tonight, however, he seemed preoccupied, and more subdued than usual.

Then quite out of the blue, he said, 'I was speaking to Henry Hodson this morning. He will be calling upon you tomorrow to pay court and make you an offer. See that you're ready to receive him. Put on your prettiest frock, the jewellery your mother left you, whatever you young ladies feel appropriate for such an occasion.'

His tone was cold and matter-of-fact, as if he were discussing a business proposition and not a possible marriage for his daughter.

'I would like to have this little matter resolved fairly soon. Time is of the essence, Lavinia. You are no longer the young girl you once were, nor so attractive a proposition in the marriage mart as you might imagine. And you really are far too opinionated for your own good. Fortunately, Henry Hodson has known you long enough to be able to ignore these flaws. As a wealthy young businessman, he can also afford to overlook such trifles as your lack of dowry. See that you make an effort to receive him with good grace and charm, and bring him nicely to the point, if you please.'

Having settled the matter to his own satisfaction, Josiah rose to his feet, dusted a few stray crumbs from the swelling dome of his stomach, and made a move to retire to his study to partake of his usual glass of port and smoke a cigar. Once the engagement was announced his debts would be nicely settled and the accounts could go hang. He might then employ a clerk to take that particular chore off his shoulders.

Livia could barely comprehend the words. *Little matter! Too opinionated for her own good! Bring him to the point!*

She sat stunned, open mouthed, shocked to the core, and only when the door was about to close upon his departing figure did she jump to her feet and summon up the courage to respond.

'I can't do that, Father. I won't!'

He turned on her, his voice a roar of displeasure. 'You can and you will.'

'No. Never!'

He raised a fist, his face livid with anger. Livia braced herself for the blow, but then he seemed to stop himself. Perhaps he realised that a young woman with a black eye or bruise on her chin would not look half so attractive to a young suitor. With immense difficulty he brought himself back under control.

'You'll do what I say, miss, or pay the consequences.

And you well know what those will be.'

Livia tilted her chin as father and daughter confronted each other, eye to eye, neither prepared to be the one to back down. At length, Josiah told her quite coldly and calmly that he would be at the store all the following day until seven-thirty as usual. 'You may call in and tell me the result of the interview at any time. You'll find me in my office. Once I know this matter is settled I shall begin to make the necessary arrangements.'

Then turning on his heel, he left her.

Livia remained where she was, shaking, although whether with rage or fright, she wasn't quite sure. Josiah Angel had made his wishes known, and, like it or not, as a dutiful daughter she was expected to carry them out. She must accept Henry Hodson's offer, whatever her own feelings on the matter.

Amos left Ella alone the second night, and the one after that. Every night she lay in bed expecting him to come, but he never did. Listening with acute attention for the slightest sound, she could almost hear him breathing as he paused at the bedroom door, then his step would continue onward and upward. She assumed he slept in the attics above.

She felt cold and lonely in the strange bed, the darkness seeming to press in upon her. Why did he not come? Was it that he found her unattractive? Why couldn't he make love to her?

Somewhere out on the empty, silent fells an owl

hooted, reminding her of their isolation, and she shivered. The sounds at Angel House had been so much more comforting: servants quietly going about their business, the clip-clop of horses' hooves in the street as carriages returned home late after some party or soirée. She longed for her own room, her things about her, her own bed, knowing her sisters were close by.

What were they doing right now? Staying up late and whispering together, giggling and being silly, as they had used to do on high days and holidays? Such delights were closed to her now. She was a wife. Amos could return to her bed whenever he chose. He had that right, as her husband, and she would be expected to carry out her wifely duties, whatever they might entail and however disagreeable. She didn't even know whether to be glad or sorry that she'd had no opportunity yet to discover.

Was he punishing her for mentioning Danny Gilpin? He seemed convinced of her guilt despite her protestations of innocence. Tension mounted in her as she waited.

One morning, Ella was brought roughly awake by a hand shaking her. Dawn was breaking, casting an eerie light through the thin bedroom curtains. What was he doing in her room? She sat up in panic. Had he at last come to claim his conjugal rights? But then she noted the grimness of his face. 'What is it? What's happened?'

'Get up, it's snowing.'

'Snowing? In *May*?'

'It's not unheard of in these parts and a late snow can do untold damage to the lambing. We have to get out on them fells and check on the flock.'

'*We?*'

A man of few words, he didn't trouble to reply, and paying no heed to the shock in her voice he simply ordered her to put on her warmest clothes and look sharp about it. Trained to obedience by her father, Ella did as she was told and what seemed only moments later she was trekking up the fell behind him, clad in boots and waterproofs, in freezing temperatures with snow falling all around. Beside him were his trio of working dogs, old Beth having been shut up in the house, much against her wishes.

'We're going up by the Tongue,' he called to her, which meant not a thing to Ella. Her lips felt stiff with cold, and despite the woollen hat and gloves he'd insisted she wore, her cheeks and nose were absolutely frozen. What on earth were they doing walking out in snow at this hour of the morning? Was he mad?

They'd crossed the river at a shallow, narrow point and now they skirted what looked like a huge cliff rising out of the snowy ground. From here they began to climb, fording a tiny beck and continuing up a slippery slope pitted with rocks and boulders. Ella was gasping for breath before they'd been walking for ten minutes, thought she might very well expire, and Amos's boots were little more than a blur in a white-out of snow ahead. Trying to keep those sturdy feet in view and watch where she put her own seemed well nigh impossible. Amos had given her a stick to help her, but it was long and clumsy, and she couldn't seem to handle it right. She stepped on an icy stone and her feet went from under, sending her crashing to her knees in the ice and snow.

She called to him. 'Amos, wait for me. Wait! I need to rest.'

He paused for no more than a moment, just long enough for her to scramble to her feet and reach him, panting for breath and with a stitch in her side. 'You must keep up, Ella.' Then he was off again, striding up the mountainside as if it were no more than a Sunday afternoon stroll. Ella was very nearly in tears. She was not only exhausted but her wet skirt was flapping against her legs, soaking her to the skin. And only a short time ago she'd been warm and asleep in her bed.

By the time they reached the top of the Tongue, Ella was weeping, wishing she'd never come to this godforsaken place, never married this dreadful man. What was he thinking of to bring her up this mountain pass in this awful weather? Did he want to get her killed?

As they reached the summit, climbing the last few feet in a series of zigzags, she realised to her relief that the snow had stopped falling and, as if by way of reward, the sun peeped out from behind a fat grey cloud, illuminating the scene. Ella gasped in astonishment. A panoply of mountains stretched out before her, their tops crested in a cloak of snow and ice, seeming to ripple into infinity. The beauty of the scene filled her with awe.

Amos took her arm and led her to a rough shelter of stones and at last allowed her to catch her breath and rest. If she looked back she could see the Kentmere valley, and to the north yet another dale, even more remote than their own. Amos told her this was Mardale, and the small lake she could see was Haweswater. Despite herself, Ella was entranced. She could see a wooded hillock, a cluster of farms and cottages that looked very like dolls' houses from this distance; a church and inn, and what must be a school. A whole village cast down in the middle of nowhere. She could see tiny people going about their business.

Did they ache to live in the town, as she did, or were they content with their lives? Did their fathers bully them and organise them without even a by-your-leave, or did they get to choose whether they stayed or left the dale? Her thoughts were interrupted as Amos was again on his feet.

'If you've got your breath back now, we need to press on. We must check every ewe, make sure no lamb is lost in the snow.'

'But what can *I* do?'

'You can help. Sheep tend to shelter beside dry stone walls, so take your stick and gently probe wherever the snow lies thick. If you find a sheep or lamb under there, give me a shout. Come on, there's a deal of ground to cover.' Then he was striding away from her, the dogs fanning out at his command, and it suddenly occurred to Ella that she was on her own. She'd been given a task to do and she must do it, however unjust and unfair it might seem. What did she know about sheep? Nothing! He had absolutely no right to bring her up onto the wild mountaintops and leave her to hunt for possible dead or injured sheep. What was the man thinking of?

It was the longest morning of Ella's life. She was miserable with cold and fatigue, and it seemed to go on interminably. She plodded back and forth over the huge expanse of fell, searching, prodding and poking, once startling both sheep and herself as a ewe she thought must surely be a goner suddenly reared up and skittered away with a lamb at its feet. She called him when she found a ewe with twin lambs huddled in a snowdrift and Amos helped her to scrape the snow from her body and urge her back to life, and soon the lambs were suckling again and all was well. Seeing they were safe, they both returned to the search.

Her whole body ached, her fingers and toes no longer had any feeling left in them and her nose felt red raw with the cold. Just when she thought she could take no more, Amos appeared at her side, his arms full of lambs.

'This one's an orphan,' he said, pushing the frail creature into her arms. 'And these two have just been born and need attention. We'll take them home with us. The mother will follow and we'll put them in the barn overnight.'

Ella stood mesmerised, instinctively cuddling the lamb

in her arms, gazing into its doe-like eyes.

'Well, are you coming?' He was already heading off down the track, back the way they had come, then he turned and suddenly grinned at her. 'Tha's done a good job today, lass. Now let's go home and have some of Mrs Rackett's hot soup.'

Ella found herself grinning back and, giving the bleating lamb a reassuring hug, she set off in his wake.

Chapter Ten

Livia's meeting with Henry Hodson did not begin well. He'd obviously come dressed for the occasion, being formally attired in frock coat and top hat. Livia had so effectively banished the coming interview from her mind that she was on her knees pulling weeds beneath the lilac tree in the back garden, wearing her ordinary gardening frock and green apron when he arrived.

While Kitty took his hat and gloves and showed him into the drawing room, she quickly washed her hands in the cloakroom, but decided against changing her gown. It was far too late to worry about that now. She simply took off her apron, tucked a few stray curls into place, and swept into the drawing room with a smiling apology for her appearance.

'Henry, how lovely to see you,' as if she hadn't been warned of his visit, or its purpose.

He was standing by the fireplace, hands behind his back with a proprietorial air about him. Livia waved a hand at one of the over-stuffed armchairs and suggested he make himself comfortable. The sooner they got this interview over with, the better. She talked of the weather – unseasonably wet for August – and repeated her father's concerns about trade being slack; mentioned a new line of gabardine motoring rugs lined with a camel fleece that completely enveloped a lady's skirts which the store now had in stock, and were really quite the rage. But the conversation was more stilted than normal, just as if they were strangers instead of friends of long standing.

Kitty brought in the tea and Livia set about serving it with a delicate slice of lemon and a warm buttered scone, which Mrs Snape, the cook, had made especially. She thought he might never stop eating. He consumed two scones and several cups of tea, gulping them down and spitting crumbs as he talked about the new yacht he'd acquired on Lake Windermere.

'You must come over and see it for yourself, Lavinia. We'll take it out for a sail round Belle Isle and back.'

'Indeed.' My word, 'Lavinia' indeed! He *was* being formal.

Mentioning the yacht perhaps reminded Henry of his real purpose for coming to see her this morning, and all of a sudden he set aside the china teacup to take up a stance on the hearthrug, very straight and correct. Hands clasped behind his back, he rose up on his toes as his voice filled with self-importance. His gaze was fixed somewhere just above Livia's head as he began to outline his assets rather like a shopping list: his new motor car – a Panhard no less – membership of the golf club, plus various properties he owned both in Kendal and the Central Lakes. He described in painstaking detail the improvements he'd made to the family home on Lake Windermere, as if this would win her over instantly and clinch the deal. Then he proceeded to emphasise his standing in the community before outlining several projects that were, in his own words, 'simmering in the pot and coming nicely to the boil'. Livia was clearly expected to be impressed that these would add to his already considerable fortune.

Unfortunately for Henry, Livia was not even remotely tempted by any of these benefits. She felt desperately sorry for the man, wishing he would shut up; wanting only to let him down lightly without causing offence.

Twice she attempted to interrupt but he overrode her hesitant words, too busy explaining how many servants he kept, and that her domestic duties would not be onerous. 'I still live with my mother, a widow, as you know, but as she keeps largely to her own rooms she's really no trouble at all. So long as her meals are provided on time and she's perambulated around the gardens once a day, she is quite content.'

It sounded very much like caring for a pet dog.

'You must be fully aware, Lavinia, that I've always had a soft spot for you, and I flatter myself that you're also rather fond of me.'

Livia gulped, recalling all the dreadful practical jokes she and Ella used to play on Henry when they were children growing up together. He was probably five or six years older than herself, and had always seemed to be a plump, clumsy boy with sandy hair, freckles, and very few friends. Maybe that was why he was forever hanging around the Angel sisters, perhaps feeling more comfortable with girls rather than the big boys who could be somewhat rough.

They had definitely taken advantage of his dog-like devotion, bossing him about shamelessly, making Henry carry their bags or swimming things if they were going on a picnic, or run for the ball when they were playing tennis. At times they must have made the poor boy's life a complete misery. They'd slip frogspawn down his neck, pinch his sweets when he wasn't looking, and once got him very drunk by lacing his ginger beer with Father's whisky.

'Yes, of course I'm fond of you, Henry, but...'

'I know what you're going to say, that you aren't in love with me, but I'm sure that will come in time. We've always been such jolly good pals, eh? I realise that you're an independent young woman with a mind of your own, Lavinia, and that's fine by me, so long as you don't get involved with all of this suffrage nonsense. Think I'd draw the line at that, don't you know. And I would point out that most gels these days are engaged before they reach twenty, so you'll very soon be on the shelf.'

'How kind of you to remind me of the passing years, Henry,' Livia remarked dryly.

'You once promised that you would marry me, once we were grown-up, if you remember.'

'I was a child, Henry, how could I appreciate what I was promising?'

'I believe most women would consider me a good catch,' Henry replied sulkily, then twirled his moustache and gave a wicked little wink, as if hinting that he had a whole gaggle of them just waiting for the opportunity, did she but know it.

Livia dropped her head to hide a flicker of a smile, and recalled she had always disliked that moustache, being very red and bushy. She also noticed that his comfortable lifestyle seemed to have added considerable pounds to what had always been a somewhat chubby frame. Not that Henry noticed her amusement, for he was still talking.

Livia tolerated his lecture, this essay in self-congratulation, for several more long minutes and then her patience finally snapped. She got abruptly to her feet, keen to end the interview as quickly as possible. 'I do not doubt your sincerity, Henry. May I at least have some time to consider?'

He looked momentarily stunned that she should dare to interrupt his flow. 'I haven't finished speaking yet, or properly done the deed, gone down on one knee and all that stuff.'

'But you were going to, weren't you, Henry?'

'Yes, I was actually, old thing, once I'd—'

'—worked yourself up to it, I know. Well, I'd far rather you didn't. I'd really prefer to leave things as they are between us, for the present, if you don't mind. Although naturally I will give your undoubtedly flattering offer all due consideration.'

It was a lie. She'd dismiss it from her mind the moment he walked out the door, and she could see from the startled expression in his pale blue eyes that he knew it too. Nevertheless Livia held firm, certain she'd made her feelings on the subject perfectly plain. Only a stubborn fool would fail to recognise that she was tactfully refusing him. But then Henry had ever been stubborn, though not necessarily a fool, or the good-natured idiot he liked to make himself out to be.

Henry Hodson was an astute businessman, no doubt about that, every bit as ruthless as her own father in some respects, certainly when it came to getting something he wanted. Perhaps because he was an only child she knew him also to be spoilt and totally self-centred, and that he possessed something of a peevish streak. He wasn't above pulling a few sneaky tricks himself, such as the time he'd 'accidentally' stood on her train and ripped her dance frock when she'd refused to allow him a third dance at the Mayor's ball the other year.

Now he was frowning, scowling at her quite crossly in fact, looking very much like he'd used to when Ella had finished off all the ice cream without allowing him a single lick. 'Your papa seems to think it's long past time you and I named the day. He will not be pleased if you put me off yet again.'

Livia arched her brows in a show of mild surprise. 'Have I put you off before, Henry? I don't recall you ever actually getting round to popping the question. Not that you have today, even now.'

A scarlet flush started somewhere around his stiffly starched collar and began to rise slowly up his chubby jowls. Seeing his embarrassment, Livia regretted her uncharacteristically caustic remark. He was surely a victim of their father's ambitious manipulations every bit as much as his own daughters were. She heard Henry's helplessness in his whining tone.

'It has been implied, don't you think? Rather taken for granted for years, or so I always thought, that you and I would get together one day, Livvy.'

What had happened to the more formal Lavinia, or the customary Livia? He only ever used her pet name when he wanted something.

'Ah, yes, that may well be the case so far as Father is concerned. But I'm a big girl now and am surely allowed some say in the matter. Where is the passion, Henry?'

'The what?'

'Passion! It is generally needed in a marriage, don't you think?'

He looked seriously discomfited, as if she'd used a rude word that should never be spoken in polite company. 'Oh, I say! I'm sure we could summon up a bit of that, when called for.'

Livia experienced a sudden desire to collapse into fits of giggles, but managed to stifle the urge as it would be too cruel. She dearly longed for passion in her life. She wanted to fall in love, and to be loved passionately in return. And however much Henry might sulk and fall into tantrums, she had no intention of being rushed into a marriage which she did not heartily embrace. She meant to wait until she found the right man. And then a small voice at the back of her head said that perhaps she'd found him already.

But she supposed this was about as romantic as one could expect from Henry and she smiled, feeling a great urge to pat him, as if he were a slobbering Labrador in need of careful petting.

'I must ask, Henry, concerning this alleged proposal I assume you are making for my hand, are *you* really in love with *me*?'

He grinned at her then, far more at ease with this question. 'Yes, of course I am. I adore you, always have. Couldn't imagine having anyone else for a wife. You're the one for me, old thing.'

Because you've always taken me for granted, and nobody else would have you, Livia thought with sad resignation, although she managed not to say as much out loud. She sighed. If Henry Hodson were the last man on God's green earth, nothing would persuade her to marry him, no matter what reprisals Father might devise to inflict punishment upon her.

Adoring and devoted though he may be, in his way, Livia had never found Henry entirely dependable. Like his father before him, who had built up the family wool business and property empire, Henry always had an eye to the main chance. He paid his outworkers – the knitters and weavers he supplied with yarn – the very minimum in wages for their work. Livia knew that for a fact, had remonstrated with him on the subject many times. And his tantrums as a child had been stupendous and great fun, but would be far less edifying in a grown man.

Livia moved towards the door, making it clear that the visit must draw to a close. She could see he was not pleased by her apparent dismissal, either of his presence or his proposal. He attempted to kiss her cheek but she neatly avoided him and offered him her hand instead.

'You will consider our union most carefully, I trust, Livvy?'

'Of course, but please do not be too hopeful, for I doubt I can accept. I intend to eschew marriage and all that romantic nonsense and settle for working for my living.'

'Goodness me! How?'

'I'm not sure yet. I may learn typewriting or ask the redoubtable Miss Caraway for a job in the store.'

He looked shocked, as if she'd suggested she might go on the streets. 'Don't be ridiculous. There'd be no need for any of that nonsense as my wife.'

'But that's the whole point, Henry; I don't think I'm cut out to be anyone's *wife*. Besides, I rather think I would enjoy working. And no matter what my father has led you to assume, I feel that old friends of long standing, such as ourselves, rarely find lasting happiness in marriage. I don't quite see you as a lover, I'm afraid, Henry. More of a brother.'

She'd shocked him again, but this time his blush was one more of anger than embarrassment as his expression turned oddly mutinous. It was almost as if she'd issued him with a challenge. Her attempt to put him off seemed to have tightened his resolve rather than weakened it, and his mood had visibly darkened.

'It would be foolish, Lavinia, for you to refuse my offer out of hand. You would only live to regret it.'

There was something in his tone that brought her chin up, and Livia narrowed her gaze as she considered him. 'Goodness, Henry, that sounds very like a threat. What are you saying exactly?'

'That this matter has long been agreed between our two families and *I* think we'd suit very well.' He offered her a stiff bow and, before making a somewhat undignified withdrawal, calmly informed her that he would allow her a little time to reconsider and would return the following week for her answer.

'I won't change my mind,' she warned, sounding more sure of herself as she followed him out into the hall.

Henry swivelled on his polished heels, scowling at her from beneath beetled brows as he collected his silk top hat and gloves from the stand. 'If you wish your family to thrive and prosper, I'd recommend that you consider the matter most carefully. Very carefully indeed. Your father, in particular, would not be pleased were you to persist with this refusal. And you can be sure of one thing, Livvy. I'll not let you go easily.'

Ella had experienced an unexpected surge of pride for what she'd achieved that day. She'd climbed what she now knew to be Nan Bield Pass, helped check on the sheep and assisted in bringing some distressed lambs home. The two newborns recovered well with their mother, and Mrs Rackett warmed the orphan by the fire and showed Ella how to feed it with a baby's bottle. Fortunately, the snow quickly melted and spring returned as bright as ever, if a little frost nipped. And with lambing now over, they could surely relax a little, although Amos continued to walk out at intervals from dawn to dusk every day, just to make sure all was well.

But for Ella, life on the farm continued to be both cold and harsh.

Out in the woodlands pools of bluebells appeared, wild daffodils bloomed along the lanes, and the first bees began to gather nectar. But the days of young love, of lying in the sweet long grass making daisy chains and letting Danny Gilpin steal kisses were, for Ella, quite over.

She spent her days mostly confined to the dairy, and with its slate floors and thick stone walls, it was freezing cold, even now, for all spring was well advanced and the longer days of summer already on the horizon. Within only a few hours of working her fingers would be so numb she felt certain they might snap off at any moment. Ella felt overwhelmed by the bewildering battery of equipment, which was entirely a puzzle to her – most of it looking as if it had been there for a hundred years at least and really quite alarming.

There were cheese presses, butter pats and markers, yokes and buckets, and wooden frames in which the milk was held that were known as 'chesfords'. A round barrel-like box with a handle was apparently the butter churn, and Mrs Rackett, who was called Nelly but insisted on the more formal title, began by describing its use.

'It can be reet fickle to make, can butter.'

The milk was apparently brought each morning, fresh and frothing in a big metal milk can and left to settle until the cream could be skimmed off and left to 'ripen', as Mrs Rackett termed it. Experience, she assured Ella, would tell her when it was ready for churning.

'Tha puts the ripened cream in the churn with some watter, then turn that handle. You'll happen have to do a fair bit of churning afore it comes.'

'And how will I know when it does "come"?' Ella wanted to know, a question that earned her a blisteringly disapproving glare, making it clear what she thought of farmers stupid enough to take on a town girl as a wife. The older woman smartly warned her she'd learn more if she asked fewer questions and paid proper attention, just as if she were a silly schoolgirl and not a young matron.

But the moment she embarked on the explanation, Ella wished she hadn't asked as it was so long and convoluted, the whole task sounding decidedly confusing and very hard work.

She was outraged that she had to work at all. Father had assured her she'd be mistress of a large manor farm with over a hundred acres, not an ancient farmhouse in the back of beyond that simply held rights of grazing over the fells and actually owned less than half of that acreage. He'd promised her a comfortable life in the country with a well-to-do farmer who owned a substantial number of sheep and some beef stock and poultry. Nothing whatsoever had been said about her acting as an unpaid farm labourer. Had Ella known what would be demanded of her, she'd have put up a much tougher stand against the marriage, wouldn't she?

And how would you have done that? asked that small weary voice in her head.

Mrs Rackett was now instructing her to listen to the sound butter made as it swished about in the churn, which had something to do with knowing when to stop so that it didn't curdle. Ella hadn't been properly listening so was really none the wiser.

'After that you drain off the buttermilk, add more cold water to wash it, then we salt it to make brine and finally work the butter in order to squeeze out any remaining water and pat it with them "Scotch hands".' Mrs Rackett indicated two pieces of wood that looked like paddles. 'It all depends on the weather, of course, and making sure the churn isn't bewitched, so you have to take care you don't…'

Ella hadn't understood more than one word in ten, and by the time Mrs Rackett had finished her lecture on how to prepare the feed for the calves and described what was involved in killing, plucking and cleaning hens and geese, she was ready to pack her bag and return home upon the instant, no matter what retribution she might face at the hands of her father.

Within a few short weeks of her new life, Ella was in despair.

Sometimes, during the day, she would become aware of Amos casting her sidelong glances as she went about the house, watching closely as she rolled up her sleeves to reveal bare arms when she washed lettuce or peeled vegetables. His eyes would seem to glaze if her breasts should accidentally brush against him as she passed by, or be riveted by the sight of her neat round bottom as she leant over to smooth the tablecloth upon the table.

And as closely as he watched her, Ella would watch her new husband with equal curiosity. He was not a handsome man, but neither would she describe him as ugly. Plain perhaps, rangy, with a weather-beaten complexion, and although the skin of his hands was rough and hard as horn, she'd seen how tenderly he could hold a lamb and bring it to the teat. And his old dog Beth certainly adored him, following him everywhere he went.

Poor and shabby as the farmhouse was, badly lacking a woman's touch, he was constantly tidying and straightening things, careful to wash his hands before and after any task. His fetish for washing troubled her slightly, although she couldn't think quite why. Amos was also extremely parsimonious in his use of candles or lamps, which must not be lit until it was quite impossible to see without them. And he was utterly devoted to his scriptures. He'd sit for an hour or more most evenings reading his Bible, and seemed to expect Ella to do the same.

As she studied him, Ella made a supreme effort to judge him fairly, and not to be too influenced by her father's part in all of this, which had naturally put her against Amos Todd from the outset. Yet he was not a bad man. She'd made a mistake by mentioning Danny, and hadn't the first idea how to put that right. And his efforts in the bedroom department had been a dismal failure. But he hadn't really hurt her, just been rather clumsy and unromantic. How could it have been any different when he clearly wasn't in love with her any more than she was with him?

True, she'd expected to marry someone who would love her, even if it couldn't be Danny Gilpin. She was used to being loved and adored: by her sisters, and her dear departed mother, and even at one time by her father. So why couldn't her new husband love her too? He saw her only as an unpaid skivvy on his farm, a mother for his children.

At times Ella found it difficult to comprehend that she was a wife at all, a married woman no less, and also, it appeared, a mother. She'd seen little of her stepchildren thus far, as they stayed with their aunt during the week while they attended school in the village. There was a school in the dale, but Amos said it was too far for them to walk the four miles there and back every day, and he didn't have time to take them in the cart. Ella complained that only seeing them at weekends didn't allow her much time to get to know them properly, but in her heart, she was rather relieved, knowing nothing about children and caring even less.

Amos merely scowled at her, as serious and thoughtful as ever and told her she'd learn soon enough what was involved in mothering. It felt very like a threat.

Chapter Eleven

As instructed, following Henry's disastrous visit, Livia collected her bicycle from the garden shed and pedalled off down Gillingate into town to face her father with the unpalatable truth that she had turned the marriage offer down.

She might well get involved in women's suffrage. Whyever not? No matter what Henry might say, it was a worthy cause, and Livia felt in sore need of a new challenge in her life.

Oh, but the interview had been exceedingly difficult, and the one she now faced with her father would be even worse.

She really needed to convince him that his wish for a match between them was simply that: wishful thinking on his part. Nothing more than castles in the air. He simply mustn't be allowed to go on organising their lives in this tyrannical way. Couldn't he see that she wanted to make him proud of her? How could she ever achieve that if she wasn't to be allowed to flourish and do things in her own way?

* * *

At that precise moment, Josiah Angel was poring over his account books and studying them with frowning displeasure. The end of each financial year was always an anxious time and this one had been more difficult than most. Profits were down, and his plans to improve the store by installing lifts had again been put on hold for lack of funds. It irked him to realise that Angel's was losing some of its former glory and falling behind the times. The London stores – Dickens and Jones, Debenham & Freebody, and Harrods, of course – were producing their own designs, hand-labelled in gold lettering. They were catering for duchesses and foreign princesses, while he could do no better than the spoilt rich wives of the county set. And most of those good ladies could take as long as six months to settle their accounts.

Josiah knew the situation was growing ever more desperate.

The sale he'd held in January, when he'd bought in stock at especially low prices to sell on at maximum profit, had not gone as well as he'd hoped. The kind of high-class customer enjoyed by Angel's clearly saw such items as unworthy of their attention. And it had never occurred to the snobby Josiah to encourage the ordinary man or woman off the street to enter through his rather grand portals, so why would they think of coming to his sale? The enterprise had been a complete failure, and what had seemed like a way to a quick profit had left him in an even worse situation, since the shop was now overstocked with unsaleable goods. Even bustles, or improvers as they were called, had fallen out of fashion, and the stock rooms were bursting with any number of those.

On top of all this, his debts were mounting daily. Josiah was becoming more and more dependent upon his daughters for getting him out of these financial difficulties. Livia in particular. Once again he glanced at his pocket watch, every moment seeming to drag as he waited for her to call with the news that she'd accepted Hodson's offer. He heard the click of the office door and looked up in hope, only to find it was Miss Caraway with some damn fool question or other. Josiah snapped at her and the woman wisely went away again.

Josiah and Henry Hodson had been involved in several projects together over the years, buying land and building and selling property, but their relationship had taken a turn for the worse of late. Josiah owed the younger man a considerable sum of money, having accepted a loan from him to pay off a rather large gambling debt. Gambling, like women, had ever been a weakness of his, but Josiah saw this indulgence as one a man of substance such as himself was entitled to enjoy. He certainly worked hard enough. But after yet another dismal trading year, and having suffered further losses at the Kendal trotting races, the hound trails, and at Cartmel, he'd found himself even more financially embarrassed and quite unable to repay the loan.

Consequently, he'd readily agreed to Hodson's suggestion that he give him Livia's hand in marriage in return not only for wiping out his existing debts but furnishing him with a substantial investment in the business for future improvements. This would allow Angel's to move on into this new century in a much healthier position.

It had seemed like the answer to his prayers, but Livia, as always, was proving difficult.

As if three legitimate daughters weren't difficult enough to handle, he'd then had that other one pop up out of nowhere, threatening to be a thorn in his side. And all thanks to stupid Florrie. Still, he'd sorted her good and proper. Shut her away where the sun didn't shine, and seen to it she stayed there. A fistful of notes in the workhouse master's back pocket had done the trick nicely. She'd bother him no more.

But there was still Livia to deal with.

Josiah really couldn't see why the girl was making such a fuss. Hadn't the pair been inseparable when they were youngsters? He seemed to recall her once suffering a childish crush on the older boy. Josiah took out his pocket watch. It was well past midday, so the interview would be long over. She'd better have accepted him, or she'd live to regret this day for the rest of her life.

By the time Livia had negotiated the heavy traffic along Stricklandgate and Highgate, and propped her bicycle against the kerb at the store's entrance, her courage had begun to fail. She smiled at the line of small dogs, left by their lady owners chained to the rail at the entrance. She bid the chief floor-walker a polite good morning as she swept inside, but paused to linger over a particularly charming display of summer prints, wondering why there wasn't a buzz of young girls doing exactly the same thing. Why did Angel's Department Store feel like a dusty mausoleum instead of a vibrant, exciting place to shop?

Her pace slowed as she crossed the floor, and by the time she reached her father's office, her nerves had got the better of her completely. Livia paused, her hand poised over the mahogany door knob and decided that for now, at least, she'd play safe and simply explain that Henry had agreed she should have time to consider his offer, that he would be back in a week for her answer.

A great deal could happen in a week.

It came as a great shock to Ella to discover that Amos expected her to rise early every single morning and *work*! Day after day, after day. She could hardly believe the demands he made upon her. Never in her entire life had anyone asked her to so much as lift a finger before. Weren't there always servants to do all of that? Really, it was most unfair!

Even Mrs Rackett was a trial to her, actually laughing out loud one morning when she came downstairs in a pretty blue silk gown.

'Where you off to, a dance?'

Ella lifted her chin. 'I see nothing wrong in looking smart.'

'Suit yourself, only you and me has to muck out the calves this morning.'

Ella stamped back upstairs to change.

'You should employ a lad for dirty jobs,' she objected

to Amos later. 'Or do the work yourself. You're the farmer, not me.'

'Calves and poultry are women's work.'

'I don't see why. Hens are smelly, nasty creatures, and the geese chased me this morning. They were really quite vicious.'

'Good guard dogs, are geese,' and he smiled at her, as if he'd said something funny. When she didn't laugh too, he said more soberly, 'I expect they were hungry and wanted feeding.'

'Well, I shan't go near them again.'

'Then feeding could be a problem and they might take to chasing you more often.'

He really was the most infuriating man. This morning he was again complaining that the hen house must be cleaned out and the dairy needed a good scrub, telling her that she might get both jobs done before tea. 'If you look sharp about it.' A phrase she had come to loathe.

Ella didn't feel in the least bit sharp. Nor did she intend to leave this sofa, old and scratchy though it might be, where she was comfortably ensconced with her book. She felt tired and cross, and she had a headache starting. She certainly had no wish to spend an hour cleaning out the hen house. Just the stink of the place made her gag. And the dairy was clean enough. She'd hardly made a mess this morning by pouring milk into a few bowls, and the cream could surely wait another week before she tried, and no doubt miserably failed, to make another batch of butter.

Ella intended to make it very clear that she had no

interest in the traditions of farming. 'You need a dairymaid to make the butter and cheese, and a servant to clean the house. I really shouldn't be expected to do those tasks at all.'

'Why not?' Amos stood with his fists on his hips considering her with a slight frown on his face, as if he couldn't quite understand what she was saying. 'Are you ill?'

'No.'

'Then why won't you work? Esther, my first wife, was happy to help all she could, as all farmers' wives are, and the children were home in those days as they were too young for school. Round her feet for the entire week they were, yet she coped well enough.'

Tearful now, Ella had the urge to scream at him that she wasn't his first wife, and they weren't her children. But that would have been unkind since the poor lady was dead. 'Well, I'm too tired to do any more today,' she sulked. 'I have a headache.' As if this settled the matter, she flounced off to her room in a pet, to spend the entire afternoon reading *Jane Eyre*, which she'd read five times already but absolutely adored.

But all of this ill feeling, her husband's coldness, served only to add to her sense of loneliness and misery. Ella felt desperately homesick, longed for a friend to talk to, someone who had a kind word for her, or would give her a hug of affection. There was still no sign of that from Amos, who continued to sleep in the attic. She could hear him most nights pacing the floor.

Exhausted by her emotions and her aching limbs from

all the work she was forced to do, Ella snuggled down in bed and slept, but her respite was short-lived. She woke to find Amos standing staring down at her in ominous silence.

For one awful moment Ella thought he might be about to make another attempt to consummate their marriage, but then he calmly informed her that supper was ready.

If the week was hard and work on the farm relentless, Ella found the weekends even more of a challenge as the children returned home from school. Sundays in particular proved to be an absolute nightmare. Amos insisted that she must rise at eight, despite the fact she was tired after working all week. She would be obliged to eat porridge with his round-eyed, silent children, instead of a little bread and butter and coffee in bed, which she would infinitely have preferred.

Day after day, night after night, Ella ached to go home. She longed to see her sisters and gossip with her friends, take tea on the lawn, visit the library for the latest romance, and of course enjoy the many delightful shops in Kendal town. But whenever she complained that she was bored, Amos would find her yet another task to do, or suggest she peg a rug, for goodness sake, as Mrs Rackett did of an evening. Or take up embroidery, which was apparently a passion of his first wife. She couldn't tell him that she was bored sick with hearing about the wonderful Esther, his beloved first wife.

'Won't you be visiting Kendal soon to go to the auction mart?' she persisted, but he shook his head as if annoyed she should ask, saying they would go in a week or two, when the lambs were fat enough to sell.

'We could at least visit the market. Don't we have eggs and milk to sell?'

'My neighbour, Mrs Jepson, sells them for me. She's always glad to help.'

Ella had met Mrs Jepson on her first visit to St Cuthbert's church, which the entire family was expected to attend three times every Sunday. Mrs Rackett was excused, as she had to cook Sunday dinner, although most of the work for it had been done the night before, as none could be done on the Sabbath. They were all bundled into the farm cart and bumped back along that endless road until they reached the tiny church Amos had pointed out to her on the day Ella had first arrived.

That first service had seemed to go on interminably. Hours and hours so far as Ella could judge. And all the while she was aware of people turning to look at her, remarking to each other in loud whispers that she must be the 'new wife'. Ella didn't feel in the least bit new. She felt old, worn out, exhausted, and desperately unhappy.

Now, weeks later, she was still waiting for Amos to give permission for their neighbour to call. Ella had broached the subject many times but he always demurred, insisting he didn't care for strangers calling unannounced.

'Why don't I go with Mrs Jepson next week and help her to sell the eggs, a few vegetables, maybe a chicken or two, whatever produce we can find. Won't that help? Don't we need the money?' She wasn't in the least interested in spending a day standing in the market trying to sell their wares, but a day in town would be wonderful. Marvellous!

Amos scowled. 'So that you can see your lover, Danny Gilpin?'

Ella's cheeks flamed. 'Not at all. That's not what I intended.' Oh, but it was, it was. She simply ached to see Danny.

His mouth twisted into a smirk of disbelief. 'Don't you need to make the cheese first, my dear, before you can sell it?'

This was a fact Ella hadn't considered. In her desperation to avoid the dreaded task, she'd even taken to pouring good milk down the drain. Surely he hadn't found her out, had he?

She hated her life out here in the back of beyond, thought it deeply unfair that she was cooped up at the farm the entire week. She felt desperate to escape, to tell her woes to sweet, patient Maggie, to weep and seek comfort in Livia's loving arms. She really must persuade Father into allowing her to return home for a while, for a short visit at least. She would write and get the letter posted or delivered somehow.

In the meantime, perhaps she'd better learn how to make cheese, if only to give herself the opportunity to go into town.

Chapter Twelve

'How will you ever break it to Father that you have no intention of marrying Henry?' Maggie was gazing at Livia, her clear grey eyes wide with fright. 'He's not going to like it.'

Livia gave a little puff of exasperation. 'I've already warned Father that I'm prepared to consider Henry's offer but I'm making no promises, which should suffice for the present.'

'Yes, but that won't hold him off for long, will it?' Maggie sounded doubtful, as well she might, knowing their father's ill temper.

It was almost a week since Henry's visit and he was due to call again any day for Livia's answer. The two sisters had walked over to Serpentine Woods, their favourite spot, the hedgerows clotted with lady's mantle, pink campion and bright blue forget-me-nots. They sat on a limestone rock pitted with yellow lichen, eating wild strawberries as they gazed out over towards the Kentmere Horseshoe and thought about Ella. They wondered how she might be faring and why she hadn't called to see them in all these weeks.

Since there were no answers to these questions, Livia returned to the issue most obsessing her right now. 'I don't care whether Father likes it or not, I've no intention of marrying Henry Hodson simply because he wishes to get his hands on some property deal or other. I'm sure that is what's behind this scheme. It certainly isn't about some silly childhood promise. Look at poor Ella, for goodness sake. Is she happy? How would we know? Why doesn't she ever come to see us? Why doesn't she write proper letters instead of scrappy little notes? I worry about her, Maggie, but I won't allow Father to sell *me* off so cheaply. We really must stop allowing him to bully us in this way. We're grown women. We should stand up to him more.'

'Easy to say—'

'I know, I know. How about you, are you feeling all right? Your cough seems to have cleared up.' Livia tucked an arm about her sister's waist and gave her a squeeze.

Maggie gave her a patient smile. 'I'll survive.'

'Of course you will.' Livia smiled in return as she anxiously studied her sister's frailty, the dark smudges beneath her eyes, which seemed to indicate many sleepless nights. Maggie wasn't classically beautiful, nor perhaps as lovely as Ella, but the girl possessed a natural charm with her sweet, heart-shaped face. There was a serenity about it with its pearl-like translucence, and eyes such a clear grey it was as if you were looking into a pool of water.

But from her earliest years there had always been a

fragile vulnerability about little Maggie. She'd never quite recovered from a childhood dose of measles which, coupled with a bad chill, had in turn led to a bout of pneumonia. Even now Livia would often hear her coughing in the night.

They sat in silence for a while, nibbling on the strawberries as they gazed out over the old grey town, dreaming of freedom as they so often liked to do. In truth Livia was the dreamer, the one who talked of travelling to distant lands, of earning her own living or even joining the women's suffrage movement. Maggie would merely listen and smile, the kind of girl who would have been content to stay at home for ever, had circumstances been different. But with things as they were, she too longed for escape every bit as much as her more adventurous sister.

'How would we do it?'

'Stand up to Father?'

'No, escape. We can't possibly stand up to him, you know that, Livvy. All we could do would be to leave, to run away and disappear from Kendal altogether. But where would we go? How would we survive? Live rough in the mountains? Run away to London?'

Livia was silent for a long moment. This was the vexed question that churned endlessly in her head, one which couldn't be ignored indefinitely, but to which she could find no answer. There were times when she almost envied Ella, who seemed to have made an escape of sorts. She hoped and prayed that her sister had indeed found happiness with this husband their father had chosen for her, and that was the reason she didn't write more regularly, because she was too busy enjoying life.

Maggie interrupted her thoughts. 'It's a pity we don't have aunts or uncles or cousins. Didn't Mama have a sister somewhere?'

I believe she did, yes, but having lowered herself sufficiently to marry her father's former apprentice, her family never spoke to her again after the death of her father, and never acknowledged her existence. When the marriage went disastrously wrong, as predicted, she had no one to turn to.

'Poor Mama.'

'Indeed, poor Mama. I miss her so much.'

'Me too. Thank goodness we at least have each other, the three of us, or did until Ella left. But why did their marriage go wrong? Mama never explained. Didn't Father adore her? Everyone else did. Wasn't he at least a little in love with her when he married her?'

Livia smiled at her youngest sister's naivety. 'I don't think so, Maggie. I believe Father considered she would be useful to him, as an asset. He knew she would be left with a sizeable business and inheritance. How could he resist taking advantage of that fact?'

'How cynical you have become, Livia.'

'With just cause.' Livia sighed. 'Whatever happens, Maggie love, if – no – *when* we do leave, we'll go together.'

Maggie blinked away tears, her face so pale and sad Livia ached to take away whatever pain haunted the sixteen-year-old girl. 'You will take me with you then?' she begged.

Livia hugged her tightly. 'Of course I will. How could you think otherwise? I'd never abandon you. You are my beloved sister.'

'The thing is, Livvy, I'm not sure I can take much more. What he does to you – to us all – particularly when he's angry, tears me apart.'

Livia kissed the younger girl's soft cheek. 'Don't worry, I can take it, just so long as he doesn't lay a finger on you, my precious one. I promised Mama I'd take good care of you, and I have, haven't I? At least *you* are safe from his vile temper, eh?'

Maggie turned her haunted gaze away to stare vacantly out over the old grey town tucked in the valley below. Livia's thoughts were once more gnawing upon the vexed question of what she would say to Henry and didn't even notice that her question hadn't been answered.

Henry called first thing the following morning for his answer, and on receiving it turned on his heel and stormed off, this time without even showing her the courtesy of removing his hat.

'Oh, dear,' Livia said, watching from the window as he climbed back into his trap, flicked the whip at the poor horse and departed at quite a lick.

Now she'd done it. Now she would have to tell Father the truth, that she had absolutely no intention of marrying Henry Hodson, and had just told him so.

Livia resolved to present herself forthwith before the redoubtable Miss Caraway and humbly apply for a position. All she had to do was to make her request with modesty and good manners. If that good lady agreed to her being considered as a possible trainee, then on what possible grounds could her father object?

What did she have to lose?

Livia loved visiting the store and, as always, she paused before entering to allow herself time to carefully examine the windows for anything new or exciting. Privately, she considered the display somewhat overcrowded and busy, but she particularly admired a wide-brimmed hat, which was a delightful confection of feathers and chiffon for sale at a ruinous three guineas. But then Angel's Department Store catered very much for the discerning customer, as her father frequently pointed out to her.

Not that Livia could ever see herself actually wearing such a hat. She wasn't the sort of girl who went in much for extravagancies. Dressed this morning in a stiff-collared shirt blouse, and a skirt bound with leather around the hem to protect it from the dust, she felt perfectly comfortable in herself. Her cheeks aglow with fresh air and exercise, and her own robust health, heart singing, Livia felt bounding with confidence, as if she could take on the world.

Once inside, she found herself surrounded by ladies of class delicately discussing the relative merits of lace or ribbons for their peignoir, the optimum width of a petersham belt in order to make a waist appear smaller, with just the right silver clasp of course.

As Livia passed by, she heard an assistant assuring one young lady that sleeves were being worn much narrower this year, and that boleros were all the rage, while another promised that an item could most certainly be put onto madam's account. Livia marvelled at being allowed the opportunity to buy whatever you liked and pay for it whenever you wished, something the Angel sisters had never been permitted to do, despite their seeming affluence.

But then these ladies would think nothing of changing their gowns four or more times in a day. They'd start by taking breakfast in a silk dressing gown, change to a tailored outfit for a shopping expedition in town, or whatever was deemed suitable for a hack or game of tennis. An afternoon dress would follow for paying calls, then they would slip into a loose tea gown in which to relax afterwards before dressing for dinner.

Livia tugged at her own skirt, feeling really rather plain and shabby in the face of such exotic creatures, not to mention the glorious displays of ball gowns, fans, gloves, shoes and mantles on stands and mannequins set about the store. In this very respectable and proper establishment, she almost giggled as she remembered she was wearing cycling knickerbockers beneath her sensible skirt, which were surely anything but proper, being really rather racy, for all she also wore white frilly bloomers beneath those.

Oh, but how she would love to be a part of this exciting scene, free to explore the delights of the myriad tiny drawers behind each counter, to assist a young girl to choose her bridal gown, or to find a middle-aged matron something stylish and warm for winter. It all seemed such fun.

All sense of youthful happiness deserted her as she faced the ire of her father.

'You did *what*?'

Livia swallowed, took a breath, and quietly repeated what she'd just confessed. 'Henry called again this morning for his answer and I told him no, that much as I like him, I can't marry him. I've declined his offer.'

'You've *declined*?'

'Yes.'

'And what possible reason did you give, might I ask?'

Josiah's tone was dangerously calm, but Livia was determined not to be put off by this, or let him see the fear that was starting to creep over her. She straightened her shoulders and opted for sweet reason. 'I realise you were keen on the match, Father, but I don't love him, you see. I shall never love him. And I'm quite sure you wouldn't wish for me to be unhappy, would you?' She wasn't sure of any such thing, but it seemed the right thing to say. 'I don't believe he really loves me either.'

'What the hell has love to do with anything? And who gave you the right to make decisions on such important matters?'

Livia saw red at this. 'I believe, as a woman of twenty-two, I have that right. You might be able to bully Ella, Father, and Maggie too for that matter, but not me. I'm old enough to make my own decisions now.' She took a step towards him, her beautiful eyes challenging, even as she clasped her hands together as if in prayer.

He struck her. Livia fell backwards, banging her head on the claw foot of her father's hat stand. Not allowing her time to catch her breath, he hauled her to her feet and hit her again, this time keeping a firm hold of her wrist while he slapped her back and forth across her face over and over, shaking her all the while as if he were a terrier and his daughter nothing but a mouse.

Livia cried out, unable to stop herself. She heard the office door open and a frightened voice apologise for the intrusion before it was quickly snapped shut again.

'I'll make you sorry you ever defied me, girl!'

Livia was distraught. She'd walk away from her father's door gladly, this very minute, were she capable of escaping his grip, and if it didn't mean leaving her darling Maggie. Oh, God, but she was in a pretty pickle! What could she do? Henry, too, had seemed to see her refusal as a form of defiance. He'd warned her that she'd regret her decision as he'd stamped from the room like a petulant child deprived of a treat. But standing up to Henry was as nothing compared to defying her father.

Grasping her by the arm, Josiah marched her from the room, along a narrow passage and out through the stock room, where shocked and curious eyes swivelled to follow their progress. Then pulling open the door, he threw her down the back steps into the delivery yard beyond. Livia fell on the cobbles, in the filth and the dirt, wincing as pain shot through her shoulder.

Josiah followed to yank her up and shake her. He struck her again, making her ears ring, then flung her once more to the ground. 'Get back to Henry this minute, and tell him you've changed your mind. Otherwise, don't bother to come banging on my door begging me to let you come back home.' Livia curled herself protectively into a tight ball.

What followed happened so quickly she could hardly believe it. There was the scrape of running feet on the cobbles, then the figure of a man hurtled out of nowhere and launched himself at her father. Livia screamed. Even as she did so she knew nobody would come running to offer assistance. The overworked souls inside would not risk their jobs by getting involved in a dispute between their employer and his daughter. They'd even closed the door so that they couldn't hear what was going on.

Yet here was one man who wasn't afraid of the great Josiah Angel.

Livia recognised him instantly: Jack Flint!

The older man was no match against his young, fit assailant, hampered as he was by a cumbersome belly and sagging muscle. Fists flew, bones crunched, and there was the sound of hard knuckle meeting flabby flesh. Within seconds Josiah was flat on his back, and Jack had one arm across his throat, pinning Josiah to the ground.

'Let him go!' Livia screamed, trying to pull Jack away. 'Get off him!'

'He was about to bloody kill you.'

'No, no, he wouldn't. Let him go, he's my father. *Leave* him alone!'

'I know who he bloody is! He's the man who's been squeezing the life out of his tenants on Fellside.'

But Jack Flint did ease his grip fractionally, long enough for Josiah to drag himself to his feet, push his attacker away and fling a punch or two of his own, landing squarely on the young man's hard belly. They made little impact, being more like hitting a stone wall. Sweat was pouring down his face and Josiah could feel his energy fast slipping away, his chest tightening. He was not the man he used to be. He preferred more subtle ways of control these days, but he'd be damned if he'd let some flea-bitten youth get the better of him.

The final punch came out of nowhere. Livia was aware of a great roar of fury then the young assailant charged the older man. Fist met jowly chin with a crack and Josiah went down like a tree felled.

'My God, you've killed him.'

Chapter Thirteen

Livia came round to find herself lying in a narrow bed covered with a plaid blanket. A large woman with a mop of white hair, dark eyes, and precious few teeth was seated by her side, smiling kindly down at her. A small child was asleep on her ample lap.

'By heck, it's good to see you back in the land of the living.' The woman half turned and called to someone behind her. 'She's come round, lad, tha can stop fretting.'

'Where am I?'

'You're safe, lass. Whoever did this won't think to come looking for you here. You're with friends now. Do you fancy a bit of broth, love, to warm yer?'

Livia struggled to sit up and the woman handed the sleeping child to a girl of about fourteen or fifteen so that she could assist Livia, plumping up a flock pillow behind her head. The mattress was nothing more than a straw-filled sack, but it was the room she found herself in that appalled Livia the most.

It was small and bare, and other than the bed she occupied, the woman's chair and the odd wooden crate, which obviously served as both table or stool according to need, the only other item of furniture was a large handloom, operated by a boy, which seemed to fill half the available space. In one corner stood what must be a slop pail, as for all it was covered with a wooden lid the stink coming from it was nauseating. No doubt it saved them from many trips down the endless flights of stairs to the privy out the back, the state of which she didn't dare to even consider. Here and there were heaps of sacks, some filled with straw, which must serve as beds, and a strip of pegged rug that someone had troubled to make, perhaps to give the room a brighter, more homely feel. It hadn't worked.

While going about her charity work, Livia had frequently visited the homes of those less fortunate than herself, but she had never seen anything as bad as this. This was the most miserable room she had ever seen in her entire life. She could hear scratching behind the wainscot and guessed the whole place was verminous. There might even be bugs in the very bed in which she was lying. Yet try as she might, she could not move a muscle. She felt disorientated, giddy with pain.

And all around her were countless pairs of eyes, which Livia viewed through a mist of floating lint, which seemed to fill the air. Her scrambled brain eventually identified these as belonging to children, clearly curious to meet their guest. 'Where am I?' she asked again. 'How did I get here? Who brought me?'

'Our Jack carried you, lass.'

Livia looked shocked. 'Carried me?'

'Claimed you was light as a feather, but then he allus was a bit of a show-off where ladies are concerned.' The woman, who introduced herself as Jessie, chuckled; a deep joyous sound that rumbled up from the heart of her, and one that brought a smile even to Livia's mouth, sore as it was. 'He certainly couldn't leave you where you were, happen to be knocked about again. No, don't explain, love. None of our business how you come by them knocks, but I've cleaned yer cuts and bruises, and tended them with herbs, now we must leave it to time and the Good Lord to help them heal. So, come on, sup up, lass. A drop of broth will help set you on your feet.'

Livia's mouth felt as if it were twice its normal size and she tentatively ran her tongue over her teeth to check none were missing. Father had certainly socked her hard enough to loosen a few, but fortunately all seemed to be well. The last thing Livia wanted right at that moment was to eat but the woman was so kind that Livia felt it would be churlish to refuse. And after a sip or two of the broth, which was filled with vegetables and absolutely delicious, Livia discovered to her surprise that she was hungry after all. When the bowl was empty Jessie took it away, urging her to get some rest.

'Afore you nods off again though, our Jack would like a word, if you feel up to it.'

Livia was vaguely aware of a man stepping out of the gloom. She could hardly see him in the poor light from a piteously small window but the familiar husky male voice brought her head up sharply, too sharp, and she winced against the pain.

'Whoa, no sudden movements. I reckon you'll need to take things easy for a day or two.'

Livia cleared her throat. 'How dare you attack my father?'

'I believed I was defending you.'

She fell silent, deeply ashamed that this man should witness her humiliation, almost wishing he'd walked on instead of so arrogantly taking control. And why had he brought her here, to this room, for goodness sake? Livia struggled to find the right words to explain her predicament. 'It was an unfortunate incident, a family squabble, nothing more. I could have managed perfectly well on my own, I do assure you.'

'I doubt it, and there's really no need to thank me,' he dryly remarked, since she'd made no attempt to do any such thing.

'Wouldn't it have been far more sensible not to resort to—'

'Fisticuffs? I didn't see any alternative. You'd have been mincemeat by the time any other help came.'

Livia shot him a furious glare, wishing she didn't feel duty bound to defend her father, yet it was a habit she'd followed all her life. 'And why did you bring me here to…to this place…wherever it is?'

She was aware this sounded ungrateful, even curt, but Livia was privately appalled at finding herself in this predicament, and shuddered as a rat ran over the feet of a sleeping child where he lay curled up on a sack.

Jack took his time answering, then quietly leant forward in the chair, elbows on knees. 'I saw what he did to you, your father, Josiah Angel. I saw him throw you out the door then start to beat the sh…the living daylights out of you. The marks of his fist are still plain to see on your face. You don't really imagine I could stand by and do nothing?'

Livia was humbled into silence, her cheeks colouring with embarrassment. 'I'm sorry, that was ungracious of me. My father, he…well, he isn't an easy man. He can be impulsive and quick to anger at times. I'm sure he'll regret it tomorrow, he generally does.'

'Until the next time?'

She didn't answer this, since it was of course unanswerable.

'What did you do to offend him?'

'I refused to do as he asked.'

'I see.' Jack saw rather more than she appreciated. In fact, he thought he might know a good deal more about dear papa than this girl did herself. He returned to her earlier comment. 'He's quick to anger, you say. So if a young girl were to come to his store seeking work, perhaps claiming she was his *illegitimate* daughter – what do you reckon he would do about that? Because so far as I can tell,' Jack blithely continued, 'when my friend Mercy did exactly that, she vanished off the face of the earth.'

Livia listened in shocked silence as Jack explained, very succinctly, about Mercy being the child of Josiah's mistress. Her first instinct was to shout a denial, but the sincerity and pity on his face held her mute.

It was difficult to take in all that he was telling her. Livia knew her father to be a tyrant and a bully, the kind of man who liked to control his women, yet not for a moment had she guessed that he'd actually fathered a love child. But why would he not? He was a cruel, unfeeling man who cared nothing about heaping misery on his own family, in beating them into submission in order to make them do his bidding. His rule was law. Livia thought of her poor mother, and her heart bled. What pain this mistress must have brought her. He'd bullied and hurt her fragile mother, reduced her to an unhappy invalid, and now she could see why.

In that moment, Livia marvelled that winning his approval and approbation had ever mattered to her. She felt nothing but hatred for him now, even if he was her own father. How could she not, after what she had just learnt?

And who was this girl, this child who was, she supposed, her half-sister? More importantly, *where* was she?

'I know my parents' m-marriage was not a good one,' she stammered, still in shock. 'More one of convenience than love, I believe. But I wasn't aware that Father had actually betrayed her in such a disgraceful manner. He's a bully, yes, but still I thought him a man of honour.'

Jack gave a cynical snort. 'Why would you think such a thing?'

Livia looked him steadily in the eye. 'Because I am his

daughter and despite everything he has done, I love him. At least, I suppose I do. I've spent my entire life wanting him to love me, to be proud of me, as I am proud of him. Or was, until now.' Again she paused, thoughts and emotions she'd always taken for granted growing confused and muddled. 'He came up from nothing to be one of the wealthiest businessmen in Kendal, in all of Westmorland, why would I not be proud?'

Jack and Jessie exchanged a speaking glance, but made no comment to this. Jack continued with his tale. 'It's possible, and I'm not saying this is the case as I have no proof, but it's possible that he's had more than one mistress over the years. I've heard of at least two more.' Was this the moment to tell her that some didn't even justify that nefarious title, being nothing more than ladies of the night, as they were more politely named? Perhaps not.

Livia put her face in her hands, as if to shut out the pain of this new knowledge, and Jack quietly told her the entire story. All about how Josiah had abandoned Florrie to her own devices when her child, Mercy, was still only an infant. How the pair might both have starved had his own mother not taken them in and taught the poor girl the age-old skills of weaving and knitting.

'Evidently Florrie Simpson had become an embarrassment to him, and, as Josiah Angel rose in stature in the town, I dare say he decided to protect his own reputation, rather than hers. When Mercy's mam died of consumption back in the spring, she left the girl a letter of introduction in the hope Josiah might still hold some regard for her. She fondly imagined that his cold heart might soften sufficiently to grant her precious daughter a job at Angel's Department Store and salvage what looked like a bleak future.'

Livia had become so engrossed by the tale she'd quite forgotten her own ills, and had pushed herself up into a sitting position to hear all the better. 'So what happened? Did she get the job?'

Jack took a breath. 'I thought you might be able to tell me that, since you're his daughter. I wondered if he might have mentioned her visit.'

Livia shook her head, a frown creasing her brow.

Jack went on, his tone caustic, his expression dark with anger. 'That's what I was coming to ask him today, as I did once before if you remember, at your sister's wedding.'

Livia gasped. 'You never mentioned any of this then.'

'It didn't seem an appropriate moment, as I believe you yourself pointed out. Nor has your father agreed to see me since, despite my calling on numerous occasions to request an interview.'

Jessie intervened at this point. 'Aye, and if the lass had been given a job, and the accommodation to go with it, she would have come to see us to tell us her good fortune. She has no one, d'you see, but us? Me and my kids worship the lass, and we're everything to her. Them shop assistants surely gets a day off now and then, in this fancy store your father owns?'

'Of course, every Thursday, and Sundays too, of course.'

162

'So why hasn't she come to see us, her family, or as good as? Where is she, our little Mercy? We've seen neither hide nor hair of her since that day.'

Livia thought this was a fair question, but one she hadn't the first idea how to answer.

George, or Georgina as he preferred to be called, was given six cuts of the birch for obscene behaviour. This didn't greatly trouble him (or her) and he endured his punishment with stoic goodwill, although it upset Mercy greatly.

She did her best to save him by explaining to the woman in charge that the patients, many of them merely boys, had acted out of simple curiosity, or else it was a joke that had got out of hand. Mercy assured her that she hadn't felt in the least bit threatened, which wasn't strictly true but she really couldn't see how punishing them would help. It had been harmless fun in their eyes.

The woman did not agree, and made it very plain that she was letting Georgina off lightly.

'I could have given him a dozen, not six lashes, or set him stone-breaking for a week. I will not have such lewd behaviour on my ward. He deserved every stroke.'

The birch resembled brooms used for sweeping up leaves, the twigs bound together to form a long stick or rod. There were differing weights, Mercy discovered, for different ages. The older the boy suffering the punishment, the bigger the rod. Mercy was appalled by the very idea of such a vicious punishment for such a slight offence, but apparently the birch could be given for something as

163

simple as not wearing bootlaces, or talking to a girl.

'And for it to be really painful,' her friend Prue explained, 'it might be soaked in water first. It's all carried out in the privacy of the office so no one can be sure that the set number of strokes, usually six, are adhered to, and the poor victim is not in any position to argue.'

'But that's dreadful!' Mercy was horrified. Where had she come to, and how on earth was she ever to get out of this place?

But worse was to come.

Her own punishment was to stand outside in the yard, naked from the waist up, with the words '*I like men to do shameful things to me*', painted in red chalk across her breasts. Mercy had never known such shameful humiliation in all her life. It was a relief when the rain started and the chalk letters began to run into each other, forming rivers of red streaked across her bare breasts, although the change in weather did nothing to protect her nakedness. She still wasn't allowed to move, or cover herself, until the end of the morning. Six solid hours of utter shame and degradation.

Mercy was mortified at having to stand exposed in the yard with half the inmates gawping and giggling at her, making lewd remarks as if she were stone deaf and couldn't hear what they said.

How had she come to this? Poor as they were, she and Mam had been perfectly content on Fellside with their bit of weaving and knitting, and their good friends close by. Mercy's world had been turned upside down the day her beloved mother had died, made worse when she'd called on her so-called father for help.

All she had asked for was a respectable job in a respectable shop, not to be incarcerated in the workhouse as a destitute. And she certainly didn't deserve to be treated like some common whore.

Those boys had been rude and silly to lift the hem of her dress to see if she was wearing drawers. But at least George, or Georgina, had finally rescued her from the one who was humping himself upon her. *And none of that had been her fault!* So why had she been punished too? Nor did she regret attempting to defend them.

'I'll not stand by and see someone browbeaten by a bully, so help me,' Mercy vowed silently to herself.

A small voice whispered in her ear, and a gentle hand touched her shoulder, making her jump. 'It's all right, Mercy, it's only me. Look, you've missed your dinner but I've fetched you summat.'

It was Prue, and she was holding out a slice of bread and dripping, a big grin on her face. 'Go on, take it. I've been sent to fetch you in. One of the lads has been sick and the ward needs scrubbing again. Anyroad, it's been decided that you've no doubt learnt your lesson by now.'

'But *I* didn't do anything wrong. It was that woman, Nurse Bathurst, the great bully. Why should I be the one punished?'

'I know how you feel, love, but look at it this way, it could be worse.'

'How?' Mercy gratefully wrapped herself in the shawl her new friend had brought.

'I don't know, do I, but I'm sure it could. I allus say that to meself when I'm in trouble. I mean, you could have been standing here in your flannel drawers with not even a skirt on, then the whole world would have known what underwear you wore.'

Both girls fell into a sudden fit of giggles. Even Mercy couldn't help herself, Prue was so funny.

'That's better, now eat up your bread and dripping and live to fight another day.'

And with tears of laughter as well as sadness in her eyes, Mercy did just that.

Chapter Fourteen

Livia felt a deep unease, a creeping fear that chilled her. Had the girl really managed to gain access to her father's presence? And if so, what had gone on, and what had happened to her? She experienced a dreadful sense of foreboding. Surely he wouldn't actually harm the girl?

'It would be a waste of time to ask Father; he'd never tell me,' she said, speaking her thoughts out loud.

'Then ask someone else, do a bit of snooping,' Jack suggested. 'There are always ways and means. I'm hoping we can rely on your assistance to find her. Mercy is an innocent in all of this, remember, just as you are.'

Livia had the grace to see that was the case.

Yet still she clung to the hope that her father wouldn't do the girl any real mischief. She might be all too aware that he was a brute and a bully, but there was surely a limit to how far even he would go?

'What exactly are you suggesting he did? He would never do anything really terrible, anything...against the law.' She couldn't bring herself to use the words *kill* or *murder*, yet she could see this thought reflected in Jack's dark gaze, and Jessie's clenched, fretting hands.

Jack scowled, impatient with her resistance, her denial. 'I don't know, do I? That's why we need you. He might've spirited her away some place.'

'But where, and for what purpose?'

'Out of shame perhaps, or fear of losing his good reputation and high standing in society. It wasn't Mercy's fault she was illegitimate, and she had every right to expect some support from her natural father following the death of her mother. She must be somewhere,' Jack said, for the umpteenth time. 'A person doesn't just vanish into thin air.'

'All I'm saying is that we should keep an open mind on the subject. I'm not making excuses for my father, why would I? And I'm certainly agreeable to speaking to one or two people at the store, discreetly of course, in case anyone has seen her. But I have to say that I don't hold out much hope. We can't be certain my father is involved until we've investigated further. He should be considered innocent until proven guilty.'

They met her pleading gaze with silence and Livia ploughed on with her somewhat over-optimistic defence, desperately clutching at straws. 'He might not be involved with her disappearance at all; the girl could have come to grief in the streets and alleys of Fellside.'

Jack instantly rebuffed the idea, insisting that wasn't possible. 'We've asked around, searched every nook and cranny, and everyone hereabouts knows who Mercy is. She belongs in this neck of the woods, has lived on

Fellside ever since she was a bairn. Besides, no one would dare touch a friend of Jack Flint.'

Livia gave a wry smile. 'I dare say they wouldn't.'

'My lad isn't some ne'er-do-well villain what bullies and frightens people, so don't suggest that he is,' Jessie heatedly interposed. 'He's done a lot for folk round here, unlike some I know. And he's still battling with that father of yours, trying to get our rents reduced afore we all die of starvation trying to survive on a pittance.'

'Yes, I do realise that,' Livia soberly agreed. 'I'm sure what you say is true, but my father has to make a living too, I suppose. Perhaps he doesn't appreciate quite how bad things are for you.'

'He knows right enough,' Jack snapped. 'He's just a greedy selfish cove,' and turning from her in disgust, he began to pace the room like a tiger locked in a cage, his anger barely contained, as if he held her personally responsible for their difficulties.

'*My* father was a drunk who died in the gutter after a bar room brawl. That isn't going to happen to me. I like a glass of beer same as the next man, but nothing is more important to me than my family, and no one, not Josiah Angel, nor that Henry Hodson with his crippling commission charges on the weaving we do for him, will break us. No matter what the cost, I'll fight till my last breath for me and mine. Without my family, and I include Mercy among their number, what do I have worth living for?'

Livia said nothing in response to this passionate outburst, but quietly and respectfully absorbed the powerful emotion behind the unexpected confession. Besides, it was true what he said. Her father was greedy, and selfish, thinking only of himself. She really should stop defending him. Jack Flint might be rebellious and assertive, the kind of man who revelled in danger, or even courted it. He certainly wouldn't be troubled by the normal rules of convention. Yet he also appeared to be deeply caring, supportive and protective, so far as those he loved were concerned.

It crossed her mind to wonder how it would feel to be loved by Jack Flint.

'I know that you think I've had things easy, but that's not strictly true. I do understand what you're up against with my father, really I do.'

And as both Jack and Jessie considered her with an expression of total disbelief, Livia let out a heavy sigh. 'All right, I promise that I'll do my best to discover the truth. I'd really rather like to meet this girl myself, since we must be half-sisters,' Livia mused. 'How very strange life is.'

Jessie and Jack together devised a plan. The idea was for Livia to go back home and apologise to her father for upsetting him, then at the first opportunity start asking questions at the store.

'How do you feel about going back home, lass, after what he did to you this morning, and to your mam all them years ago?' Jessie quietly asked, as she helped the younger woman on with her coat.

Livia managed a wry smile. 'Resigned. I've no choice

but to go home. I couldn't possibly abandon Maggie. My sister needs me. As for what he did to my mother, I need to think about that.'

She kissed the old woman's soft cheek, thanking her for the care she'd taken of her. Livia couldn't pretend not to be shocked by their living conditions, or the evidence of poverty all around her, but these were good, kind people. Despite what her father had drummed into her day after day about the poor being feckless and lazy, Livia couldn't believe this woman was entirely responsible for her own misfortune.

'I'll see you safely home,' Jack offered.

'I'm sure I can manage to find my own way up the hill and across town. I'll go along Low Fellside and up Beast Banks.'

'I'd rather you didn't try doing anything of the sort on your own, not in this locality. We've lost one girl, let's not risk losing another. In any case, I think we should go down rather than up. We'll head for Stricklandgate, then you can wait for me by the Town Hall while I run back to the shop and fetch your bicycle. How would that be?'

'Excellent, then I can cycle home as if nothing at all had happened. Father would no doubt prefer it if the matter was forgotten.'

They walked down Stony Brow and round by Grandy Nook without speaking. Livia was shaken by the evidence of need she saw all around her, by gaunt-eyed women standing at their doors, many working their knitting sticks, half-naked children rolling in the muck, dogs scavenging in gutters that ran with effluent. Hands

171

tugged at her skirts, desperate voices begged for a penny. Livia began to search in her pockets but Jack stopped her.

'They'll rip you apart if they think you 'as a bit of brass on you.'

'Oh, but...'

'No, buts. A penny won't make much difference anyroad. It's decent homes they need, and honest employment.'

Livia walked on in silence, subdued by the day's events. Yet she was acutely aware of Jack swinging along beside her, pacing his stride to hers. She found it hard to resist the urge to link her arm into his. Jack Flint, she rather thought, could become quite a good friend, but would that be such a good idea?

As they took a short cut through Woolpack Yard into Stricklandgate, she felt a strange reluctance to part. Watching him as he strode off to fetch her bicycle, she couldn't help thinking what a fine figure of a man he was. A real man, not one who had to rely on money or status to make an impression. There would never be any question of Jack Flint being ignored in a crowd. He was tall and commanding, possessed high levels of energy, and was evidently a bold, dominant, leader. The kind of man who thrived on a challenge and in living on the edge. Yet she had been given evidence of a gentler side to his nature, and it moved her.

It surprised her that she even liked the man, let alone trusted him sufficiently to believe this convoluted tale he'd told her. What if it was all a trick, some ploy to discredit her father in order to win this battle he was waging over the rents?

But how could she think such a thing? How could she resist him? He was undoubtedly good-looking in his own idiosyncratic way, even if he was in need of a haircut, and quite the sexiest man she'd ever met.

He was back within minutes wheeling her bicycle, and as she took it from him their fingers briefly touched. It was as if an electric charge shot up her arm. Startled, Livia looked Jack square in the face, feeling a blush warming her own. He returned her gaze unblinking, his dark mahogany eyes unreadable.

'I can manage now, thank you.'

There was a tremor in her voice as she took the hand Jack stretched out towards her. It was large and square, with spatula-shaped fingers and surprisingly clean nails. His grip was firm and warm, powerful but really quite comforting, and she felt oddly reluctant to let it go. Livia smiled up into his eyes, and some fierce emotion squeezed her heart.

She took a steadying breath, struggling to focus, and in an over-bright voice said, 'Right, off I go then, and thanks again for all your help. I'm still reeling over what you've just told me, but I'll do my best, Jack, I promise. Although how am I ever going to find the excuse to ask questions about this girl?'

'You'll think of something,' Jack said, and his smile sent her on her way, wobbling dangerously on her bicycle in a dizzying spin of confused emotions.

* * *

The children made it very clear by their stubborn silence, and by the dark resentment in their eyes, that they would pay heed to their sister Mary, but not to Ella. Each weekend progressed as miserably as the one before, with the older girl making it plain she was the only one allowed to do anything for her siblings. Ella was strictly forbidden to so much as touch them. Should she reach for a towel to rub Tilda's hair dry after her Saturday bath, Mary would snatch it from her hands with that fierce anger in her eyes.

'I can do it!' she'd snarl, pulling her small sister out of Ella's reach.

They made it very plain that they'd no intention of ever accepting her as a stepmother. Not that Ella had the first idea what was required of her in that role. What did she know about children? Nothing. But she longed to help, if only because they looked so sad and unhappy, and so much older than their tender years.

The boy, Emmett, in his short grey trousers that fell from armpit to knee, presumably to allow room for growth, appeared locked in some private world of his own. Ella would often see him talking to himself, his small face a picture of misery. The younger girl, in a faded cotton print dress that had obviously already been well worn by her older sister, never uttered a word so far as Ella could see. And Mary herself, in a dress that stretched tightly across her budding young breasts and should have been dumped in the rag bag months ago, bore an expression taut with anger on her young-old face.

She did her best, even took them for a walk one

afternoon, and what happened? The little monkeys led her right into a bog and left her wallowing almost up to her knees in mud while they ran home giggling. The more she struggled, the deeper in the mud she sank, and of course fell full length in the end.

By the time she reached home, in dire need of a bath, Mrs Rackett claimed the hot water would take an hour to boil up, and the children could barely speak for laughing. Even Amos looked as if he were struggling to remain sober-faced. How she hated them all.

Yet once she was clean and warm again, she forgave them. They were only children after all, and really she felt quite sorry for them. They were not permitted to play with toys or games. She'd never seen them draw or paint, do a jigsaw, or read a book other than the Bible. Even though they were home only at weekends, their father made no effort to allow them a little fun. Instead, they were expected to get on with their chores without complaint.

No work or chores of any kind were allowed on the Sabbath, of course, not even knitting or sewing. Then Ella really was truly bored, and so were the children. During one particularly long, dull, wet Sunday afternoon she could bear the silence no longer and, clapping her hands together, brightly announced, 'I know, why don't we play at making soap bubbles?'

Her suggestion was met with a glum silence.

'It's such fun,' Ella assured them, doing her best to sound enthusiastic. 'I used to love blowing bubbles with a clay pipe when I was a girl.'

'We have no clay pipes here,' Amos tartly informed her, 'since we don't hold with smoking. It's a filthy habit.'

'I only wanted to amuse them with a game,' Ella said, sounding defensive, despite her best intentions not to. 'They've worked hard all week. Children need some time to play.'

'"It is good for a man that he bear the yoke in his youth,"' quoted Amos.

She realised it was useless to argue further as the children had already been led away by the over-protective Mary, insisting it was time for their afternoon nap. Sighing, Ella gave up, thinking perhaps a nap might be a good idea for herself too, and retired to her room for the rest of the afternoon to lie on her bed with her book. It felt such a relief to be away from the children's critical gaze, and their visible resentment at her presence in place of their beloved mother.

After supper, which comprised the usual cold meats and bread and butter, Amos took out his Bible and read to them. Lamentations of Jeremiah was his choice of text tonight, from which he'd quoted earlier. By the time the clock struck seven and it was their bedtime, the children were very nearly asleep. Bored out of their mind, she shouldn't wonder. But they needed a good night's sleep as they'd all be up at five the next morning. The moment milking was finished at six, Amos would drive them back to their aunt's house in Staveley, ready for another week of school.

Mary always took the children up to bed, but tonight

Ella offered to tuck them in. 'I could tell them a fairy story.'

'Tha'll not feed lies to my childer,' Amos sternly informed her.

Ella looked at her husband, outraged. 'Fairy stories aren't lies, they're lovely, imaginative, magical tales with happy endings.'

'I don't hold with magic, nor other devil practices.'

'There's no harm in a little magic, and *Cinderella* is my favourite.' She turned to Tilda, at just five she was a small, round-cheeked child with large brown eyes. Really quite adorable. Surely she must be interested in fairy stories. 'Wouldn't you like me to tell you a story of a beautiful princess who fell in love with her Prince Charming?'

'No, she wouldn't,' her father answered for her, before the little girl had time to even nod.

Ella was cross, and for once allowed her feelings to show. 'Oh, for goodness sake, Amos, don't be such a spoil-sport. Is it so wrong to believe in love and happiness?'

There was a telling silence and she could see at once that she'd said the wrong thing. It went on for quite some time, broken only by a loud snore from Mrs Rackett, who was pretending to be dozing by the fire.

'You've made it clear what your views are of love, that it should be freely given.'

'Amos, please...' glancing anxiously at the children, '...this isn't the moment. And don't change the subject.'

'"Who can find a virtuous woman? For her price is far above rubies."'

Ella flushed with embarrassment and caught a glimpse of Tilda's little face as she turned to slowly climb the steep stairs. She looked so sad and disappointed, revealing that the child would indeed have loved a tale of magical nonsense with a happy ending. Perhaps she was as tired of dry biblical quotations as herself. Ella longed to protest further, but bit her lip and said nothing more, afraid Amos might twist that too. She did, however, manage to offer the little girl a smile as Tilda made her way upstairs, as if secretly promising to return to the subject another day.

Why was the man so cold, so cruel? What was his problem? Had she merely exchanged one tyrant for another?

Chapter Fifteen

Breakfast, like every other meal at Angel House, was filled with tensions. The breakfast room itself, with its panoramic views of the distant fells and mountains beyond, was scented with the lavender wax polish applied by a diligent housemaid who rose at five to clean out fire grates and beat the dust from cushions and rugs. The table might look a picture of respectability with its pristine starched linen, sparkle of glass and pretty vase of violets, but the air positively bristled with undercurrents of emotion. Beneath the superficial gloss of good taste and civility, resentment and hostility simmered.

This particular Monday morning, Kitty, the parlour maid, entered in something of a flurry and set a dish of smoked kippers on the sideboard. She was late, having been held up by cook scolding her for not having warmed the butter, which meant it was too hard for the family to spread on the soft fresh rolls.

Mr Angel demanded long hours and high standards from his servants, but he loved his kippers, insisting upon them for breakfast every Monday morning. Yet another task for Kitty: finding time to scurry over to the fishmonger by seven sharp to buy them. She checked that everything was as it should be, bobbed a curtsey, and fled before he could give her another telling-off.

Fortunately Josiah didn't notice the shortcomings of his maidservant on this occasion as Maggie had still not come to the table, a crime set to put him in a temper before ever the day had begun.

He sat glowering at his watch, drumming his fingers with impatience upon the table, refusing to allow the kippers to be served until Maggie arrived. Worse, when she finally did come rushing in, looking pale and distressed, she didn't seem to have any appetite and turned up her nose at the fish.

Josiah was not amused. 'You cannot begin the day on an empty stomach.'

Maggie glanced at the greasy kippers and felt her stomach heave. It had been doing that quite a lot lately, which was most unsettling. 'I shall ask Kitty for a lightly boiled egg, Father. I really can't face fish this morning.'

'Kippers have been provided and kippers are what you will eat. Livia, serve your sister some breakfast.'

Livia did as she was told, although she was concerned, sensing Maggie was suffering from some malady, otherwise she would never have dared to defy him. For all she'd never been fond of fish, even as a young girl, her younger sister was ever the appeaser, the one forever urging them to do as their father bid them. Josiah viewed sickness as a sign of weakness and a self-induced affliction. He certainly did not consider ill health a cause for sympathy.

Maggie was so gentle that if anyone should say something unkind in her presence she would look at them in startled surprise, her rosebud mouth falling slack with dismay.

Apart from her dislike of fish, there had been times in the past when Father had been known to stand over her when she baulked at the strong gamey taste of pheasant, or a slice of rare meat that pooled blood on her plate. Livia knew that her youngest sister would never hurt a soul, nor could she bear the thought of any living creature being hurt. If only Livia knew what it was that was hurting her now.

'Perhaps Maggie has eaten something that disagrees with her.'

'Stuff and nonsense! She eats the same as everyone else in this house, and I will not have good food wasted.'

Livia couldn't help but smile. 'No food is wasted here, Father. The servants finish off every scrap we leave, we all know that for a fact.'

Josiah looked outraged. 'I don't work my fingers to the bone to feed lazy servants, or recalcitrant daughters. Do as you're told, girl. Eat!' Taking her obedience for granted, he proceeded to tuck into his own fish with gusto.

Livia picked half-heartedly at her own food while watching with pity as Maggie made a valiant attempt to eat the now cold kippers. She did her best, uttering not one word of protest, only too aware, as was Livia, that if she didn't eat the blessed things they would be brought before her yet again at lunch, and at dinner, until every scrap had been consumed.

Unfortunately on this occasion she'd barely consumed more than a couple of forkfuls when, realising she was about to be sick, she slapped her hand to her mouth and made a dash for the door.

Josiah flung back his chair with a roar of fury, reaching her before she'd even set foot on the stairs, and dragged his now weeping daughter back to the table. 'You leave when I say you may, miss, and not before.' He thrust her, still trembling, back into her seat, and taking up her fork attempted to shove a portion of fish into her mouth. Maggie began to cry. Livia was on her feet in a second, protesting vigorously.

'Stop that, Father. Leave her alone. She's clearly ill.'

The words were no sooner out of her mouth than her sister vomited all down the front of her father's grey silk waistcoat.

Josiah's rage was incandescent. Grabbing his daughter by the hair, he marched her up the stairs with Livia racing breathlessly behind in a desperate bid to secure her sister's release. It was quite impossible, of course. He paid not the slightest attention to her protests, and, on reaching the landing, Josiah flung Maggie into the tower room and locked the door.

'You'll stay there, madam, until I say you may leave! You'll get no lunch today, nor any dinner, if that is the way you treat good food.'

Maggie lay in a crumpled heap on the floor, sobbing hysterically.

Livia was in despair. This was certainly not the happy

family breakfast she'd hoped for, nor the moment to ask him any questions about what he might have done with an alleged illegitimate daughter.

Livia was deeply thankful when her father finally left for the store, much later than his usual time, and at once hurried upstairs. She tapped on the door.

'Are you all right, Maggie?'

The reply was muffled, but as on previous occasions when one or other of the Angel sisters found themselves locked in for one reason or another, Livia wasted no time. She 'borrowed' the spare key from Mrs Snape, the cook-housekeeper, and within minutes was by Maggie's side, offering what comfort she could. If her darling sister was to be forced to spend all day incarcerated in her room, then Livia would share the punishment with her.

She soothed her brow with rose water, read to her, and even held her head when she was sick again. By late morning she was feeling better and Kitty sneaked up the back stairs to smuggle in a sandwich for them both.

'Is there something wrong? Are you ill?'

'No, of course not. It's as you suggested. I've eaten something that disagrees with me.'

Over dinner a few evenings later, the moment Maggie retired early to bed, again claiming to feel unwell, Livia determined to grasp the opportunity to speak to her father. She wanted to ask about Mercy, if he'd seen the girl and what had happened to her? She longed to demand that she be allowed to work at the store, but she'd tried that before and never got anywhere, and this wasn't the moment to do battle. Jack had warned her to exercise caution, fearing that if they didn't tread carefully, Mercy might be the one to suffer.

Livia had made up her mind that the only way to placate him was to seem to agree to his terms, then he would stop watching her every move and she would be free to investigate this mystery unchallenged.

Even so the words seemed to stick in her throat. 'I have decided, Father, that I am prepared to reconsider Henry's offer of marriage, after all.' It was bribery, pure and simple.

Josiah, momentarily silenced by this surprising reversal, allowed a nervous Kitty to serve the apple pie and custard. Wild as his eldest daughter was, he clearly hadn't lost his ability to control her.

'I'm glad to see that you've come to your senses at last.'

The instinct to refute this comment was strong, yet somehow she managed to smile with a degree of serenity. 'You could say that.'

'Excellent! I will report to Henry that he can start planning your wedding. We are agreed then?'

Livia swallowed the protest that leapt intuitively into her throat, smiled into her father's eyes and nodded. 'That would be perfectly splendid.'

She only hoped she could find the answer to this puzzle quickly, and that in the meantime the girl was safe, wherever she was.

* * *

Maggie set aside her diary which she'd been writing to stare at her sister, aghast. 'How could you agree to such a thing? You told me that wild horses wouldn't be enough to persuade you to marry Henry Hodson. What's happened? What has Father done to make you change your mind?'

'Nothing.' Livia turned away from her probing gaze to stare out of the bedroom window at her favourite view of the town. She could just make out the tip of the church tower, and the lazy curl of the River Kent beyond.

'Don't lie to me, Livvy. I'm not blind. I did notice the cuts and bruises on your face the other day. If it's me you're protecting, then don't, I'm fine, just a bit off colour, that's all.'

'I'll admit we did have a bit of a barney the other morning, and Father let his fists fly, as usual, but nothing I haven't had to put up with a thousand times before.'

Accepting this comment without question, Maggie asked, 'So what else has happened? What has made you change your mind about marrying Henry?'

'I've just told you, nothing. This is all a ruse, a pretence.' Livia came over to kneel by the bed and grasp her sister's hands. She had no wish at this juncture to discuss the real reason behind her decision; to tell Maggie about the girl who might be their illegitimate half-sister who had gone seeking a job from their father, and apparently disappeared off the face of the earth. It might upset her, and worryingly she had this morning again claimed not to be feeling well. It would be soon enough to tell Mercy's story once the girl herself had been found.

'I have absolutely no intention of going through with this marriage, I swear. But I'll promise anything if it means he keeps his fists to himself, at least until I find a way out for us both. I'm not the patient sort like you, Mags.'

'Don't I know it.' Maggie laughed as her sister went back to her pacing, pausing to glance out of the window, or to cuddle one of Maggie's favourite dolls and soft toys arranged on her window seat, then to rearrange the ornaments on the mantle shelf. Restless, fidgety, discontented, and yes, always impatient. 'But what about Father? He won't take kindly to being fooled, or lied to.'

Livia shrugged. 'We won't tell him.'

'So what happens when Henry finally discovers that you've led him on? You can't seriously allow the man to start planning a wedding and then turn round and say it was all a *ruse* to stop father bullying us, and that you never meant to go through with it?'

Livia turned bleak eyes upon her sister. 'I could say that I'd changed my mind, got cold feet or something.'

'Ice cold, I should think. More like hypothermia.'

Both girls giggled, then Livia flopped on to the bed beside Maggie to wrap her arms about her. 'Let's not worry about all of that now. One day at a time, eh?'

She was determined to find out what misfortune, if any, had befallen poor Mercy Simpson, and to protect her sister, no matter what the cost.

Chapter Sixteen

Amos suggested that Ella learn to spin. Most evenings, after supper, he would work his loom, often propping his Bible against the frame so that he could read at the same time. And Mrs Rackett would sit by the fire and spin, saying nothing very much as usual.

'Farmers have been involved in weaving ever since there were sheep,' Amos explained when Ella cast him glances of astonished disbelief that a man should be engaged in such a task. 'Happen we produce sturdy cloth, rather than fine, but it's none the worse for that. And we make it more for our own pleasure these days than for commercial purposes, but thee might find thyself less bored of an evening if thee were to join us in the task.'

Ella looked down her nose at the old woman seated on the settle, her spindle rhythmically spinning, needing only a pointed hat to complete the image of a witch. 'I have plenty of work to do, thank you very much, without adding any more chores. Besides, I'm tired.'

'Thee might find thee enjoys it.'

'I would also be obliged,' Ella said, in her clearest, firmest tones, 'if you didn't constantly address me as thee, or thou. I find it very…very discomfiting, and really rather archaic. This is the twentieth century, after all, not the sixteenth.'

'I beg thee… I beg your pardon.'

Ella was surprised to see his cheeks flush bright red, though whether with embarrassment or anger, she wasn't quite certain.

Mrs Rackett sent him a sideways look of concern, stopping her spinning for a moment to speak with unusual firmness to Ella. 'He means no harm by it. It's just his way, so you mind your manners, young lady.'

Did the old witch expect him to fly off the handle because she'd dared to criticise him? Ella found she was clasping her hands very tightly in her lap, half expecting him to turn and slap her for refusing him, as her father might have done. But he made no move to do so, and slowly, after several tense moments, she relaxed.

Yet Ella still burnt with resentment. Did she have no say at all over her own life? How dare he expect her to work every hour of the day? Was that the only reason he married her, in order to acquire a skivvy?

And he might not care for criticism himself, but he was quick enough to chastise her if he thought she had transgressed in some way. He'd been cross when she'd declined a request to become involved in arranging flowers in the small church, or setting out the hymn books before a service. Ella had insisted it was too far for her to walk, and she really didn't have the time.

Amos accused her of being un-Christian, which had stung.

The fact she might quite have enjoyed helping the other ladies, since she did like arranging flowers, only made it worse. When would she have time to walk four miles there and four miles back on top of all her other chores? Her days were full as it was. Like all men he was thoughtless, and utterly selfish. Just like her father.

Even more petty, the other day he'd pointed out that her petticoat was showing beneath her skirt by the merest fraction of an inch. She'd yanked at the waistband, tried to right matters but only succeeded in making things worse and been forced to apologise.

'Sorry, but this slip is rather long for the skirt, I'll admit, but it's the only one I have clean at the moment, thanks to our primitive wash conditions.'

It was Mrs Rackett's task to scrub floors and clean windows, to help with the cooking and wash the clothes. She would boil the sheets and shirts and the combinations Amos wore in a large pan that hung from a hook over the fire. She'd scrape in a few flecks of soap then stir it with a long stick from time to time, until the sheets billowed and bubbled.

Ella would watch in amazement as she would then carry the scalding hot pan outside to the pump to rinse the sheets with cold water. Finally the old woman would wring them out with her large capable hands and hang them over a hawthorn hedge to dry. She didn't have a mangle, nor even a washing line. And if it was raining, as it so often was up here in this damp valley, then they would have wet sheets dripping from the clothes rack above the fire for days on end.

Because of the difficulties involved, Amos was encouraged to make one shirt and one pair of combinations last for the entire week, and Ella was allowed one blouse, one petticoat, and one nightgown. It was all most unsatisfactory, a long way from the efficiencies of the laundry at Angel House where nobody would have dreamt of laying down such restrictions.

Even worse, the very same pan in which Mrs Rackett did the washing, she would then use for making broth or boiling a shank of bacon, not necessarily remembering to scour it out first, which would give the resulting dish a somewhat soapy taste.

Ella grew weary with nagging the woman to be more hygienic or efficient. Where was the point in arguing when it never got her anywhere? And much of the time she was too exhausted to do battle, wanting only to get the hated chore out of the way so that she might find five minutes alone to put up her feet and rest.

Spinning indeed. Flower arranging. Didn't she have enough to do already? Ella thought she would never get used to this life, never!

Life continued to be tough in the dale and Ella felt perpetually tired, worn out by an endless succession of chores: feeding the geese and ducks, the chickens that scratched in the dirt around the farmhouse, and the calves. The farm cats, too, seemed to be constantly demanding saucers of milk.

Ella deeply resented the fact Amos expected so much of her. He'd even demanded she help with the sowing of the oats and barley, traipsing up and down the meadow for hour upon hour scattering seed from a basket. Did he think she had the stamina of a donkey? And she'd made it clear from the outset that she didn't like cows, was really quite nervous of them, yet he insisted she go with him into a field full of them to collect a calf he could perfectly well catch by himself.

'You need to get used to the beasts, Ella,' he told her, 'and they need to get used to you.'

Then there were the black cattle, huge, ugly animals that glowered menacingly at her whenever she passed by. He seemed to find her dislike of them amusing.

Oh, how she hated the farm, and the dale.

Ella felt as if she were working from dawn to dusk, with scarcely a minute to herself. She would sneak an hour or two off in an afternoon, true, for a rest or a walk in the fresh air, even if she did hate the oppressive silence of the mountains looming down at her. But she surely deserved this precious time to herself?

Her day never varied.

After breakfast Amos would take a tin bottle of tea and a hunk of bread and cheese and go off over the fells to tend his precious sheep, or down to the pastures to see to the cows, or mend his dry stone walls. Ella wouldn't see him again until late in the day when he returned for his supper, thankful that he didn't come home for a midday meal as she had more than enough to keep her occupied.

There was a small vegetable garden behind the house and it was apparently Ella's responsibility to tend it and keep the family supplied with potatoes, onions, cabbage and green beans. Surely a hopeless task. Ella had never done a day's gardening in her life.

Cooking had to be done on an open fire and the boiler beside it kept constantly filled with water. Mrs Rackett would make a thin oatmeal porridge each morning, which they would all eat after the milking, followed by plain bread and butter. Breakfast never varied and Ella longed for a taste of raspberry jam. It might even be worth working the garden, she supposed, if she could grow some raspberries, which were said to do well in these hills. Or rhubarb and blackcurrant perhaps? Gooseberry pie was delicious. Ella began to make one of her lists, planning what plants she would like for her garden. She had several of these, all waiting for that much longed-for trip to town.

Unfortunately, with Amos still convinced she meant to run off with her lover, this was still a distant dream. Serve him right if she wrote to Danny and ran off anyway.

Ella was collecting some feed from the barn one morning when she thought she saw something move out of the corner of her eye. 'Tilda, is that you? Are you hiding in the straw?' Surely not. It was a Monday. Hadn't Amos already taken all three children back to their aunt's house, ready for school?

And then, perhaps startled by the sound of a human voice, a nose and whiskers emerged, sniffing the air.

Ella stepped closer, wondering what it was, when suddenly a rat emerged from the straw and ran across her feet.

Ella screamed. Dropping the bag of feed all over the floor she fled out into the yard and ran pell mell straight into Amos. He caught her to him as she flung herself into his arms. 'What is it, Ella. What's happened?'

'It was a rat, a rat! It jumped out at me. Oh, it was awful.'

He began to laugh. 'There are always rats in the barn. They go after the animal feed.'

'Well this one came after me.' Cheeks flushed, Ella struggled to free herself from his grip, but for some reason he held on to her arms, not willing to let her go. 'You must do something about it, Amos. I refuse to go in there again until you do.'

'Oh, Ella, have you any idea how very delightful you look when you are cross?'

'I am not *cross*, I am furious!'

'Of course you are. I think I rather like thee furious,' and suddenly, quite out of the blue, he kissed her. His arms were tight about her waist so there was no hope of escape. He hadn't shaved yet this morning and the bristles on his chin rubbed quite painfully against hers, but the kiss itself was astonishing, not at all what she might have expected from such a quiet, serious-minded man. His mouth moved over hers in a most demanding, exciting manner, stirring something deep within her that she'd thought quite dead. And it was over far too soon, leaving her breathless.

Amos grinned down at her. 'I promise I'll see to the rats, just as soon as I can spare the time.' Then he walked away, still laughing. Ella put trembling fingers to her lips and wondered what had just happened to her.

The mere that had given Kentmere its name, and was once found in the lower dale between Kentmere Park and Green Quarter, had been drained over fifty years ago by the Victorians. In its place had been built a reservoir to provide water for the bobbin mills and paper-making industry in the villages of Staveley and Burneside in the valley below. High and remote, it must surely be the loneliest spot in all of England. Merely to stand within the amphitheatre of those mountains and look upon the steel grey glimmer of its surface brought a chill to Ella's heart. The silence of the place was profound, with not even the call of a lark or rustle of a leaf in this treeless setting. She avoided it like the plague. If she walked out at all, which wasn't often these days, she went down the dale, her feet instinctively leading her in the direction of the village and civilisation.

With her husband, it was quite the opposite. He preferred the tranquillity of the upper fells, could stride up Froswick as if it were a mere anthill and not a mountain of over two thousand feet with steeply forbidding slopes.

Most of all he loved the river. A mere infant when it entered the reservoir, it rapidly grew into a rushing force as it gathered pace down the dale, and having served the local mills, would rush through Kendal and onward to Arnside, bursting into the sea at Morecambe Bay.

Amos claimed that the tarn must once have been a fine spot for fishing, and he rather regretted never having experienced its charms. Nevertheless, there were other places on the river in this part of Kentdale where he loved to fish.

One morning, as he packed his tea can and ham sandwiches, he informed Ella that he would not be on the fells with the sheep today as he intended to go fishing. He hoped to bring home a fat trout or salmon. She was only half listening, being far more concerned with the length of time the kettle was taking to boil when she was desperate to wash her hair.

From the corner of her eye, she saw Mrs Rackett give him a jab with her sharp elbow, whereupon a strange invitation burst out of his mouth. 'I were wondering if thee – if you would care to join me. It's a bonny day, not too much sun for fishing, but warm and pleasant all the same. I've put up enough food for two.'

Ella looked at him in amazement. 'Fishing. You want me to come fishing?'

'You might enjoy it.'

'I don't think so.' She laughed, and then wished she hadn't as she saw the old woman's mouth pinch into a tight line of disapproval and saw again that betraying flush on her husband's cheeks.

'Thee could… I meant for you to watch. I thought happen you might enjoy a change of scene. But if you'd be bored, forget it. Anyroad, I'd best be off.' Draping his bag across his shoulders, he picked up his rod and tackle and was striding out the door in a second.

'You daft happorth,' the old woman snapped. 'He were only offering you an hour or two off from the work because you've been complaining about having too much to do. Why won't you give the lad a chance?'

Ella realised with a small shock of surprise that she was right. He'd been attempting to be kind by suggesting she accompany him, even offering to share his picnic. Now she'd said the wrong thing and it was too late to back down.

Mrs Rackett spat in the fire in disgust, her spittle hissing on the coals. 'Sometimes, madam, you'd cut off your own nose to spite yer face.'

Ella ruefully remembered her own mother saying much the same thing.

Later that day, after she had washed her hair and bathed herself in the tin bath, which Mrs Rackett thought she did far more often than was rightly called for, Ella found herself walking along the lane towards the spot where she knew Amos had gone to fish. The great hump of Ill Bell, dark against the silver blue of the sky, was at her back. Ahead was the smooth sweep of Kentmere Pike, to her right Rainsborrow Crag rising from the green earth like a giant fortress fashioned by God's hand.

Ella kept on walking, for once almost savouring the silence, watching with interest as puffy white clouds bounced like soft bags of wool before the wind. She heard the lone cry of a curlew, spotted a tiny shrew disappear among a heap of larch and pine needles, no doubt seeking seeds for its supper.

She was heading for the bridge and that part of the river where the waters would be running deep, due to recent rains. Ella saw his bag first, lying abandoned on the bank, neatly fastened and with his rod leaning against it, his old jacket in a crumpled heap beside it. She hesitated. Was he done with fishing already? Had he changed his mind and gone off to see to the sheep after all? In which case he could be anywhere. A sweeping glance of the panorama of mountains all around her revealed no sign of him. And then Ella heard a splash, and there he was.

He was in the river, lying on his back in the fast flowing current, his head thrown back as he gazed up at the blue arc of sky. And he was naked. Flustered to find him thus exposed, Ella stepped quickly back behind a stand of spindly pines, yet couldn't resist peeking out around the side of one. Even as she watched, he sank his head back under the water, then rose to shake the water from his hair, laughing out loud as the dog, Beth, did the very same thing. Laughing, he threw a stick and the old dog bounded into the water to fetch it, a game that looked as if it had been going on for a while.

Ella was entranced. Man and dog seemed to be having such a good time. Amos looked happy, relaxed, quite different from the serious man who scowled and quoted the scriptures at her.

Before she had time to realise what he was about, he rose from the river like some sort of water god, and for the first time Ella saw the man she had married. She was stunned. In his shabby farming clothes he was nothing special at all. A spindly thin, tired farmer who worked too hard and didn't have time for fussing over clothes and appearance.

He was standing with his back to her, thank goodness, but she could see that he wasn't thin at all. He was lean and hard, his shoulders broad, and with muscles rippling in arms that could easily lift a full grown sheep. His body narrowed to slim hips and long, strong legs. He was, without doubt, a fine figure of a man, and something very like desire started somewhere deep inside her, spreading outward like the ripples in a tarn.

He wiped his face with the flat of his hands, stood for a moment with arms outstretched to the sun as if in quiet homage, then rested his hands on the top of his head as he gazed at the mountains above, perhaps savouring their beauty. Ella stood enthralled.

Remembering that kiss, and looking on this man, this demi-god who was her husband, for the first time Ella thought that perhaps she might not object to sharing her bed with him after all.

Chapter Seventeen

Josiah had scarcely given the girl a thought since he'd dispatched her to the workhouse, though it did cross his mind that perhaps he should pay a visit to the workhouse, to make sure there was no question of her ever being allowed out. If the girl were set free to gabble her tale to all and sundry, then his carefully built reputation would be in tatters.

It was wrong of Florrie to tell the child that he was her father, and to take it into her silly head to send the girl along to him, seeking favours. He certainly didn't in any way feel obliged to concede to the request. The very idea of offering his by-blow employment in his own store was ludicrous.

They'd had their little fling, and what fault was it of his if there'd been an unfortunate result in the shape of a baby? He'd pretended an interest, for a while, but once Florrie herself had begun to bore him with all her conversation taken up with teething and milk jellies, he'd been glad to walk away. She should have taken more care to avoid such accidents, as others had done before and since.

He was hoping to be made mayor by next year at the latest, and later taken up as a Member of Parliament, ultimately a knighthood no less. And why not? Didn't he deserve it for all he'd done for this town? For the annual treat he helped to fund for the poor souls in the almshouses if nothing else. He certainly had no intention of allowing it to become generally known that he had a love child, a bastard, for goodness sake!

Josiah's reputation was everything to him, and he would not allow it to be tarnished by some fly-by-night whore, which is what Florrie had turned out to be despite her claims that he'd taken a sweet virgin and used her for his own ends. Utter nonsense! All that talk about her *being in love* was just so much tosh. What young woman doesn't know what she's letting herself in for when she lifts her skirts?

Right now, though, he had more important matters on his mind.

Josiah stared down at a letter spread out on his blotter. It was from the bank manager, dated a week ago, asking him to call in to discuss the state of his account. He hadn't obeyed the request, which was tantamount to an order, although he couldn't ignore the problem for much longer. The situation was growing serious and the bank could easily decide to call in his loans, an outcome that didn't bear thinking about.

Why did events always conspire against him? Horses that fell at the last fence, profits that failed to materialise, property that cost more than he'd bargained for and never got completed because he couldn't make the final payments to an over-demanding builder. Even the land he'd acquired from his new son-in-law had not proved to be the investment he'd hoped for. Josiah no longer had the money to build on it, and so far had failed to find a buyer willing to take it off his hands. Everything was going wrong for him in this difficult market, and he really had neither the time nor the patience right now for obstinate daughters. He was up to his neck in problems, the pressures upon him mounting daily.

Josiah felt again that familiar tight breathlessness in his chest, which he experienced whenever he allowed things to get on top of him, as he was doing now. He really shouldn't worry so much. This would all be resolved once the girl was safely married, which it looked as if she was about to be, praise the Lord. He just had to hold tight a little longer and all his troubles would be over.

What bothered him the most, of course, was that Lavinia was a sly little minx. Unlike Ella, whose protests had soon buckled once he'd ratcheted up the pressure, his eldest daughter was quite capable of saying one thing and doing another. Or of changing her mind at the last moment. Josiah was no fool and didn't trust her fervent assurances, not for a moment.

What he needed to do was speak to Henry Hodson, man to man. It should be possible, if the two of them worked together, to ensure she carried out her promise with all speed. The sooner the pair were wed, the better.

Josiah recalled how fortuitous it had been the day he'd

met Amos Todd, quite by chance, at the County Hotel. The two men had become engaged in conversation over lunch, and he'd very soon discovered that while the farmer was in need of a mother for his three children, having recently been bereaved, he was also in possession of a choice piece of land on Sedbergh Road suitable for building purposes. Josiah had invited him to a function he was holding that very afternoon at Angel House, and it had been remarkably simple to come to terms, once the farmer had seen Ella handing round canapés.

Later, on the day of the wedding itself in fact, Josiah had felt duty bound to enlighten the fellow as to his daughter's faults as well as her many attributes. He'd pointed out that the girl was somewhat lazy and vain, scatter-brained and empty-headed

'She might prove to be a bit skittish at first, but keep her on a tight rein and she'll soon come to heel,' Josiah had advised. 'I wouldn't recommend you let her out of your sight for a while, not until she's grown used to her new harness, as it were.' Thereby sealing his daughter's life as a prisoner at Todd Farm for the foreseeable future.

Lavinia, however, was far less malleable and nowhere near as foolish as her younger sister. Nevertheless, she too had her head in the clouds with nonsensical dreams about becoming a 'modern woman', whatever that might mean, and could easily take it into her head to do something daft. But she wasn't nearly so tough when the happiness and health of her dear sisters were at stake. And although he might no longer have any power over

Ella, Livia would soon come to heel if she thought her precious Maggie was at risk.

All he had to do, with Hodson's help, was get her to that altar. Surely not beyond his ingenuity? The moment their union was achieved, all his debts would be settled, and the loan the younger man had made to him considered void. He could then pay off the bank and all would be right with his world.

Josiah lit up a cigar and leant back in his chair to consider his options, savouring his dreams for a prosperous future once this current cash-flow crisis was over.

A tap on the door, which opened immediately, interrupting his thoughts and Miss Caraway marched in without him even giving permission for her to enter. He really should sack the woman, she was far too full of her own importance. A real busybody if ever there was one. Very nearly insubordinate. He would dismiss her, if only she wasn't so damned efficient.

'Sorry to interrupt, sir, but it's the bank manager. He says he'd like a quick word if you're free, and I see that you are, so I'll show him in.' Before he could protest that he was actually extremely busy, let alone extinguish his cigar, the man himself came marching in as if he already owned the damn place.

Maggie was once more vomiting up her breakfast in the water closet, yet it was her sister she was worrying about. Livia ached to find a real purpose in life, something she'd been fretting over for months, and dreaded being married off to anyone, Henry in particular.

Maggie felt sure she'd made this promise only to protect her. If only she knew the truth. She could only hope that she would find some way to wriggle out of it before it was too late.

Their father was a difficult man to fool when it came to pulling the wool over his eyes, and if ever he discovered that Livia had tricked him, there would be all hell to pay.

He never considered the feelings of anyone but himself, not staff, servants, or even the happiness of his own children. Poverty, bereavement, ill health, all left him entirely unmoved. His own needs were paramount. He hadn't shown the slightest sympathy when she'd been too sick to eat those dratted kippers, a malady which seemed to have lingered on ever since.

Now Maggie wiped her mouth, retrieved her diary from its hiding place and crawled back into bed. As she began to write, filling in the commonplace day-to-day happenings, a butterfly she'd seen, or what they'd had for tea, she worried over what illness it was that plagued her. What could she have eaten to upset her stomach so badly and produce this dreadful bilious attack? At first she'd put it down to the late summer heat, but it had been going on for weeks now and was getting no better.

As always, the nausea seemed to go off a little during the course of the day, which was something of a relief, although she still felt generally below par, not at all herself. Then every morning Maggie would find herself once more with her head in the bathroom sink, throwing up the contents of an empty stomach.

Unable to concentrate on her writing, she lay back against the pillows and closed her eyes, utterly exhausted, recalling how often this had happened over the last week or so.

This was the moment when reality struck.

Some memory of her mother being sick in exactly the same manner seeped into her mind. It had been during one of the many pregnancies that had ended in tragedy, yet another miscarriage in her efforts to present her husband with the much longed-for son. Now the truth seemed to strike Maggie as if she'd been shot between the shoulder blades.

She leapt to her feet and ran to stare at herself in the dressing-table mirror. Her own shocked eyes gazed back at her in horror, and she knew without a shadow of a doubt, despite there being no visible signs to prove it, exactly what was wrong with her. She was pregnant. Dear God in heaven, she was carrying her own father's child.

Oh Lord, now what was she to do?

She knew instinctively that this was one problem she could never share with her sisters. Ella was too far away to be of any help, and was in any case completely scatter-brained with no experience of such things. She was also far too selfish and wrapped up in herself, so very like Father in that respect. The silly girl was, at times, her own worst enemy. It would be useless asking Ella.

As for Livia, her beloved elder sister fondly believed with absolute certainty that she'd successfully protected her from their father's brutality, as she'd promised their mother she would. Maggie knew that it would hurt her badly to discover that she'd failed. She was even now planning some miraculous escape, which they both knew to be impossible. Their father would never let them go. She would be deeply distressed if she ever learnt the truth about what Maggie had suffered for years at Josiah's hand.

And the shame Maggie herself would feel if it all came out would be too much to bear. No matter what the cost, this was a secret she must somehow manage to keep all to herself.

Chapter Eighteen

Mercy had come to loathe Nurse Bathurst, hated everyone in fact, in this dreadful place. The woman insisted on absolute discipline at all times, would poke the boys with a stick if they didn't jump to it when she issued an order, or stop their noisy banter when she told them to shut up. Batty Brenda liked peace and quiet in her ward, and would make them stand with their hands on their heads for hours on end, until they were whimpering with distress, or until the air was rank with the smell of urine leaked during the overlong restraint.

All that pain just to teach them the value of obedience.

Mercy saw one young boy locked in solitary confinement for two whole days for taking a handkerchief that didn't belong to him.

'I think he took it by mistake,' she protested, as always coming quickly to her charge's defence. 'He couldn't read the initials in the corner. Maybe I could teach him his letters, would that help?'

'There's no point in wasting time and money on teaching this lot anything,' came the predictable response.

'You should learn to keep your mouth shut, or it'll get you in worse bother,' her friend Prue would warn her.

Mercy couldn't deny it. It was her big mouth which had got her shut in here in the first place. What had possessed her to make those demands of Josiah Angel? She must have been mad. He'd abandoned her lovely mother, so why should he care a toss about her?

'I'm sorry, but I can't just stand by and say nothing when that woman intimidates and ridicules those poor patients,' Mercy objected, as the two girls made their way back down the corridor. 'Them lads don't understand and get upset when she makes jibes at them. They're just a bit young and daft, that's all. It's so unfair.'

'Huh, life is unfair,' Prue snapped. 'Haven't you learned that by now? Just keep out of the woman's way in future.'

Easier said than done.

One of the boys, not much younger than Mercy herself, had a bad squint. Batty Brenda called him 'squint-eye', or 'cock-eyed Jamie' and never let up badgering the poor boy over his deficiencies from morning till night.

Sadly, his handicap made him clumsy and one morning while trying to set down his mug of hot chocolate, he missed the table altogether and it fell to the floor, smashing the pot mug to smithereens, the dark milky substance pooling across the clean linoleum.

Nurse Bathurst came marching over, fury in her voice as she berated the hapless boy. 'Now look what you've done, you squint-eyed idiot,' and she smacked the lad across the back of his head, making him even more cross-eyed.

Mercy was on her feet in a second. She wished with all her heart that Jack were here. He'd soon sort out this Batty Brenda person, but since he wasn't, she'd tackle the woman herself. 'Don't you dare smack him, and don't call him names neither, it's hurtful. It's not Jamie's fault his eyes wander all over the place so that he can't properly see what he's doing. Why can't you leave the lad alone, you great bully!'

There was an awed silence, even those who paid little attention to what was going on around them stopped giggling and gossiping to take in the full import of her words. Nurse Bathurst's gaze was one of outraged fury that this strip of a girl should dare, yet again, to cross her, and in such a way.

Mercy could feel her cheeks growing all hot and red, and wondered what devil possessed her to keep constantly putting herself in such jeopardy? When would she ever learn to keep her lip buttoned? She tried to redeem her mistake by running to grab a cloth to mop up the mess. The woman waited until the floor was mopped clean and every shard of broken pottery swept up before fixing Mercy with her gimlet gaze.

'My office, Simpson. Now!'

This time the punishment wasn't scrubbing the floor twice over, or being deprived of her supper. Nor was she sent out into the yard with shaming words chalked across her breast, which much later Mercy thought would have been far preferable. She was stripped of her clothing right down to her birthday suit, then dressed in a large coarse potato sack, thrown into a small dark cell, and left in solitary confinement for four days and nights on plain bread and water.

At first she sang to herself, or recited the poems and stories her mother used to tell her. But in the end the silence won. She curled up like a hibernating animal, and simply waited for the time to pass. Mercy was of the firm belief that during this period she gradually began to lose her mind, which perhaps accounted for what happened later.

Mercy would watch the visitors arrive on the first Saturday of every month, but none ever came to see her. She would read the diet sheet on the wall promising untold delights, and then eat the thin porridge or the bread and gruel without comment. And then one Wednesday in late September the patients were instructed to put on clean shirts or aprons and present themselves with clean hands and faces for inspection, as they were expecting an important visitor that afternoon.

As they lined up in the hall to greet their visitor, Mercy's heart leapt into her throat as she saw who their esteemed guest actually was. None other than Josiah Angel himself was standing before them, smiling and nodding at all the upturned faces before him, scanning the lines as if looking for one face in particular. Mercy thought she might be sick with the excitement of it.

He was looking for *her*! He'd come for her at last. Why else would he be here? Filled with hope that he'd suffered a change of heart, Mercy pushed back her shoulders and stood up very straight, knowing that at any minute he would see her, and all would at last be right with her world. He must regret sending her off with a flea in her ear that day, and had come to make recompense by rescuing her. She could hardly believe her good fortune.

She nudged Prue, standing in line beside her. 'It's him, my dad. Didn't I tell you he'd come?'

Prue cast her a quick glance of anxious disbelief, clearly thinking she'd lost her marbles, before quietly shushing her. 'What are you talking about? That's not your father, that's Mr Angel. Mr Josiah Angel from the big department store.'

'I know who he is,' Mercy insisted. 'And I tell you he *is* my father.'

A hissed whisper from behind. 'I thought you said your da were the prime minister, or was it Baron Rothschild? Or happen it's King Edward himself. How about that? Why didn't we realise we had a princess in our midst?' A fit of stifled giggling broke out, quickly silenced by a fierce glare from Nurse Bathurst.

Josiah was drawing nearer, moving along the lines as if he were a major general inspecting the troops. Without pausing to consider the consequences of such an action, Mercy stepped out in front of him.

'Good morning, Father. I'm so glad to see you've come for me at last.'

211

You could have heard a pin drop. The silence in the great hall was profound.

Mercy was looking up into his face and didn't see how Mr Cardew, the master of the workhouse, and Matron, who stood beside him, positively seethed with fury. But the silence was beginning to make her feel uncomfortable. It had this affect upon her ever since that spell in solitary, the longest four days of her entire life. She could see that Josiah Angel didn't look quite so pleased to see her as she might have hoped. His face was changing colour, from ruddy red to ashen white, and then a ghastly purple. It was at this point that Mercy came to her senses and, too late, saw the mistake she had made.

'What did the girl say? Are her wits addled?'

Panic and anxiety was almost palpable as Matron said something about her being a problem from the first day she'd arrived; that the girl did not appreciate how fortunate she was to have a roof over her head, food in her belly and regular employment.

Mr Cardew was almost falling over himself in his eagerness to agree with his wife's assessment. A large hand reached out to snatch Mercy by the collar and she found herself being roughly shaken as phrases such as 'ungrateful child', 'rude and obscene', 'a cheeky little troublemaker who leads men on', were being bandied back and forth.

'The chit is certainly a fantasist and a liar,' said Josiah, speaking as if from a great height. 'Such insubordination must be dealt with.'

Now he was bending his head to engage in a whispered

212

conversation with the master, his eyes boring into hers as he did so. Mercy was beginning to shake with nerves. He hadn't come for her at all. He'd come to check that she was still safely locked up. Or more likely he'd completely forgotten about her existence until she had stupidly reminded him.

'Yes, indeed, sir,' the master was saying. 'I do so agree. An example must be made.'

Seconds later, Mercy was being frogmarched out of the hall.

To be branded a liar by your own father for speaking nothing less than the truth was bad enough, but what followed was harsh beyond even Mercy's imaginings.

Much later she learnt that it was at Josiah's suggestion she be given a dozen lashes instead of the more usual six. Mercy stared in wide-eyed disbelief as the master reached for the birch. She was held down over a chair by two assistants, her skirts lifted, her drawers pulled down and her bottom bared. She soon realised that, wriggle and protest as she might, there would be no escape. The pain of the first lash was excruciating and she cried out, the thin sharp sticks of the birch cutting deeply into her flesh, and her body jerking violently with each new stroke. Four more of these and Mercy was beyond pain, aware only of a red mist forming before her eyes in which furious faces leered at her then faded away, mouthing words she couldn't hear. On the eighth stroke she blessedly passed out, and when vinegar and water failed to revive her, Matron judged it best to proceed no further, for fear they might have a dead girl on their hands.

Instead she was thrown back into solitary and left to lie in a pool of her own blood, fading in and out of consciousness for what felt like an eternity.

It was her dear friend Prue who was finally permitted to take her back to the dormitory, although not till the following morning. She bathed Mercy's wounds and staunched the bleeding with cold water, since she had nothing else. But by then it was too late. The lashes and the dark solitary hole had done their work. Mercy felt completely numb, as if they'd finally broken her spirit and robbed her forever of that vital spark of happiness and faith in the world that had been a natural part of her personality.

Chapter Nineteen

Maggie was becoming increasingly morose, almost falling into a depression, yet could offer no explanation for her black mood. At least the sickness seemed to be passing, which had saved calling out the doctor.

Even more worryingly, they still hadn't seen Ella, not since her wedding. Whenever Livia wrote and urged her to visit, she would give some excuse or other: the weather, the work in the dairy, or not being able to leave the livestock. Livia sighed. Ella's letters were so vague, so unlike her sister's usual chatty nature that she did wonder if Amos censored them. A chilling thought!

How easy it had been to make that promise to Mama to protect them, and how difficult to carry it out.

Neither had Livia forgotten her promise to Jack Flint to enquire about Mercy, the young girl who was also, apparently, a sister, albeit a half one. Livia was still coming to terms with this shocking revelation, but her father had always been secretive, in many respects. He had never divulged where he went on the evenings he was not at home.

She'd begun her quest by talking to the shop assistants, particularly those who worked in the back rooms unpacking and sorting stock, or engaged in the making up of customers' orders, sewing gowns or whatever.

They were all too busy, they assured her, to lift their heads from their work to ease aching backs, let alone pay any attention to what was going on around them. Or too wise to gossip. They made it very clear that they didn't much care to be interrogated by the boss's daughter, as if she were checking up on how effectively they were carrying out their own jobs. They seemed to believe that she meant to tell on them to her father, and she'd had to back off pretty quickly.

It was all becoming rather embarrassing and far more difficult than she'd hoped.

Livia left Miss Caraway until the last, out of cowardice she ruefully admitted, yet she was the one most likely to know the answer to the puzzle.

'We have many girls enquiring after positions,' the older woman responded in her usual tart manner when Livia finally plucked up the courage to ask her the question.

'And have there been any lately, that you remember?'

Miss Caraway looked at her askance. 'And why would I trouble to remember the tribe of hopefuls who trek through my door with little or no hope of proving suitable? They are generally of the lower classes with dirty fingernails and no brains.'

Livia stifled a sigh. Miss Caraway was at times even more snobby than dear deluded Ella. 'And have you ever been approached by a girl with clean fingernails and evidence of some small degree of intelligence? One, perhaps, with fair hair and turquoise blue eyes?'

'I do assure you that the colour of hair and eyes is quite immaterial when choosing staff, and I ceased to hope for intelligence years ago.'

'I'm sorry, Jack, but I'm not sure how much longer I can go on. I've done my best, but no one seems to have seen her, and old Caraway is being stubbornly vague on the subject. I've quite run out of ideas what to try next.'

They generally met up by the river, as they were doing now. They'd walk from Nether Bridge along Colonel Walk past the parish church where Ella had been married, and on past the old grammar school and Abbot Hall.

Today they were sitting on a grassy bank watching the ducks squabble over crusts of bread that children were throwing to them. The sun was shining on this lovely October day, and, despite the bad news Livia had to impart, she felt curiously happy and optimistic.

Jack plucked a stalk of grass and thoughtfully chewed on the end of it. 'Why is that? Because this Caraway woman knows what happened to her and doesn't want to tell?'

Livia shrugged, her eyes on his mouth, wondering what it would feel like to have it pressed against her own. 'It's possible, I suppose, although I mentioned no names, merely the barest details, so she didn't have much to go on.'

Jack tossed the grass stalk aside to respond with one of

his captivating smiles. 'Maybe, but *she* should remember that one day you might actually be running the store, then where would she be?'

Livia gurgled with laughter. 'I very much doubt that could ever happen. Father will most certainly make sure that it doesn't.'

'You don't have any brothers though, do you?'

'No, but that doesn't mean I would inherit, so you can forget that notion at once. Father would much rather leave it to some distant cousin, I'm sure, so long as they were male.'

Livia felt a faint stirring of unease that Jack should think in that way about her – as someone who might inherit a thriving business. But then he was probably only teasing her in that droll manner of his. She really mustn't be quite so sensitive, and he was, after all, her friend.

At least that *was* all she wanted from him, wasn't it? Friendship. Lounging on the grass with his long legs stretched out, Livia experienced a great longing to lie beside him, to feel the warmth of his body curl about hers. She tucked her arms about her knees and quickly changed the subject.

'So what shall we do about poor Mercy then? I seem to be getting absolutely nowhere by asking these questions, except to make a nuisance of myself. And I'm nervous of arousing Father's suspicions if I push too hard.'

They sat in glum silence for some long moments, contemplating possibilities. Then Jack's face cleared and he sat up, suddenly fired with an idea. 'Why didn't I think of it before? Florrie provided Mercy with a letter of introduction. What happened to that, I wonder?'

Livia frowned. 'Father would have thrown it away, surely?'

'What if he didn't? What if he just left it lying about? Maybe you should look for that letter instead.'

Livia was appalled. 'You want me to sneak into my father's office and start searching through his papers? Are you mad? How do you imagine he'd react if he caught me snooping?'

Jack had the grace to look concerned by this prospect, nevertheless his answer brought little comfort. 'You'll just have to make sure that he doesn't.'

'Thanks!'

He brushed the back of one hand against her cheek in a gentle caress. 'I wouldn't want you to take any risks, so choose your moment with care, when he's safely off the premises.'

Livia was so taken aback by the touch of his fingers against her skin that she could scarcely formulate her thoughts into any sensible order. 'I will...of course...I – I'll take care.'

'He hasn't...hit you again, has he?'

'No.'

He frowned. 'Sure?'

'Absolutely. I promised to marry Henry, after all, so he has no reason to.'

He sat up to stare at her in startled surprise. 'You did *what*? You aren't serious?'

'It was the only way to stop him from harassing me, and to protect my sister, who isn't too well.' Her brow puckered with concern as she thought of Maggie. 'Not that I've any intention of fulfilling my promise,' she blithely continued.

'So the word of you nobs can't be trusted, is that it?'

Livia chuckled. 'It was only a little white lie.'

'It was a whopping big black one. Still, I'll let you off in the circumstances. You had me worried for a moment.'

'Why should it worry you whom I marry?' Livia regretted her question almost the moment she'd voiced it, as it sounded so arch and contrived, as if she were fishing for compliments. And could that be a flush creeping up his neck? Had she embarrassed him? Or stirred something else in him, something rather wonderful? His face suddenly seemed to have come much closer to her own, so that she could see the reflection of her own image in his big brown eyes. But then he half turned away with a casual shrug of the shoulders.

'I suppose everything you do concerns me, at the moment anyway. Aren't we friends, united in a quest?'

'Because of Mercy, you mean?'

He held her gaze for some long seconds before answering. 'What else could I mean?'

Livia was now the first to break the gaze. 'You've no need to worry about me. I've no intention of marrying at all, not Henry, not anyone.'

He smiled. 'You intend to remain a spinster stuck on the shelf?'

'I hate both those expressions. I am not a spinster, whatever that might be, and I'm certainly not stuck on any shelf. I intend to do other, more useful things with my life than pander to some male,' she said, her tone ringing with resolve and self-satisfaction. 'I've had enough of that sort of thing already with my father, thank you very much. I've certainly no intention of exchanging one bully for another.'

'Not all men are bullies,' Jack said, in that low, husky voice which had such an odd effect upon her insides.

Livia fixed her gaze firmly upon the ducks as she mumbled that really she had no intention of taking the risk. If only he wasn't sitting quite so close. His very nearness was making her feel flustered. Spinster indeed!

'You might change your mind, about marrying I mean.'

'I won't.' She looked at him, her eyes fierce. 'Not ever. Men are not to be trusted.'

'We'll see, shall we?'

'In the meantime,' Livia said, 'I'll search for that dratted letter and do what I can to locate your friend. Where the hell do you think she is?'

Mercy and Georgina, or George as she preferred to think of him, had become firm friends and happily shared secrets and gossip. He said little about his own background and Mercy had the sense not to ask, but she confided in him her grief over the death of her mother. One afternoon as they circled the ward together, shuffling round and round in their usual listless fashion, she told him the truth of her birth, and how she'd taken Florrie's carefully penned letter to Josiah Angel's Department Store in a bid to secure a job from the man she'd discovered was her father.

'So when you stepped out in front of him on the day he came visiting, you were speaking the truth?'

Mercy shrugged. 'I was a fool. Speaking the truth sometimes isn't such a good idea. I should've realised he didn't give a toss.'

'So you went to him to ask for help and all he did was send you to this place?' George was outraged.

'Like I say, I'm stupid.'

'But he's your da. Not that mine was much better.' George told her then how he'd spent his youth avoiding his own father's heavy hand. 'Which had a habit of landing on my backside. We lived out in the wilds beyond Keswick, where he worked in the lead mines. One day, when I was about thirteen, I stupidly told him I'd no intention of following his example and going down the mines. He nearly killed me. There was a carter leaving that night for Kendal, so I went with him.'

'Didn't you manage to find work here in Kendal either?'

'Nope. I didn't have no character, did I? No reference, no training, couldn't read and write, useless I am. I nicked a pie off a market stall and got caught. It was either the clink or the workhouse. I opted for the latter, pretending to be soft in the head, threepence short to the shilling.' George chuckled as if it were all a fine joke, then quickly sobered as he went on to apologise to Mercy for his high jinks on the day she'd arrived, which was what had got her into trouble in the first place. 'I didn't mean you no harm, I just like playing practical jokes, hence the dress. It lightens the boredom.'

Mercy looked bemused. 'But why would a good-looking man like you want to dress like a woman?'

George laughed. 'I find it helps to appear more stupid than I actually am.'

Mercy's eyes widened. 'Why? I've certainly discovered that what Prue told me was true. If you want to survive in this place, don't fight, don't argue, and keep your mouth shut. But I never thought you'd need to pretend to be something that you're not.'

George winked. 'Being classed as an imbecile has proved very useful, I can tell you. Better than breaking stones or being sent to the reformatory. They think I'm so stupid that I can't even find my way around this place, which I encourage by constantly "getting myself lost". Such excursions have allowed me to check out the layout pretty thoroughly, and I have, in fact, learnt of a way out.' He half glanced over his shoulder to check there were no eavesdroppers. 'Why don't we make plans to leave, eh? There's a whole world out there, Mercy, just waiting for you and me to grab it by the throat.'

Mercy was the one laughing now. For the first time since the birching and those terrible dark days in solitude, she felt a lifting of her spirits. Maybe she did have some strength left in her, after all. 'You're on,' she said. 'Just show me the way.'

Chapter Twenty

The moon looked pale as a pearl in the black velvet sky, the stars a scattering of diamonds as Ella crept up the stairs to the attic. Ever since her walk to the river to join her husband fishing, which had led to her secretly watching him bathing, Ella had been tormented by the image of him standing proud and naked before her, albeit unaware of her presence. He was a man not given to demonstrations of emotion, a private man who preferred to keep his grief and private worries to himself. But he was her husband, and Ella understood that if this wall he'd erected between them was ever to be breached, she must be the one to take it down, brick by brick if necessary.

A floorboard creaked as she stepped into the room and she halted, holding her breath in case he should wake. No sound came, and stepping softly on the soles of her feet, Ella edged forward. The bed he slept in was narrow, made for one, not two, but as luck would have it he was turned with his face to the wall, the blankets rucked up.

Very slowly and carefully, Ella pulled back the covers and slipped in beside him.

A shaft of stray moonlight coming through a narrow window cut into the roof above revealed that he was naked from the waist up. He wore nothing but his long johns. Ella lay silent beside him, her breathing soft and quiet as she struggled to control her nervousness. Very gently she rested the flat of her hand against his back, then she placed her lips against his warm bare skin and kissed it. Next she slid her hand around his waist, caressed the hardness of his belly, the velvety smoothness of him, and heard him groan as he turned to her. Then he was kissing her, every bit as demanding as that very first time when she'd been frightened of the rats in the barn, and he'd surprised her with a kiss. He was pulling her beneath him, his breathing growing ragged with need.

Ella stroked the hair at his nape, wrapped her legs about his narrow hips and flung back her head in sheer delight as he caressed each nipple with the tip of his tongue. So he did want her after all, as much as she now wanted him. The preacher man was full of surprises.

And he hadn't even thought to wash his hands first.

He was warm and strong and hard, and possibly still half asleep. Ella didn't care whether he thought this a dream or not. Like a miracle, he slid inside her and took her as sweetly as though they'd been made for each other. She cried out in ecstasy, knowing she'd longed for this moment ever since she'd seen him in the river that day, and as they moved together with an instinctive rhythm, her heart sang.

Could this be love? Was this how it felt to really love someone? Full of awe and fear and pulsing excitement?

When it was over, they lay with limbs entwined, utterly spent. Ella waited for him to speak, to tell her how beautiful she was, but was disappointed instead to hear once more the steady rhythm of his breathing. Her husband had fallen asleep. Smiling softly, she tucked herself into the curve of his warm body and slept too.

It was Ella who woke first, with shafts of a pink dawn piercing the darkness as she turned to kiss him on the tip of his nose. It was as if she had branded him with a red hot iron. He leapt from the bed in an instant, one moment contentedly asleep beside her, the next standing shivering on the bare boards, glaring down at her. 'What the... What are you doing in my bed?'

Ella made no attempt to move. She merely grinned at him and pulled the blankets up to her chin. 'I am your wife. I believe I'm fully entitled to be in your bed.'

He made a grumble of contempt deep in his throat. '"With her much fair speech she caused him to yield, with the flattering of her lips she forced him." Get ye gone.'

Ella sat up, not caring that the blanket fell back to reveal her to be bare breasted, although she heard his quick indrawn breath. 'I forced no one. I am not the devil, Amos, my father was for marrying me to you when he knew there was no love between us.'

She saw how his eyes were riveted to her nakedness, hot with need. 'Who do you think you are, woman, Eve, or Bathsheba?'

226

Ella chewed on a fingernail and pretended to consider. 'Wasn't Bathsheba seduced by David, rather than the other way around? And I believe you too had a part to play in last night's events.'

Amos changed his line of attack.

'Thy father informed me of your fall from grace. I have yet to meet a virtuous woman, one who is not willing to steal into a man's bed and bring him down like an ox to the slaughter, as it says in Proverbs, chapter seven—'

'Oh, stop that at once, Amos.' Ella was out of the bed in a second, standing before him with not a hint of embarrassment as she stamped the floorboards with one bare foot. 'Stop hiding behind the scriptures and be a man, why don't you? But all right, if you don't want me, so be it. Stay in your narrow little bed with the company only of your narrow little mind, and see if I care. To hell with you, Amos Todd, and your moralising.'

And she stormed off, tears rolling down her cheeks, quite forgetting she'd left her nightdress behind. Amos snatched it up as if to chase after her with it, but then changed his mind and buried his nose in it instead, breathing in the essence of her.

Mercy was trudging across open fields, doing her best to keep pace with George's long-legged stride. They'd been walking for days and she was bone-weary, her feet a mass of blisters and every muscle screaming with pain.

Escaping from the workhouse had turned out to be far easier than she'd feared. George had shown her a tiny window with a loose catch in the boiler room, just big enough for her to squeeze through. George himself, tall and broad-shouldered, couldn't possibly escape that way. Instead he'd adopted his Georgina role, and in dress and bonnet managed to somehow mingle with the visitors and walk out of the door as bold as brass. Mercy thought it a miracle he wasn't spotted, or even searched – though if any of the staff had seen him, they might have assumed it was Georgina being simple again. Whatever the reason, and against all the odds, the plan worked.

'We got away with it!' she cried, when he'd hunkered down beside her on Kendal Green.

'Not yet,' he'd warned. 'We still need to get down into town and find transport.'

In fact, they'd been fortunate to discover a line of farmers' carts trundling up Windermere Road, and it was the simplest thing in the world to hitch a lift. They'd pretended to be mother and daughter on their way home from market. That first cart took them as far as Windermere, where George had divested himself of the dress. Beneath that he was wearing the trademark canvas trousers and shirt that marked him out as a workhouse inmate, but a scout around the backstreets soon produced a washing line with a pair of trousers and shirt that fitted.

They walked for several miles to Ambleside, following the shore of the lake for part of the way, before slipping under the tarpaulin of yet another farm cart as it lumbered past.

George reckoned they must now be in the Langdales, the most westerly range of mountains in the Lakes, and that the last village they'd driven through a few miles back was Chapel Stile. When the cart had slowed for the driver to open a farm gate, the pair of them slipped out over the tailgate and hid in a ditch until it had gone.

'Now where are we?' Mercy cried, gazing around at the sweep of brooding mountains. It looked very much like alien territory so far as she was concerned, yet she was transfixed by the sheer beauty of the boulder-strewn landscape: by the purple carpet of heather, the looming mountain peaks, the spindly pines that leant into the wind, and everywhere she looked there were sheep. Dark and round-bellied with rough white faces, they didn't look like proper sheep at all.

George told her they were called Herdwicks, and were believed to have been brought over to Lakeland by the Vikings many hundreds of years ago. 'They're thick-boned, provide good wool and the sweetest meat you've ever tasted.'

Both their mouths watered at the mention of food. George had managed to steal half a loaf of bread from the dining room, and Mercy a hunk of cheese from the kitchen. They sat down at once to eat a little of this, saving the rest for later, knowing they would be even hungrier by then.

'Once we find shelter, a barn or something, I'll set a trap for some real food,' George promised.

That had been yesterday, or was it the day before? Mercy was beginning to lose track of time. One night they had indeed found a barn and had slept well, warm as toast, another time they'd slept under a hedge, and last night they'd huddled close together for warmth beneath the canopy of an old beech tree.

But now the valley and the stream where they'd quenched their thirst and finished the last of the bread and cheese at breakfast were miles behind them. Mercy noticed a lone buzzard circling overhead and fell to her knees in fright, thinking it a vulture, which amused George greatly. But then she'd lived all her life in Kendal, on Fellside. She wasn't used to wild places.

George didn't seem in the least troubled by the remoteness of the spot. The mountains were rugged with high peaks and crags that seemed to tower over her. He named them for her: Langdale Pikes, Bowfell and Crinkle Crags, and promised to take her walking up them one day. Mercy declined.

'I prefer to keep my feet firmly on solid pavements and cobbled streets, thanks all the same, not slippy, sharp rocks that hang over a precipice into which I might fall and crack me skull.'

She was almost glad when heavy clouds obscured the mountaintops in a thick fog. George might call them noble but Mercy saw them as menacing, and made sure she kept pace with him as he strode along, nervous of getting left behind.

'We need to keep off any main roads, just in case someone should come looking for us.'

Mercy thought this highly unlikely but what alternative did she have except to follow him? Besides, she trusted him implicitly, even if it did sometimes feel as if they were going round in circles. He, at least, knew where he was going.

In this she was sadly mistaken. George had been lost for some time, but had kept on walking out of necessity, or habit, hoping he'd come across a village where he might find work, or a likely spot for them to settle for a while, then he could catch them a rabbit for supper. He had a box of matches in his pocket for lighting a fire, which he'd thieved from the boiler room, and his belly felt as if it was sticking to his rib cage. He could tell Mercy was hungry too because her pace was slowing. Tonight he meant to make them a proper lean-to shelter, in case those threatening clouds fulfilled their promise and brought rain.

They came at last to a copse by a small tarn. The rich colours of the rowan, heavy with their scarlet berries, looked so beautiful they warmed Mercy's heart. A thin mist was creeping down the fells like an old man's beard and she could hear the clear bright song of a robin, the gentle bleating of the Herdwicks, and the rustle of wind-blown leaves.

'And where are we now? I swear I've seen that mountain before.'

George was looking distinctly uncomfortable, wondering if she was right. 'Even if we are lost, isn't this better than being locked up in that flamin' workhouse? It's beautiful. I can't think why I ever went south to the town in the first place? I must have been mad.'

'If you hadn't done that, you'd never have met me.'

'True, which would have been a pity.'

Something warmed inside her at his words, and she grinned back at him. 'We were destined to meet, you and me, eh? Still, this place is desolate and we belong in the town. We'll starve out here with no food, and it's getting colder by the minute.'

George was beginning to feel desperate for some rest and flopped down on a hillock of moss, closed his eyes and was almost instantly asleep. Mercy had never known anyone with the ability to fall asleep quite so quickly. She envied him this as she stood looking down at him, shivering in the chill wind, but then she too sank down onto the mossy bank and snuggled up against the warmth of his bulky body.

She liked George a lot. He was good-looking in a rough and ready sort of way, though his nose was a bit crooked and his brown eyes deep set. His mouth was wide and full, the kind she would very much like to kiss, had she not still nursed doubts about his fondness for wearing that dress.

She heard a rustle in the undergrowth and, glancing up, spotted a deer. It was quietly feeding in the dusk, unaware of her presence, and Mercy kept very still, anxious not to startle it. As she sat watching the creature in awe, she suddenly caught sight of a feast of blackberries cloaking a thorn hedge, and gave a little squeal, quite unable to stop herself. Startled by her cry, the deer leapt away into the undergrowth.

Undeterred, she gave George a shake. 'Look, look, brambles. Supper!'

They ate till their mouths were black with the berries

and their stomachs could take no more. By the time they'd collected branches for a makeshift shelter it was already growing dark and George had grown oddly silent. Mercy brought bracken to use as a mattress, laying it under the lean-to just as the rain started, relishing the prospect of curling up beside him as they had done on previous nights.

George set a trap using his bootlaces and some forked twigs, since that was all he had, in the vain hope of catching a rabbit for breakfast. Then he lay down beside her. Mercy snuggled close, fitting herself against the warmth of his body like a pair of spoons in a drawer.

She was almost disappointed that yet again he didn't try anything on. Proper gent, was George. Or else his desires ran in an entirely different direction, which troubled her more than she was prepared to admit. Mercy was beginning to suspect that she was falling in love with George, which wouldn't do at all, if that were the case.

The bracken was scratchy and not half so soft and comfortable as it had appeared when she'd first laid it down. Nor was the lean-to shelter as waterproof as they'd hoped and the rain soon seeped between the branches, soaking them through. After a largely sleepless night, they woke at dawn to a biting cold, gnawing hunger and a still empty trap. Even George no longer saw their escape as a romantic adventure and agreed there was only one answer. Today must be make or break. They either found themselves a job, or tomorrow they must return to Kendal.

* * *

To Ella's great joy she received a letter from Livia encouraging her to come any time she cared, assuring her that Father had agreed she could stay for as long as she liked. Amos, however, was not in favour of her staying even for one night. They'd spoken scarcely more than a few essential words since Ella's visit to the attic, and she knew that he was deliberately avoiding her. Yet he did agree, at last, to a short visit, for one afternoon, no more. Perhaps this was by way of reward for all her hard work these last months, or by way of an apology for his failure to be a true husband to her. Whatever the reason, Ella was simply grateful for this opportunity to spend some time with her sisters, and at once fetched paper and pen to write back to Livia to tell her that she would be there Thursday week.

Chapter Twenty-One

Livia had kept putting off the search of her father's office, delaying the moment as she sought to summon up the necessary courage. He would be sure to find out that she'd been rooting through his things. Father possessed an uncanny knack of knowing everything that was going on around him. He might even catch her in the act. But if it was true that Mercy had presented him with a letter from her mother, then it must be found. One way or the other, Livia needed to know if Josiah had found some way to silence the poor girl.

She'd just about gathered the nerve to take the chance, when word reached her that a riot had broken out on Fellside. Livia was at once concerned for Jessie and Jack.

She snatched up her bicycle and pedalled hell for leather along Highgate.

The streets of Fellside were in turmoil. The simmering discontent of recent months had boiled up into a communal rage, and tempers were running high. A crowd had gathered in Fountain Brow and bricks and bottles were being thrown, windows smashed, and men were fighting with their bare knuckles or whatever came to hand. And amidst the mêlée a few frantic policemen were running around blowing their whistles and having very little calming effect whatsoever. If anything, the disturbance was worsening. And then Livia spotted Jack.

He'd climbed onto a low roof over an outhouse where he stood with his arms raised, calling for quiet from the crowd gathered around him. The stink from the privies almost made her gag, nevertheless Livia pressed forward to listen along with everyone else, finding herself a safe perch on the corner of a wall.

'We've had enough of being treated like animals,' he shouted, and the crowd roared their agreement. 'We live with lice and rats in absolute squalor, breathing in the foul stink of dung pits and cess pools. The pigs are better housed than we are.'

'We want fresh water in our taps for our kiddies,' yelled one woman.

'Aye, and enough privies for everyone.'

'We want our rubbish collected regular like.'

'We do indeed,' Jack yelled, 'and rents we can afford to pay. Right now we get nowt for the brass we hand over each week, and the sum we pay is increasing beyond our means, particularly considering the pitiful wages we earn. We're being ripped off by the landlords and the hosiers. Some of us are paying as much as three shillings to live in a hovel not fit for swine, yet they claim the rents don't cover the cost of repairs. But why would they care? So long as they can sell on the property for a nice fat profit, the landlords come up smelling of roses. I, for one, have had enough of being used as fodder to make rich men richer.'

Another roar from the crowd, filled with outrage at this indisputable but unpalatable fact.

It was then that the rain started, the kind of relentless, driving rain that seemed peculiarly native to Lakeland. The skies suddenly opened and it came down in torrents, hammering like nails upon their heads, drenching the assembled crowd in seconds. Some of the women grabbed their children and ran for cover, while most of the men and some of the more determined women remained. Jessie among them.

The police seemed to take this exodus as a good sign and began trying to herd the rest of the stragglers back to their homes. Their efforts were far from welcome and most fiercely resisted. It was as if war had broken out and the embattled constables soon found themselves being pelted with stones and muck picked up out of the filthy gutters and dung heaps.

Far from dispersing the crowd, other folk came rushing to join in and the mob soon doubled in size. The howling, baying throng weren't listening to Jack any longer, and surely bones as well as windows were now being broken, children getting caught up in the panic.

One child of about four or five fell headlong on the cobbles, and would have been trampled underfoot had not Jack quickly jumped down from the roof and plucked him from the crush. He handed him over to his relieved mother, then helped the pair of them to the corner of The Syke, so named for a syke, or stream, that had once run down it. Now this had become an open drain, clotted with the kind of filth it was best not to examine too closely, and surely proved the neglect endemic in the district. When finally free of the throng, the woman clutched the child to her breast and began to run.

But not before Livia saw her give Jack a quick kiss on his cheek. Was that simply by way of thanks, or something more? She felt a pang of sorrow in her heart, anxious that it might be the latter.

Jack didn't hang around to watch the young mother safely home, but turned back to assist Jessie, who'd started to unfurl a huge banner, presumably one that proudly declared the purpose of their campaign. Livia jumped down from the wall and set off to fight her way through the crowd, intent on helping, but at the same moment she saw her father, Josiah Angel.

He came up Low Fellside and burst into Fountain Brow with a group of armed militia on his heels. Frantic now, she tried to reach her friends and urge them to escape. But then someone hit her over the head and everything went black.

They were spared a bloodbath by the quick thinking of Jack and other leaders of the Fellside community, as well as the common sense of the militia. The former had everyone running for cover within seconds, and the latter were slow to respond, largely ignoring the instructions of Councillor Josiah Angel, who seemed to want the running figures cut down in a hail of bullets.

Once some sort of calm was restored, Jack picked up Livia in his arms and carried her to Jessie.

One man had suffered a broken arm, another crushed ribs, and several folk nursed cuts and bruises, but nothing really serious. The people of Fellside returned to their homes, strangely subdued and ruefully aware that they'd achieved nothing. No doubt their landlords would punish this small rebellion by raising the rents still further, rather than lowering them as they'd hoped.

Livia soon recovered from the blow to her head and returned home, incandescent with rage, wasting no time in tackling her father on the subject. The moment dinner was over that evening, and Josiah had returned to the drawing room following his usual cigar and glass of whisky, she began her attack, determined to take up the cudgels on her friends' behalf.

'Why will you not reduce the rents you charge to a more economic level, Father? One the residents can afford to pay.'

'And leave myself worse off? Don't be ridiculous, girl.' Josiah was so irritated by the question that he poured himself a cup of coffee, not even thinking to demand that one of his daughters do this for him, as they usually did.

Maggie handed him the sugar, casting her sister a reproving glance. 'Perhaps this isn't the right moment for such a delicate discussion, Livvy. It's all rather too raw and recent.'

'It is precisely the right moment.' Livia waited until he was settled in his wing chair before continuing with her argument. 'Why won't you at least carry out some repairs?'

'Because I'm not made of brass, although some folk might think otherwise.'

'You are by comparison with the poor souls who have to live in those damp, infested hovels. Have you even stepped inside one, Father? Do you know how those poor people are condemned to live day after day? They need clean water, more lavatories, and the kind of rubbish-free streets and decent sewerage system that is benefiting the rest of the town. Surely that's not too much to ask?'

Josiah set down his untouched coffee on a nearby table with a snap. 'I trust you aren't going to turn into a radical, girl. The last thing I need is a suffragist for a daughter.'

Livia bridled. 'This has nothing to do with me being a radical, nor was that riot anything to do with women's rights. It was about the rights of honest people, the need to provide decent accommodation for respectable human beings.'

This comment seemed to amuse him as he put back his great head and roared with laughter, eyebrows twitching, the jutting chin wobbling alarmingly. 'Honest people? Respectable human beings? What, the likes of Jack Flint? You must be mad. He represents the lowest of the low.'

'At least Jack cares about his family, which is more than can be said for you, Father.' It was the bravest, most reckless remark she had made to him in a long while, and

240

Livia sensed rather than heard her sister's quick indrawn breath.

Josiah stared at his daughter for a long moment, then pushing himself up from his chair with the agility of a man of much younger years, he came over to where she was seated by the fire. Livia's book lay forgotten in her lap, and picking it up he glanced at the title: *The History of the Roman Empire*. He tossed it aside with a scornful growl, then grasped her firmly by the chin, almost spitting in her face as he responded.

'Who am *I* then? Nero? You think I'm fiddling while Rome burns? Well, maybe I am. Maybe I enjoy the role of tyrant. I deserve it after all I've done for this town. But if you ever go near that man, the notorious Jack Flint, who has been a thorn in my side for more years than I care to count, you'll be the one thrown to the lions. You have my word on that.'

'Father, please don't!' This from Maggie, who had leapt to her feet, as always distressed when her father's temper grew heated. He turned on her, his face dark with anger. 'I'll have no more of this obstinacy, from either of you. I'm damned if I'll be lectured by my own daughters. Get upstairs to bed, the pair of you, or you'll be spending the night in less conducive surroundings.'

Both girls scuttled away without another word. Maggie was trembling with nerves, knowing he would come to her later, if only to re-establish his control, and he would be in an especially foul mood.

Livia stormed to her room seething with silent fury. Sadly, the poor of Fellside had achieved nothing by their

241

rebellion, and herself even less by trying to help them, despite her courage in standing up to her father.

But if nothing else, the confrontation had helped Livia to make up her mind on one thing. She would visit Father's office at the very first opportunity and find that dratted letter. She would discover what had happened to that poor girl, no matter what the cost. He seemed to imagine he possessed the power to manipulate the lives of others simply to suit himself, well he was wrong. No matter what the risk involved, she was determined to take it.

She chose the very next afternoon, a time when she knew her father would be out enjoying lunch with his friends and colleagues. The store always closed for one hour from twelve-thirty until one-thirty. Once she was certain that all was quiet within and all the assistants were upstairs in the dining hall, she crept back along the myriad corridors till she reached her father's office.

The door was closed fast, as she'd expected. It might well be locked and a part of her half hoped that it would be, so that she need go no further with this dangerous quest. But as she turned the shiny mahogany knob with trembling fingers, the door creaked open. Within seconds she was on the inside, pressing it closed behind her, her heart beating loud and fast in her breast. What on earth was she doing? Had she completely lost her reason? If Miss Caraway should take it into her head to come and check on her, she'd be the one in the soup.

Livia glanced wildly about the room. The office was

remarkably untidy with papers strewn everywhere, but then her father had no servants here, as there were at home, to wait upon him. It didn't look as if he even allowed Miss Caraway to touch anything, which wasn't so surprising. He wouldn't want that busybody poking her nose into his private concerns. He had absolutely forbidden his own daughter access to the store's accounts, refused even to discuss his buying policy with her, so he was hardly likely to risk a mere employee getting sight of anything personal or important.

So where should she begin to look? Where would he keep such a private document as a letter from a former lover which contained the kind of information that could ruin him, if made public?

Tiptoeing swiftly across the room, Livia opened a mahogany filing cabinet and looked inside, her heart sinking as she saw the bewildering collection of files. They didn't even seem to be in any sort of alphabetical order. She quickly leafed through several, doing her best to return them to the same position she'd found them. Nothing. But then what had she expected? A file marked PRIVATE LETTERS just waiting to be opened? She closed the drawer with a sharp click that seemed to echo loudly in the empty room.

Glancing back at the closed door she half expected it to open, and for Miss Caraway to appear, eyes glaring. Thankfully, it remained blessedly closed.

Once her heart had quietened to a more normal beat, Livia started to search hastily along the bookshelves. She riffled through the drawers of her father's desk, at least those that were not locked. Since she could see no sign of a key anywhere, there wasn't much she could do about the others.

The task was hopeless. Even if the letter had ever existed, it was gone now, probably thrown away long since. Livia found herself searching through the waste basket, just in case, but of course that was foolish as it was emptied daily, and it must be months since Mercy's visit. The whole thing was a complete waste of time.

She froze as she imagined she heard a footfall on the corridor outside. Was that Father coming back early, perhaps the worse for sherry and port? If she hung around here a moment longer than necessary she could well live to regret it. If she lived at all. He would surely want her head on the block if he caught her snooping.

Livia swept her gaze one last time over the items on his desk: pen and ink stand, blotter, newly installed telephone, and then, quite by chance, she glanced at the most obvious place of all. The letter rack. A quick riffle through and there it was. A single sheet of crumpled paper that had obviously been quickly folded and stuffed hurriedly behind a wodge of old receipts. Livia's eyes widened as she quickly scanned the contents, which confirmed all that Jack had told her. Then, just as she was tucking it safely away in her pocket, she heard the door handle turn.

Chapter Twenty-Two

Amos drove Ella into town on the farm cart, and as he dropped her off at the gate to Angel House, he promised to collect her at four o'clock sharp.

'Aren't you coming in to pay your respects?'

'When I return, happen. I've some jobs to do in town. I can't sit about blathering with womenfolk.'

Ella regarded her husband from beneath her lashes. 'Don't think to spy on me, Amos. I have no intention of seeking out Danny Gilpin, or doing anything I shouldn't. You have nothing to fear on that score.' And she climbed down from the cart without waiting for his reply, knowing that she'd caught him out and that was exactly what he'd intended. But before she got halfway along the drive, the front door burst open and Maggie and Livia came racing to meet her, and all such concerns flew out of her head.

The three sisters fell upon each other on a burst of laughter and joy, all talking at once and none of them listening to the other. It took several cups of the tea that

Kitty brought them before they calmed down sufficiently to begin to take in all their news.

Livia told them the story of the riot. 'It was really quite dreadful. It's a wonder more people weren't injured or someone killed, and the weather didn't help of course.' For some reason she chose not to mention Jack Flint, keeping the memory of the part he played that day to herself. Not out of shame, because she was proud of his heroic acts that day, more a fear that she might too easily reveal her growing attachment to him. 'Father, of course, brought the militia and would have had the rioters all shot if he'd had his way.'

'Typical!' Ella grumbled. 'But why do those poor people stay in that dreadful place? Why don't they go to live somewhere else?'

Maggie and Livia looked at their sister askance. Livia said, 'Ella, have you no sense at all? Where could they go? Do you know of anywhere in Kendal with cheaper rents, as well as better conditions? And some of these people are managing on very little money, thanks to the likes of Henry.'

'You need to speak to Henry then,' Ella said, flushing slightly over her own foolishness.

'Yes, I think you do,' Maggie agreed. 'You are the only one he's likely to listen to.'

Livia frowned, not much caring for the sound of this plan but reluctantly agreed that her sisters might be right. Certainly something needed to be done.

Ella said that she was far from happy in her work on the farm, and still battling to bring some light into the lives of Amos's young children, then frowned at her younger sister.

'You're looking almost as peaky as I feel, but then I'm working from dawn to dusk so I've a good excuse. Are you taking proper care of yourself, getting the right nourishment and enough fresh air and exercise? It can't be good for you hibernating in this dreadful house day after day, with only the servants for company.'

'I'm quite all right, thank you. Stop fussing, Ella.'

'But have you no news of any sort?' Ella persisted and Maggie wondered how they would respond if she told them that she was pregnant. And by their own father.

'No,' she smiled. 'I have no news of any kind, save for making petticoats for the poor girls in the workhouse. Father has generously donated this bolt of pink flannel. Would you like to help me cut them out? See, I've pinned on patterns cut from old newspaper.'

'Oh, for goodness sake,' Ella objected with her customary pout. 'Work, work, work, that's all I ever hear back home. I've come to see *you*, to chat with my adored sisters, not to do yet more work. I'm glad to escape it for a while, thank you very much. Besides, I've only got a couple of hours before his lord and master returns.'

'I don't mind helping,' Livia offered, picking up the scissors to start the cutting. She smiled at Ella. 'Don't worry, I can listen at the same time. Tell us all about the farm. Amos doesn't really lord it over you, does he? How are things between you two?'

* * *

Ella talked and talked, a huge outpouring of self-pity and tears. She told her sisters about all her concerns and worries, her jealousy of a dead wife, her failure so far to reach the distant Mary, the loneliness of her empty marriage bed. She told them everything, save for the vision of her husband in the river, and their encounter in the attic. These incidents she believed too private to share.

At a loss to know how to deal with so much trauma, Livia abandoned the cutting-out to hold her sister close, to stroke her hair and wipe her streaming eyes. And she worried over the further burden she would add to her lot before the afternoon was over when she told her two sisters about Mercy.

'Marriage is not at all as I imagined,' Ella huffed.

'Do you love him?'

'I don't know, do I? I haven't really had much chance to find out.'

'Do you like him?'

Ella considered. 'I don't *dislike* him.' Excitement stirred in her even now as she recalled his lovemaking, although Amos seemed to be filled with shame since, as if they'd done a shocking thing.

'Has he hurt you?'

Ella shook her head, tears bright in her lovely eyes. 'He never so much as touches me, not willingly. I sleep in the big bedroom, he sleeps in the loft.'

'Aren't you at least grateful for that?' Maggie quietly asked.

'No, I want a proper marriage. I want love and affection. When he's not telling me how much better the wonderful Esther managed things, and what she might or might not have approved of, its all "do this", "do that". I have the poultry to see to, and the calves. I must clean the dairy and the hen house, and all of that on top of helping Mrs Rackett with the cooking and the cleaning. He even expects me to help him bring in the sheep when he needs to dose or worm them.' Ella shuddered. 'I never have a minute to myself from dawn to dusk. And in the evening he reads his Bible the whole time, or works his dratted loom. He never *talks* to me.'

'Perhaps,' Livia tentatively suggested, 'you might help with the weaving. At least you'd be doing something together and may grow companionable.'

'*What?*' Ella pouted. 'He did have the cheek to ask if I was interested in helping to spin the wool into yarn. I told him I had quite enough to do already, thank you very much. He has never asked again. The impertinence of the man.'

Livia and Maggie exchanged a brief speaking glance. If Ella was taking this attitude it did not auger well for the future of the marriage. And yet she was their sister, and they loved her and wanted her to be happy.

'I might just as well not be there. He doesn't want a wife at all, only a dairymaid, and a mother for his children. And if I complain about how lonely I am, how utterly *exhausted*, he just looks at me and says life isn't all tea parties and romance, that as a farmer's wife I'm expected to do all of these things.'

Livia tried to stifle a smile as for a brief second she saw the situation from Amos's point of view. Instilling any sense of duty and work ethic into Ella would not be easy. She herself had tried on numerous occasions, and failed miserably.

'Are things getting any better with the children?' Livia hoped that mention of her stepchildren might lighten Ella's mood. Not so. The question only brought a fresh spurt of tears and recriminations, which needed to be mopped up with copious clean handkerchiefs and several more cups of soothing tea.

'I believe I could win over little Tilda, if the older girl would only give me half a chance,' Ella said. 'Mary is so like her father, so cold and distant. I think she's glad I'm unhappy.'

'Don't be unkind, Ella,' Maggie gently scolded. 'And what about the boy?'

'Emmett is quiet, very placid, and still grieving for his mother, I think.'

'Of course he is, poor child. It's barely fifteen months, I suppose, since she died. Not very long. I do wonder if Amos, too, might still be grieving,' Livia suggested.

'Then he shouldn't have married me.'

'No, you're right. He should have waited till he was properly ready.'

Maggie said, 'Why not concentrate on the little ones first. If you win them over, then Mary might soften too. Younger children are surely much easier to deal with. Although you didn't actually give birth to them so how can you feel...' She stopped, seemed to flinch, as if she might have said the wrong thing, then fell silent, gazing into space.

Ella and Livia waited patiently for her to finish whatever it was she'd been about to say. When she said nothing more, Livia decided to snatch her opportunity. The hour was flying by at record speed and she was growing anxious that she might never find the right moment to drop her bombshell.

Paying no attention to Maggie's dreaminess or the sulky droop to Ella's lip, Livia began. 'If I may change the subject for a moment, there's something important I need to tell you both. And I'm afraid you aren't going to like it very much.'

Maggie at once set aside her sewing. Ella glanced at the clock on the mantelshelf, sighed dramatically and said, 'Oh, all right, what have you done that's so wonderful? Ah, you've met a man. You're in love; I can see it in your eyes. Who is he? Go on, tell us all about him. I promise not to be jealous, well, not too much anyway.'

'It's not that at all. I certainly haven't fallen in love or anything of the sort,' Livia protested, nonetheless blushing to the roots of her hair as an image of Jack Flint came unbidden into her mind.

She had no wish to confess to this growing fancy she had for him. If she was behaving like a lovesick schoolgirl then not for a moment would she admit as much to her sisters. Besides, the news she had to tell was far too serious.

Livia briefly explained all that Jack had told her about their father's dalliance with various mistresses, and of Mercy being their half-sister; of her losing her mother and going to him for help. It didn't take long, only a few telling moments to blow their last hopes of normality right out of the water.

Clearly shaken, they were both looking at her as if she were speaking a foreign language and hadn't understood a word. Livia finished by explaining how she had very nearly got caught looking for the letter in Father's office.

'There was nowhere to run so I hid under Father's kneehole desk, my heart beating loud enough for anyone to hear. The door opened. Silence. Was someone looking in, I thought, or even now walking towards me? I can't begin to tell you how scared I was. I held my breath, praying that it wasn't Father, that he wouldn't come over to sit at the desk. Then after the longest moments of my life, although it was probably only a matter of seconds, the door closed again and I knew by that different sort of silence that I was alone again, and safe.

Ella was wide-eyed. 'Oh, my goodness! Was it Father do you think?'

Livia shook her head. 'I suspect it was Miss Caraway. Fortunately, she failed to see me tucked under that big kneehole desk. Look, here it is,' she said handing over the letter for them to read. 'I know it's a bit of a shock to discover we have yet another sister, albeit a half one, but what do we do about the fact she is missing? And where do you think I should look next?'

Ella, appalled by the whole shocking tale, quickly read through the short letter then handed it over to Maggie. Her sister seemed oddly subdued and distracted, saying nothing as she stared unseeing at this incriminating piece of paper. No one had any advice on what to do next. Livia realised they were too stunned to think straight, rather as she had been initially.

Ella made a few suggestions, none very helpful, and then surprisingly it was Maggie who finally came up with the answer. 'That poor girl. Poor, poor girl,' she said again. 'And none of this is any fault of her own. Try the workhouse. If she was found wandering about the streets with no job and no money, that might be where she'd end up.'

Livia wasted no time the next morning in cycling over to the workhouse, asking to speak to the master in person. He was most respectful, knowing he was speaking to the daughter of one of the town's most upstanding citizens. Livia doubted he would have been quite so deferential had Jessie or Jack Flint come asking the same questions.

Sadly, it turned out that she was too late. To her complete dismay Livia learned that Mercy had indeed been in the workhouse for some months, but had run away a short time ago with one of the other inmates.

'When she is found, as she surely will be, Miss Angel, I fear she'll be facing a custodial sentence.'

'Let us hope not,' Livia crisply responded, and left. Oh, but she could kick herself for being so foolish. Why hadn't they thought of the workhouse before? They'd wasted all this time when it was surely the obvious place to look? Now what should she do? Where did she go from here?

As she cycled wearily up the drive to Angel House

she knew at once that something was wrong, if only by the wails of distress coming from within. Flinging the machine to one side Livia raced into the house, knowing in her heart it was too late. She saw Maggie the moment she entered the hall. She had hanged herself with her dressing gown cord from the topmost banister.

Chapter Twenty-Three

1909

Everything changed when Maggie died. Something inside of Ella also shrivelled and died that day. Perhaps that was when she started to grow up, when it finally dawned on her that this life was all she was going to get and, like it or not, she must make the best of it.

Despite Amos's disapproval, she turned instinctively to Mrs Jepson. As a near neighbour, the older woman offered not only the comfort Ella craved during that initial period of shock and sadness, but also the kind of support she needed in the dark months following it. Consequently, Ella learnt much from her new friend, and she would regularly take tea in her parlour, or chat in Wilma Jepson's kitchen as she made soup or jam or pickled beetroot.

Twelve months on Ella was coping much better, and despite it having been a long, hot summer, her garden was flourishing. She'd picked her first luscious raspberries, blackcurrants and gooseberries, as well as the blackberries that grew wild in the dale. Ella and Mrs Rackett had spent hours in the kitchen making preserves, so they now had raspberry jam to put on their toast at breakfast.

Ella was also an expert in the dairy now. She would put the milk from the family's small herd of shorthorns into earthenware bowls and leave them standing overnight, for the length of three meals, dinner, supper and breakfast, before skimming off the cream. When the cream had been kept for a week or two, she would churn it into butter, knowing instinctively when it was ready. Mrs Jepson, who took it into Kendal for her each week to sell, along with the eggs and cheese, declared it to be the creamiest butter she'd ever tasted.

Ella was flattered by the compliment, and found an odd sort of satisfaction in the rhythm of the task, enjoying the hour or so of solitude and peace in the cool dairy, away from the dust and heat.

Oh, but how she envied her new friend. How Ella wished she could go with her into town each week.

Since the funeral, Amos had allowed one brief visit to Kendal each month to see Livia, but he still refused to let Ella travel alone, or visit the shops where she might be tempted to waste his hard-earned brass, or to personally attend the weekly market to sell her produce. Why he was so hard on her, or saw Kendal as some sort of Sodom and Gomorrah, she had no idea, but since the death of her lovely sister, Ella had lost the will to fight. What did it matter if she was trapped in a sterile, loveless marriage?

She accepted her lot now without question or argument.

But the deficiencies of the farm continued to irk her. Ella was frequently forced to walk an extra half mile to fill her water buckets at the spring because the private water supply from the pump had dried up, as it did every summer. Amos kept promising to dig a new well, or fix the leaks, but never got around to the task. And even this precious resource must be kept for drinking only. Water for washing had to be collected in rainwater barrels, or drawn from the river, yet another long walk.

Ella hated the earth privy round the back of the house, little more than a wooden shack with a zinc roof hidden in a clump of nettles. Whenever she had to face that trek on a dark wet night, she would recall with longing the smart modern bathroom at Angel House with its high ceramic bath and gold taps. She would remember how carelessly she had taken such wonders as hot running water entirely for granted.

Mrs Rackett's laziness was also a source of great irritation. The old woman could often be found in her clogs and shawl and cotton poke bonnet, sitting in the orchard doing nothing at all, or hiding in the wood shed smoking a twist of tobacco in her clay pipe.

The first time Ella had caught her smoking, she'd been astonished, recalling how she'd once asked for a clay pipe for the children to blow bubbles and been told there wasn't such a thing in the house as Amos didn't approve of smoking, it being a filthy habit. But when she challenged her on the matter, the old crone paid not the slightest attention. The woman was either stone deaf or pig-ignorant so far as Ella could see, for she never responded to instructions, and only heard half of what she was asked to do.

This afternoon on her walk, Ella stubbornly set down her water buckets, lay back on a hump of grass beside the beck and gazed around at mountains and sky. The skies here seemed endless, constantly changing and always rushing on as if to some other, better place. When Ella had first come to the dale she too had longed to go with it. Now she accepted that this was where she lived, and where she must stay. She must make of her life what she could, and not give up on it as darling Maggie had done.

She heard the plaintive whistle of a golden plover, the slap and gush of water bubbling over the boulders in the stream, and these familiar sounds brought a strange sort of comfort.

Clouds were gathering over Rainsborrow Crag, indicating, as its name implied, that there would be rain later. The flank of Yoke, its near neighbour, seemed to loom ever closer as the sky darkened. Glad as Ella would be to see an end to this heat, a change in the weather presaged autumn and the cold winter ahead, a season when the loneliness of the dale nearly drove her mad.

A year or more ago, when she'd first driven up the valley with Amos in the cart, she'd found little comfort in her surroundings, the steep slopes of the surrounding mountains too dramatic, their silent presence sombre and disturbing. Now she could appreciate their majesty and beauty. She saw how fortunate she was to live in such a spectacular setting. Even so, there were times when the solitude of the place made Ella want to scream, simply to hear the sound of a human voice.

To her surprise, she'd discovered a passion for walking. Not the adventurous kind that would take her climbing over the summit of Ill Bell or Froswick, but she loved to meander by the river, skirt the heaps of slate waste to explore the old quarries. These Sunday rambles gave her precious time alone with her thoughts to remember Maggie, and to think about what was happening in her own life.

Unencumbered by water buckets, she would have liked to have walked further this afternoon, perhaps to climb the craggy outcrops as far as the waterfall, or to gaze upon the glimmering waters of the reservoir. Once, Ella had again climbed Nan Bield Pass, albeit in better weather, to take the children to see the wild fell ponies on Lingmell Fell. It had felt like the end of the world. But it had been worth the effort because even Mary had been entranced by the sight of these sturdy beasts. Today the weather was too uncertain, and her time limited.

Instead, she sat hugging her knees and let her thoughts turn to Maggie. She rarely had a minute to herself, a private moment to remember her beloved sister.

How they had all got through those dark days following her death, she'd never know. First came the horror, then the blame, and most horrendous of all, the funeral, with everyone asking the same question: why would she do such a thing? Why would such a lovely young girl take her own life?

There seemed no answer to that, and Ella still couldn't believe that her young sister was dead, that she would never again see her sweet smiling face, never hear her bubbling laughter, nor see those soulful grey eyes as clear as a mountain stream. Her patience and tolerance, her sweet nature, were legendary, and her love for her two older sisters unquestioning.

Ella's mouth curved into an instinctive smile as she recalled how Maggie would scold Livia if she should scramble up a tree in Serpentine Woods to grin cheekily down, as if challenging them to prove they were half so agile as she. Maggie would be unimpressed, too afraid that she might fall.

She would sternly scold Ella that she really had no need for rouge or artifice, that she was beautiful and elegant, and any young man must fall in love with her at first sight.

As they had done, and she with them. But what good was beauty when her own husband saw it only as the devil's work, and hated the sight of her?

Ella let out a sigh, heavy with sadness. Maggie had thought little of herself. She'd never claimed to have Livia's energy, her ambition or intelligence. And she saw her own prettiness as a feeble thing by comparison with Ella's lovely elegance. She'd taken refuge in a private world of her own. She would write little stories, talk to her stuffed toys and dolls, reveal her thoughts only in her secret diaries, and neither Livia nor Ella would ever dare to invade this need of hers for privacy. Since her death, Livia had searched every scrap of paper, trying to find a clue to their youngest sister's state of mind. So far as Ella was aware, she'd found nothing.

The tragedy had ripped them to shreds. Livia was beside herself with grief, quite unable to remain at home. For some reason she blamed their father. Not so surprising, perhaps, since they all knew him for a bully. But what he had done to Maggie that was any different to his normal bullying – what trigger had finally made her snap so that she could bear no more – Ella had no idea. It was all quite beyond her, but the pain was no less to bear now than it was twelve months ago on that sunny autumn day when a neighbour had come galloping up the valley on his old mare to tell her the dreadful news.

Amos had at once taken her back to Angel House, and she and Livia had clung together, sobbing with bewilderment and grief. What had gone wrong? Why hadn't they noticed how depressed she was and been able to help her? They didn't even know what had caused the depression in the first place. So far as Ella could see, it was a complete mystery, coming right out of the blue.

But then Maggie had been far too good for this world. Ella and Livia may have grown inured to their father's constant bullying and iron control, but it had clearly been too much for the more fragile, vulnerable Maggie. Her tolerance and saint-like patience must finally have snapped. She simply hadn't been able to take any more.

Ella suspected she might never get over their sister's

death, that she and Livia would forever carry a sense of guilt because they hadn't been there on that last fateful day to help her deal with her final cry of despair.

Ella returned to the farm with her water buckets, setting them in the cool of the larder and praying the rains would come soon to refill the private reservoirs closer to the house. It was a Friday and she was baking a cake for the children, who would be home this evening as usual. Wilma Jepson had given her the recipe for a Victoria sponge and it had become quite a favourite.

Ella had made some progress with Tilda and Emmett, although not as much as she would have liked. They at least talked to her now, and the older girl, Mary, was not quite so over-protective. But they maintained their distance, never wanted a cuddle or thought to come to Ella with their worries and concerns. They still attended school in Staveley and were away all week, except for Mary, who had gone into service at Whitsun, having been taken on as kitchen maid by a doctor. Ella hoped her relationship with the younger children might improve now they had only their stepmother to turn to.

Each Friday they were brought by a neighbour of their aunt's in a trap to the end of the dale, where they were dropped off by St Cuthbert's church. From there they walked the rest of the way to Todd's Farm, a distance of some four miles.

Ella had been keeping a lookout for them for some time now, a pan of hot broth and herb dumplings simmering on the hob in readiness for their supper. She kept going over to the window to glance along the lane, anxiously watching the great black clouds roll up.

As she took the cake from the oven and set it to cool in the larder, she noticed that the rain had indeed started. By the time she had split the sponge and filled it with raspberry jam and butter icing, which they loved, it was coming down in stair rods; the kind of relentless downpour they were well used to in the Lake District.

When the first crack of lightening came, swiftly followed by a huge clap of thunder, Ella turned to her husband. 'There's a storm starting, Amos. You'd best go and meet the children. Tilda will be scared.'

Amos was seated at the table reading his Bible, as he usually was after a long day on the land. He didn't even look up when she spoke.

Ella tried again. 'Amos, did you hear what I said? There's a storm brewing and you know how nervous Tilda gets when there's thunder and lightening. They'll both be soaked in seconds, it's absolutely bucketing down.'

'There's no point then in us all getting wet, is there?' he said, and turning over the page, continued reading.

Ella stifled a sharp retort. They were his children, after all, not hers, as he frequently reminded her. Their regime of school and weekend chores was as unchanging now as it had been when she'd first come to the farm. And if she ever suggested that perhaps they might be allowed a little more free time to play, it was explained to her that Todd Farm had been in the family for generations and would one day belong to Emmett. It was therefore imperative that he learn from the start what would be required of him. Tilda, too, must be taught certain chores so that when she was old enough to wed she would be a good help to her husband.

These arguments were irrefutable, but it seemed a bleak sort of life to Ella. She assumed that Esther, Amos's first wife, had set down the regime, perhaps disapproving of bringing children up soft. And it was true in a way that you needed to be tough and self-sufficient on these fells.

But Ella was weary of Esther's rules, which still reined supreme in this household; no books allowed save for the Bible, no games and toys for the children to play with, no fairy stories. All of this and more was apparently down to Esther's fierce brand of Puritanism, which Amos continued to follow to the letter. Ella longed to bring some joy into their little lives, to hug them and show them some love and affection, tuck them up with a kiss and tell them bedtime stories, none of which was allowed either.

But she could at least save them from the rain.

Ella wrapped her shawl about her head, picked up a handful of sacks and without another word to her husband, lifted the latch and let herself quietly out.

Amos had been quite correct, of course. It was pitch black outside with no sign of a moon, and within seconds Ella was drenched to the skin. Nor did the lamp she had picked up as she passed through the porch offer much light beyond her own feet. As if on cue, a crack of lightening suddenly illuminated the path ahead, empty for some distance so far as Ella could see. A great clap of thunder followed almost at once, proving Kentmere must be close to the eye of the storm.

The rain was a tumult, bouncing off stones and turning the dirt track into a quagmire. The river would be flooding its banks soon, if she was any judge, and its swollen waters racing down to the weir at the foot of the valley. Ella pulled a sack over her head and set off on the long trek to the church. If the weather seemed bad to her, how much worse must it be for two small children?

She found the pair unwisely huddled beneath the old yew tree in the church yard, too frightened to go any further. Tilda was crying, and brave Emmett was doing his best to comfort and calm his little sister, but the presence of so many gravestones, poking out of the earth all around him like broken bones, wasn't helping.

Ella gathered them to her in an all-enveloping hug and for once neither of them protested or attempted to wriggle free, as was their wont. They clung to her, both crying by this time. Ella did her best to soothe their fears, wiping the rain from their tearful faces, kissing their frozen cheeks, then she draped folded sacks over their heads and shoulders in a vain attempt to keep off the worst of the rain.

'Come on, my ducks,' she said with a cheering smile. 'Let's swim home, shall we?'

And with one child tucked under each arm, they set off back to the farm.

Ella did everything she could to get the children warm and dry, with some assistance from Mrs Rackett but none at all from their father. She stripped them of their wet clothes, called for hot water to be poured in the tin bath, adding a good dose of mustard as an extra precaution. Then, after a brisk rub dry, and with their bellies full of the warming broth, she tucked them into their beds, a hot brick at their toes. For the first time Ella broke her husband's sacred rule and told them a fairy story. It was the one about the giant turnip, which she hoped would make them laugh. Long before she'd reached the part where it had to be tugged out of the ground, both children were fast asleep. And by morning it was clear to them all that Tilda was ill, very sick indeed.

Chapter Twenty-Four

It was amidst the poverty of Fellside that Livia attempted to come to terms with her loss. She was slowly learning how to live again. Not that it was proving to be an easy process. She'd spent much of those first weeks after Maggie's death in a state of shock, or sobbing her heart out. It had all seemed so unreal. How could she be dead? Her sister was far too young to die, barely eighteen years old, and with so much to live for.

Every morning during those first painful days Livia would wake and feel disorientated, wondering where she was, and what she was doing sleeping on a straw pallet in an airless loft with ten other people, the stink of the night soil bucket pungent in her nostrils. And then it would all rush back to her.

Maggie had hanged herself.

Why would she do such a thing? And why had she felt unable to turn to her sisters for help? But then Livia had discovered the answer to these questions, and almost wished she hadn't.

As if coping with her sister's suicide and funeral wasn't bad enough, she'd been the one faced with the unpalatable task of dealing with Maggie's belongings. Livia had shut herself in her sister's bedroom and with tears raining down her cheeks, had set about folding away her favourite dresses, putting her much-loved teddy bears and childhood books into boxes to give to the poor. It had been utterly heartbreaking. Quite against her better judgement, she'd also flicked through her sister's personal papers and diaries.

It was while she was engaged in this painful task that she'd found the letter. It was addressed to herself. Maggie must have slipped it into her diary, knowing only Livia would look in there. Opening it with some trepidation, the note was even more shattering than she'd feared. In a few short sentences it stated that she was pregnant, and named the father of her child.

Shock and disbelief had misted Livia's vision, blurring the stark cruelty of those devastating words so that she'd been obliged to read them over and over several times before she was able to accept their veracity. Then Livia had run to the bathroom and vomited down the lavatory pan.

It couldn't be true. Surely such depravity was beyond even her father's capacity, much as he enjoyed inflicting hurt on his three daughters. Yet there it was, in black and white. And as if to prove it, Maggie was dead. She'd preferred to take her own life rather than live with the consequences of what her own father had done to her. Livia couldn't find words strong enough to express the horror she felt at this discovery. Her lovely sister must have felt debased, corrupted, her young life ruined.

That very same day Livia had packed her belongings and left with only what she could carry in a Gladstone bag and a string parcel. She'd run from her childhood home in a state of shock, without even pausing to speak to her father. Unable to think where else to go and with no money of her own, no aunts or cousins to turn to, she'd come to Fellside, where Jessie and Jack had welcomed her into their home without the need for any explanation whatsoever.

Livia had made a pact with herself that day, vowing she'd keep this particular vile piece of information to herself, for now at least, until she could find the strength to decide how best to deal with it.

Her first reaction had been one of disgust and mind-numbing anger. She'd wanted to go in search of her father, to drag him from whatever debauchery he was indulging in while his youngest daughter had hanged herself, and force him to confess his crime. But then the anger had drained away leaving her spent and shaking with shock, far too overcome by grief to have the stomach for any confrontation with him right then.

But this was *incest*, for God's sake!

The torment of her grief had very nearly destroyed her, her mind teetering on the brink of madness as Livia faced the reality of what that man had done to his own daughter. All those years in which she'd imagined she was protecting Maggie from his beatings, shielding her from the worst of his sick punishments. While all the time… Livia could hardly bear to think of it.

She told herself to shut it out of her mind, to put it in a box and lock the evil away until she was able to deal with it. Livia thought she might never forgive herself for letting Maggie down so badly. But then why should she hold herself responsible for her father's evil? She was but a young girl, ignorant of what had gone on. How could she have stopped him? Yet in her heart, Livia was convinced that she'd failed her vulnerable young sister. Why hadn't she paid more attention when it was obvious she was troubled over something, when she was being sick? Why hadn't she investigated further? Her own naivety was a bitter pill to swallow, and one she must live with for the rest of her life.

She considered rushing straight over to Ella, to tell her sister what she'd discovered and share the agony with someone who loved Maggie as much as she did. But somehow she couldn't quite bring herself to do so. Hadn't Ella enough to contend with? A cold husband and sterile marriage foisted upon her by that very same father, stepchildren who resented her presence in their home, and grinding hard labour on a farm out in the wilds. A life far from the luxurious one a frivolous young Ella had once dreamt of enjoying.

Livia decided that she really couldn't burden her with more misery. Wasn't grieving for the loss of her sister bad enough? The whole truth was far too dreadful and best kept secret, for now. Until one day it could be used against the person who really was to blame: their vicious, corrupt father.

A few short months after Maggie's death, Josiah Angel was appointed town mayor. It made Livia sick to her stomach to see him preening himself in his new role. He wallowed in the sympathy of the townsfolk of Kendal, as if he wasn't the one responsible for this terrible tragedy, and for the destruction of his entire family.

People talked, of course they did, puzzling over the whys and wherefores. They couldn't understand why Maggie had chosen such a terrible path, why rumour had it one sister was deeply unhappy in her new marriage, and the other had run away from home.

Let them talk. Livia didn't care what anyone said or thought. Although what they would have to say if they knew the whole story, she couldn't begin to imagine.

From the day she'd walked out of Angel House, Livia felt that she was on her own, or would have been were it not for the generosity of the Flint family. For the rest of her life she would be eternally grateful for their kindness, despite the sight and smell of the place making her gag at times. They may be living in squalor, but her new friends at least had a code of morals way above those of her own, much richer, parent.

Jack Flint had become an important part of her life. There had been much flirting and covert sideways glances, and an acute awareness of him whenever he came into a room. They enjoyed laughing and talking endlessly together, content in each other's company. And on Sundays, when Jack was free, they spent the whole day together.

Things had gone on this way for months. In the end

Livia realised that this attraction between them would remain unacknowledged unless she did something about it. Jack Flint, for all his confidence and pride, his courage when it came to fighting for his rights and protecting his family, was less certain when it came to crossing the boundaries of class. Unfortunately, he saw Livia as someone above him in status.

Livia knew she couldn't grieve for ever, and Maggie wouldn't wish that for her. And she could barely be in Jack's presence for more than five minutes without wanting to touch him. Livia was mesmerised by him, dreamt of him day and night, ached to taste the heady sensation of his mouth moving over hers. Longed to be held in his arms and loved.

She made the decision that it was up to her to make the first move.

Livia chose a Sunday afternoon in late October, just twelve months after her beloved sister's death. She suggested a walk over Scout Scar, from the top of which they would be able to enjoy wonderful panoramic views of the Lake District. To her delight, Jack agreed, and as she'd warned Jessie in advance of her little scheme, the older woman managed to deflect the children from begging to go too with the bribe of an ice cream if they'd walk with her by the river to the church and back.

It was one of those crisp, sunny autumn days when the leaves are proudly displaying their finest colours of russet, gold and saffron, and white clouds danced across a brilliant blue sky. A perfect Lakeland day.

The walk took them past Serpentine Woods, which

brought painful memories of the happy times Livia had spent there with her sisters, but she made no mention of those sad feelings now. This must be a happy day, and mark a new beginning in her life.

Skirting the woods, she led Jack up a steep incline then along a grassy path from which there was a good view over the town to the Howgill Fells and Whinfell. From here they traversed several fields, scrambled over walls and outfaced a few cows, Jack laughing at her nervousness as the animals plodded after them in typically curious fashion. After an hour or two of walking they reached the cairn at the top of the fell, and with the wind in their faces, turned to gaze back over the town nestling in the valley below, and at the vast panorama of mountains all around. Jack pointed out Coniston fells, High Street and Shap, Bowfell and Fairfield.

'Would you ever live anywhere else?' Livia sighed, feeling a swell of love and pride in her home country.

Jack said, 'A man would give his life to protect such a land.'

Livia slipped her hand in his. 'Don't say such things. We won't speak of death, not today, not any more. Only life and...'

He smiled knowingly at her. 'And what?'

She laughed. 'Come with me. I want to show you something.'

Spinning on her heel she ran up the hill, Jack racing after her, both giggling as if they were children. Breathless now, she stopped only when she reached an old iron kissing gate. It gave access to the open fell and a path leading over the crest of Scout Scar. Leaning over the gate she demanded a kiss before she would let him through.

He laughed. 'Is this what you wanted to show me, this kissing gate?'

'It is.'

'And this is the toll I must pay, just one kiss?'

'And cheap at the price. Not that I am cheap,' she corrected herself.

A shadow crossed his face. 'No, Livia, no one could ever say you were anything but the finest quality. High class, and very beautiful.'

She smiled provocatively at him, her heart racing with the fear of rejection. What would she do if he turned away, if he didn't ache for her as she ached for him? And then his mouth was on hers, his arms were tight around her and it was as if a whole cascade of emotion erupted inside her. Livia had never known such bliss, such complete happiness. Except that it was over far too quickly.

'Oh, that wasn't nearly enough. I should have demanded more. The toll has just gone up. The price today is two kisses.'

Jack chuckled. 'Make it three if you like, or four, but no more while we're standing here with this iron gate between us. Let me through, Livia, and you can name your price and I'll double it.'

They found a sheltered spot beneath a stunted old thorn tree, and sat with their arms about each other. From here they could have admired the view south to the Lyth valley, to the Kent estuary and Morecambe Bay. Or west to Coniston Old Man, Black Sails and Wetherlam. North to Kentmere, where Ella was even now preparing Sunday dinner for her husband and stepchildren. But they had eyes only for each other.

Jack was kissing her again, her eyes, her throat, her mouth, as if he would devour her. And Livia was matching his passion with her own. They fell back into the long grass and she gasped with pleasure when he slid his hand over her breast, wanting more, needing him, knowing this was the man she'd been waiting for all her life. Jack Flint.

She helped him to unbutton her blouse, revealing only a chemise and no corset. Livia had never been one to follow the rules.

Nothing would stop her from loving this man, certainly not an accident of birth, or her bully of a father. He may well be a humble working man, but he was worth two of the likes of Josiah Angel. She felt proud to know him, and while they took care not to have any unwanted repercussions from their coupling, Livia gave herself up to loving him without a moment's regret.

From that moment, Livia made no secret of the fact that she and Jack were lovers. Since the gossip-mongers of Kendal assumed they were already living shamelessly together as man and wife, what did they have to lose? In any case, marriage, for the moment at least, was quite out of the question.

Livia would have been more than content to become Jack's wife and live with him in a rented cottage somewhere, with not a penny in her pocket and nothing but the clothes on her back. But Jack wouldn't hear of it. He insisted they couldn't marry until he'd gained promotion at the factory. He wasn't earning enough yet to support a wife, or the children that would surely follow. They must be patient, he warned her. They must save up. Where was the rush?

In the meantime they were careful. They loved each other deeply and made the most of each precious hour, every single moment they had together.

Livia was aware there were other matters – more serious issues – still to be resolved with regard to her father. Not that she spoke of these to Jack. She did not allow herself to dwell on them much at all, knowing that the rumours of her love for Jack Flint would infuriate and offend her father to distraction.

There was some pleasure in that, at least, and one day she would have the satisfaction of getting justice for Maggie, she was sure of it. Her moment for revenge would surely come, one way or another.

Chapter Twenty-Five

Ella nursed the little girl day and night, piling on blankets when she shook with cold, soothing her hot aching head with a cold compress of vinegar and water when she burnt with fever. Amos insisted they soak a sheet in vinegar and hang it over the bedroom door to help prevent the spread of whatever infection she might be suffering from.

'We don't know that it is an infection,' Ella told him, pooh-poohing the notion, but he was adamant that this must be done. He also insisted they keep a bowl of warm water and lye soap in the bedroom and wash their hands before and after they touch her.

'She doesn't have the plague,' Ella said. 'It's only a bad chill, because of the soaking she got. Which might not have been so bad had you gone to collect her in the cart, or carried her home.'

Amos looked stricken, but stuck to his point over the washing ritual. 'You do as I say in this.'

'Call the doctor if you're really worried.'

'Doctors do no good at all,' he growled. 'They're more

likely to bring infection into the house than cure it. Soap and water and vinegar, that's what we need.'

Seeing his agitation and anxiety, Ella agreed to do as he suggested, and these sensible precautions were duly put in place.

And then the coughing started, harsh and bronchial, which caused the little girl considerable pain and distress, making it quite impossible for her to rest. Mrs Rackett now proved herself to be a veritable expert on old country remedies, and Ella welcomed her assistance as she was at her wits' end.

The old woman plastered Tilda's skinny little chest with goose grease and pounded cabbage leaves, kept in place with a layer of brown paper. She also made a concoction from the flowers of the hoarhound, sweetened with honey, which Tilda was expected to drink four times a day. For sustenance she was given beef tea flavoured with thyme, considered to be an excellent remedy for bronchial ailments, as well as an antiseptic for the throat.

'If'n she don't start to show any improvement soon, we'll boil up some thyme and give it to her on a spoon every two hours.'

This they did as nothing seemed to be working and with each passing hour the little girl grew ever more exhausted by the coughing, sinking further into a torpor, her skin pale and waxy looking, and with big purple bruises beneath each eye. There were times when Ella feared for her life. She was terrified the child might suddenly start having convulsions or the bronchitis might turn into pneumonia.

Amos finally agreed to call the doctor the night she started hallucinating. Tilda was convinced rats were running around her room, even on her bed, which terrified the little girl and frightened the life out of Ella too. She herself had never quite recovered from her experience with a rat, despite its aftermath. But it was all in the child's imagination. Ella called for Mrs Rackett to fill the hip bath with cold water and they sat Tilda in it in a desperate bid to bring down her temperature. By the time the doctor arrived she was back in bed sleeping peacefully for once, and he congratulated them on having done the right thing.

He produced a tincture for the cough, instructed them to keep the child warm and give her plenty of fluids, making sure they always boiled the water first, and left.

'You can get some rest now,' Amos told Ella, but she shook her head.

Mrs Rackett went off to her own bed, Ella having reminded the old woman that she'd need to be up early as she must continue to manage the dairy and the other chores on her own until Tilda was better. Then she made herself comfortable for the long night ahead, too afraid to leave her alone for a second.

Ella was slumped in a half doze perhaps an hour later when Amos returned with a tray. He'd made her a pot of tea and a ham sandwich. It was the first kind act he'd ever done for her through all these long awkward, difficult months since she'd arrived as his bride. Ella was deeply touched.

279

'Thank you, that's most thoughtful.' She noticed how his ears went pink at the tips from the compliment. 'Would you like to sit with her?'

Amos did so, sitting in silence, as was his way, his large hands that could birth a calf or coax a lamb to its mother's teat hanging loose between his knees.

Much as he might lavish care on his animals, he'd never demonstrated any affection for his children, no kisses or cuddles, rarely even a smile or show of interest in whatever they were doing. He seemed to see them only as an extra pair of hands to deal with the chores. Yet Ella saw evidence of that love now. It was clear that he was desperately worried about Tilda.

The face she'd thought bland now looked drawn, and gaunt with pain. The square, capable hands began to fidget. One would scrape over the stubble he'd forgotten to shave off his chin, or both would rub his knees or his thick strong thighs, pluck at the bedclothes or pick up the medicine bottle to read the label for the umpteenth time. He could hardly bear to sit still, clearly wanting to put things right but unsure how to go about it.

At one point his favourite collie, Beth, nosed her way into the room, circled for a moment with drooping tail, then curled up with a quiet sigh at his feet. And for the first time ever, Amos did not automatically respond to her devotion by patting her head or ruffling her ears. He simply sat gazing at his daughter, willing her to get better.

Ella ventured a question. 'Has Tilda been ill before?

Did Esther ever have to sit with her like this for some other childhood disease, measles perhaps or chickenpox?'

Amos shook his head. 'She's never ailed nowt until now.'

Ella tucked the sheets closer about the little girl's chin, worried Amos might be blaming her in some way. If so, he surely had no right to do so. He should have gone to collect the children himself. 'She's at that age now, I suppose. She'll catch everything, I expect, one by one, and we'll just have to cope as best we can.'

He got up then to go to his own bed as he too had to be up at five for the milking, but at the door he turned to her and said, 'She's in good hands. Not even her own mother would have taken better care.'

Ella was so startled by this unexpected praise that two huge tears sprang into her eyes, spilling over on to her cheeks. It was the first compliment he'd ever paid her, and the only time to her certain knowledge that he'd expressed a word of criticism over Esther.

Amos was a strange man, intensely private, slow to respond even to his own troubled thoughts, obsessive over this fetish he had for cleanliness, and with the kind of self-imposed stoicism that seemed to be bred in men in these parts. Yet he was a strong man, and as hard on himself as he was on Ella and the children. In the following days, he began to show signs of softening. He never failed to call in on his daughter two or three times each day, and would sit with her for an hour or more of an evening, his face etched with concern.

And bringing trays of tea or snacks for Ella as she

kept vigil became a regular habit. After almost eighteen months on the farm, she was at last given a glimpse of his human side, and marvelled.

The day came when Tilda suddenly opened her eyes one morning and announced that she was hungry.

Relief washed over Ella, and she smiled. 'Are you, dearest? That's good. What would you like? Toast and jam or eggy bread?'

The little girl's eyes lit up. 'Ooh, eggy bread, please,' and Ella kissed her.

'Eggy bread coming up then, and I'll cut it into soldiers for you.'

She ate every scrap and from that day on, with the resilience found only in small children, her recovery proceeded at a pace. Within twenty-four hours she was complaining about being bored and wanting to come downstairs.

'Perhaps for an hour or two this afternoon,' Ella promised. 'But you go straight back to bed when I say you must, no argument.'

Tilda nodded her agreement, eyes shining.

Ella played paper and pencil games with her: noughts and crosses, squares, and crazy mazes. She played I-spy and a silly game, 'For my dinner I ate ample apples, boiled buttercups, crabby cabbage, dirty dishcloths...' By the time they reached S for stewed sausages, they were all in fits of laughter, the little girl's cheeks at last glowing pink, and with no sign of a cough. Mrs Rackett sat nodding and smiling in her rocking chair, watching this healing process with satisfaction in her faded eyes.

'Esther will be turning in her grave. I've never seen that child laugh so much in all her short life,' she commented when, at four o'clock, Ella lifted Tilda up in her arms to take her up to bed.

The remark touched Ella, and yet she found it deeply troubling. Why was there never any laughter in this house? Why had the wonderful Esther never prescribed it for her children? Did religion have to preclude joy? And would Amos begin to relax a little more, now that he'd finally revealed that he really did care for his daughter?

More than anything, Ella was determined to ensure that Tilda knew what it was to have the love of a father. Would that she knew such joy.

Josiah sat in his office at Angel's Department Store, staring at the letter in his hand. It was from Hodson, calling in his loan. It had come three months ago and he knew every word by heart. There was no doubt about it, he was facing ruin. He'd done everything he could think of to raise the cash, and now on the last day of October, he had to accept that time was running out. Here was a further message from Hodson, delivered this very morning, asking him to be so good as to call on his way home from the store, saying there were important matters they needed to discuss. It didn't take a genius to work out what they would be.

Josiah felt as if his world was falling apart. The house echoed with empty rooms. Most of the servants had left for a more congenial establishment, presumably where daughters of the house were not found hanging from the banister. Even his eldest daughter had deserted him.

Whenever anybody asked why Livia had left, he'd say, 'The poor lass was confounded by grief. Since then she's got caught up in her own obstinacy and is afraid to lose face by crawling home with her tail between her legs. But she'll tire of her "good works" and social conscience soon, then she'll come back home, see if she doesn't.'

In truth, Josiah suspected that his eldest daughter had learnt something about Maggie's death. Perhaps she'd found a suicide note or some such. If so, then she had kept its contents to herself. She certainly hadn't discussed the matter with him, although the very fact she'd vacated the family home within twenty-four hours of the funeral spoke volumes.

The doctor dealing with the post-mortem had quietly informed him that his daughter Margaret Anne had been pregnant at the time of her death. Josiah had managed to appear shocked and upset, as any father might in response to this news, and the doctor had assured him that the poor girl's reputation would be protected by professional confidentiality. The matter would never be referred to again.

Josiah had understood then why Maggie had taken this irrevocable step. He felt no guilt, no sense of blame. She had chosen this way out of her own volition, and had raised few objections to his twice-weekly visits to her bed over the years.

At the beginning she'd been too young to understand, admittedly, and later as she'd grown older she'd fussed a little, almost run off once or twice, striving to show her independence. But he'd impressed upon her how it was her *duty*, as his *daughter*, to make her father happy. He'd found it necessary only once to chastise her. On that occasion he'd tied her to the bed head with a pair of her own stockings, face down, and taken her that way instead. It had really been quite titillating.

She'd never objected again, although she was free to leave at any time, should she have wished to do so, so long as she had the funds to provide for herself. The fact she stayed proved she really quite enjoyed their little sessions, despite her feeble protests.

Hodson, so far as he could tell, was not aware of the reason why Maggie had killed herself. Josiah was almost certain that Livia had not told whatever it was she'd discovered. Too ashamed probably, prissy little madam. Gullible Henry probably thought the girl was unbalanced, or depressed. That's if he thought about her at all. He seemed far more interested in getting his hands on Livia, and on Angel's Department Store.

Which brought Josiah back to the letter in his hand. He crumpled it up and flung it in the waste-paper basket.

So far as Josiah was concerned, Henry was welcome to the girl, and to use whatever means necessary to win her. But he would never allow him to possess the store, not while there was breath left in his body. Josiah had worked too hard, paid too high a price, to lose it over something so trifling as mere money.

All that mincing and fawning to win over his former employer for a start, and then having to set aside personal inclinations to court and marry his whey-faced daughter. Since then there'd been his wife's failure to provide him with a son, and recalcitrant daughters who'd been the bane of his life ever since.

As for that little madam in the workhouse, his heart had near failed him when she'd called out, addressing him as Father, for some ridiculous reason imagining he'd come to rescue her. Thank God everyone else had simply deemed her to be mad. He'd said as much to the workhouse master, pointing out that the girl was either a rogue and a charlatan, or had completely lost her senses. The man had not demurred when Josiah suggested the birch might curtail her vivid imagination, which had resolved the problem most satisfactorily. Mercy Simpson had been dealt with as she deserved, and there was an end to the matter.

Lavinia, however, was still to be dealt with, and so far as Josiah was concerned, Hodson could have her any way he chose, whether she was willing or not. He was adamant about only one thing: the store would remain firmly in his own hands.

Chapter Twenty-Six

Tea with Mrs Jepson had become a regular feature of Ella's week, but she hadn't seen her since Tilda had fallen ill. One afternoon, desperate to get out of the house after being confined for so long, Ella suggested they walk down the lane to see her. She took Tilda with her, judging she too would benefit from a breath of fresh air.

Ella was also suddenly keen to learn more about her predecessor. Up until now she'd considered Amos's first marriage to be none of her business. He'd held up the wonderful Esther as some sort of saint and paragon of virtue, and was clearly still grieving for the woman. Otherwise, why else would he have turned his back on his second wife? Ella really hadn't wanted to think about Amos's first wife any more than was absolutely necessary. She'd been an ominous presence in their marriage, almost as intrusive as her own father. Now, following the remarks made by both Amos and Mrs Rackett during Tilda's illness, she was filled with curiosity to know more about her.

Wilma Jepson was delighted to see them both. As a widow who lived alone, she was more than ready to pop the kettle on and partake of a cup of tea and enjoy a bit of crack. 'There are few enough people to talk to round here, so I've missed a good gossip these last couple of weeks. Now, what can we find for this little lass?'

She found Tilda an iced fairy cake and, after rummaging through her dresser, an old colouring book and packet of crayons. Tilda was beginning to think that being sick was really quite a treat, something to be savoured and enjoyed.

'How is the little lass then? She still looks a bit peaky.'

'She's making a good recovery at last. Comes downstairs for two hours every afternoon now, when we play lots of silly games.'

'Games?' Mrs Jepson said, her mouth falling open with shock.

'We've been very silly, Aunty Wilma,' piped up Tilda, brown eyes shining. 'Giggling and laughing and all sorts.'

'Giggling and laughing? My word, have you indeed? Well, I'm glad to hear it. There's nowt like a bit of silliness to get over being poorly.'

When the little girl had settled herself on the rug with Mrs Jepson's cat, enjoying her cake and happily colouring in the pictures, Ella ventured a question. 'Did their mother ever play with them?'

'Esther? Nay, that vinegar-faced woman wouldn't have known how to smile and have fun if you'd paid her.'

'I must say I've searched the entire house from top to bottom looking for some harmless game to entertain them. Snakes and Ladders perhaps, or Ludo, but have drawn a blank. Not even a pack of cards.'

Mrs Jepson laughed. 'You'd not find owt as sinful as cards, not in a Methodist household. Eeh, but I reckon I might have a set of draughts somewhere, what our Maureen used to play with when she were little. She's married now, with childer of her own.'

The older woman got up and began to search through the dresser again. It seemed to be stuffed with books and papers, baskets of half-finished knitting, bags of buttons, and any amount of detritus. 'Here it is, and a Snakes and Ladders too by the look of it. You're welcome to both.'

'Won't your grandchildren want them when they call?'

'Nay, they consider themselves far too grown-up for childish games nowadays. Go on, tek 'em, them kids need summat to lighten their little lives.'

Over tea and gingerbread, Ella ventured to ask the question that had been nagging her for some time. 'So what was she like, Esther?'

Mrs Jepson sipped at the tea in her best china cup, and considered. 'The kindest thing you could say about that woman is that she couldn't help the way she was because it was all bound up in that religion of hers, and of course she were allus ailing summat.'

'Oh, I'm sorry to hear that. My mother was an invalid for years, though we never quite knew what it was that ailed her. Her heart perhaps, or some weakness of the blood, I'm not sure. She died when I was quite young, so I do understand how it feels to lose a mother. I wish I could explain that to the children.'

Mrs Jepson was looking sympathetic, and patted Ella's hand gently. 'I'm sure you'll find a way, you're a good girl, a good wife to Amos, if he but realised it.'

Ella gently brought her back to her question. 'Were they happy together, Esther and Amos?'

Mrs Jepson laughed. 'Oh aye, I'm sure they were in their way. He worshipped the ground she walked on, did everything he possibly could for that woman. But, like I say, I'm not sure she ever understood the meaning of the word happiness. Moan, moan, moan, from dawn to dusk. Nothing were ever right. When I say she was allus ailing, what I really mean is that she imagined she was. There's a name fer it, hypo-summat.'

'Hypochondria?'

'That's it. If she heard tell of some illness or other, a flu epidemic, tummy upset, rheumatic fever, even pleurisy or neuralgia, she'd be sure to catch it, or think she had. For years she insisted she had ammonia.'

'Do you mean she was anaemic?'

'Aye, summat of the sort. I allus thought it were Esther's way of avoiding work. She left most of the hard graft to Mrs Rackett. There were nought Esther liked more than sitting with her feet up, even if she didn't do anything more exciting than eat currant sad cake and read her Bible. But she were very particular about how things should be done, wanting the house to be clean as a new pin with not a cushion out of place. Nay, not a cushion in sight, more like, as they might harbour germs.

'She was a Puritan of the worst sort, was Esther, issuing daft rules for the childer: no nursery rhymes or stories, or toys of any sort, as if they were a sin sent by the devil. Right little spoilsport she were. It all started from the time Amos would come home roaring drunk. The pubs were open till midnight and he'd go from one to the other, then he did it once too often for her liking. Esther did not approve.'

'Amos got roaring drunk?' Ella could scarcely believe it.

'All the farmers did. Nothing unusual in that, but Esther put a stop to it and insisted he sign the pledge. After that she became obsessed with religion, wanting complete silence for her prayers and meditations with no noisy childer racketing about. I suppose Amos joined in out of shame, and he were that grateful she'd not left him. Anyroad, he could see no wrong in her and believed all that gobbledygook she spouted at him. He adored the woman even though she played him for a fool.'

'What do you mean by that? In what way did she play him for a fool?'

Something closed in Wilma Jessop's face. 'Nay, I've said too much already.' But then apparently gave the lie to this statement by blithely continuing, 'Anyroad, after she'd enjoyed bad health for years, she really did fall sick, which she didn't enjoy at all.'

'Why, what happened?'

'The pair of them went into Kendal, as they generally did every week to attend the market, only on this occasion there was an epidemic of scarlet fever starting. Esther had never suffered from owt worse than a bad cold up until that point, despite her imaginings, but she caught summat that day. It was terrible to see the poor woman suffer. Poor Amos did everything he could to save her.

'The doctor called, issuing instructions about how to restrict the spread of the infection by keeping the children out of the way, hanging a vinegar-soaked sheet up at the door, all of that stuff. He told Amos to keep his hands scrubbed scrupulously clean, then he left, insisting isolation on the farm was the best thing for her.'

'So that's why he insisted I put them up for Tilda?'

'Oh, aye, Amos followed the doctor's instructions to the letter, and from that moment nursed his wife all on his own, wouldn't allow anyone else near. Mrs Rackett looked after the childer and practically ran the farm single-handed for a while. By the time Esther died the poor man had become so fixated with cleanliness and fighting the infection he couldn't seem to stop. He's still the same to this day, so far as I'm aware. Neurotic on the subject, he is.'

'I've noticed that he can't seem to stop washing his hands,' Ella agreed.

'It's partly out of fear for the children, of course. He's terrified they too might get sick and then he'd have no one. That's the reason he holds himself back and won't show them the least bit of love or affection. He daren't risk it in case he loses them too.'

'Oh, Mrs Jepson, that's dreadful.' Ella had listened to this sorry tale with deepening horror. 'Does he blame himself then, for his wife's death?'

'Oh, aye. He sees Kendal market now as a den of iniquity and won't go near it. That's why I offered to take his produce in to sell, for the sake of them poor bairns if nowt else. He needs the income. He thinks the doctor failed her too, which is a bit unfair. Many others died of that dreadful disease at the time, and if it's God's will there's nothing anyone can do, that's what I say.'

Ella leant forward in her seat, her eyes brimming with tears as she saw the misery that had engulfed this small family for years. How the poor man must have suffered. 'So what can I do to help? How can I make things better for the children, and for their father?'

Mrs Jepson gently patted her hand. 'It might not seem so by the po-face he carries on him, but that man is besotted with you, lass. He does want to please you and make you happy, it's just that he doesn't know how. He's far too serious for his own good, and a bit shy and lacking in confidence.'

'Shy?' Not for the world had Ella imagined any man could be termed shy, not with the kind of father she had. And she certainly hadn't considered Amos would suffer from such an affliction.

'Indeed he is, and taciturn, as many farmers are in these parts. He doesn't see enough people to buff up his social graces. You'll have to teach him how, dear. But look at that child, at her rosy cheeks, and how content she is playing wi' them crayons. I'd say you don't need any advice from me. You seem to be managing very well by yourself.'

* * *

Later in the week, the blacksmith called on one of his regular visits to shoe the horses and Ella asked him if he would make the children a hoop and stick each for them to play with. Losing Maggie, and almost losing Tilda, had taught her how precious life was. And talking to dear Mrs Jepson had given her the courage to decide that it was time to stop kowtowing to the edicts of a long-dead woman.

'Children need to play,' she stoutly remarked, lifting her chin as if daring anyone to defy her.

Amos was clearly startled by the unexpected request, and Ella saw that his first instinct was to open his mouth in protest. But then she saw something change in his eyes, and he closed it again. He said nothing as the blacksmith laughingly agreed he'd be delighted to make them each a hoop and stick. He'd get right on to the job first thing in the morning and see they had them by the time Emmett came home on Friday, by which time he hoped Tilda would be well enough to play with it.

When Friday came, Tilda and Emmett were so thrilled by the gift they could hardly speak for joy. They both glanced nervously at their father, wondering if perhaps he might issue some rule that they could play with it only at certain times, or if he might take it away from them altogether. But to their surprise and delight he said, 'Aren't you going to thank your stepmother for this lovely present? I should think she deserves a kiss at least.'

A kiss? Unheard of in this household!

Tilda instantly flung herself into Ella's arms to hug her tight around her waist and Ella duly bent down to receive a smacking kiss. Emmett followed his sister's lead more slowly, but offered her a shy kiss on the cheek, and then blushed to the roots of his tousled brown hair.

'Now your turn, Pa,' Tilda said, her young face bright with mischief.

'I wonder if that would be wise,' Amos replied.

Ella half turned away, embarrassed by Tilda's forwardness, but then, to her complete astonishment, she saw that Amos was smiling. His whole face seemed to light up, revealing an entirely different man from the one she'd come to know. His blue eyes crinkled at the corners, his flat cheeks lifted and he looked almost reborn.

'Perhaps you're right, Tilda. I need to thank Ella for taking such very good care of you. I should show how much I appreciate all she has done for us these last weeks by bringing our precious girl back to life.'

And then, before she could protest, Amos caught Ella's chin in his hand and kissed her soundly on the lips. There was a shyness to it, a fumbling embarrassment between them and a bumping of noses. It wasn't anything like the kind of kiss Ella remembered from their previous two encounters. Oh, but it felt so good.

Ella was dimly aware of the two children laughing and cheering them on, and when he lifted his mouth from hers, he smiled at her again.

'Thank you,' he said. 'Not just for Tilda, but for…for everything. For being here…with us.'

Ella was so astounded she couldn't think of a thing to say in response. Turning to the children, she said, 'Come on then, you two, let's see how good you are at bowling that thing.'

And with a shout of laughter the children snatched up their new toy and set off around the farmyard, slapping and striking the iron hoop in an effort to make it roll. They were soon all in fits of laughter, even Amos, as the hoop bowled anywhere but where the children wanted it to. Emmett struck his so hard it set off down the lane at a dangerous lick, heading straight for the river. Fortunately, he managed to catch it in time. Tilda's actually rolled right over her at one point, knocking her to the ground, and both Ella and Amos rushed to pick her up, still grinning from ear to ear, colliding with each other in the process so that Amos had to catch her in his arms to steady her.

By seven o'clock, when Ella called them in for a supper of hot milk and buttered Chorley cakes, they were near-masters at the skill. Simple happiness had at last arrived at Todd Farm, and with it had come the realisation that something else had changed too. Ella had fallen in love with her husband.

Chapter Twenty-Seven

Once those first fragile weeks were behind her, Livia knew she must contribute something to the household for her keep and asked Jessie to teach her how to knit, to spin and to weave.

'Nay, tha doesn't want to do that,' Jessie had protested. 'There's no money in weaving these days, nor in the knitting. It's all dying out.'

'Surely it can't ever die out, though I accept things might change.'

'Mebbe, but there's no money in it any more. We pay through the odds for the yarn and get paid nobbut a few coppers for labouring all day over a pair of stockings for the soldiers or sailors. And with no wars on, for which we are truly thankful, there's not much call for them right now. Nay, you find yourself a better job, lass. You could walk into one of a dozen.'

But Livia found that she couldn't. Employers either demanded references or were highly suspicious of why the eldest daughter of the town's most prominent businessman and present mayor was in need of such common employment. They assumed it was either a put-up job and she was being sent to spy on them, or Livia was simply seeking to amuse herself, which wasn't quite proper with her sister dead. No one would take her on.

So by way of payment for the meals and care her friends offered her, she set about learning these skills herself. She wanted to share in their labours as they knitted, or treadled their loom. It was a long hard road she trod, and Jack would often laugh as she became frustrated with her own clumsiness and silly mistakes, or if Jessie apologetically rejected the piece she'd laboured over for so long, making her unpick it and start all over again. The work had to be of top quality or it wouldn't be accepted; bad work wouldn't sell.

The knitting stick seemed to have a life of its own, so often disgorging all the stitches she'd so painstakingly put on. Then Jessie would tighten her toothless mouth and shake her head in mock despair before patiently helping her to put it right. Livia hated to be a trial. Time and yarn was money. This wasn't some foolish game they were playing. This was all about survival.

'Na then, it's not like ordinary knitting where you use two needles, you has to let yer body move with it. It's a bit tricky but you must persist if you want to learn the rhythm, lass.'

'Oh, Jessie, I can but try. Maybe I should learn something else, the weaving, or the spinning. Is that any easier?'

'Find me some raw wool that doesn't cost a small

fortune and I'll show you how to card and spin it. We buy the yarn from the hosiery company, which is expensive. And the weaving doesn't pay as well as it did.'

'I see. Yes, of course.'

The factories of Lancashire and Yorkshire could do it better, and far cheaper, with their steam-operated power looms. The folk of Fellside had mostly been employed in weaving linseys, and Jessie could remember the days when it was common to see men carrying home the huge bundles of yarn to be woven into the fine woollen cloth. But all of that was gone now.

Jessie would often reminisce about the good old days. 'I learnt all I know from me mam. She'd sit rocking to and fro on her stool, swaving she called it, using this very same crooked pin and knitting sheath that I use to this day. See, me da carved them rose petals and leaves in the wood the day he wed her.' The old woman wiped away a tear. 'I miss them still, bless their dear hearts.

'Mam would allus let us childer do a bit, the welt happen, or a thumb in a glove, same as I do wi' mine. And when I were a bairn she used to tie a bit of string round her ankle so she could rock me cradle while she treadled the loom, and still work her bobbin back and forth. Me da would read his poetry from a book propped up against the frame. Eeh, it's all changed now. I never thought to see the death of such a busy industry.'

'It's not dead yet,' Livia protested.

'Near enough. Hodson doesn't need us now,' Jessie mourned. 'Not now that factory of his is doing so well.'

She was right. Henry was the one ultimately responsible

for the workers' situation. He had again increased the cost of the yarn he provided to a prohibitive sum, yet had reduced the price he paid for finished goods.

The yarn for the stockings was normally handed out either by hosiers, agents from the military – of which there were very few at the moment, as Jessie pointed out – or a local woollen firm. Henry owned one of the largest in town and greedily swallowed up most of the profit. He'd started by putting out work to hand-knitters only, hundreds of them in Kendal alone. Now that method of operating had largely disappeared and he was more interested in machines. They were cheaper, faster, and he had greater control over the workers as they were all under one roof, in his factory.

They slaved from six in the morning till six at night, Jack included. They were given no share in the profits, were merely wage-earners with very little say over pay and conditions. And if they complained about the long hours, they were sacked.

But for those who wished to continue knitting in the traditional way, times were even harder.

'I'm sorry to say that your father has put our rent up yet again, *and* we've been threatened with an eviction notice. It'll be the workhouse for us soon,' Jessie mourned, starting to cry. 'We're done for.'

'Not yet we aren't,' Livia said through gritted teeth. 'Not if I've anything to do with it.'

She couldn't put it off any longer. It was long past time she confronted her father and made him see sense, perhaps even issued a few threats of her own.

But before she was able to make her move, Jack got word that Mercy had been found, walking with a friend on the road into Kendal. The pair were apparently hungry, wet and cold, but otherwise well.

'Thank goodness,' Livia gasped. 'That's the best news we've had in months. Perhaps things are starting to look up for us at last.'

Josiah sat sipping an excellent whisky, smoking a fine Havana cigar which Hodson had offered him, listening with careful attention to what he had to say. There was a great deal of what Josiah could only term 'flannel'. How reluctant Henry was to pull the plug, how he'd put off the moment for months, mindful of Josiah's grief. How he regretted their friendship reaching this pretty pass.

Josiah allowed the young man to prattle on for a good ten minutes or more. It always did take him an age to get to the point. By then he'd heard enough.

'So are you telling me that you are no longer interested in marrying my daughter?'

A short, startled silence. Henry, standing on his own hearth rug with his back to the fire, floundered a little, as if he'd been caught out in a secret desire, lusting over an unattainable prize. 'No, indeed, I – I'm not saying anything of the sort, but I can't keep waiting indefinitely. It isn't fair,' sounding very like a petulant schoolboy.

Josiah snorted his disdain. 'Never give up, boy. Never give up. But I'm hardly likely to help you win her, am I, if you make me bankrupt and take over my business?'

Henry scowled. 'I doubt there's much chance of

that happening now. I – I'd rather given up hope, to be honest.'

'Nonsense, there's generally more than one way of killing a cat besides drowning it.'

Hodson shuddered at the analogy, but his interest was alerted nonetheless. 'So what do you suggest?'

Josiah sucked on the cigar for a second or two longer, as if considering. He had to hand it to the boy, he possessed excellent taste. This was a first-rate Havana. 'Have you considered force?' The suggestion was calmly offered as if using violence on a girl was a perfectly normal way to set about persuading her to marry you.

Hodson's eyes narrowed. 'What do you mean, exactly, by force?'

'There are always ways and means of bringing a woman to heel,' Josiah commented, drawing deeply on the excellent cigar. How he would enjoy seeing that high-minded daughter of his brought low. Serve her right for being so full of herself and causing him so much bother. 'It's important, I believe, to show a woman who is boss right from the start. And most are gagging for it, in any case. Just remember there's one thing they fear above all else, and that's the loss of their reputation. It wouldn't be the first shotgun wedding, would it? Get the girl with child, Hodson, isn't that the phrase? She'll marry you fast enough then.'

Hodson stared at the older man, at first aghast and appalled by the suggestion, but then, as he considered how it would feel to carry it out, with the added benefit of a successful outcome, he began to see positive advantages.

Yet he could see one or two possible problems. 'How do I charm my way into her bed when she'll barely remain in the same room as me for more than twenty minutes? She's barely spoken to me since that stupid riot.'

Josiah gave the younger man a measuring look, one lip curled upwards into a sneer. 'What has charm got to do with anything? You tried charm and that didn't work. I expect you to be a man. I don't care how you do it. I'll help if you like by setting the lure. But, not to put too fine a point on it, you get the lass pregnant with or without her permission. Am I making myself clear? She'll make a dash for the altar fast enough once the job is done.'

Henry looked blank-faced for a moment and then smirked, the idea was becoming more attractive to him by the minute. 'And the price for your assistance in "setting the lure" for this bit of chicanery?'

Josiah eased himself back in Hodson's comfortable leather chair, pretending to contemplate this knotty problem while he allowed the younger man to savour the pleasure of his intended prize a little longer. 'It would be a quite straightforward exchange, as we've agreed from the start of this mission. You cancel my debt, consider the loan paid off. *I* agree that you can take my daughter, with my blessing, any way you choose, but *you* must agree to keep your grasping hands off my business.'

A small silence while Henry walked over to the side table to refresh his whisky glass and refill Josiah's. He'd already put the squeeze on Livia's so-called friends by dropping the price he paid for finished woollen goods. Hodson was aware that he'd always paid less than any other manufacturer or hosier in Kendal, but he'd tightened the screws even more lately in the hope she'd finally buckle and come to him begging for help. So far she'd obstinately resisted and he'd grown irritated and impatient, and finally lost heart altogether.

Now, this new plan was most definitely growing on him. He rather relished the prospect, in fact. How could he not? Willing or not, he was certainly man enough to take her. He carried the refreshed whisky glass over to Josiah.

'So how do we set this lure when Livia deliberately avoids my company?'

'I believe I could persuade Lavinia to return home for a short visit, on the pretext that her sister is coming. Do we have a deal?'

Henry paused for only a fraction of a second before leaning forward to clink glasses. 'We do.'

Jessie was like a mother hen when one of her chicks has been lost and found again, clucking and fussing with feverish excitement. The poor girl had looked close to collapse when Jack first brought her into the loft, together with a young man who said his name was George. But a dish of Jessie's soup had already begun to banish the bruises beneath her eyes as well as the hunger pains from her belly.

Mercy was soon relating the tale of their escape and how they'd stolen a ride in a farm cart, eventually reaching the Langdales where they'd very nearly starved in those first few weeks of freedom.

'We gave up at one point and set off back to Kendal, but then George found himself a job as a farm labourer, and the farmer's wife took me on as a dairymaid. They offered us a room over the stables so we pretended to be man and wife.'

'Not that we were sharing a bed.' George, who until now had been sitting quietly sipping his soup, making no attempt to interrupt, finally spoke up.

Mercy gave a philosophical wag of her head. 'George slept curled in a blanket on the floor, so I had a big comfortable bed all to meself. I argued about this decision at the time, saying I really wouldn't mind in the least if he joined me in it, that I trusted him implicitly and didn't he need a decent night's rest as much as I did after a long day's work?'

George smiled. 'I made sure I treated her proper, like. Mercy had suffered enough without me taking advantage.'

This had been a great disappointment to Mercy at the time, as she'd thought George wonderful. Her hero! He was lively and cheerful, cheeky and fun, and she'd absolutely adored him.

'Then we had a sort of tiff and I stalked off and left him.'

'And I chased after her.'

Everyone was smiling as she cast George a shy glance from beneath her lashes, and he gallantly finished the story for her.

'Aye, well it all turned out fine and dandy because the farmer held us jobs open for us. Mebbe I'll tell you the full yarn one day, but what I will say is that it serves me right for being such a daft cluck with me practical jokes. No wonder she thought the worst of me and I nearly lost her. Anyroad, it all ended happily, thanks be praised.'

They looked into each other's eyes and everyone sighed at the sight of the undeniable love between them.

'Aye, so we made up quick, and I decided it were high time I did the honourable thing by her.'

Jessie gasped. 'You're married?'

Mercy was blushing now, her cheeks a delightful rosy pink, and George was grinning from ear to ear. 'I'd've asked her sooner, only I wanted to have some money saved afore I declared meself.'

There were cries of 'aaah' all round, and Mercy finished the convoluted tale by assuring her friends that since she'd no family left, they'd felt no reason to wait so had married in a little church out on the fells. 'God knows where.'

'But we had a real vicar, and there was a proper congregation, hymns and everything, so it were all done right and proper. The farmer helped me get the licence and make all the arrangements,' George assured them. 'He were very good about it.'

Then Mercy was blushing again as she remembered that first night when George had at last joined her in the big bed, and offered full proof of his manhood.

Following this wonderful news the bride and groom had to be kissed and hugged and congratulated, then Jack insisted on going to the pub to buy jugs of ale for everyone. Jessie set out the best she could offer in the way of supper, and they all had a merry time together.

Listening to the girl's happy chatter Livia found herself smiling. She'd fully expected to dislike this unexpected sister but instead was instantly captivated by her. She reminded her so much of Maggie that the very sight of her brought a lump to her throat. Mercy had the same heart-shaped face, and fine long fair hair very like her sister. And if the full, rosebud mouth pouted a little more than Maggie's had, it was nonetheless as beautiful. The eyes were different, Mercy's having a quality to them as if you were looking into a deep ocean rather than the clear grey of a stream that had been Maggie's. She was also feisty and funny, and strong-willed, and, judging by the tales she was telling about her time in the workhouse, not one to suffer fools gladly.

There was no sign of Maggie's vulnerability or fragility in the sturdy way this girl had dealt with the trials that life had flung at her, nor of Ella's giddy selfishness and exotic beauty. She seemed to possess rather an impatient, impulsive nature, the kind of girl eager to grasp a problem by the throat and deal with it.

Yet there was a wariness about her, which, Livia suspected, may be partly due to her own presence in the loft. The girl seemed pleased to be back with her friends, but kept casting dark glances in Livia's direction, as if she were slightly resentful of this new half-sister who had somehow supplanted her place in their home.

Livia wanted to reassure her on that score, point out that Mercy had never been forgotten, but decided it was best to say as little as possible at this stage. Mainly because Livia herself was having some difficulty growing accustomed to the idea of a new sister, and there was no doubt in her mind that this girl was undoubtedly their father's child.

Chapter Twenty-Eight

Ella was making substantial changes and feeling remarkably pleased with herself. Today she was at a farm sale, buying a mangle and boiler, a new clothes rack, and other useful bits and pieces that might make her life easier. Amos had given his permission without a word of protest, putting a wad of notes into her hand with a warning only to be cautious not to flick an eyebrow or raise a hand unless she fully intended to buy a particular lot.

'Otherwise, you might find yourself bidding for a rusty tin kettle, or a dozen chickens you never wanted.'

'I might very well buy more chickens to boost our egg supply,' she stoutly responded, chin high. 'But I'm no fool, Amos, so don't treat me as one.'

Amos merely smiled, in that enigmatic way of his, saying nothing.

Ella had also insisted that he either sink a new well or mend the one they had so that it didn't leak, and she wanted him to pipe the water into the house and dairy.

'This is the twentieth century,' she'd told him in her firmest voice, 'and high time this farm was brought up to date.'

She'd expected resistance, sulks, an argument about how tight money was, but he'd simply given her his slow smile and said, 'Whatever you like, dear. I'll get Tom Mounsey over to help me tackle the job.'

Ella couldn't quite believe what she was hearing. She was beginning to see strengths and depths in this husband of hers she'd never noticed before. And he was really being most agreeable. But then she too had perhaps been a little more reasonable lately, making special dishes for his tea, walking out with him on his evening walk and not being prone to heavy sighs when he talked endlessly of the cattle or his fishing. Were they at last beginning to tolerate each other a little more, perhaps even reach some sort of understanding?

One evening, about a week after the sale, as Ella sat watching Mrs Rackett ply her spindle in the time-honoured way, she suddenly asked if she would teach her the rudiments of spinning, a task she'd fiercely resisted in the past. The older woman was surprised by the request, but at once began to talk about wool, explaining the difference between short 'staple' and long.

'First it has to be sorted into top quality and not-so-good, then cleaned of hay seeds or any ticks.'

Ella found it strangely satisfying to pull the fleece gently apart with her fingers, transforming the clumps of fleece into a fluffy mass ready for 'carding'. The lanoline or 'suint', as Mrs Rackett called it, softened her work-roughened hands, and soothed the red raw skin made sore from all the scrubbing and cleaning she did.

'Next we do the carding,' Mrs Racket explained, demonstrating with a pair of wooden 'bats' that were covered with rows of tiny sharp hooks. Ella found this task harder to do than it looked, the older woman's skill clearly one born of long practice. And if she'd hoped that Amos might compliment her for her efforts, Ella was soon disappointed. He sat quietly working his loom as he often did of an evening, his Bible propped up against the frame, making no comment whatsoever, not even watching how she got on.

'The fleece has to be pulled so that the fibres all lie in the same direction. When we've got a nice long sausage, then we can begin.'

The spinning was done using a spindle or 'distaff', a spinning wheel considered to be far too expensive for a farmer to own. In any case, Mrs Rackett thought it unnecessary as she was more used to the simple spindle.

'That's why they call women the "distaff" side of the family,' the older woman informed her, 'because they use the spindle.' It was a highly decorated stick with a disc at the top held on a thread by a hook. The carded wool had to be attached to it in a particular way before the spinning could actually begin. Mrs Rackett expertly worked her stick so that the weight of it turned at just the right speed, pulling out the wool at the same time so that the resulting yarn wound neatly onto the spindle.

Ella struggled to emulate her expertise but soon became

frustrated by her own inadequacy. Either the spindle wouldn't spin properly, or it would constantly change direction, the yarn refusing to evenly wrap itself around the stick, or it would become snarled and tangled. She couldn't even decide which hand to use, and they both very soon became all sticky and sweaty.

'Oh, it's hopeless, I'll never learn,' she cried, as the fibre bunched up into another useless lump.

Mrs Rackett chuckled as she leant over to help untangle the mess. ''Course you will, given patience and practise. Just let the spindle unwind a little, that's it, now spin it again. Don't tug too hard or you'll break the yarn. You know what they used to say: cross patch, lift the latch, sit by the fire and spin. You can't be angry when you spin because of the steady rhythm of the job. It's very relaxing after a hard day's work.'

Ella thought it unlikely she ever could relax, but after a while she did begin to get the hang of it, and became quite absorbed by the task, however flawed her work was in comparison to the older woman's. Surprisingly, it was Amos who called an end to the lesson.

'That's enough for one evening. Tha's made good progress. You can try again another night. We all need our sleep now.'

And he was right. She was indeed tired, yet Ella went to her bed with reluctance, and with a heavy heart. Every night it seemed lonelier than ever. If only she had a proper marriage, with a man who loved her. She listened to her husband's heavy footsteps climbing up to the attic above and wished, as she did more and more

312

these days, that Amos cared for her just a little.

There had been a time when she'd feared him as she had her own father, when she hadn't wanted him in her bed. She'd so resented being forcibly married off she hadn't properly given their marriage a chance. Ella saw that now, and regretted it. Of course Amos too had made mistakes, with his lack of trust and refusal to take her into Kendal, his assumption that she was no virgin and would play him false, not to mention the unrelenting work routine, which had come as a great shock to her system.

But ever since she'd instigated their lovemaking when he'd been half asleep, Ella had never been able to erase the wonder of that moment from her mind. She wanted him, now more than ever. And since Tilda's illness he'd shown her great kindness and respect, and Ella knew in her heart that she loved him. If only he could love her. Would they ever be man and wife in truth, as well as in name? If only she could learn to spin some happiness for the pair of them.

Mercy was delighted to be home but filled with a bitter resentment over Livia's presence. What on earth was she doing here when she'd had the kind of privileged upbringing that Mercy could only dream of, stealing all the love from their father that had been denied her simply because she was illegitimate? Not for a moment did Mercy trust that I-am-your-best-friend attitude which the other girl seemed to have adopted. And just because she didn't have a patronising, nose-in-the-air attitude, didn't mean she wasn't far too full of herself. Didn't the quality always think themselves better than everyone else?

Now unemployed, Mercy felt she was right back where she'd started, in dire need of a job and a decent future. There wasn't even much in the way of weaving and knitting. Life was really quite depressing.

And so she took out her resentment on Livia.

Mercy enjoyed queening it over this more fortunate sister of hers, and since she knew the neighbourhood so much better than Livia, she'd pretend to show her the secret parts of Fellside. 'It's not wise to take short cuts on your own. You can quickly lose your bearings,' she warned.

'So Jack informs me.'

Mercy despised that calm, unruffled manner of hers, that hoity-toity, I-know-it-all attitude.

Sometimes, as she went about visiting old friends, Mercy would deliberately lead her into unsafe places through a maze of dark alleys and ginnels. Then she'd hide in a doorway, watching as Livia began to panic on finding herself alone, grow confused and get thoroughly lost trying to find her own way back. Or she'd take her into shady corners where groups of youths would throw muck and stones at them, or hover threateningly close so that Livia would grow nervous. Mercy would frighten her with tales of what they intended to do to them, then urge her to turn tail and run, while she would remain with the lads, laughing her head off.

Irritatingly, Livia soon grew wise to these tricks, and began to be amused rather than put off by them. And she remained obstinately kind.

Mercy was also jealous of Livia's obvious friendship

with Jack. What Jack saw in her, Mercy couldn't comprehend. They weren't suited at all, didn't even come from the same world. Why couldn't he see that she was only amusing herself with him? Mercy said as much to him one day.

'She'll drop you the moment she gets a better offer.'

Jack had looked at her, smiled, and said only, 'Maybe she won't get a better offer than me. I'm pretty damn good, you know.'

Mercy had her lovely George now, of course, but she still thought of Jack as her own very special friend, and resented Livia taking him from her. She wanted him to hate the Angel family every bit as much as she did.

George too was having difficulty finding employment since he'd only ever been a farm labourer, his true calling, she supposed, and he loved the work. But there wasn't much call for tending sheep here in Kendal itself. Between them they didn't have a penny to their name, having used up the last of their savings while on the road, driven back to town by Mercy's homesickness. It certainly wasn't going to be as easy to earn a living here as she'd first hoped. And without a job there was precious little chance of them ever being able to set up home together. In the meantime they had to be content with sharing a straw pallet on Jessie's hard floor.

Mercy found this particularly hard to accept when she considered that this posh, so-called half-sister of hers must be loaded with brass, yet quite clearly kept it all to herself.

* * *

'I think it's time we talked, don't you?' Livia said to Mercy one day. 'There are things you should know about us, your new family. I'm sure there must be lots of questions you want to ask. Finding out you even existed has been something of a surprise so far as I'm concerned, and it must be even more so for you. I didn't realise I had another sister until Jack told me about you. We've all been looking for you ever since.'

Mercy snorted her disbelief. 'I can't see why you'd care.'

Livia raised questioning brows. 'Why wouldn't I? And why wouldn't I be concerned that my father had started bullying you too?'

A small silence while Mercy digested this remark, uncertain as to its true meaning. Was she saying that her father had been known to bully other girls at the store? Or did she mean that as well as abandoning Mercy and her mother, Josiah Angel had then started to bully her too?

They were sitting on the steps that led up to Fountain Brow, a group of bare-bottomed children playing in the dirt nearby. A man with a handcart rumbled by, hawked and spat into the filthy gutter, and Mercy noticed how Livia quickly pulled her skirt away in case he spattered snot on it. The gesture almost made her laugh out loud. It proved how fancy and fastidious she was.

'You don't belong in these parts. Why don't you go home to yer posh house, your rich friends and yer doting papa? What are you doing slumming it here wi' us lot?'

Livia sighed. 'Let me tell you about my doting papa.' And she did. In a few blunt sentences, well laced with bitterness, Livia described the years of abuse at her father's hands. She told about Ella's forced marriage, Maggie's suicide, although she claimed the reason was that she'd been driven to the point of despair by their father's bullying. The facts about the pregnancy were still very much her private secret, and would remain so until she'd found the courage, and the right moment, to confront her father on the subject. Livia went on to explain that this was the reason she'd finally walked out, and as she talked, Mercy's mouth fell open.

'But I thought—'

'That we'd led a spoilt, sheltered existence, pampered and cosseted by an adoring father?' Livia's sigh this time was heavy with sadness. 'I wish that had been the case. I wish I could take you home to him now and say, "Father, here is a welcome addition to our family, a new daughter to treasure." But he doesn't even treasure his legitimate daughters, seeing us only as pawns to move about the chessboard of his life to his own advantage. He has damaged us all by his cruel treatment of us, by his resolve to exercise power over our lives, having first destroyed our mother. It is no surprise to me that he turned on you too, bullying you and having you beaten and locked away. It's typical of him.'

Mercy struggled to readjust her thoughts. 'But why do you let him get away with it? Why don't you stand up to him?'

Livia shook her head in despair. 'With what? As his daughters living at home we had no say over our own lives. He had all the power.' She told Mercy then about the cage in the tower room, the shackles and the butcher's

317

hook, the strap he used on them regularly.

The younger girl's eyes widened in shock, hardly able to take in what she was hearing. This was the last thing she'd expected. By the sound of it she'd been the fortunate one, after all. At least Mercy had been loved and cared for by her darling ma, whereas Livia's mother had died years ago, leaving those poor girls with a brute for a father.

Who'd've thought it? The quality were even more of a mystery than she'd bargained for.

Livia said, 'He'll be furious when he finds out you're back in Kendal. I'm afraid that he'll see you as a threat to his precious reputation. Stay well clear of Angel House, Mercy. Don't ever allow him to lure you in there. I beg you never to trust him.'

Mercy shook her head in disbelief. 'What you say may well be true, but Josiah Angel as good as killed my ma by his neglect, and one day I mean to tell him so. I want to give that man a piece of my mind.'

'Just forget him,' Livia urged. 'Seeking revenge will do you no good at all. I wish I had money to give you, a job to offer, but I don't have a penny to my name. I swear I'll find some way to help you and George, to help all my friends who live here on Fellside. Trust me, I'll do everything I possibly can. In the meantime, I would so like us to be friends. To be real sisters. I've lost one already, I don't want to lose another.'

Livia put her arms around her, and Mercy allowed herself to be hugged. She went through the motions of making friends, even if deep down she struggled to believe this tale that Livia had spun.

Chapter Twenty-Nine

Not only was Josiah making plans with Henry, but as extra insurance in his efforts to bring his daughter to heel, he sent round one of his rent collectors to issue an eviction notice.

It stated that Josiah wanted the Flint family out by the end of the month, claiming they'd missed too many payments. Jack explained to Livia that this was untrue, that he'd argued with the rent collector on this point, even fetching out the rent book to prove that, difficult though it had been at times, they'd always met their obligations. But for some inexplicable reason the Flint family rent book did not match the entries in the ledger the rent collector carried, and their word alone was considered untrustworthy.

'He's accused us of altering the entries in the book, which is outrageous! And if we refuse to budge, then Mr Angel will evict every tenant in the entire building, and bulldoze the lot to the ground. Says he's had enough.'

Jack believed the man to be perfectly capable of doing

such a despicable act. He was not to know that Josiah would not be able to carry out this threat any time soon, as he had financial troubles of his own. He simply couldn't afford to hire the necessary machinery, let alone replace the building with anything else at present. The threat sounded real enough, and none of them had any reason to doubt his word.

Livia was furious. She knew that her father would enjoy seeing her friends run like rats from a terrier. How dare he threaten them in this way! He still seemed to imagine that he could control other people's lives exactly as he pleased. She was the one he wanted to punish, the one he was angry with, for refusing to obey his every whim and marry Henry as he'd decreed. Now he was taking revenge for that bit of rebellion on her part by destroying Jessie and her family.

She was already trying not to be a nuisance by eating as little as possible of their precious food, and doing her bit with the knitting, but life was hard. If only they could find alternative accommodation, and a cheaper supply of raw wool. Then they could perhaps knit something more saleable than the traditional thick stockings and gloves. And sell to someone other than mean Henry.

Livia wondered if she could persuade Miss Caraway to take a few knitted motoring scarves, or perhaps thick warm sweaters and woolly hats to sell to walkers in the sports department; that wouldn't necessarily be sufficient to earn the Flint family a decent living, but it would be a start. They could surely find other shops interested in their goods, perhaps in towns such as Keswick or

Ambleside? People needed warm sweaters in this county, didn't they?

She began to feel almost optimistic. Maybe it would work if she could but lay her hands on a supply of wool at a reasonable cost, and perhaps a couple of the new-fangled hand-knitting machines. Would Henry lend her the money to do that? she wondered. Could they set up some sort of co-operative?

Livia felt she could put the evil moment off no longer, but first she must tackle her father.

Following Maggie's death, she'd sworn never to speak to him again. Yet Livia knew that there really was no alternative but for her to swallow her pride and confront him. The thought made her feel sick to her stomach, but she had to make him withdraw this eviction notice. Mercy was right. They couldn't allow him to get away with his bullying any longer. It was long past time she stood up to him. Livia thought of all the other times she'd tried to do so in the past, and failed bitterly. Why would it be any different now, things being as they were between them? Yet for the sake of them all, she surely must try.

The first sight of her father shocked Livia to the core. He had aged in this past year more than she would have thought possible. Surely he wasn't suffering from guilt? No, more likely an excess of indulgence. He'd put on weight and looked less well groomed than usual, positively unkempt. There were food stains on his silk cravat, his hair looked in need of a trim and he'd grown a beard. His eyes appeared bloodshot and more askew than ever, and he stank of whisky and stale cigars. But then he no longer had loyal servants or daughters around to see that he ate sensibly and wore clean clothes.

There was a new maid, Peggy, and he waited until she'd poured two glasses of sweet sherry, bobbed a curtsey and departed.

Livia glanced about her at the familiar room where she and her sisters had spent so many evenings, her gaze going at once to Maggie's chair. Her eyes filled with tears, which never seemed far away these days. How she longed to see her beloved sister still sitting there, sweetly smiling as she worked at her sewing, her pink flannel petticoats for the poor. How could she be gone? How could she be dead? The familiar rage swelled in her breast, firing up the hatred Livia felt for their father. It was all his fault. He drove Maggie to do that terrible thing.

'So you've come home at last,' was his opening remark.

Livia took the glass he offered, straightened her spine, and resolved to come straight to the point. 'No, Father, I have not come home, nor ever will. I've come to take issue with you about this eviction notice. It is completely unfair. The Flint family have never missed a single payment, have gone without food on their table rather than miss paying rent due. I know why you have chosen to persecute them. It's really me you wish to punish, me you are angry with. But if you have a modicum of compassion, think of the children of the family. You have no quarrel with them.'

He pulled a walnut from his pocket and cracked it in his palm, as she'd seen him do many times before, then quietly sipped his sherry while he considered her. 'I take it you're still not ready to obey your father then, as a good daughter should.'

Livia almost snorted her disdain and set down her glass with a snap, untouched. 'Nor ever will be. Don't think you can bully me any longer, Father. I'm free of your tyranny now. I'm my own person and refuse to be intimidated. I only beg you, please do not involve my friends in this vendetta you're conducting.'

'All they need do is earn more money, then they'll have no trouble in paying the increased rent.'

'But it's an entirely unreasonable sum. Quite impossible, a fortune for what is nothing more than a hovel. They've barely enough money to survive as it is, let alone pay more in rent. Henry, too, seems intent on taking out his disappointment over my rejection of his proposal by exploiting the innocent. He's cut the payments he makes to them for finished work down to a penurious level. Does the silly man have no idea of the problems he is causing these people by his callous disregard of their rights to a decent living? I shall have something to say to Henry about that next time I see him.'

'Why don't you tell him now? I sent the stable lad for him when I saw you arriving on your trusty bicycle.' And before Livia had time to protest, or point out that nothing had yet been agreed between them about the rent or the threatened eviction, Henry himself was in the room and her father was softly closing the door as he departed.

'I'll leave you two lovebirds alone, then you can talk in private.'

Livia stood frozen to the spot. This was the last thing she'd expected. To face up to her father had been difficult enough, to cope with them both at once was almost more than her nerves could stand. And she hadn't even broached the subject of Maggie's death yet.

Jumbled thoughts raced through her head. It seemed highly convenient that Henry should be nearby to come running the instant he was called. Had her father planned this? She'd assumed that he'd issued the eviction notice in order to punish her, but had he simply wanted to lure her here? Livia was beginning to feel that she might have been duped, which made her very angry indeed. And if Henry thought he could persuade her into a change of heart over his proposal, he was very much mistaken.

But was it possible for her to induce him to pay more for the finished work he purchased? She admitted doubts on that score, since the business he did with the knitters of Fellside was diminishing by the day.

Henry was thinking that this visit was going nicely to plan. He pecked a kiss upon each cheek, relishing the prospect of more later. 'Livia, what a lovely surprise. You were the last person I was expecting to see today. What can I do for you? Is there some particular reason for your visit, or is this simply a social call? The latter I hope,' he burbled, his mind racing over possibilities.

'I came to see Father on a particular matter.'

'Of course, and, I hope, to inform me that you're willing to reconsider my offer for you and I to...' He left the sentence unfinished with a slight upward curl to those full moist lips, in the hope she might pick up the thread without his actually needing to.

This was the last thing Livia needed, and she instantly set about quashing any dreams Henry might nurture on a possible union between them. 'I don't want you to be under any misconceptions. I'm afraid I haven't changed my mind. I simply don't see you as a potential husband, Henry dear.'

His mouth visibly tightened and Henry thrust his hands behind his back, clasping them in a tight fury of disappointment. 'I see, well, I appreciate your frankness.'

Livia detected an icy coolness creeping into his tone but decided not to trouble herself over it. She had other, rather more important issues on her mind. She was determined there must be some way she could help her friends to earn an honest living, and if that meant she must beg favours of Henry, as well as her father, then it was a price she was prepared to pay.

Oh, but it was really quite preposterous, considering how wealthy the Angel family was supposed to be, the size of this house for a start, not to mention the land and property her father owned, that she had no money of her own. Not a penny. If she had, then she would use it to set the Flint family up in business on their own account. But she had nothing and was obliged to swallow her pride and make the best of it; otherwise she, together with the entire Flint family, would be the ones in the workhouse, not just Mercy.

She settled herself in her favourite chair, striving to be calm, and began by describing her concern for the residents of Fellside, explaining that many of them had no other employment but the knitting and weaving, and were in dire straits.

Henry looked unmoved. 'I fear the world is changing, Lavinia. We cannot halt progress.'

'I do realise that,' Livia agreed, quite sharply. 'Nevertheless, it seems to me that since there must still be a market for knitted goods, albeit a changing one, a fair price should at least be paid for their labours. They've done so much for me, nursing me when I was out of my head… I don't wish to go into all of that, but I want to help them. They deserve better.'

Henry's smile had become stiff and forced. He strolled over to take up his usual stand on the hearthrug before the blazing fire, almost as if he owned the place. 'I can see that you have become rather tied up with the petty concerns of these people. Of course, we both know that there really is no need for you to be living on Fellside at all.' He looked at her as if she lived in a whorehouse. 'If there is some reason you don't yet wish to return here to Angel House, you could come and stay at my house. It would be perfectly proper since Mother could act as chaperone.'

'Henry, I thought we'd just agreed—'

'I don't mean as my fiancée, although I would still welcome you in that capacity, were you to experience a change of heart. I meant as a friend. You would be much more comfortable there than living in such grim conditions, at least until you felt able to return home.'

'I have no intention of ever returning home, so you can put that idea right out of your head.' Livia clasped and unclasped her hands with growing impatience. 'Henry, I really have no wish to engage in an argument with you. The point is, you pay only sixpence for an item that might take all day to knit. I'd like to ask you, to beg you, to increase your payments. A shilling, at least, would be a much more appropriate price.'

He raised his eyebrows in alarm. 'A shilling! I think not. My own costs have risen exponentially. Do you appreciate the time and trouble involved in delivering and collecting the wool, and selling those hand-knitted stockings? My factory can knit thousands in a week, instead of the pitiful quantity a hand-knitter can supply. It's a specialised market now.'

'Is it indeed? And to hell with the needs of the people, is that it? Let them starve, eh?'

His expression turned sour as he dropped all show of politeness. 'They can always seek employment in one of the woollen factories in town, although I confess I have no openings at present in my own.'

Livia took a breath. 'I did think of encouraging my friends to start their own business, knitting sweaters and scarves and so on. I don't suppose you would consider making me a loan to set that in motion, would you?'

'No, I don't suppose I would.'

There was a frigid silence for the length of one

heartbeat. 'Well then, now *I* must thank *you* for being so frank. I'm sorry to have troubled you.' Livia rose from her chair and walked to the door. Henry made as if to follow her, but she put up a hand to stop him. 'Please don't disturb yourself. I believe I know the way out of my own home. Stay and finish your whisky.'

'Livia, for goodness sake, don't dash off in a huff just because I refuse to help with your cock-eyed scheme.'

'Cock-eyed?' She whirled around to face him, all social niceties gone, temper bright in her eyes. 'That's not how *I* see it.' Then turning on her heel she marched out into the hall.

'Wait, I need to talk to you. I miss you. You're still the only girl for me. I still want to marry you, Livvy. And I may yet agree to assist with this foolish...this new enterprise of yours.'

She paused. 'On what terms?'

'Obviously I'd see the matter in an entirely different light if you were to accept my offer of marriage. A wife is generally permitted one or two pet charities to occupy her.'

Livia looked at him with open contempt. 'Blackmail, is it now, Henry? Please explain to my father that I had to leave. Good day to you both.'

She snatched up her cape and hat, so anxious to put these two painful interviews behind her that she didn't even trouble to pin the latter in place. Livia had almost reached the porch when she was halted by a familiar booming voice from behind.

'Are you going to just let her walk away, or behave like a man for once?'

'Father, please, don't stir up any more trouble. I came to ask you – to beg you – for help. Both of you. I should have known better. Good day to you.'

But Henry was beside her in a second. He caught her wrist as she reached for the big brass door knob and twisted her round to face him.

'I *mean* to marry you, Livvy. Stop being so damned obstinate and admit you've made a mistake in refusing me.'

'Let go, Henry, you're hurting me.' Livia strove to pull herself from his grasp, very nearly succeeded, but he was so much stronger than her, and filled with a rage born of rejection. 'I will have you, woman. Damn it, I'll show you whether or not I have passion.'

The image she would remember in the moment of realisation that he had no intention of allowing her to leave was of her father standing in the hall laughing his head off.

Chapter Thirty

It was a Thursday and Jack was concerned that Livia wasn't at home, wondering where she might be.

'She went out hours ago.' Jessie was equally concerned, and about to serve the evening meal, the usual broth with herb dumplings, this time with a few tasty bits of bacon in it which she'd got cheap on the market.

'Yes, but where to? Where did she go?'

'I'm not sure.' Jessie placed a brimming dish of broth before her son, and his nose twitched with appreciation as he savoured the delicious aroma.

'Has she gone to her father to ask for a stay of execution on the eviction notice? She hasn't gone to beg him for money?' Jack slammed down the spoon he'd only just picked up. 'I hope she hasn't been so stupid as to risk seeing him alone? Is she mad?'

Jessie shook her head and shrugged, looking more and more troubled as her son continued to fire questions at her. 'Don't ask me; I know nowt. She just wanted to know if I'd found us anywhere else to live yet, and when

I said no, I hadn't, she became very distressed and—'

Jack was on his feet in a second, his hunger forgotten. 'Dear God, that confirms it, she has gone to see him.'

'Calm yerself, lad, I'm not so sure about that. We went on to talk about Hodson, and his penny-pinching ways of doing business. I mentioned that Hodson had dropped his payment by another threepence for that last batch of stockings I made. She was livid, seemed to believe it was because of her that he's turned nasty, that Hodson is trying to punish her through us. Isn't he an old flame of Livia's?'

Jack frowned. 'Hodson is her father's choice of husband for her, yes. But she refused, or so she told me. I doubt she's suffered a change of heart.'

Jessie chuckled at the very idea. 'Not with the pair of you unable to keep your hands off each other, not unless I'm a pig's uncle. Nay, it's this business of the knitting and the weaving that's got to her. She's that determined to help it's more likely she's gone to give him a piece of her mind. You know how she is, always says what she thinks right up front. She were annoyed he was squeezing yet another few pennies out of us and promised to sort it out, once and for all.'

Jack ran for the door, shouting to his mother to keep his supper warm till he returned. 'See you save enough for two. I shall bring Livia back with me.'

How she came to be in the conservatory Livia had no idea. Following those last bitter words between them there'd been an undignified tussle in which she'd desperately attempted to effect an escape. And utterly failed to do so. Had Henry, with her father's help, really propelled her to the conservatory, her arms pinioned to her sides? Yet here she undoubtedly was, among the potted palms and ornamental ferns, the door locked, her father gone off still laughing, and the pair of them alone once more.

Henry was now in his shirtsleeves, having thrown off his fine frock coat, and had her backed up against a wall. Amazingly, he was attempting to tug her skirt up above her knees.

'What are you *doing*?' Livia tried to grab his hand, to stop him, but he was so much stronger than she remembered. She'd never had any trouble controlling him when he was a boy and they were squabbling over who was to ride her bicycle. 'Stop this nonsense, Henry. At once, do you hear?'

His laughter chilled her. 'You think I'm such a fool, don't you? Good old Henry, lead him on, tease him, what does it matter? He's quite harmless, and so *useful* to have around to fetch and carry.'

Livia cringed at the way so effectively emulated their tone when she and Ella had been silly young girls. 'It's not like that, not any more at any rate. I'm sorry if we were cruel to you when we were young, but we were only *children*.'

'You promised me,' he hissed in her ear, and his warm breath, smelling strongly of whisky, made her almost retch. 'You *promised* you'd wed me, and you *will*, damn it! If you won't keep your promise voluntarily, I'll *make* you. You'll be glad enough of my offer when you find yourself carrying my child.'

Livia gasped. 'You're *mad*!'

His eyes glittered dangerously. 'You're right, I am. Mad with love for you.'

Before Livia had the chance to frame any sort of reply to this outrageous remark, his mouth crashed down on hers, cutting off her protests, stifling the start of a scream somewhere deep in her throat. His fat fingers were feverishly ripping apart the pearl buttons on her blouse, pawing at her breasts, again searching beneath her skirts, seeking that private, secret part of her, oblivious to her efforts to break free, her squeals and cries begging him to stop.

Dear Lord, she couldn't believe this was happening to her. This was *Henry* after all, her oldest friend. She'd thought of him as a brother. What on earth did he mean to do to her? Had he quite lost his reason?

Henry's next words explained all, the icy tone of his voice sending a chill down her spine. 'This was your father's idea. "You can have her," he told me. "Take her any way you choose, willing or not, by force if necessary. You have my permission."'

And she'd fondly imagined she could make her father feel guilty for what he'd done to Maggie?

Gathering every vestige of her strength, Livia shoved him hard, slapping at him frantically with the flat of both hands. But it was like a fly trying to bat away an elephant. Henry was a big man, growing bigger every day by the look of him. All she succeeded in doing was dislodging a plant pot that had been balanced precariously on a marble pillar close by. It went crashing to the ground.

'Don't think to alert anyone by knocking stuff over, and no point in screaming either.' He clapped a hand across her mouth, just in case she should try. 'Most of your father's servants have either been given their marching orders or left of their own accord. There's only a daily, and Peggy, who you saw just now, and she's already left. As for the neighbours, they know better than to interfere with whatever goes on in the house of their new mayor.'

Livia felt sick at the thought, all too aware that he spoke the truth. The house was too big and solid, and the grounds too large for neighbours to hear anything going on, even in the conservatory. There was no one around, save for her father, and he would do nothing to save her. She couldn't get the sound of his laughter out of her head, or the way he'd helped Henry to drag her away from the door, for all he must have been fully aware of what was about to happen. Yet why should she be surprised by his malice, wasn't he completely amoral?

Henry seemed to echo that laugh now, and the sound chilled her. 'Didn't you once ask if I was capable of passion? Well, I'll damn well prove to you that I am.'

Pulling her roughly to him, he devoured her mouth in a punishing kiss, raking it with his tongue, nipping at her lips with his sharp teeth as he sucked at her. 'Is that passionate enough for you?'

If he saw how her eyes begged him to release her, he gave no indication. He was far too absorbed in dealing with the intricacies of her undergarments. When she

334

fought him, he shoved her back hard against the house wall among the grapevine, which had never yet produced any fruit, only clinging tendrils that clawed at her hair. His breathing grew ragged, grunting alarmingly like a rutting stag in autumn. He ripped her petticoat apart with both hands, then set about her French silk knickers, which Ella had once assured her were very much the coming thing.

Oh, Maggie, how on earth did you cope with a similar violation, *from your own father*?

Livia screamed.

Sadly, he'd been right about the neighbours. No one came running in answer to her cries. Nor did anyone appear when other plant pots went flying as he tumbled her to the ground to finish the job properly. Livia's fingers scrabbled frantically in the rubble, seeking something substantial to hit him with, anything, a desperation now in her efforts to free herself. But the world might as well have been deaf, blind and dumb for all the good her cries made.

The butler who answered the door at Henry's house on Serpentine Road was not, at first, particularly helpful. He looked down his nose at Jack and informed him that he had no right to even set foot on their front doorstep, that he should use the servant's entrance at the back or better still remove himself from the premises altogether. He soon changed his tune, however, once Jack had slammed him up against the door-frame and threatened him with a clenched fist, and had finally admitted that the master was in fact visiting Mr Josiah at Angel House.

'You could have saved us both a great deal of time and trouble had you told me that in the first place.'

Jack heard Livia's cries long before he reached the house. All the lights were blazing in the front drawing room, although one glance through the window as he charged past revealed that it was empty. He couldn't see Livia anywhere, but he headed for the side of the house, in the direction of those desperate cries, instinct driving him on.

The glass door to the conservatory was locked so he smashed it with his fist to reach for the lock inside and open it. Jack swept aside palms and ferns, trampled a particularly rare orchid, which Livia's mother had once nurtured, and she had cherished because of that. He broke through the jungle of Edwardian horticulture only to be presented with the sight of Henry's bare backside mooning before him. And beneath the mound of his gross body, amidst the soil and broken shards of pottery, lay Livia.

Jack didn't stop to think. He didn't pause to consider that this was his employer he'd caught in the act of rape. He grabbed hold of his shirt collar and dragged Hodson off. When his fist connected with the flabby jaw there was a crack which resounded satisfyingly loud in the confined space. He followed it with a second, and then a third, and kept on punching and thumping, a red mist forming before his eyes as his temper got the better of him.

Hodson sank to his knees. Caught off guard by the sudden unexpectedness of the attack, and failing to return a single punch, he begged for mercy. But then a man was hardly in a position to throw decent punches with his trousers around his ankles.

The final blow landed squarely, breaking Hodson's nose and sending blood spurting everywhere. Henry went down like a felled tree, legs sprawling in a most undignified fashion. Jack wasted no time over him, one glance at Livia cowering among the shards of broken pottery and shredded plants making his heart plummet. She was weeping uncontrollably, desperate little gasps and sobs as he gathered her into his arms, his worst fears confirmed. Had he arrived too late? Hodson must surely have done the deed, slaking his lust on her, as he'd always intended.

Chapter Thirty-One

Ella had made many changes at Todd Farm. With water now piped to the dairy and the outhouse next door, she designated the latter as the washhouse. Amos, with the help of Tom Mounsey, installed the boiler Ella had also bought at the farm sale, which provided masses of hot water for the washing. It was still rather primitive, a fire needing to be lit beneath it well in advance and kept well stoked with wood, but far better than boiling up shirts and sheets in the old tin pan on the rattencrook hanging over the fire. Ella now insisted that Amos change his shirt every Wednesday, as well as Mondays, and keep a special one for Sundays.

She'd given the walls of the kitchen a fresh coat of limewash, scrubbed out every drawer and cupboard, and set the prettiest pieces of pottery out on the dresser shelves. She even added a display of rowan twigs bright with berries in a blue jug on the table. The whole place looked so much cleaner and tidier, as if someone cared for it at last.

'I might sew some cushions for the settle.' She glanced across at her husband, rather anxiously. 'What do you think, Amos? Would you mind?'

'Why would I mind?' he asked, his face as inscrutable as ever.

'Esther didn't care for cushions, did she?'

After the smallest pause, he said, 'It's not Esther's kitchen any more, it's yours.'

Ella felt a small glow of happiness inside at these words.

Mrs Jepson came round regularly and helped Ella to stock the larder with pickles and jams and preserves, bottled plums and damsons, all ready for the coming winter. She even managed to nudge more effort out of Mrs Rackett, by gently bullying the old woman out of her chair now and then to help.

The dairy was scrubbed scrupulously clean every single day, and Ella finally put her foot down over the rats in the barn, which were growing in number. 'They'll be infesting the house soon if you don't do something to get rid of them.'

Amos regarded her in that quiet, thoughtful way of his, the shadow of a smile twitching the corners of his mouth. Then he called in Tom Mounsey with his two terriers, and the rats were duly dealt with in speedy fashion.

Ella had come to love the dale, almost welcomed its quiet solitude, her fear of it quite gone. She no longer felt overawed by the steep slopes of Froswick and Ill Bell, the cold greyness of Rainsborrow Crag or the fickleness of the weather that would soak her almost dry sheets in seconds. She loved the constant gurgle of water as it rushed in ever widening rivulets down to the River Kent. Nor did she mind the boggy ground that would catch her unawares and suck off her boots, the silent watchful sheep or the dour black cattle. These elements that had once alarmed her now seemed to be a vital part of its wild, magical beauty.

She had her own secret places and would walk out most days either up to the waterfall by the reservoir or down to the packhorse bridge in the hope of spotting salmon swimming upriver to spawn, were it the right time of year. She'd call out to the men toiling at the old quarry workings as she passed by, although was sufficiently mindful of Amos's feelings not to venture too near. She knew where the badger setts were, could differentiate easily now between a buzzard and an eagle, mistaking neither for a vulture, and liked nothing better than whiling away a happy half hour sitting by the river watching an otter at play.

Ella loved everything about the dale: the yellow lichen that crusted the dry stone walls, the mists that feathered the mountaintops. She loved the way the bracken formed patches of russet amidst the grey jumble of rocks, looking for all the world like splashes of paint from an artist's palette. The valley was to Ella a place of beauty, a perfect haven of peace and tranquillity.

And she'd also come to love this ready-made family of hers.

Life at Todd Farm was most definitely improving

for the better. If only she could say the same for her marriage.

On this particular afternoon they were down at the riverbank, celebrating Emmett's eighth birthday. Amos no longer expected Ella to share in his love for fishing, although he considered it much more than simply a sport when it produced a fine plump trout for their tea. He would occasionally ask if she'd like to help by passing him the net.

Today, since this was a special occasion, Ella had brought a picnic and Emmett and Tilda were giggling and having fun as they dabbled in the shallows, hoping to catch a trout with their bare hands. Tickling, they called it. Amos had bought his son a rod for his birthday and had spent the past hour teaching him how to use it. Now he seemed content to let the boy play, a sign of the more relaxed way in which Amos was treating both his wife and his children.

Ella lay back on the grassy bank, smiling at the antics of a red squirrel performing its acrobatic tricks among a cluster of ash and larch. Beth, the Border collie, was flopped beside her, as she so often was these days. The old dog largely left all the chasing about to the younger dogs now, confining her energies to a little gentle chivvying of the sheep, which never seemed to tire her. But when the master was engrossed in some occupation that did not include her, Ella was her first choice of substitute now.

The sky was a rain-washed blue on this lovely autumn day, marred only by a few streaks of white cloud that very much resembled the skeleton of a fish, filling Ella with a deep contentment. Life was good, on the whole, yet deep in her heart she was aware of a growing ache. She longed for a child of her own, if only her husband could love her enough to help her make one.

Mrs Rackett was dozing, but without opening her eyes she suddenly said, 'Patience is a double-edged sword. On the one side good enough to blunt pain, but on the other it can cut off the hand that wields it. Sometimes, thee has to grasp the metal and fight for what you want.'

Ella looked up at the old woman, startled. Was she a witch, able to read unspoken thoughts? And what did she mean exactly with this talk of a double-edged sword? It was typical of the sort of rambling nonsense she often spouted, yet there was a certain twisted logic to it. Was Ella being too patient waiting for Amos to make the first move? Should she object to his still stubbornly climbing those stairs to the attic every night? Should she grasp the metal, or was it the nettle, however the proper saying went?

And if she did, would he reject her again, as he had once before? Dare she try one more time, or might she live to regret taking the risk? Ella decided she needed to think a little more about this to be sure it was what she wanted.

Amos caught three fine trout which would provide them with a splendid meal later. Once the fish were properly dealt with and safely stowed away in his basket, Ella spread the cloth and got out the fresh bread she'd baked specially that morning, the cheese and pickles, spicy currant pasties, and the children's favourite, a

Victoria jam sponge. On this occasion it was smothered with white icing in honour of Emmett's birthday. She placed eight tiny candles on the top, ready to light when the moment of celebration arrived.

They feasted well, the children happily chatting about school and the favourite meals that their aunt would sometimes make for them during the week.

'Aunty Molly is very kind but she isn't as good a cooker as you, Ella.'

'Cook, not cooker. Though I'm quite certain she is. She has been doing it for years, while I am still learning.'

'Then you are a very able student,' Amos said, biting into the crusty bread spread liberally with Ella's own butter. As always, the rare compliment brought a flush to her cheeks. His mouth lifted slightly into the ghost of a smile, transforming his usually plain face into one that, if not exactly handsome, was filled with kindness and joy. A look that warmed her heart. Then his gaze shifted to linger upon her mouth, before he turned quickly away to cut himself another chunk of cheese. Ella felt suddenly flustered and her heart skipped a beat.

Quite out of the blue, or perhaps as a means of changing the subject, she asked a question that had been on her mind for some time. 'Why don't the children go to the little school in the valley, the one down by Kentmere Hall? Wouldn't it be marvellous to have them home with us all the time?'

'It's too far to walk every day,' Amos grumbled.

'I wouldn't mind taking them and bringing them back.

Wouldn't you like to live at home?' she asked them, seeing how their little faces had lit up at her suggestion. But they glanced anxiously across at their father, not quite brave enough to agree that they would.

'And what about when it rains? Look what happened when Tilda got soaked that time. Do you want her to get sick again?'

'Of course not,' Ella said, but she could see that he'd made a valid point. She turned the problem over in her head as she nibbled her bread and butter. 'I don't suppose we could buy a pony and trap? I could handle one of those so much better than the big farm cart. Wouldn't that make things easier? Or you could buy us a fell pony each next time there's an auction. I can ride, you know. Father paid for me to have lessons. That's something good he did do for me.' She looked at him hopefully but Amos made no response, just kept on stolidly eating his bread and cheese.

'If I had a trap, I could take the eggs and cheese into Kendal myself, without troubling Mrs Jessop,' she mused. 'Or we could go in together, she and I, taking turns to drive. It really is time I took more responsibility for the marketing, don't you think, Amos? And I'm sure I'd be perfectly safe, so long as I didn't go in the heat of the summer when there might be fever about. I know my way around very well, of course, having been brought up there.'

He looked at her, frowning, saying nothing.

'What do you think?' Her heart was pounding, wondering if she dared hope.

'I'll take you into Kendal again, if that's what this is all about.'

'Oh, but you've said that before and then something crops up and it gets forgotten. I know you're busy, but I only had an hour last time. I've had a letter from Livia, begging me to come, wanting me to spend longer next time. Oh, and Tilda is in dire need of new boots before winter sets in.'

'We'll go in to market next week,' he suddenly agreed, his lips twitching at the corners again, as if holding back a smile. 'I was, in any case, thinking of getting you some extra help in the house, and mebbe I'll take on a hired man.'

'Really? Oh, that would be wonderful.' Ella clapped her hands with joy, startled and pleased by his generosity, suddenly filled with excitement at the prospect of a trip into town. 'How wonderful! Something to look forward to. Now I shall light the candles, and you must blow them all out at once, Emmett, for luck. Oh, you are so good to me, Amos,' and leaning over the cake, she kissed him soundly. The children laughed out loud with delight.

Livia refused to speak of what had happened, hadn't even cried, wouldn't allow herself to show the slightest sign of weakness. She bottled up the pain deep inside, and nothing would persuade her to pick the scab off the sore and examine it. What right did she have to complain, or feel sorry for herself? Her father had done worse to his own daughter, who was now dead because of his brutality and abuse.

Yet despite her brave show and apparent outward calm, Livia was not coping well. She remained deeply shocked by the assault, and felt strangely vulnerable, not at all her usual confident self as she cycled out on her days off. She'd keep nervously glancing back over her shoulder, worried that he might be following her.

Livia had never seen the world as benign, or a particularly safe place, all too aware from her experiences at the hands of a brutish father that you had only to scratch the surface to find evil within. But she'd believed this sort of misery, so far as her own safety was concerned, was largely confined to the tower room in Angel House. Now she saw violence as endemic. It was everywhere, touching everyone. Whom could she trust, if not an old friend like Henry, or even her own darling Jack, who had completely over-reacted?

She was deeply thankful that Henry hadn't succeeded in committing rape, although it had been a near thing. Her fingers scrabbling through the shards of pottery had finally located a large, heavy pot, which she'd used to hit him over the head. He'd already been half-stunned when Jack had come smashing his way into the conservatory on his mythical white charger to rescue her.

As a consequence of this heroic act, or rather of the beating he'd given his employer, Jack had lost his job at Hodson's Hosiery factory. It had been the first thing Henry said when he'd come round, all too quickly. Livia had been furious with Jack for that, and she'd turned on him the moment they reached the loft on Fellside.

'I could have managed perfectly well. There was really

no need for you to come charging in like a bull in a china shop.'

'There was every need. He was *raping* you for God's sake!'

Livia was alarmed to find that she was actually shaking, and her teeth were chattering as if with the cold, yet she answered robustly enough. 'I'd already socked him one with a plant pot.'

'He could easily have recovered and finished what he'd started.'

'Nevertheless, you overdid it. There was really no need for you to hit him quite so many times. I cannot abide men who have no control over their temper.'

Livia was thinking of her own father, of all the times while they were growing up that he'd lashed out and hurt his daughters, and the damage he'd caused them to this day. The thought that Jack might prove to have the same problem with his temper sickened her. Livia loathed violence. She feared it, half suspected it might be prevalent in all men by their very nature. She certainly seemed destined to have her life blighted by it.

Unfortunately, Jack didn't see things in quite the same way, and couldn't understand why she was angry with him and not Henry. He instantly took offence. 'Oh, so I should have just stood back and let him assault you, should I?'

'I'm perfectly capable of looking after myself.'

'It didn't look that way to me. You should never have gone to see your father, not alone. You should have waited for me to come with you.'

'You aren't always right, Jack Flint. You don't have to play Sir Galahad for me.'

'Now there's gratitude for you. I'll remember not to bother next time.' And he'd stormed off in a huff, slamming the door behind him.

Jessie had taken no part in this argument, nor chastised Livia for putting herself in such a vulnerable position. The poor girl had surely suffered enough already. She'd set about boiling water, calmly filling the hip bath and tenderly bathing her, ready to hold her close when she sobbed. But Livia hadn't shed a single tear, not then or since.

Livia felt as if her whole world was falling apart, her life in turmoil. She was in danger of losing the man she loved, her father was controlling her life as much as ever, and she really didn't know what to do for the best. Henry might have failed in his intention to impregnate her, but he'd certainly succeeded in driving a wedge between herself and Jack, one that seemed insurmountable.

It was, however, only too clear who was really to blame for all of this, who the real perpetrator of the crime was. The attack hadn't been Henry's idea at all. He'd been egged on by her father, had admitted as much even as he'd pawed at her with his fat, greedy fingers. Henry had been talked into using violence in order to get her pregnant, which he'd naively believed would compel her to accept that fateful walk to the altar.

There was no doubt in Livia's mind that the root cause of all of this was her father's need for money. Henry must have some hold over him, some financial or political clout, or else her father needed a stash of cash to pay off some gambling debt or other. Livia was well aware of his weakness for gaming, to which it seemed she must now add a fondness for women too. And, in custom with his usual way of doing business, he was offering his own daughter as merchandise in return for some favour or other. No doubt he considered the exchange a fair bargain. Did she imagine she didn't have the wit to understand how his vile mind worked?

But how to defeat him? That was the question. The only effective way must be to publicly denounce him and reveal to the people of Kendal what a debauched, depraved brute he really was. The question was, did she possess the necessary courage to take him on? And was there any hope that she'd win, or would she succeed only in destroying herself in the process?

Chapter Thirty-Two

Throughout the long days that followed, Livia was finding it increasingly difficult to keep up the pretence that nothing unpleasant had occurred. This dark unnamed fear seemed to grow inside her like a canker, and she couldn't rid herself of a constant sense of unease and anxiety. She felt dirty, violated, even though she'd been spared the worst. She almost wished that she could cry, then she might dislodge this solid pain that seemed to have lodged itself somewhere below her breast bone.

And the peace she'd strived so hard to achieve following Maggie's death was now lost.

Livia understood that she could have Henry charged with attempted rape, as Jack urged her to do. But she refused point-blank, and so they embarked upon their worst row yet.

'Why do you protect him?'

'I'm not, I'm protecting myself. I have no wish for my personal life to be bandied about, or appear in the gossip columns of some local rag.'

'It's *his* reputation that would suffer, not *yours*.'

'Henry would claim that I'd led him on, that I'd wanted him really. Rampant for it, as he himself accused me of. He'd say that I'd changed my mind at the last minute but then I'd hit him with the plant pot without allowing him the chance to retreat. Then you came charging in, hell-bent on attack, when really he'd already backed off. He'd accuse you of losing your temper and refusing to stop and listen. It's no good pretending otherwise, Jack. They'd believe him, not me.'

'Rubbish. Not all men are like your precious Henry!'

'He isn't *my precious Henry*, and please don't shout. So far as I can see, all men are exactly like my father. There's no question that he is the one behind this latest plot. Men are despicable, bad-tempered and foul-mouthed, born bullies and bursting with aggression. And their view of women is low, the only consolation being that women generally hold men in even worse contempt!'

She had to stop to catch her breath after this outburst, but her bitter words etched deep sadness in his face. He made no attempt to defend his gender, as she continued with her point.

'Consider how it will appear to anyone not aware of the true facts.' Livia held out her hands as if to plead with him. 'My father is supposedly grieving, having lost his youngest daughter in the most dreadful circumstances, yet I've left home and deserted him, for no reason anyone can quite understand. More shocking still, I'm having an affair with a man known for being a rabble-rouser, shamelessly behaving as if I were his wife when there is in fact no ring on my finger. I am, in their eyes, a fallen woman.

'Henry, on the other hand, is a respectable, prominent businessman in town. He owns a fine house where he lovingly cares for his widowed mother. Now who do you imagine they are most likely to believe? Forget it, Jack. It's simpler to say nothing and let it pass.'

Josiah was suffering more than Livia might have appreciated. He sat in his office at the back of the store with his head in his hands, not knowing which way to turn. Both the bank and Hodson were pressing him harder than ever, his choices reduced to either allowing the one to foreclose or the other to take him over lock, stock and barrel. And all because of a lack of a bit of ready cash, some liquid funds to buy himself out of a hole.

All he needed was sufficient money to pay off the mortgage and overdraft at the bank, plus the extra loan he'd foolishly taken out with Hodson. Why was that so difficult?

Falling into Henry's grasping, greedy hands had obviously been his undoing.

At two o'clock that afternoon, precisely on time, as promised, Henry called in to remind him that his patience was running thin. Josiah bluffed and blustered, insisting he needed more time, that he fully expected trade to pick up, and for his circumstances to improve.

'I've recently been asked to stand for Parliament, for God's sake,' he bawled, pointing out that he was a man of stature in the town, a man who was going places. 'I feel sure I'll be put forward for a knighthood next. I think you really should appreciate how very important I am.'

Henry merely smirked, then added insult to injury by calling him a has-been, a yesterday's man, with no future of any consequence, so far as he could see.

Josiah was outraged by this evident lack of respect from the younger man, and instantly went on the attack. 'How dare you speak to me in this manner, after all I've done for you? I've entertained you in my home, allowed you to court my daughter, acted like a father to you, for God's sake. I cannot believe you allowed her to get away! Why didn't you finish the job while you had the chance? Does red blood run in your veins, or only milk and water?'

This was not the first time Josiah had taken Henry to task over his failure to actually carry through his intentions and finish what he'd started with Livia. As on previous occasions, Henry refused to rise to the bait. He calmly placed his final demand on Josiah's desk, and clearly stated his terms.

'No bride, no further extension on the loan. I'll take the business instead, Josiah, and make more of it than you ever could. You have till the end of the year, two months from now, to vacate the premises, that's if the bank don't get you first.'

It was as simple as that.

As Hodson walked away, a decided swagger to his step, Josiah could barely contain his anger. He was incandescent with rage. Unwilling to resort to fisticuffs, since he'd be sure to lose, he instead took out his ire by sweeping everything off his desk in a fit of temper. He sent his letter tray, blotter, pens and pen holder, papers and ledgers, hurtling to the floor. Even the tray of tea and biscuits that Miss Caraway had brought them now lay in pieces on the rug.

Who did the fellow think he was, imagining he could walk in and take control of a person's life, his business, even his home, and all because he'd defaulted on a paltry debt! The man was a charlatan.

But losing his temper solved nothing, and Josiah had to admit he'd put his case with more bluster than logical argument. He'd never felt so beleaguered, as if his entire life were teetering on the brink of collapse. He was about to lose everything he'd ever worked for. A lifetime of effort lost. It was as if all his worldly goods had been put up for auction, about to be sold off to the highest bidder whether he liked it or not. And for the first time, Josiah knew he was not in control of his own destiny. Worse, he felt bone-weary, defeated by events.

Josiah was also furious to discover that Mercy had arrived back in Kendal, apparently fit and well and with a young man in tow, who, rumour had it, might or might not be her husband. He'd spotted the pair of them walking arm in arm along Highgate and had been quite unable to believe his own eyes. If that little brat started gabbing then the last precious bricks of his entire empire would fall about his ears. He'd be done for.

In stubborn defiance, and wishing to cock a snook at the bank, Hodson, and his recalcitrant daughters, the whole flaming lot of them, Josiah issued a further eviction notice, this time not just to the Flint family, but to every single occupant in Angel Buildings. He gave them the same terms that Henry had offered him. They had until Christmas to pay the new higher rent or get out. If he was going down, then he might as well take as many people as possible down with him.

The second eviction notice arrived later that same day, care of the weaselly little rent collector. Livia took it straight round to Mr Blamire, the family solicitor, her temper high as she slammed it down on his desk. 'My father has no right to do this.'

The solicitor considered the notice with ponderous care. 'I'm afraid he does, my dear.'

'No, I won't have it. Make him stop.'

The old solicitor sighed. 'I'll do my best, but he is within his rights to do as he pleases with his own property.'

The man had been their family lawyer for as long as Livia could remember, and always dealt with Josiah's affairs. Now she begged him to persuade her father to allow Jessie and her friends more time to find alternative accommodation. To be fair, the man looked as if he'd had no prior notice of the eviction notice, and confessed that he had no personal knowledge of Mr Angel's intentions with regard to the buildings he owned on Fellside.

Livia was adamant. 'Whatever his intentions, he cannot be allowed to treat people in such a draconian fashion. I beg you to help.'

Perhaps it was because he'd always been entranced by those gentian eyes, that perfect heart-shaped face and golden hair, or that he could still remember Livia as a small child smiling sweetly and thanking him politely for the mint humbug he would give her as she sat patiently waiting for her father to conduct his business. Whatever the reason, the old solicitor agreed to look into the matter for her, and naturally he wouldn't dream of charging her a penny. Hadn't he been the Angel family solicitor since time immemorial? Livia thanked him warmly, and was at last able to take her friends some real hope.

As a precaution, Livia went along to the town hall to ask about rooms to rent, and to the newly built Carnegie Library in case they too might have details of likely accommodation for the Flint family. Neither could offer any help other than the workhouse. Even the vicar had no useful suggestions to make beyond the obvious that she'd tried already, and Livia did not dare approach any of the charities in town over which the mayor held authority, since that would bring her into direct conflict with her father.

She was at least successful in helping them to launch their new business enterprise. Livia had sweet-talked Miss Caraway into buying some of Jessie's hand-knitted sweaters, which seemed to be selling modestly well in the sports department. These were thick and warm and popular with walkers. It wasn't enough, of course, as the profit on each garment was low, but it was a start. But they desperately needed to cut the cost of the basic material, the price of the raw wool still rising thanks to Henry's meanness.

'We need to buy direct from a farmer,' George suggested. He and Mercy were also helping with the knitting, George more in the way of fetching and carrying, although he seemed quite handy on the loom. They were still desperately seeking a room of their own to rent, one that wasn't running with damp or infested with cockroaches and vermin. Not an easy task, even in affluent Kendal, at the kind of rent they could afford to pay.

Livia thought this a good idea. 'Ella is coming on Friday afternoon, and staying over until Saturday. Did I mention it?'

'Only twenty times,' laughed Jessie.

'We could ask Amos. He might know of someone with good wool to sell.'

Livia was encouraging them to use a finer wool to knit fashionable cardigans and woollen jackets, and expressed a wish to one day see them invest in a knitting machine.

'Woollens will always be in fashion and there's absolutely no reason why you shouldn't build yourselves a good little business in time, Jessie. Maybe enough work for Mercy and George too, in due course. Let's hope the solicitor can keep Henry and my father off your backs. But we really must start looking for other outlets. Being dependent upon my father's store is not a good idea. If he ever found out that Miss Caraway was buying goods from us, he'd put a stop to it at once. I might cycle over to Windermere or Ambleside, and ask around the shops there.'

'That's a fair ride,' Jessie warned, looking concerned.

'Particularly with winter coming on. I don't reckon that'd be wise, not a woman on her own, on a bicycle.'

Livia frowned. 'Oh, if only we had better transport, which we'll need anyway for deliveries so far away. How I wish I had the wherewithal to help you all properly. I'd ask for a loan at the bank, except they'd be sure to tell Father.'

'You've done enough; we'll cope fine on us own,' Jessie told her, busily directing her older children in the art of cable stitch.

Sadly, Jack was less appreciative of her efforts. He was barely speaking to Livia these days, let alone cooperating with her on the new venture. Since being dismissed by Hodson, he'd found himself a job labouring on the same building site where George was working. Not at all what he wanted to do, but the best he could manage in the circumstances. Hodson seemed to have blacklisted him not only from his own hosiery factory but from those of his competitors as well.

Today, he listened to the conversation between Livia and his mother in silence, then caustically remarked, 'I can understand why *you* don't fear ending up in the workhouse. Obviously the threat of dire poverty wouldn't include you, one of the precious Angel girls. If things got really bad, you could simply swallow your pride and return home to your fine house at the top of the town. Or dear Henry might finally get his wish and you would agree to marry him after all.'

'Stop it, Jack. Why are you behaving like this? I

hate it when you're being deliberately cruel.'

He got to his feet, overwhelming the small loft suddenly with his glowering presence. 'Then have the bloody man arrested, Livia! Prove to me that the girl I fell in love with still exists.'

'I – I can't.'

'You mean you *won't*! I believe you *are* in love with him after all.'

'Don't be ridiculous!'

Jack shook his head in disgust. 'I never saw you as a snivelling coward,' and turning on his heel, he walked out.

It near broke Livia's heart for him to treat her with such cold disdain, as if he believed she'd deliberately welcomed Henry's attentions. How could she convince him that charging Henry would only create greater problems for everyone?

Yet there was a doubt growing in her mind. What if Jack had a point? Was she indeed behaving like a snivelling coward? Was her reluctance to charge Henry with attempted rape really because she thought his word was more likely to be believed than her own? Or was it simply fear that held her back? Did she think there was a risk that Henry, or more likely her father, might possibly try to attack her again? What had happened to her ebullience, her confidence, her courage? Had her father and Henry together effectively destroyed her, after all?

If Jack wouldn't help, and the family solicitor wasn't even able to prevent the Flint family from being thrown out onto the streets, what more could she do? Time was running out.

Oh, but Ella would be here for a visit at the end of the week, Livia thought, with a spurt of optimism. Perhaps she would have some ideas to offer.

Chapter Thirty-Three

It was Friday afternoon and the two sisters were delighted to be together again and sat with their arms about each other in the County Hotel, enjoying afternoon tea and happily exchanging news. It was just the three of them, as Ella and Amos had left the children with their Aunt Molly in Staveley. It was just as well, as Ella became quite distraught when she heard what Livia had suffered with the attempted rape. She was soon in tears as she listened to the tale, despite Livia having cut the details to the bare minimum.

'Look, I'm perfectly all right. He didn't finish the deed, thank God.'

'No, thank Jack for saving you.'

Livia bristled slightly. 'Actually, I'd already clocked Henry one over the head with a plant pot by the time Jack came galloping in, so was well on the way to saving myself.'

'Even so...' Ella said. 'It could have been much, much worse, had he not appeared just when he did.'

'Love and lust can do terrible things to a man,' Amos remarked, and they both turned to look at him, slightly startled by this quiet intervention.

'Have you reported Henry to the police?' Ella wanted to know. 'You really should, even if he didn't quite go through with it.'

'Oh, don't you start. Jack keeps on and on about that, but I'd really rather not involve them. He won't try again, I'm quite certain of it.' Livia instantly made the decision not to mention their father's role in all of this, except perhaps quietly to Ella later when they were alone. Since Amos was a fervent Methodist, he might well start preaching to her about the need to honour her father, something which was quite beyond them both.

Instead, she briskly changed the subject and began to tell them all about their efforts to find more work for the hand-knitters of Fellside. Livia described the range of goods they were hoping to offer, the orders they'd received so far and the problems involved in finding a wider market. Amos seemed quite interested and asked several pertinent questions concerning the costs involved, and their supplier.

'Ah, there's the rub. Henry is our only supplier, and so far we have been unable to find a reliable alternative.'

Amos rubbed his chin in that thoughtful way he had. 'I might be able to help you there. I know quite a few farmers who'd be only too happy to sell you wool direct. I could let you have a bundle or two meself.'

'Really? Oh, but that would be wonderful.'

'Have you somewhere to store it? A shed or summat?

It's best to buy it at clipping time, tha knows.'

'Oh, dear!' Livia shook her head, thinking hard. 'I hadn't thought of that. Until we get the accommodation problem resolved, perhaps the wool could be brought out a bundle at a time when the farmer in question was visiting Kendal market?'

Ella excitedly intervened at this point. 'Oh, I'm sure we can work something out. We could store the wool in our barn, and bring it out as you need it. I could do that, couldn't I, Amos?'

Amos looked at his wife, saying nothing. The details were finalised and they ordered a second pot of tea and buttered teacakes, to celebrate. When they were finally replete Livia offered to take them to meet Jessie and her brood.

As the two girls walked together arm in arm along Stricklandgate and up Allhallows Lane, Amos striding along ahead of them, Livia whispered, 'Mercy will be there.'

'Oh good, then I'll meet her at last. What is she like?'

'Spiky, still nursing some imagined resentment against us, and itching to take revenge on Father.'

'If you and I don't get to him first.'

Livia smiled wryly. 'I'm trying to win her round, little by little. We can but hope.' A short pause and then, 'Does Amos know she's our half-sister, and illegitimate?'

Ella flushed with embarrassment. 'Um, I haven't actually got around to explaining all of that yet. He can be very prissy about such things.'

'I see.' Another thoughtful frown. 'Don't you think it would be advisable to tell him? It doesn't seem quite right to have secrets between husband and wife. And he is part of our family now.'

'You're probably right, but it won't be easy. He'll feel duty bound to issue a lecture, and it won't help relations between himself and Father, although they've always got on surprisingly well. I'll wait till he's in a mellow mood, then I'll try telling him.'

'Good girl! We'd best keep off the subject today then, if we can.'

This presented no problem as Mercy kept remarkably silent while Jessie happily demonstrated and displayed her work to the visitors, making them all welcome even as she apologised for the humble nature of their home.

Livia hugged the older woman and told her the loft looked as clean as a new pin, and to stop fussing. Indeed it was evident that Jessie had taken considerable trouble to clear the straw pallets away into a neat stack, had scrubbed the floor and with no night soil bucket on view and the narrow window open to catch the breeze, the air was almost sweet, apart from the usual fog of lint which nothing would cure.

Amos seemed oblivious to the poverty of his surroundings and was getting on famously with Jessie. He was interested in comparing her loom with his own back at the farm, discussing the intricacies of the weave, and whether or not she used the jacquard pattern. He admired the finished woollen goods, and the knitting in progress.

Livia excitedly butted in to explain about Amos's offer to help supply raw wool, and they all began to discuss at some length the various benefits of short or long staple, Herdwick, Swaledale or Masham, and whether they'd be interested in investing in knitting machines one day.

Amos seemed appreciative of the happy hum of work among the older children, but couldn't resist expressing concern that perhaps the younger ones should have been in school.

'Education is important, Jessie,' he gently informed her.

'Amos, please,' Ella scolded. 'It's really none of your business.'

For once he looked chastened by his wife's words and swiftly apologised. 'I'm sorry, that was unpardonable of me. I've got too much into the habit of preaching, but Ella is teaching me the error of my ways.'

Everyone looked a little surprised by this confession, not least Ella herself.

'I'll take them tomorrow,' Jessie promised, giving a cheeky grin. 'Though they'd much rather stop at home and help with the knitting, till the work gets too hard, then they want to play. That's children for you.'

Amos actually smiled. 'My own are just as bad, and will do anything to avoid learning their letters. But they are healthy and strong, and that's what matters most, is it not? Ella is a good mother to them, although she too has had a great deal to learn since coming to live on the farm. Now she can make butter and cheese, preserves and excellent cakes, and has recently learnt to spin, isn't that right, Ella? She's made great progress these last months.'

Ella had been listening almost open-mouthed with astonishment to this string of compliments, and now found herself flushing bright pink as his gaze rested proudly upon her. Was Amos at last beginning to appreciate her efforts?

Later, over a glass of ginger beer, Jessie, Livia and Amos began to work out the details of the operation. Ella noticed Mercy huddled on a sack in the corner all by herself, clearly feeling rather left out, and went to sit with her to ask how she was, and if she'd found employment.

'Not yet,' Mercy mumbled, her mouth falling into the familiar sulk she always adopted whenever one of the Angel sisters was near.

'What would you like to do?'

'Huh, folk like me don't get to make choices in life. Only rich folk like you have that sort of power.'

Ella laughed. 'I'm not at all rich, but I agree that money does help you to have more opportunities in life. But I've also discovered that even if life doesn't go quite as you'd planned it, things can turn out to be surprisingly good in the end.'

She didn't notice Mercy's disbelieving scowl as she glanced across at her husband, still deep in conversation with Jessie and Livia. He looked really rather smart in his setting-out suit, as he called it. Farmers always dressed well when they came to town, and his hair was all slicked back and glossy instead of its usual tousled state, with very nearly a smile on his face. She again turned to smile at Mercy. 'It might take a bit of effort, of course. Then life can surprise you.'

'Or it can hammer you into the ground,' Mercy quipped.

At that moment Jack and George arrived home, tired after a long working day, and both damp from having stuck their heads under the pump outside, to rid themselves of the accumulated dust. George came over to Mercy and kissed her on the lips. 'Hello, love. How are you?'

Mercy wrapped her arms about his neck and kissed him right back, then uncurled herself from the straw pallet upon which she'd been sitting, and went to find some food for the two men.

Jessie was telling Jack about the plans they'd made for the supply of wool, and although he kept glancing across at Livia, she refused to meet his eye. George flopped down to sit cross-legged on the floor, and when Jessie asked him if he'd had a good day, he simply gave a philosophical shake of the head, as if that were a foolish question to ask.

Ella surprised everyone, particularly herself, by suddenly walking over to her husband, putting her hand on his arm and suggesting he take on George as his hired man.

'You were looking for someone anyway, and Mercy could perhaps help me in the house.' She didn't mention the nature of her relationship with the other girl, judging this wasn't the right moment. But then keeping family secrets was ingrained in Ella's nature, following years of living with a brutal father.

There was a small, stunned silence, one that was finally filled by Amos himself, who turned to George and asked if he had much experience. The younger man was on his feet in seconds talking of the work he'd done on his father's farm as a boy, then with Mercy on the farm out in the Langdales. 'I'm particularly good with sheep, but I can deal with cattle too.'

'Then you'll do for me,' Amos said, and his whole face creased into a wide grin as he stuck out a hand to shake on the deal. 'Looks like you were right to insist we come into town today, Ella. It's all worked out rather splendidly. I've a bit put by and wouldn't mind investing in this new woollen business. I'll let you have some wool, Jessie, to get you started, and you can pay me when the money starts coming in. If all goes well, we might try buying one or two of them new-fangled knitting machines. We must try to keep up with the times, mustn't we, my love?' he said, putting an arm about his wife's waist.

'Yes, indeed,' Ella agreed, somewhat weakly, since he'd never used any sort of endearment with her before. 'I suppose we must.' Really, this husband of hers never ceased to amaze her. He was a man with hidden depths.

They stayed at the County Hotel on Friday night (Amos for once having left his livestock in the care of a neighbour) and on Saturday, while Amos went off to deal with a matter of business, Ella took the opportunity to visit the store with her sister.

It was so exciting to have money to spend, a rare treat. She bought some boots and a new frock for Tilda, plus a little rag doll for her to dress up and cuddle. For Emmett she bought a warm blue checked shirt and a football. She didn't forget Amos and bought him a new cap and warm woollen scarf. She believed it was one that Jessie had knitted, so there was a double benefit in buying it. Ella took Mercy with her, and had her fitted for a dark blue day dress, although got little thanks for it.

'I'm quite happy with the one I've got.'

'But you'll need another to wear when that one's in the wash,' Ella sensibly pointed out. 'Or you can wear this one for church, if you like.'

Mercy sulked, obviously wanting to disagree but finding the argument irrefutable. Ella was almost relieved when the girl insisted on going back to Fellside, as she needed to pack up the few things she and George would be taking with them. As she watched her flounce off, the parcel tucked carelessly under her arm, Ella recognised that she wasn't going to be easy to live with, but prayed it would work out. She'd be glad of another woman's company as Mrs Rackett spent most of the day nodding in the chair.

After a few other essential purchases, Ella treated herself to a new blouse, and then the pair of them went upstairs to discuss the finer points of underwear. They giggled so much over camisoles and petticoats, it was almost like old times when they'd been girls together.

'Oh, I wish Maggie were here. She was so wise, so patient, and so good with advice when I needed it.'

'And what advice would you be asking her for now, were she here?' Livia gently enquired, knowing that she too missed her loving, affectionate sister. There wasn't a day that passed when her heart didn't ache for her.

'Oh, only for a suggestion on how to make my husband fall in love with me.'

'Ah,' said Livia, with a mischievous twinkle in her eye. 'I believe I might have an idea about that.'

One other purchase was made that day, but that was made by Amos. When they all met up again, preparatory to leaving, Ella discovered that he'd bought a pony and trap at the auction, exactly the right size for a woman to drive two children to and from school.

Ella could hardly speak for joy. She had never known such happiness, and, quite unable to help herself, she flung her arms about her husband's neck and kissed him most thoroughly. And he really didn't seem to object one bit.

Amos allowed her to drive it back to Kentmere herself, with him sitting beside her offering advice, of course, while George and Mercy followed in the old farm cart. Ella thought that life was really looking up at last, and she felt filled with a new optimism.

Chapter Thirty-Four

Josiah was standing behind his desk, the light from the green-shaded lamp on his desk casting a slanting shadow over her face. Despite the poor light Livia thought he looked ill, his complexion sallow, the brow deeply furrowed as he stared at her in grim silence. He was a big man, and seemed somehow larger than ever in the gloom.

She'd received the summons to come to his office only this morning, and had readily agreed. She felt safe enough here at the store, rather than at Angel house, and there was a great deal she needed to say to him. The last thing she wanted was to appear afraid. Livia straightened her spine and faced him.

'Good afternoon, Father, you wished to speak with me.'

'I wish to put an end to this stupid defiance of yours. I've waited long enough for you to come to your senses and do your duty, but I've finally reached the end of my patience.'

371

'Is that why you ordered Henry to assault me?' Livia had her hands clasped tightly at her waist, lest they trembled. She was determined not to allow him to see how very afraid she was.

'He had to find some way to get past that obstinate pride of yours.'

'By *raping* me?'

'Don't exaggerate! You've only yourself to blame. Had you done what was expected of you in the first place, it would not have been necessary for him to use such methods of persuasion.'

'*Persuasion*! Is that what you call it? You speak as if this were still the Dark Ages and I a mere chattel to be bought and sold in your feudal empire. Well, let me tell you, Father, that the world has moved on apace since then. I am my own woman and will marry or not as *I* choose, not simply to suit your purposes.'

'*You will do as I say*! How many more times must I tell you? You *will* marry Henry Hodson!'

She actually laughed in his face. 'What do you intend to do, drag me to the altar by my hair?'

'If necessary.' Josiah began to unbuckle his belt, and Livia's knees suddenly turned to jelly. Only by summoning every atom of will power did she manage not to reveal her fear. 'It will take more than brute force to make me do your bidding. Why are you doing this? Is it a debt? Has Henry threatened to take you over, or bankrupt you?'

She saw by the way his face became suffused by a terrifying purple rage that she'd guessed correctly. But then it hadn't been difficult to work out. Everything her father did always came down to money. His daughters' happiness had never been part of the equation.

He slapped the desk with the leather strap, scattering papers and ledgers everywhere, and making Livia jump. 'This is a family business, and like it or not, girl, you are a part of it.'

'Really?' She took a step towards him, fists clenched, the anger inside firing up to boiling point, as she'd known that it must one day. 'Only as a bargaining tool, a piece of merchandise to give away to your creditors in lieu of debt. But then why would I expect anything else from you? You've devoted your entire life to ruling our home with a rod of iron, determined to bend and subdue the women in your family to your will, no matter what the cost. You've beaten, bullied and abused us, your innocent daughters, for the crime of not being the son you always wanted. You betrayed my mother with God knows how many mistresses, and when the offspring of one turns up at your door asking for help, you lock her away and have her beaten too, just so that it never gets out that Councillor Angel, Mayor, and would-be Member of Parliament, has an illegitimate daughter.'

She could see how his face was working into a fury, but she didn't pause, not for a second.

'As if all of that wasn't enough to earn you a passport to hell, you order your own daughter to be raped in order to force her into marriage with the man who is threatening to make you bankrupt.' Her face contorted with disgust and rage, she spat the words at him. 'You are despicable! Depraved! Debauched! Vile! I can't find words bad enough to describe you. Just being in the same room with you makes me want to vomit.'

She half turned away, as if about to leave, but filled with a demonic fury he lashed out at her with the strap. By some instinct, some inner resolve never to submit to his bullying again, Livia lifted her arm at just the right moment, and with one vicious tug caught the strap, dragging it from his hand and into hers.

Josiah roared his fury like a lion deprived of its kill.

Livia thought of Maggie hanging from that banister, of her mother choosing to end her days in a drugged haze rather than face the day-to-day reality of a blighted marriage. She thought of Henry's fat questing fingers, and the urge to strike out and put an end to that agony, to have her revenge at last, was overpowering.

But she couldn't do it.

Not because she was afraid; she wasn't, not any more. She saw her father for what he was: a miserable, pitiful creature, quite incapable of loving anyone but himself. Revenge would solve nothing and only make her as bad as him. She tossed the strap away with a contemptuous curl to her lip.

'I'll be damned if I'll sink to your level. I'm worth more than that. But don't you dare come near me ever again, and keep Henry away too, or I'll shout all your dirty little secrets from the rooftops.'

Then she turned on her heel and walked away.

There was nothing strange or new about the work expected of Mercy on Todd's Farm. The cows needed milking in exactly the same way as those on the farm in the Langdales, the dairy operated a similar routine, and the ground needed tilling for vegetables with exactly the same kind of hoe, the weeds growing just as fast. And when she wasn't found work to do on the land or in the dairy, there was always the house to sweep, the pans to scrub, although what that lazy old woman, Mrs Rackett, did all day was quite beyond her.

As Mercy settled into the loft over the barn, hanging their few clothes on hooks in the wall, setting out the hairbrush she'd bought for herself, she embarked upon these daily duties with grudging resignation. This was not where she wished to be, although if it made George happy then she would tolerate it, at least for now.

George was still a flirt and a practical joker. He was good looking and likeable, and couldn't resist putting on an act, particularly to a new and grateful audience. Whether it was wearing a dress and pretending to be stupid, or chatting up Nurse Bathurst so that she would allow him some treat or other, it was like a performance.

Now he made a bee-line for Ella's vulnerability. Perhaps he recognised her innate loneliness, her desperate need for company and attention, and took advantage of it.

He would always be there for her if she needed water carrying, or logs stacking. He'd tell her how beautiful she looked of a morning, even when she was pale and tired with anxious bruises beneath her eyes. He'd flatter her about her cooking, no matter if there was gristle in the stew or her cakes had gone flat. And he'd stop whatever job he was doing in an instant, simply to take the time to talk to her, which her husband rarely seemed to find time to do.

Mercy had been paying careful attention and without doubt Amos neglected his wife. He never praised a meal she cooked for him, or told her she looked nice even when she'd clearly gone to a great deal of effort to please him. He took her entirely for granted, as if she were a paid servant and not his wife at all. Yet he watched her with a smouldering look in his eyes whenever she wasn't looking his way. She couldn't quite work out what was wrong between the pair of them, but something most certainly was. No wonder she lapped up the extra attention George gave her.

But if that madam thought she could steal her man, she was very much mistaken. Just let her try and she'd rue the day, half-sister or no.

It was also infuriating that Ella had made a point of explaining that she must not mention the fact she was illegitimate. Mercy had instantly taken offence, and told this so-called sister of hers, quite bluntly, that she had nothing to be ashamed of.

Ella had looked quite distressed. 'I wasn't implying that you had, only Amos is so – so very condemning over any issue concerning morals. I will tell him, as soon as I find the right moment, I swear. Until then, I'd be grateful for your discretion.'

Mercy took her revenge by being deliberately uncooperative. If Ella asked her to feed the calves, she would linger over her breakfast, coming to the task in her own good time. She would pretend not to understand

and pour the milk into the wrong dishes, taking great pleasure in seeing Ella fall into a panic because her system had gone all wrong. Serve the silly woman right for having had things easy up until now. Mercy didn't believe half those tales Livia had told her about beatings, or locking her in a cage. More likely the result of a fanciful imagination than plain fact. No father would treat his daughters thus.

What reason did Ella have to complain? She'd lived in a fine house with servants to do her every bidding, her every whim indulged, provided with beautiful clothes to wear, money to spend and delicious food to eat. Meanwhile, Mercy's own mother, and herself too, had nought but rags on their backs and been near starvation more times than she cared to recall. She saw it as only justice if now this pampered girl was obliged to toil long and hard on the farm. Do her good to suffer for a change.

If Mercy could find any way of making things more difficult for this half-sister of hers, then she would do so.

Just a week or two after starting work on the farm Mercy spotted her best opportunity yet for revenge. Naughty George was lingering in the barn chatting to Ella when really he should have been taking the cows back to the pasture and checking on the sheep and cattle. So when she saw Amos approaching, Mercy made a great show of quickly shutting the door, as if she didn't want him to see inside.

'Can I help you, sir?' she asked in all innocence, bobbing a curtsey and appearing flustered.

Amos frowned. 'I don't believe so, Mercy. Is there some problem?'

'No sir, not that I know of.' It was demeaning having to do all this 'yes sir, no sir,' nonsense, bobbing and curtseying when really the man was no better than she was, and her brother-in-law to boot. Mercy stubbornly blocked his way. 'Begging yer pardon, sir, only I wouldn't go in there, if I were you.'

'Why not?'

'Ooh, it's not my place to say, sir...only...you might see summat that would upset you.' Mercy flapped her hands and put on a great show of being caught out. 'I just wouldn't, sir, that's all.'

Amos set her firmly to one side and pushed it open. He saw them at once: his wife and his hired man. They were standing close together and she was gazing up at him, a flush on her lovely cheeks, *while his hand was on her hair*. Amos saw how they instantly leapt apart when they heard the door open, Ella's eyes wide and frightened. Then she came running over, looking flustered, asking if he needed anything. Amos glared at her, then turning on his heel, strode away.

Mercy crept back to the kitchen, a secret smile on her face.

Ella was devastated by what had just occurred. What bad luck that Amos should choose to walk in at just that inopportune moment? George had been commenting that she looked tired, insisting that she take more rest now he and Mercy were here to help. Suddenly there he was, framed in the doorway, glaring at them both. She'd felt like a defenceless rabbit transfixed by the beam of a torch.

She had to admit that it had looked bad. George had been tucking a stray curl behind her ear, which he'd really had no right to do. Yet nothing had been going on. They'd only been talking, although admittedly she'd been tempted to open her heart perhaps more than she should. But then George was a good listener, and most sympathetic to her plight.

Ella wasn't in the least tempted by his flirting, or believed a word of his silly flattery, much as it might make her blush at times. More importantly she'd no wish to betray Amos, or harm her relationship with him, so why had she foolishly leapt away when he'd walked in upon them like that, making it appear as if they were guilty when that was definitely not the case?

Why hadn't she remained calm and simply walked over to him with a smile, as any loving wife would?

Ella's one preoccupation was to try and find a way to win over her husband. He wasn't an easy man, but he was honest and good. She knew that he came from a long line of yeoman stock, an independent breed with a strong sense of what was right and wrong. Amos involved himself in church and community affairs because, no doubt, his father before him had done so. Such men would often take on the role of constable, churchwarden, or justice of the peace, sit on juries or help collect rates. Yet this could often make them somewhat condemnatory of others' faults.

She'd thought recently that Amos was slowly beginning to relax and not be quite so quick to judge, and was learning to show his feelings, little by little. He was a kind man, albeit one with problems.

After her talk with Mrs Jessop, Ella had come to understand her husband better. He spoke less often of Esther, and didn't follow his first wife's rules quite so blindly. He'd even stopped endlessly quoting the scriptures at her. Then there was the surprise purchase of the pony and trap, and the fact he'd started to pay her a few compliments. Ella had really become quite optimistic of things starting to improve between them.

Now she'd ruined everything.

That night, for the first time since he'd made love to her in the attic, Amos came to her bed. Ella could hardly believe it when she heard his hand on the latch. She was excited and terrified all at the same time. What had inspired him to come? Was it out of jealousy? She wondered if she should reassure him that what he'd witnessed in the barn had been perfectly innocent, that she wasn't in the least attracted to George. And yet reminding him of that scene could be a mistake, making more of the incident than it rightly deserved. He might see her protestations as yet another sign of guilt, as if she needed to defend herself.

Oh, but she wanted so much to please him. She wanted a proper marriage and a husband who loved her. She wanted a child.

While Amos went through his usual ritual of washing, and a lengthy prayer on his knees, head bowed, Ella slipped quietly out of bed and drew from the chest the nightgown Livia had persuaded her to buy. It was a deep blush pink with an edging of coffee-coloured lace around the low-cut neckline and short sleeves, quite unlike the modest white cotton nightgown she normally wore, which covered her from neck to toes. Within minutes she'd changed and was back in bed, the sheet flung back so that as he reached to turn off the oil lamp on the side table he looked at her for the first time.

His mouth fell open, his gaze riveted to the rapid rise and fall of her breasts above the low cut neckline. Ella, breathless with hope and excitement, smiled up into his face. 'I'm so pleased you came, Amos. I've been hoping for so long that you would.'

Even as she spoke what she meant to be soft words of encouragement, she saw his face tighten with displeasure. His next words stunned her.

'Is that what you wore when you cavorted with Danny Gilpin, and with George? Did you enjoy making me jealous so that I'd fall for your shameless tricks too? Just look at you. Like a whore of Babylon in that get-up. Where is your dignity, woman, your decency? You disgrace yourself and me by such wanton behaviour.' And having delivered these blisteringly cruel words, he picked up the lamp and returned to the attic. Ella put her face in her hands and sobbed her heart out.

Chapter Thirty-Five

There was snow powdering the fells as Amos drove into Kendal the next morning, although it was only November. The hills were pin-sharp in the luminescent light, the river dancing at their feet, surging along with a chuckling glee on this first winter's morning. Amos did not share its joy. He'd spent a miserable night alone in the attic going over everything in his head. Had he over-reacted? Did he see fault where none existed? Why should loving her shame him so?

He remembered what he'd felt when he'd first seen Ella with her pale silver hair and green-grey eyes. He'd been entranced by her silky skin, the wide loving smiles she'd shared with her sisters. How he'd longed to have that smile turn upon him. It had been at some function or other at Angel House that he'd first seen her, a time when Josiah had been in the business of buying land. Those plans didn't seem to have come to fruition after all, and now his own marriage seemed destined to fail.

Yet why had he imagined she would come willingly

to his home, an isolated farm, and to his bed? He was a plain, dull farmer with nothing to recommend him at all, and she was a beautiful young woman.

And what had possessed him to think he could trust her? She was a woman. Weren't all women sinners? Hadn't she herself confessed to loving another, a Danny Gilpin?

Amos had prayed long and hard to his God, and finally vowed he could overcome any doubts and concerns he might have on the wisdom of this union. He'd wanted her, and foolishly believed he could make her happy, that she might at least come to love his children.

Now she was making eyes at another man in his own home, his own barn, and dressing like a hoyden, a harlot no less. Perhaps he shouldn't have reacted quite so strongly last night, but he'd been haunted by the thought of her wearing that very same garment with *him*, her paramour. He'd had a sudden vision of the pair of them cavorting together in that very same bed, perhaps while he was out tending the sheep. Hadn't he suffered enough? All he'd wanted to do last night, felt able to do, was to run from that knowing invitation in her eyes.

He'd spent a sleepless night, endlessly tossing and turning, feeling out of his depth, and not having the first idea what to do next. He'd risen at dawn and driven the cart into town to ask his father-in-law for help. Someone had to knock some sense into his silly young wife's head, since she showed no sign of listening to him. Who better to turn to than her own father?

* * *

Josiah listened to the tale Amos told him in aggrieved silence, enraged that yet another of his daughters was about to become involved in a scandal. What was wrong with them all? As if he didn't have enough on his plate to worry about right now without Ella creating mayhem.

Only this morning he'd received notice that the bank had frozen his accounts. They were about to appoint a receiver to look closely into his finances. He no longer had any say over the future of his own home, let alone Angel's Department Store. One or both could be sold off at a knock-down price to the highest bidder, in order that the bank, and various other creditors, could have their pound of flesh. It made Josiah sick to his stomach to see his fortunes sink so low. Very soon, when word of his financial difficulties got out, his humiliation would be plain for all to titter and gossip over.

The only consolation, so far as Josiah could see, was that Hodson wouldn't benefit from his downfall. His rival had sent round a note this morning saying that he was off to foreign climes, seeking a new future and a second fortune on the Riviera, for the sake of his dear mother's health. Hah, a likely tale! Running for cover more like, after what he'd done to Livia, or rather failed to do. No doubt terrified she might spill the beans. Serve him right for not finishing the job properly and bringing her to heel as intended. Good riddance to bad rubbish, in Josiah's opinion.

Unfortunately, Hodson's departure had not come soon enough to save the day, but at least the man wouldn't get his hands on Angel's Department Store. That dratted loan never would get repaid now, not if Josiah had any say in the matter.

There was at least some satisfaction in that.

But this could all have been so easily avoided, if only Livia had been more accommodating, and if Maggie had not carried out the ultimate disgrace. And if that workhouse brat hadn't come into his life, threatening to ruin his reputation completely. Now Ella was about to embark upon an affair with some labourer her husband had hired.

Damnation! It was more than any father should be asked to endure. Would his daughters never learn to behave with proper decency?

His first reaction was to deny responsibility, on the grounds it was up to Ella's husband to control her now, not her father. But then Amos made an interesting remark which brought him up short.

'I'd foolishly imagined that things were getting better between us, so much so that I'd taken on extra help in the house and dairy: a girl called Mercy. I also took on her husband George as a hired hand to work with me on the farm. The girl is only seventeen or eighteen, young to be married, but I've checked the marriage certificate and I'm satisfied the union is genuine. Now this George has the gall to take a fancy to my wife. I saw them together the other day and I was sickened by the way he was touching her and she was lapping up the attention. I swear I'm at my wits' end.'

Josiah became very quiet. Surely there couldn't be more than one girl of that name in Kendal? It was not a common one. Clearing his throat, he idly enquired. 'Where did you meet them, this couple?'

'It was Livia who introduced them to me at her friends' house, and I thought...I mean...they seemed perfectly respectable and...' Amos stopped, frowning, the first seeds of doubt forming in his mind. Had he said something wrong? Should he perhaps not have mentioned Livia, or her friends? He knew there was some form of estrangement between both girls and their father, something to do with their sister Maggie's death, although why they should blame him for the girl's suicide he had no idea. They had not told him the full tale and he had not asked, presuming it to be private, family business.

Josiah smiled. 'Friends of Livia's, you say? Then you may well be right that they are indeed respectable, although they could simply be some of her lame ducks. I'll have a word with Ella, if you wish. Try to find out what's going on, and remind her of the need to appreciate how very fortunate she is to have such a good husband. It's time the lass grew up.'

Amos sighed with relief, and instantly stopped worrying about Livia. She was not his concern in any case. Didn't he have enough to worry about with Ella, his lovely wife, whom he seemed to be losing just when he'd thought they were growing close at last? If Josiah could help, what more could he ask? He didn't give a thought to Mercy. Why would he? She was nothing but a dairymaid, so far as Amos was concerned.

'Thank you, Father-in-law. I would greatly

appreciate your assistance in this delicate matter.'

'Consider it done.'

Nothing on God's earth would prevent Josiah from taking this opportunity to finally deal with that misbegotten child and at least spare himself the ignominy of any further scandal.

That same afternoon, Josiah was sitting in Ella's parlour drinking tea and eating her damson pie. Ella was wondering why she'd ever felt afraid of him. He was nothing more than a sad old man. He looked deeply weary, his flabby cheeks drooping even more than usual, the eyes more twisted, the mouth slack rather than firm and determined. He seemed to have aged noticeably since last she'd seen him, but she felt not a jot of sympathy for him.

Ella sat, spine rigid, with not even a polite smile to lighten her own grim expression. Nor did she pay much attention to whatever it was he was saying to her, something about how she should appreciate her good fortune, that she mustn't create a scandal or misbehave, be a good little wife and other such nonsense. As if she would have the opportunity to be anything else out here in the back of beyond, even had she wanted to misbehave! Which she didn't, in point of fact. But how could she be a good wife if her husband wouldn't come near her?

She'd felt quite ill today, hardly able to comprehend that it had all gone wrong for them yet again. She kept hearing those words Amos had used, '*whore of*

Babylon'. What on earth did he mean? What was so wrong with wearing a pretty nightgown? She hadn't even realised she was making a mistake simply by trying to look nice for him. Wasn't she even allowed to be feminine, to enjoy being a woman now that she was a farmer's wife? A preacher's wife! She felt quite tearful at the thought, and very afraid. How would she ever reach him when he was so *good*, so morally upstanding, so bloody perfect?

Now to be forced to sit here in her own parlour and be lectured by her father was too much. Had Amos said something to him about their difficulties? She'd never forgive him if he had.

Ella watched with dismay as Mrs Rackett served Josiah a second slice of damson pie, glaring fiercely when she cut it extra large with a generous portion of cream, and banished her with a look. The older woman crept away, back to the kitchen. Ella held her tongue as her father launched into yet another lecture, this time about lack of gratitude on her part, and that of her sisters, for all he had done for them. The way he was singing his own praises almost made her laugh out loud.

She shut her ears to the sound of his voice, focused upon getting this little domestic scene over and done with as quickly as possible, and getting Josiah out of her house. Otherwise she might explode and hit him in the face with the remains of this damson pie. The visit had been unasked for and unexpected. His very presence in her parlour made her skin crawl. Ella waited with barely contained patience for him to mop up the last piece of pie, then got to her feet the instant he laid down his spoon.

'Well, thank you for calling, Father. It was interesting to see you and hear your news.' Had he brought any news? She really couldn't remember, not having paid proper attention to anything that he'd said. 'I trust you will take proper care of yourself.'

'I don't seem to have any choice since my daughters are hell-bent on creating havoc,' he grumbled. 'You bring me nothing but grief.'

The pale winter light of the afternoon was darkening, and it had started to snow again, great piles of it starting to drift and pile up against the farmhouse walls. Ella had a sudden vision of Josiah's motor getting stuck in the lane, compelling him to return and stay the night. She quickly handed him his hat and waterproof. 'I don't wish to hurry you but the weather is worsening and you wouldn't want to get caught up in a snowstorm on your way home to Kendal, would you?'

She briskly ushered him off the premises, almost dusting the mat of the imprint of his feet and quickly closing the door before he'd even reached his motor. Let him drive into a snowdrift for all she cared, so long as he didn't come back here. Ever!

But Josiah did not immediately climb into his Mercedes-Benz and drive away. Unseen by anyone in the gathering snow, he went to the barn and after hunting around for a likely spot, he set a gin trap just where George and Mercy would come down the stairs from the loft above. Half hidden by darkness and a scattering of straw, they wouldn't see it until it was far too late. Josiah didn't much care which of them got caught in it. He would prefer it to be Mercy, but seeing her husband crippled would serve almost as well. The revenge would be just as sweet.

Chapter Thirty-Six

The snow hadn't lain for long before a downpour of rain had banished it, sweeping the dale clean, and the following morning Ella woke to bright skies and crisp, clear mountain air. But not even the improved weather could lift her spirits following her father's visit. Ella felt quite low. It disturbed her to think that he was still involved in her life, still ruling and controlling her, even though it was almost eighteen months since she'd left home. What right had he to lecture her on how to behave as a wife? Had Amos been complaining about her?

She'd thought her new nightdress was really quite elegant and tasteful when she'd bought it, not at all the kind a scarlet woman would choose to wear. Why did Amos always think the worst of her? Why hadn't he thought her pretty? Why didn't he trust her?

Coming to a sudden decision, she ran upstairs to the attic, empty at this time of day as Amos was out on the fells, probably checking on which ewes still needed to be served by the tup.

The attic was gloomy, with only a little light filtering in through the narrow fanlight, dust motes floating in a shaft of pale winter sunlight. It was bitterly cold with fierce draughts blowing in through the ill-fitting window; a wonder Amos didn't freeze up here in wintertime.

The narrow bed where he'd made love to her so beautifully, albeit in a dream state, was rumpled and unmade, the single blanket thrown back revealing one worn grubby sheet, patched and thin. A crumpled pillow lay discarded on the floor. What was he thinking, living here all alone, revelling in self-pity and moral martyrdom, when he could be with her in a comfortable bed? How would they ever salvage this marriage if they didn't sleep together?

Amos Todd, like his family before him, had been born in this ancient house; had lived, worked, and would no doubt die here in the peace and isolation of these hills where none of the new breed of tourists ever trod. He was self-sufficient and independent to a fault. A quiet, introspective man who trusted no one, not even his wife, who rarely even thought to cuddle his own children. What could a woman do with such a husband?

The next instant, Ella was ripping the sheets and blanket from the bed. She tore off the pillow case, stripped the mattress bare, and gathered the whole lot into a bundle ready for Mrs Rackett to wash. Not satisfied with that, she pushed the mattress off the bed and propped it against the wall. Then she unscrewed the legs from the base of the bed, and completely dismantled it. Let Amos try and sleep in it now. He'd find precious little comfort on the bare floorboards.

* * *

Amos never went near his attic bedroom during the day, but Ella heard him pass her bedroom door and climb the rickety stairs about half an hour after she'd retired for the night. She heard the door of the loft open, his footsteps move across the floor, and imagined him carrying in the oil lamp, placing it on the box he used as a bedside table. The silence now was deafening, the only sound being the thump of her heart. What would he do? Would he come to her, or obstinately sleep with no covers on the bare mattress?

It was almost a relief when she again heard his step on the stair, and then the door of her room opened.

'I suppose you did this.'

Ella was sitting up in bed in her new silk nightgown, the light of her own bedside lamp illuminating her fair beauty as she smiled shyly at him. 'I thought it time we became man and wife proper, Amos. Or that you at least talked to me, instead of hurling insults because I simply want to look pretty for you.'

His face took on that tight, condemning look, and for a moment she thought all was lost, that he'd stalk away again, as before. But then he softly closed the door and came into the room. He looked all gangly and uncomfortable standing there, not quite knowing where to put himself, his expression almost sheepish.

'I've been wondering lately if happen I've been a bit too judgemental, like, a bit hard on thee.'

Ella couldn't help smiling at this understatement, and the way he'd slipped back into the old-fashioned 'thee' again. She patted the bed, inviting him to sit, and without

393

protest, he did so, perching on the edge as if she might contaminate him if he came too near.

'I certainly think it's time we were more open and honest with each other, don't you? I'll start, shall I, by admitting that I never wanted to marry you, and objected most strongly. I gave in only because of the retribution my father would have inflicted upon my sisters, had I not obeyed him.'

He frowned. 'What sort of retribution?'

Ella told him then about the many beatings their father had regularly given his three daughters while they were growing up, either by use of his fists, or the leather belt from around his waist. She described that day when Josiah had finally broken her resistance by hanging Livia by her wrists, like a piece of meat from a butcher's hook, in a cage he kept specifically for that purpose in the tower room. Amos looked shocked and appalled by this, at first reluctant to accept the truth, but by the time she was done explaining his treatment of her mother, and her true relationship with Mercy, he believed every word.

'He kept a mistress?'

'Several, I believe.'

'And rejected Mercy because she was the child of one? But the fault was not the child's.'

'Indeed not.' Ella almost sighed with relief that he was taking this so well. 'She is an innocent, albeit one with a huge chip on her shoulder. But then why wouldn't she when her own father had her locked in the workhouse.' Ella went on to relate the tale of the birching Josiah had ordered.

'How could he treat you all so badly, his own children?'

'I wish I knew. I suppose because he never loved us, never loved anyone but himself. Do you love your children?'

'Of course.'

She looked at him then, her gaze challenging. Ella was deeply afraid of saying the wrong thing, yet knowing that if they didn't begin to break down these barriers between them, they'd never get anywhere.

'You gave little sign of it when I first came here. It's been a real battle to even get you to allow them to play, as normal children should. And don't tell me Esther wouldn't approve, because Esther isn't here any more, but you are. They would also like it if you gave them a hug now and then. It's quite safe to love them. You aren't going to lose them, Amos. I understand your fears about sickness and infections, having learnt about Esther's final days, but you don't need to be quite so paranoiac about cleanliness, or frightened of loving them. Neither Tilda nor Emmett is going to get sick and die, as their mother did. They're healthy and strong, but you will most certainly lose their love if you don't show them yours.'

Having said her piece, what she'd been longing to get off her chest for some months, Ella held her breath and waited for his reaction, not even daring to look at him.

'Do they hate me?' he asked at length, his voice barely above a whisper. 'Is it too late?'

She smiled, and there was such shame in his face that her heart went out to him. 'No, of course it isn't. It's never too late to tell someone that you love them. Not if it's the truth.'

Ella caressed his hands, so rough and hard, yet so gentle. 'I know you love them really, and that you loved Esther. I've no wish to interfere with what you had with your first wife, but you're married to me now, and life moves on, things change. I confess I once foolishly fancied myself in love with Danny Gilpin, but that's all it was, a silly fancy, a boy and girl crush. I spoke the truth when I said we did nothing to be ashamed of. You were the one who took my virginity, Amos, the night I came to your little eyrie upstairs.'

His face flushed crimson at the memory. 'You were so beautiful, I thought I was dreaming.'

She smiled shyly at him. 'It was lovely. Perhaps we were both dreaming.'

'And I spoilt everything by mistrusting you again.'

'And throwing biblical insults at me. Not quite right to use the Bible in that way, is it?'

His flush deepened. 'I was ashamed of my own weakness in wanting you.'

'Why? It's not a disgrace to love your wife, Amos, even the Bible would approve of that.'

He looked sheepish. 'I know, but I couldn't seem to bring myself to trust you because of what happened before, with Esther.'

Ella pushed back the bedclothes and edged closer to lean against his shoulder. 'Why, what happened, Amos? Tell me about Esther.'

'She took a fancy to a quarryman. She'd often go down

there, claimed to be fascinated by the stone and watching the men work. Then I came home unexpectedly one day and found her with one of them. In this bed.'

'Oh, Amos, how dreadful!' Ella was appalled, and understood everything now. 'You must have been devastated.'

'I never could trust her after that.'

'Nor any other woman.'

'I suppose not. She took to driving into Kendal once or twice a month, supposedly to market, but I suspected her of meeting him there instead.'

Ella sighed. 'That must have been difficult for you to live with. No wonder you would never let me go into town. And then she got sick?'

'She caught scarlet fever, but I stood by her.'

'That was brave and noble of you.'

'She was still my wife, no matter what she'd done. It's Christian to forgive.'

She squeezed his hand. 'We all make mistakes, Amos, and you did indeed look after her well. I'm sure she couldn't have asked for better care.'

He put his arm about Ella, stroked her silver fair hair, then let his hand fall away, as if he didn't feel he had the right. 'But I took it out on you, and on the children. I felt so stupid, so used, not trusting anyone. I closed in on meself. I thought, why would anyone love me?'

There was such sadness in his eyes, Ella could bear no more. 'I do. I love you, Amos. I do really.'

He looked at her as if he couldn't quite believe what he was hearing.

'I know I didn't want this marriage, and behaved very foolishly when I first came here, grumbling and moaning the whole time, not being prepared to pull my weight and do my duty as your wife in any way. I was perverse and provoking, half expecting you to turn violent and hit me when I disobeyed you, as Father used to do.'

'I would never do that, although you were very stubborn at times.' He half smiled. 'And really quite funny: being chased by the geese, falling in the bog, afraid of the cows, and not making any cheese but still wanting to take it to market to sell. I liked it best when the rats scared you into my arms.'

She gazed into his brown eyes. 'That's when you first kissed me.'

'I liked that bit quite a lot.'

'Then why don't you do it again?' It was about as clear an invitation as she could give. 'I love you, Amos, and there's no shame in that. I'm not a bad woman, I'm your wife. What more can I say?'

'You could say that you forgive me, because I love you too, Ella,' he murmured, so softly she wasn't sure she'd heard him right. 'I've loved you from the first moment I saw you at your father's house.'

'Oh, Amos, I think I started falling in love with you when you rescued those new-born lambs in the snow, although I didn't realise it at the time. I also quite enjoyed seeing you bathing in the river.'

His eyes widened with shock. 'You were spying on me?'

'I was,' and she grinned wickedly at him.

Then he was indeed kissing her, and when he finally paused for breath, all she could say was, 'Oh, kiss me again. And again, and again, and again.'

Amos readily obliged, and Ella sank back on the pillows in her pretty nightgown, which he at once set about gently removing, having properly admired it first and remarked on how pretty it was. They both began to laugh with the sheer joy of finding each other, and of finally bringing down that wall of silence and distrust.

Much later, when they lay with their arms about each other in the big comfortable bed, Amos said, 'So this is what it feels like to be in love?'

Ella sighed with happiness. 'It is indeed, my love, and the best part is that it can only get better and better.' And pulling him to her once more, proved she was right.

The next morning Amos brought Ella a cup of tea in bed, kissing her and telling her to sleep in while he went to collect the cows for milking. It was George who found him some time later, alerted by his pitiful cries, caught fast in the gin trap Josiah had set.

Chapter Thirty-Seven

It took every ounce of George's strength, with the assistance of Ella, Mercy and Mrs Rackett, to prise the gin trap off him. Once used in the dale to catch pine-martins, they were somewhat frowned upon now, because of the dangers of the kind of accident that had occurred with Amos. Had he not been wearing good strong boots his leg could well have been completely severed. Even so, the wound was dangerously deep, and pumping blood. If he didn't get to a hospital soon, he could still lose it. Ella grabbed some bailing twine and tied a tourniquet above the savage gash while George ran to bring round the cart.

Mrs Rackett fetched blankets while Mercy kept repeating, 'Who would do this? Who would do such a thing?'

'This is my father's work,' Ella bitterly responded. 'He must have set the trap when he called yesterday.'

Mercy said, 'He meant this for me, didn't he? Not your husband.'

'What does that matter now?' Ella was in tears, stroking his hair as Amos lay groaning in agony, desperately trying to soothe him but not knowing how to ease his pain.

'But why?'

'Because he's the devil,' Ella almost screamed at her. 'Haven't you learnt that yet?'

They laid Amos in the back of the cart on the spread blankets, Ella and Mercy beside him, and George drove them into Kendal, leaving Mrs Rackett to mind the farm. But while doctors rushed to tend to the patient, and Ella wept, Mercy slipped away unnoticed. There were things she needed to say to Josiah Angel, and now seemed as good a time as any.

Mercy had been waiting a long time for this moment and she intended to savour it to the full. The maid showed her into a gloomy hall, and to her surprise Josiah seemed quite jovial, almost welcoming, murmuring something about how it was indeed time the pair of them met and talked properly. Mercy couldn't agree more.

She followed obediently as he took her upstairs to what he called his study. She thought it a bleak sort of room as he ushered her inside, looking about in surprise for some sign of a desk. Only when he turned the key in the lock did she realise her mistake, and her heart gave an uncomfortable lurch.

This wasn't his study. This was the tower room Livia had described to her in painstaking detail, and told her to avoid at all costs. Not that she'd believed the tale when first she'd heard it, unable to accept that a man

401

of Josiah Angel's standing would commit acts of such violence against his own legitimate daughters. Now she recognised that Livia had spoken nothing but the truth, for there, in one shadowed corner, complete with hook, was the cage. Mercy gazed at it in horror, a chill rippling down her spine.

And then she recalled the trauma of her mother's death, and her anxiety to tell her daughter the truth about her birth. Mercy remembered how, even with her dying breath, Florrie had still defended this tyrant, naively believing he would help her beloved girl to find work and a new life. How wrong she'd been, which only proved how scandalously Josiah had used and abused her innocence.

Mercy turned to face him with fresh courage in her heart. 'I thought you might like to see that I'm well, and, as you see, quite unhurt.'

He had the gall to smile, although it was more of a sarcastic smirk. 'And your husband?'

'He is perfectly well too. Your son-in-law was the one to get caught in the trap you laid, unfortunately. He's in hospital, his wounds being tended to even as we speak.'

'Amos?'

'Yes, Amos.'

'Damnation, that wasn't supposed to happen!'

'Bit careless of you then to leave a gin trap lying about where anyone could step into it. It could just as easily have been Ella, your precious daughter.'

Josiah made a scoffing sound deep in his throat. 'She's not precious to me, none of you are. Daughters!

Women! The bane of my life. If only Roberta had given me sons, as was her duty, none of this would have happened. Serve Ella right if it had been her, the little tart. It wouldn't have troubled me in the slightest. I'm surprised you care anyway, since she's having it off with your husband.'

Mercy was stunned by this bitter attack on Ella. The unexpected turn of events forced her to rethink her attitude, along with the assumptions she'd made about the Angel family generally.

'She isn't having it off with anyone. George just likes to tease, that's all. He's a flirt, yes, but devoted to me. It's good to know somebody is, since my mam is dead, and you, my own father, care so little you'd happily see me crippled. What kind of man are you?'

Josiah pulled a walnut from his pocket and cracked it in his palm. 'A powerful one! A man determined not to see a lifetime of endeavour destroyed by stupid females.' He threw away the shell and crunched on the nut with sharp yellow teeth. 'You're nothing to me. Just a bit of flotsam that has chanced by, that I can throw away as easily as that shell.'

Mercy moved a step closer, that familiar dark curl of anger starting up deep inside. 'A bit of flotsam, am I? Your contempt for women revolts me. Any decent man would feel ashamed of the way they treated my mam, but you don't know the meaning of the bleeding word. I understand that now, after what I've witnessed today. I suppose you saw my mother as just some bit of skirt for you to have fun with, and me, your own child, as an inconvenience. Is that the way it was?'

His lip curled in derision. 'Florrie knew what she was about when she opened her legs for me, and no doubt a dozen others before and since. And you'll follow in her footsteps, whore that you are.' He took a key from his pocket and moved over to the cage.

Mercy watched him, mesmerised; fear and fury warring for supremacy within, yet not for a second would she allow him to see that she was afraid.

'Is that what you want, for me to prove your theory that women are contemptible? Would it please you if I were a whore? Would you feel justified then in your treatment of Mam and me? Well, you'd be wrong! The truth is, everyone who knew Florrie would recognise it for the lie it is. She was a good, honest woman, just far too loving and trusting. She made the bad mistake of falling in love with a devil instead of a prince. And I'll make sure everyone is made aware of that fact.'

He actually laughed out loud at that. 'You think I'd allow some workhouse brat, born on the wrong side of the blanket, to bring me down?'

'Oh, I'll bring you down all right. I'm going to blacken your name and make you sorry you ever clapped eyes on Florrie Simpson. I'll tell everyone the truth about how you used her, then abandoned her with a young child. I'll tell them how she wasn't the only woman you enjoyed, tell them about this room, and this flaming cage.' She was spitting the words at him, spewing out all the fury that had festered in her over the last year or more. 'I'll prove to the whole world that Josiah Angel is really a devil in disguise. See how bleeding powerful you are then.'

'Perhaps you would, if ever you got the chance. Unfortunately, I'll make damn sure that you don't.' Apparently unconcerned by her threats, he calmly inserted the key and unlocked the door of the cage, checking that the hook was still in place. Then he turned to smile at her, looking like a cat about to gobble up its prey. 'I can see that you're very like your mother in many ways. You have her sense of humour, and her ferocious courage. She always had guts, did Florrie, and the sweetest little fanny in the business.'

Mercy flew at him, nails outstretched like talons, screaming like a banshee. But he was too quick for her, knocking her to the floor with a careless flick of one hand. She lay winded for only a second before scrambling to her feet, her bravery undaunted as she yelled her rage at him. 'I'll make you pay for what you did, I swear it.'

Josiah ignored her, his concentration focused on locating the chain he would use to bind her wrists. He caught sight of it curled on the floor of the cage, and, picking it up, turned to her with a grimace of pure evil on his ugly face.

Mercy stiffened, determined not to tremble and reveal how very afraid she was. 'And what did you do to your other daughters? Was it true that you beat them with a strap? Did you hang them in that thing, like Livia said?'

'Oh, I did much worse than that.'

'What, to that one who died?'

'Poor Maggie. Not the prettiest of my daughters, being

somewhat plain, like her mother, but all cats are grey in the dark.'

Mercy gasped. 'You're despicable, vile. But then you already know that.'

Josiah took a step nearer, the chain forming a bridge between his hands, held out like a ligature. A band almost as tight suddenly gripped his rib cage, effecting his breathing so that he staggered, feeling slightly giddy and light-headed for a moment.

Mercy instinctively retreated, keeping her back to the window. She was thinking fast. Knowing she was trapped, the door locked. Josiah Angel was far too big a man for her to tackle head on, yet a mouse could beat a lion, if he had the wit. What could she do? What weapon did she have, what skill that he hadn't? Keep him talking, that was the first thing. Maybe George was looking for her even now.

'I thought it was just me you had it in for, but it's the whole bleeding human race, isn't it? Women, in particular. You care only for number one, for yourself, not for me, not for your daughters, not for anyone except Councillor Josiah Angel, future Member of Parliament for Westmorland. The thing is, you can't kill us all.'

'Oh, yes I can.' He lunged at her, hands outstretched, still holding the chain wrapped about his huge fists. He came fast and furious, roaring with rage, a grotesque kind of fury contorting his face. The expression changed only as it dawned on him that she had stepped aside, quick and agile as a monkey, while his momentum carried him onward to crash through the tall gothic window, his balance affected by his chained hands and the fierce, blinding pain in his chest. The sound of his infuriated roar as he fell was followed by a sickening thud, and then deathly silence.

Chapter Thirty-Eight

It was reported in the *Westmorland Gazette* that Councillor Josiah Angel had tragically taken his own life while the balance of his mind was disturbed. Quoted in the local paper under the heading *A Double Tragedy*, Josiah's contribution to the town as councillor and mayor was lauded with the kind of approbation he would have loved, had he been around to read his own obituary.

'*Sadly, this self-made businessman never quite recovered from the loss of his youngest daughter, who also committed suicide. A double tragedy indeed.*'

The truth as to why Maggie had killed herself remained private, Livia deciding that revenge of that kind would hurt no one but themselves, now that her father was dead. She did, though, finally reveal her sister's pregnancy to Ella, and to Mercy.

Mercy seemed to have learnt some of the facts already during her confrontation with Josiah, but for Ella it came as a terrible shock, and she was still trying to come to terms with it.

Mercy had given them a full account of what had occurred in that tower room, and, knowing their father as they did, they thought she'd done well to get out unscathed and alive. She swore to them that she'd never laid a hand on him, that he'd charged at her, she'd stepped out of the way, and he'd been unable to get his balance and prevent himself falling through the window. It felt like a kind of justice.

A huge weight had been lifted from Livia's shoulders, with even Henry in France, and no longer a threat.

Hodson had also waived his demand for repayment of any loans he'd made to his erstwhile colleague. Quite rightly, in Livia's opinion, although Jack still had a fancy for stringing him up from the nearest tree.

The court had appointed a receiver to oversee the sale of Angel House, although Mr Blamire, the family solicitor, had assured Livia that once the mortgage, overdraft and major creditors were paid, he saw no reason why Angel's Department Store couldn't be saved. Everything possible would be done to keep the business afloat, and any outstanding debts to creditors could be paid over a period of time, under the supervision of the receiver. Livia meant to learn all she could about the business, and perhaps be able to help her friends develop theirs.

She had no sentiment for Angel House and would be glad to see it sold, unlike her father, who would much rather sell off his daughters than his palatial home. Livia decided to live above the store, as she would have no other home, and couldn't impose upon Jessie any longer.

'Love and happiness is found in people, not

possessions,' she told Jack, when they finally got around to talking about their future.

He was full of apologies for doubting her, but although they were still very much in love, Livia tactfully explained that she didn't yet feel ready for marriage. 'There are things I need to do first. Debts still to be paid off, a store to revitalise, and a new sister to get to know.'

Jack grinned at her, 'That's just as well, since I'll be busy helping Mam to build a business of our own. But I would like to make an honest woman of you one day, Livvy, if you'll let me.'

She kissed him, deep and soft and languorous. 'I shall give it serious consideration. In the meantime, I'm quite willing to risk a scandal, if you are.'

'Scandal of that sort doesn't trouble me in the slightest. You know what a devil I am with women.'

And Livia was able to laugh, knowing that it wasn't true, and that the real devil in her life had gone, tragically unmourned.

Best of all, so far as Livia was concerned, all differences between the three girls now seemed to be a thing of the past. There were now four Angel sisters, and although one was forever absent, darling Maggie would always be loved, and never forgotten.

It was Christmas day at Todd Farm. The big farm kitchen was all decked out with sprigs of holly and mistletoe, a tree trimmed with paper chains made by the children stood in one corner. They'd each put up a stocking in which they'd been so excited this morning to find an

410

orange, a bag of sweets, and a silver threepenny bit in the toe. There was also a doll for Tilda, a toy train for Emmett, and a brush and comb set for Mary, who had been allowed home for the holidays.

On Christmas Eve the entire family had gone into Staveley for a party at the Temperance Hall, where there'd been a lucky dip in a bran tub, coconut shies, sandwiches, cakes and jelly. Jessie, Jack and all the Flint children had come along too, so it had been a noisy, lively affair.

The most exciting part for Mary was when her father had thrown nuts all over the floor and the children had to scramble about on their knees to pick up as many as they could. She'd never seen him laugh so much. But then he had plenty to be cheerful about. He was recovering well from his accident, and had promised her, most faithfully, that he would soon be out of that wheelchair and walking again.

She smiled as Tilda jumped up from the rug, where she'd been dressing her doll, and ran to him now for a hug; pride and love in her eyes. It had been so long since he'd shown them any affection, but now he was forever giving them cuddles.

After the party, they'd all got wrapped up in their warmest clothes, with hats, and scarves, and gloves, and gone round the village singing Christmas carols. People would invite them inside for mince pies and something called a hot toddy for the adults. Emmett had nearly been sick he'd eaten so much. On their way back up the dale, walking arm in arm still singing, they'd called in at St Cuthbert's church for the traditional Christmas carol service held around the manger where a china doll lay masquerading as baby Jesus. Mary had felt so proud when her father had read one of the lessons.

Now it was Christmas Day and her young sister seemed beside herself with excitement. But then even Mary had never known such joy in all her short life. Everyone was here, seated like one big happy family round the long pine table. She felt pretty and almost grown-up in the new blue velvet frock with its eau-de-nil lace collar that Father had bought her. Jessie Flint and her many children were here, and Aunt Molly too of course, as well as their new relations. They were all wearing silly paper hats, even Mrs Rackett.

There was her father carving the turkey cooked by Ella, the stepmother she'd resented for so long; Beth, the old collie, standing by, tongue lolling, for any scraps that might come her way. Mary had warmed to her new mother now, and knew that Tilda loved her dearly, as did Emmett. She rather liked Ella's sisters too, who were going to be their new aunts.

Livia was funny, and full of passion and big ideas. She looked so happy pulling that cracker with Jack, even though she claimed to be tired out with working so hard in the run-up to Christmas. Mary hadn't got to know her terribly well yet because she was learning how to run Angel's big department store in Kendal all by herself, without even her father to help since he was dead. She thought that was terribly brave. Maybe when she was a grown woman, Mary would be able to do something equally daring.

They saw Aunt Mercy quite regularly, as she was living in Staveley with Uncle George. The pair of them still came most days to help Father and Ella on the farm, but also worked in the new woollen business that Jack Flint and his mother were starting up in the old mill yard.

So from only having one parent, all depressed and miserable after their mam had got sick and died, they now had a whole new family. Which was so wonderful it made her head go dizzy with joy!

A plate of turkey and roast potatoes with all the trimmings was placed before her, and Mary sighed with pleasure. Oh, but she was so happy! She didn't even mind having to eat Brussel sprouts. How could she not be happy when Father looked so relaxed and content? He'd even played Snakes and Ladders with them the other night. And Ella had promised that one day she might actually teach him to dance. Now that would be something to see!

About to tuck into her Christmas dinner, Tilda suddenly gave Emmett a nudge, and whispered in his ear for him to look at their father, who was kissing Ella again. They seemed to be doing that quite a lot these days. The two children clapped a hand over their mouths and fell into fits of giggles.

Mary smiled, then tucking their napkins under their chins, gently told them to behave and sit up nicely to eat their dinner.

Oh, but everything was suddenly so lovely and exciting, and the little ones were to start school here in Kentmere in January, with Ella taking them there and back in the pony and trap, so it was worth putting up with a bit of soppy kissing now and then, wasn't it? They had a happy family at last, and Father was laughing again. What more could they ask? ━

The Angel sisters' story continues in

Angels at War

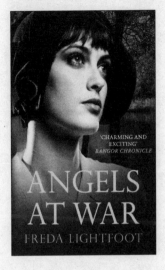

The Lake District, 1910. After a tumultuous past, the future is finally looking rosy for the Angel sisters. Livia is set to marry handsome Jack Flint, while her sisters are contentedly living at Todd Farm. Yet Livia still dreams of resurrecting the neglected drapery business which was left to her when her father died. But is she prepared to jeopardise the love she shares with Jack to achieve her wish? With the wealthy and determined Matthew Grayson standing in the way of her ambitions, Livia must stay true to her heart, or risk losing everything . . .

To order visit our website at
www.allisonandbusby.com
or call us on
020 7580 1080